UTUBE

Also by Rozlan Mohd Noor

21 Immortals: Inspector Mislan and the Yee Sang Murders

DUKE: Inspector Mislan and the Expressway Murders

UTUBE

INSPECTOR MISLAN
AND THE EMANCIPATIST
CONSPIRACY

ROZLAN MOHD NOOR

An Arcade CrimeWise Book

First North American Edition

This is a work of fiction. Names, places, characters, and incidents are either the products of the author's imagination or are used fictitiously.

Arcade Publishing books may be purchased in bulk at special discounts for sales promotion, corporate gifts, fund-raising, or educational purposes. Special editions can also be created to specifications. For details, contact the Special Sales Department, Arcade Publishing, 307 West 36th Street, 11th Floor, New York, NY 10018 or arcade@skyhorsepublishing.com.

Arcade Publishing® and CrimeWise® are registered trademarks of Skyhorse Publishing, Inc.®, a Delaware corporation.

Visit our website at www.arcadepub.com.

10 9 8 7 6 5 4 3 2 1

Library of Congress Cataloging-in-Publication Data is available on file.
Library of Congress Control Number: 2021933409

Cover design by Erin Seaward-Hiatt
Cover photograph: © George Pachantouris/Getty Images

ISBN: 978-1-950691-42-5
Ebook ISBN: 978-1-951627-92-8

Printed in the United States of America

To my children,
Reyza, Reeze, Reeziana, and Daniel:

I can provide you with education,
but you will have to seek wisdom on your own.

"Self-righteousness belongs to the narrow-minded."

Toba Beta, *My Ancestor Was an Ancient Astronaut*

1

INSPECTOR SHARIFAH AZLINA SYED Abdullah, who prefers to be called Sherry, and Detective Deena Sofea Azman from the Sexual & Child Abuse Investigation Division, D11, arrive at Putra Ria Condominium, Pantai Dalam, Kuala Lumpur. A little earlier, they had been informed that Brickfields District Police Headquarters had received report of a rape under Section 376 of the Penal Code. The complainant identified herself as Era Amilia from unit 901 of Putra Ria Condominium. Rape cases are treated as special cases and investigated by D11 officers, who are trained to handle victims' sensitivity and emotional trauma.

Standing outside unit 901, Sherry looks for the doorbell. Not finding one, she knocks on the door and waits. When there is no response, she looks at her wristwatch. It is 2:11 a.m. She knocks again a little harder and calls out.

"Miss Era, I'm Inspector Sherry from KL police."

Instantly, she hears the dead bolt click and observes the doorknob turning. Sherry doesn't see a peephole; Era must have been standing behind the door when she first knocked but didn't dare open it until she identified herself as a police officer. The door opens just a crack to reveal a terrified pair of red, puffy eyes peering at her. Sherry holds up her authority card.

"Miss Era, I'm Inspector Sherry, and this is Detective Deena," Sherry repeats. "May we come in?"

The door opens wider, and Sherry takes that as an invitation to enter. Era turns from the door, walking to the living room without uttering a word. The D11 officers close the door behind them and follow her into the living room. Era is in her early thirties, about five feet tall, not glamorously beautiful but pleasant-looking. She is slim, of fair complexion, with wavy, shoulder-length black hair with a streak of light brown on the right side. She is in a bathrobe and her hair is wet, most likely from a shower.

Showering after being sexually violated is a very common reaction among victims. The need to wash away the nauseating feeling of being physically and emotionally desecrated, to wash away the smell of the perpetrator. But to rape investigators, the act of showering immediately after the incident is like washing away crucial physical evidence. Though dismayed, Sherry says nothing.

Era sits on the edge of the three-seat sofa with her arms folded across her chest, tightly hugging herself while absentmindedly rocking back and forth. Back and forth. Her chin presses to her chest, her eyes fixed on the floor. Sherry believes she has already forgotten their presence. With eye gestures, Sherry tells her detective to move slowly so as not to startle her, and they sit at the sofa with the victim.

"Miss Era, we received a call saying you were raped," Sherry says as calmly as she can.

Era stops rocking. She gives the slightest of nods without lifting her head or looking at the inspector.

"Can you tell us what happened?"

The rocking stops and Era remains still, stiff.

The officers wait patiently as she starts rocking again. Now and then she shakes her head as if she is saying no to something playing in her head. Her damp, uncombed hair sways rhythmically with the head shakes. Sherry recognizes the behavior pattern as one of the signs of rape trauma syndrome, RTS. The involuntary rocking, shaking of the head, the distressed manner, and the long silences in between statements are indicative of the disorientation, disbelief, and shame from being sexually violated.

"Last night, I thought I finally had it all," Era eventually mumbles. Her voice is so soft that the two officers have to lean closer. "Two years . . . for two years I slogged, day and night. I had . . ." She stops mid-sentence.

Not knowing what she was mumbling about, the two officers look at each other.

Era stops rocking and says, "They took a video."

"I'm sorry, what did you say?"

"They video-recorded the whole thing, what're they going to do with it?" she asks, angrily. "Why did they video it?" She stares intently at Inspector Sherry.

"Did they use their cell phones?"

"No, not phone, they used a video cam."

The officers exchange a quick glance.

"You said *they*, how many of them were there?"

"Two."

"Can you tell us what they did?"

"His hands were pale . . . cold," she stammers.

Sherry notes Era shivering and tightening her hug. She knows the memory is vividly playing in her head.

"Was he wearing surgical gloves?" Sherry asks.

Era looks at her, her eyes blank, not grasping the inspector's question.

"He had a knife. He told me to do as I was told, or he'd practice his carving skills on my face and slit my throat," she says, almost in a whisper. She shivers again before continuing, "I begged him to take all my money, but I could see him smiling through the pantyhose covering his face."

"What did he want you to do?"

Era reverts to staring at the floor. Sherry notices she is biting her lower lip to stop it from quivering. Sherry prepares herself, expecting the victim to break down.

"He told me to take off my panties and bra." Era pauses, taking a deep breath. "When I pleaded with him again, he cut my bra straps, and then my panties, saying he's going to free me." She lifts her head to look at the officers. Her face contorts into an expression of questioning and confusion.

"Free you?" Sherry says. "I don't understand."

Era nods. "Yes, free me, that's what he said."

"You mean, he'll free you after you do what he wants?"

"No, he didn't say that . . . He said he's going to free me."

"OK, I'm not clear, we'll talk about it again. Then what happened?"

"Then he raped me."

"You mean they raped you?"

"No, he raped me . . . the one who said he was going to free me. The other one recorded it."

"And the one videoing the incident did not rape you?"

Era shakes her head.

"While he was," Era could not bring herself to say the word, "he kept whispering in my ear, asking me, how does it feel, is it nice, do I like it. It was sickening."

The two D11 officers do not know how to respond.

"I shut my eyes and he told me to open them and look at him. He told me to enjoy it and I'll be free," Era continues, her body trembling with disgust and anger. "Then he said he wanted me to come and experience the true pleasure of sex. Disgusting."

"'Come' as in climax?"

Era nods.

"Where did this take place?"

Era indicates to the bedroom with her head. "In there."

"Miss Era, I need to call Crime Forensics to process your bedroom, and I'll have to take you to the hospital for examinations. Is there anyone I can call on your behalf?"

Era shakes her head.

"How about your apartment, is there anyone I can call to look after it?"

Again she shakes her head.

"OK, Detective Deena will lock up after Forensics is done, and she will return the keys to you." Sherry reads Era's face for her understanding and agreement. "Can you show me where the keys are?"

Era motions toward the dining table.

"I need you to do one more thing for me before we go to a hospital. Can you point out to me the clothes you were wearing when you were sexually assaulted?"

With effort Era pushes herself from the sofa and wobbles to her feet. Deena jumps forward to steady her.

"Are you OK?" she asks, holding Era's arm.

Era nods and manages a "thank you" with her eyes. Deena holds on to her as Era takes shaky steps toward the bedroom. At the door, Era hesitates and leans on the door frame, breathing heavily.

"It's all right. Take your time," Sherry says, standing next to her.

"I can't," she cries, and dashes back to the sofa. Sitting on the edge of the seat, she bends over, cups her face, and sobs, "I'm sorry, I can't go in there. I'm sorry."

"It's OK, we understand," Deena comforts her. "It's OK."

2

THERE'S A KNOCK ON the front door. Era warily turn her head, glaring at the door. Her eyes are unblinking and her body stiffens. Sherry signals for Deena to answer the door, and she moves next to the victim. She tells her it must be the Crime Forensics team. They're here to collect whatever evidence they can from the scene. Deena turns to Sherry for her approval before opening the door.

"Hi," Inspector Kevin Foo greets her.

Returning his greeting, she says, "Inspector Sherry is with the victim."

Seeing Kevin's team approaching, Sherry excuses herself, telling Era she needs to speak to the officer in charge. She meets them halfway and pulls Kevin aside.

"Kev, the victim is too traumatized to be of much help. She says she was raped in her bedroom. I don't see any sign of forced entry, but I need you to take a closer look while I take her to the hospital. Deena will be here to lock up after you're done. Kev, can you bag her hands first?"

Kevin looks at Era on the sofa.

"Look like she's bathed, so I don't think you'll get anything. Externally at least, all transfers would've been washed away."

"No harm in trying. Anyway, it's procedural."

"OK."

Sherry introduces the head of Crime Forensics to the victim.

"Miss Era, this is Inspector Kevin Foo. He'll be placing plastic bags over both your hands to protect any evidence that might still be there."

Era nods without looking up. But when Kevin reaches for her right hand, she instantly pulls it away and with a throaty voice cries, "Get away from me!"

Sherry steps in between them and whispers to Kevin, "It's because of your gloves."

Kevin looks at her uncomprehendingly.

"The rapist wore surgical gloves," she explains.

"Oh."

Turning to the victim, Sherry says, "It's OK, Miss Era. Kevin's not going to hurt you. He has to wear gloves so as not to contaminate any forensic evidence on your hands."

Era starts crying, mumbling repeatedly, "Sorry, I'm sorry."

"Do you want me to do it?" Sherry asks.

Era nods. "Please," she pleads meekly.

Sherry snaps on a pair of latex gloves, takes the plastic bags from Kevin, and kneels in front of the victim.

"Miss Era, I'm going to put these plastic bags over your hands and tape them at your wrists. It's not going to hurt, OK?"

Era nods and holds out her hands.

Sherry touches the victim's right hand lightly with her gloved fingers, half expecting her to retract it. When she doesn't, Sherry carefully places the plastic bags over both hands and secures them around the wrists with adhesive tape. She signals to Kevin Foo to start his examination and gently leads the zombielike Era to the front door. Turning to Deena, she says, "Be sure to bring her handbag, phone, and pack an overnight bag with a few toiletries and a change of clothes. Don't forget to lock up properly."

As she slowly walks the victim to the front door, it occurs to Sherry that Era might get flustered when she realizes she's being taken for an invasive medical examination. Sherry could get a mobile patrol vehicle (MPV) to take her to the hospital, but she's not sure how the victim would react on seeing a police vehicle. It might be a trigger that could shatter her emotionally. On the other hand, Sherry is alone and, should the victim behave erratically, she might not be able to handle the situation. Though she believes she has gained the victim's trust, with a traumatized victim one never knows what to expect. At the door, she beckons to Detective Deena.

"Best if you come with us. After dropping us, you come back here and get Era's things."

"OK, let me inform Inspector Kevin."

———

Sherry sits in the back with Era while Deena drives. Leaving the condominium, they head for the affluent Bangsar suburb of Kuala Lumpur. Housing estates lined with bungalows and semidetached houses with price tags running into the millions, favored by wealthy locals and foreigners alike. From there they hit Jalan Kuching and go on to Jalan Pahang. The eight-mile trip takes them thirteen minutes. Detective Deena drops them off at the Kuala Lumpur Hospital Emergency and Trauma Center.

The E & T is busiest at night and early morning, as all government clinics are closed after office hours. The public has no choice but to go to hospital E & Ts for treatment.

Sherry flashes her authority card to the attendants gathered around the registration counter. She tells one of them to get a wheelchair for the victim, who is starting to look jittery. Era's steps are heavy and her eyes wild, darting around at the milling crowd, the constant flow of ambulances, and the casualties being dropped off. Letting her sit in a wheelchair will hopefully make her feel more at ease. Sitting would allow her to shut off everything around her by covering her face with her hands.

After registering the victim, Sherry follows the attendant wheeling her to examination room 2. Once they're by themselves in the examination room, she observes the victim start to relax and drop her hands to her sides. Sherry explains that a doctor will be examining her and will collect any physical evidence that may be on her. Era doesn't say anything; she just stares at her feet on the footrest. Sherry hears a woman's voice saying, "They're in room 2," and she steps out.

"Hi, Doc," she greets Dr. Geetha.

"Inspector Sherry, how have you been? Haven't seen you for quite a while."

"Usual-*lah*, Doc."

"This isn't a good sign," Dr. Geetha says.

Sherry looks at the doctor questioningly.

"You escorting the victim yourself, that's not a good sign. Normally, a detective would escort the victim."

Sherry nods. "This victim's displaying signs of post-rape trauma, so I thought I'd better stick around to make sure she feels safe."

"See, now I'm a psychic," Dr. Geetha says smilingly. "What happened?"

"I haven't taken her statement yet, but she says she was raped and the whole thing was recorded."

"Videoed?"

"Yes."

"Sickening. I hope there's a law to castrate the bastards."

"Maybe when a woman becomes prime minister," Sherry says with a tight smile. "Who is the GYN on duty?"

"I think it is Dr. Charles."

"Can we get a woman?"

"Not at this hour. But it's all right, I'll stick around during the examination to reassure the victim."

"Thanks, Doc, I'm sure she'll appreciate that."

They enter the examination room, and Sherry introduces Dr. Geetha to Era. She tells her that Dr. Geetha will be around when the gynecologist does the examination. Era nods but says nothing.

3

SHERRY ARRIVES AT HER office from the hospital at 7:50 a.m. and heads to the washroom to freshen up. She is exhausted from hours of standing in the examination room, observing the medical procedure on the victim. The process was slow because the victim at times just sobbed and refused to be examined. On the advice of Dr. Geetha, the victim has been hospitalized for observation and evaluation in order to determine whether psychiatric treatment is needed.

She makes herself a cup of tea and calls Forensic.

"Kev, Sherry. Any update for me?"

"As you said, there was no sign of forced entry. In the bedroom, we only recovered the victim's day clothes and a bra. No bodily fluid, pubic hair, or semen on the bedsheet or the blanket."

"What about the bathroom?"

"We got some hair samples, but they're too long to be from the pubic region. We ran the blue light on the bed, floor, and bathtub, but no sign of semen."

"Did you do the shower floor trap?"

"Yes."

"You said you found the bra, what about her panties? She said they were cut off her."

"Not there."

"Did you check under the bed? They could've been dropped or kicked under the bed."

"Checked every inch of the bedroom and bathroom. Nothing."

"Did you bag the bedsheet, blankets, pillows?"

"Yes, as I said, the on-site examination revealed nothing."

"Can you go over it again? Maybe you missed something."

"My team usually doesn't, but if it makes you happy, we'll go over it again."

"Thanks."

———

Deena arrives at the office in Kuala Lumpur Police Contingent Headquarters and tells Inspector Sherry that the victim was asleep when she visited the hospital. According to the nurse on duty, the doctor prescribed her some sedatives. She handed over the victim's overnight bag to the duty nurse.

"How did the examination go?" she asks.

"It was difficult. She kept pulling away from the doctor and pushing his hands away. Usually, victims just close their eyes tightly, block everything from their minds, and submit themselves to the examination, but not in her case. I've not seen anything like it before."

"I'm glad you were with her. I wouldn't know what to do," Deena says.

"All I did was try to calm her."

"Briefed ma'am yet?"

"No, but I spoke to Kevin. He said they couldn't find her panties."

Deena nods. "We searched everywhere. Maybe she wasn't wearing any. You know . . . likes it free and easy and no VPL."

"I remember her saying she was wearing a pair. Remember, she said the perp cut them off? Why don't you hang around while I brief ma'am? I'm going to request that you stay on this case."

The Head of Sexual & Child Abuse Investigation Division of Kuala Lumpur, Superintendent of Police Lillian Wong Wee Sin, is in her fifties. She is a slender, tall woman with short hair that is already showing strands of white. She just came back from a long-overdue vacation and is catching up on reports made during her absence.

"Morning, Ma'am, how was your vacation?"

"Morning, Sherry. It was good, but everything is so expensive. With the ringgit-to-euro exchange rate, you basically can't do much. Anyway, there's nothing like being back. Life is good here." Lillian smiles. "I read your twenty-four-hour report. You had a case last night."

Sherry nods and takes a seat. "The victim is Era Amilia Zabidin, thirty-three years old, vice president of marketing at Uptrend Advertising. Lives alone at Putra Ria Condominium on Jalan Pantai Dalam. Claimed she was asleep when she was awoken by a man standing over her, his hand over her mouth and a knife to her cheek. She also claimed the rapists videoed the whole incident."

"Rapists—how many of them?"

"Two."

Lilian gives a slow nod. "With their cell phones?"

"With a video cam," Sherry says, and pauses for her boss's reaction. "One raped and another worked the camera."

Lillian sighs. "They came prepared. So they took turns with her?"

"No, only one of them raped her, the other simply worked the camera."

"That's new. Can you think of any reason?" Lillian asks with arched eyebrows.

"The use of video cam or that only one of them raped her?"

"Both. For only one of them to rape her, they had to be a very disciplined team, don't you think?"

"Did not think of that."

"Have you known of a rape case where only one of them raped and the others didn't have a go?"

Sherry shakes her head, and the two officers remain silent for a moment.

"We'll know more after I interview her. I've a bad feeling about the video recording," Sherry says.

"Could be for their collection? It's well-documented rapist behavior. Relive the excitement by viewing it over and over. The fact that his partner didn't rape her bothers me."

Sherry agrees with her unit head.

"I've read of similar accounts before, about rapists getting aroused watching themselves. When the old video no longer thrills them, they make a new one."

"Extortion is also a probability."

"Possible."

"Apart from those two reasons, why else would they have videoed it?"

Sherry shrugs. She closes her eyes as if searching for a reason. "D10 reports there was no sign of forced entry," she says.

"That would indicate that she may have let them in, or they had a duplicate key."

"She claims she was asleep. That eliminates her letting them in."

"That's what they all say, initially. Dig deeper and you may find something else," Lillian says skeptically.

"D10 might have missed something. I want to go over the house again. D10 also says they couldn't find her panties."

"Trophy?"

"It's not uncommon."

"And the examination?"

"When we arrived at the scene, the victim had already showered and was in a bathrobe. Dr. Geetha did the examination, and Dr. Charles was the GYN in attendance. The victim had severe post-rape trauma, and they decided to keep her in the hospital for further evaluation. Dr. Geetha says she couldn't find anything under her nails, and there were no pubic hairs or traces of bodily fluid on her. No forensic clues at all. Dr. Charles says there are signs of bruising around the labia majora, minora, and the vagina, consistent with forced penetration. There were no traces of semen; swabs were taken and sent to the lab."

"Who is with her at the hospital?"

"She refused to allow us to inform family members or friends. Deena locked up at her apartment after D10 was done and took an overnight bag for her to the hospital. I'll visit the hospital later. And another thing, her blood alcohol level was high."

"That could be the reason for her memory lapse. Maybe she did let the rapists into the house. What about defensive wounds?"

"A hairline cut on her cheek, I guess from the blade she claimed was pressed to her face. There're bruising marks on her arms and neck. According to Dr. Geetha, they're consistent with forceful gripping."

"All right, let's get her to talk after she has rested and sobered up."

"Ma'am, there's another thing I find disturbing."

Superintendent Lillian arches her eyebrows.

"The victim claimed that while she was being raped, the perp spoke or rather whispered in her ear to enjoy it, to come . . . climax and experience the true pleasure of sex."

"Sickening."

Sherry nods. "He said he was going to free her."

"After the rape?"

"That's what I thought, too, but not according to the victim. I don't understand what was meant and will revisit it when I interview her."

"OK."

"Ma'am, can I have Deena assigned to this case?"

"Why?"

"Two reasons. One, this is my first experience with a victim with serious post-rape trauma, and the other is the video recording. We've had cases of rapists taking videos or snapshots using cell phones, but not with a video cam. At the same time, I don't think this is a case of opportunity rape. It looks like it was planned. The rape may not be the end of it. I've a bad feeling something more sinister is about to happen." She sighs, "But I've no clue what."

"All right, make the necessary changes to the roster."

"Thanks, and, ma'am, good to have you back."

4

INSPECTOR SHERRY IS IN her early thirties. Her Middle Eastern genes probably account for her sharp, well-defined features. She is five feet five inches tall, which is considered slightly tall for a Malaysian woman. Unlike most Malay and therefore Muslim female officers and personnel, Sherry doesn't wear the hijab. She goes with what's termed "free-hair." She has wavy hair just above shoulder length, with an olive skin complexion and a well-shaped, curvy body. Blessed with good looks and build, she aspired to a career in theater or modeling. She graduated with a degree in fine art and was taking a break before actively pursuing her dream. That was when she heard that one of her college friends was brutally raped after a night out. Sherry visited the friend in the hospital and was horrified at her injuries: blackened eyes, with a raptured retina in one, swollen face, cut lips, and two broken ribs. The doctor said the injuries would heal, but her friend was severely traumatized and would need professional counseling. Even then, the doctor said there was no guarantee she would fully recover.

As if that wasn't bad enough, Sherry later found out that no arrest was made. It was because her friend had been intoxicated and passed out. She was found the next morning by joggers and taken to the hospital. According to the police, she couldn't remember even leaving the club, let alone with whom. The police interviewed those at the party, but everyone was too wasted to remember anything. The friend she'd come with claimed she left with a man she hooked up with at the club. The CCTV cameras at the club were all dummies.

She was speechless. That was when Sherry abandoned her dream of modeling or the theater and decided to join the Royal Malaysia

Police. After passing as probationary inspector, she put in a request to be assigned to the Sexual & Child Abuse Division.

It is 2:45 p.m., and Detective Deena is already waiting at the hospital nurses' station when Sherry arrives. They walk to Era's room, finding her sitting in a chair by the window, staring out at the skyline.

"Miss Era, how are you feeling today?" Sherry greets her from the opened door. Her greeting startles Era more than she expects. "Sorry."

Era turns away from the window, her eyes hollow as if she's not there. She inhales deeply, staring at the intruders. Sherry sees recognition dawning in Era's eyes, and she flashes them a nervous smile. The officers step in, and Era resumes staring out the window.

"Do you have everything you need? Is there anything else we can get you from your apartment?"

"I have everything, thanks to your detective."

"Good. I need to record a statement from you. Are you up to it?"

Era nods and pushes herself out from the chair by the window and moves to the bed.

Sherry pulls the visitor's chair nearer to the bed, and Deena stands by the window. Shifting the over-bed food tray toward herself, Sherry lowers its height and uses it as a writing desk. Era shifts her position to the middle of the bed and sits cross-legged. She keenly observes the inspector. Sherry opens her folder and takes out several blank statement forms and a pen, placing them on the food tray. She begins with recording Era's personal details, her employer's details, cell phone number, and email address. Then she asks Era to say in her own words what happened that night. During the interview, she again notices the long silences as Era revisits her nightmare. She tolerates Era's wandering mind as she patiently tries to bring the victim's thoughts back to the incident. When Era finally finishes narrating the incident, Sherry asks if she needs a break or something to drink.

Era shakes her head. Sherry notices there are no drinks, not even mineral water, at her bedside locker.

"If you'd like a drink, Deena can go down and get something," Sherry offers.

Era nods and smiles a thank-you. Deena leaves them to get some drinks.

"Would you answer questions related to the incident?"

Era nods.

"Does anyone else have a key to your apartment?"

"My friend, Tim."

"Your boyfriend?"

"Tim's a woman, Fatimah, but I call her Tim. I mean, all our friends call her that."

"Can I have her full name and contact details?"

Era scrolls through her cell phone contact list and hands it to the inspector.

"Anyone else? Like a part-time housekeeper?"

"No."

"Is the apartment rented?"

Era nods.

"Does the landlord have a set of keys?"

"I suppose so."

Sherry makes a note to get a detective to check on the landlord. "How long have you stayed there?"

"Almost two years."

"You know most of the residents?"

"No, just a handful of them that I met in the elevator and say hi to."

"Our Crime Forensics team didn't find any sign of forced entry. I know this sounds silly, but do you recall letting anyone into the apartment after you got home?"

Era shuts her eyes and remains silent. After a long pause, she says, "I had a little too much to drink that night, but I'm very sure I didn't open the door for anyone. When I awoke, the stocking-faced man was above me." The recollection makes her shiver, and she folds her arms across her chest.

"When we arrived at your apartment, I heard you turning the dead bolt before releasing the doorknob lock. Do you normally lock the dead bolt when you're home?"

"Yes, but that night I can't remember if I did. After they left, I peeked from the bedroom to make sure that they'd gone and noticed the dead bolt was unlocked. So I locked it."

"If the dead bolt is locked, how would Tim enter when she comes home?"

"It's a key dead bolt. You can open it from outside if you have the key, which is different from the doorknob key. Tim has both."

"Sorry, I didn't notice that. May I know what you wore to bed that night?"

"When I got home, I was too exhausted, and my head was spinning from the drinks. I'm not a drinker, just occasionally when it's required," she adds as if embarrassed at not being able to hold her liquor. "So I didn't shower or change into my pajamas. I slept in my undies."

"The doctor said your blood alcohol level was high. May I ask who you were out drinking with?"

"We, I mean the company, had a small party to celebrate a new account I'd secured." Era smiles as she recalls the company's celebration—celebrating her. "I guess I had a little too much to drink. You know how it is, with every one of them proposing a toast."

Sherry nods.

"The Crime Forensics team was also unable to locate your panties. Can you describe them?"

"I was wearing a red Belabumbum Copacabana lace G-string. I remember, because Tim bought it for me when she was in Europe."

"Dr. Charles, the gynecologist, said he didn't find any traces of semen."

"He had a condom on."

"How did you know?"

"I saw him put it on," she replies, cringing.

"Did you see him taking it off after the . . ." Sherry stops as she doesn't want to use the word *rape*.

"No. I'm sorry. I closed my eyes, praying and hoping they'd leave. I was sure the one videoing would be next."

The D11 officer nods. It wasn't uncommon for rape victims to close their eyes as they attempted to disassociate themselves from what was happening.

"Miss Era, you don't have to be sorry for anything. This is not your fault, and you've not done anything wrong. In fact, I'm sorry for having to ask you all these questions, for making you relive the horrible memories."

Era nods, but she's looking past Sherry to the window, out to the skyline. Deena returns with two bottles of mineral water. She hands one to Era and puts the other on the side table. Era thanks her, uncaps the bottle, and takes a sip.

"The Crime Forensics team couldn't find it, the condom or the wrapper. I suppose he must have taken it with him to be disposed of elsewhere."

"Inspector, I don't know how to say this," Era suddenly says, followed by a long silence, her eyes still fixed to the water bottle.

The officers wait patiently.

"I don't want this to get out," Era continues, her voice trembling with fear.

"I understand. Please be assured that all personal and pertinent details will not be released to the press, even if they come to know of the case."

"I don't mean that. I mean I don't want anyone to know about this," she reiterates adamantly.

Sherry and Deena look at each other, baffled.

"Miss Era, there's no way for us to hide this case. It'll eventually come out. The hospital, your neighbors, your friends, we can't control them, especially if the case goes to court."

"Last night was a glorious moment in my life. I did tell you that I'm the new vice president for marketing, right?"

"Yes, and congratulations."

"Last night's party was also to celebrate my promotion." Era closes her eyes and takes several deep breaths. "If this comes out, I'll be ruined. All the years of hard work will be for nothing. Can't you see?" she asks, staring directly at the inspector.

"Miss Era, do you know who did this to you?" Sherry asks, suspicious at her sudden insistence. "Was it someone from the party?"

"No, it's nothing like that." She shakes her head.

"Is there, then, any particular reason for your request?"

"How can I face my colleagues, bosses, family, and friends? I was raped."

"Yes, you were, and it was not your fault. You mustn't blame yourself," Sherry tries to console her.

Era turns toward the bed and throws herself down, pressing her face into the pillow and sobbing uncontrollably. With a jerk, she turns onto her back, grips the front of her hospital robe, and gasps for air. Deena runs out to call the duty nurse, who rushes in and raises the alarm for the doctor on standby. The officers step outside and watch anxiously from the door as a doctor attends to the emergency. A nurse wheels in a blood pressure machine and starts working on the victim's arm. She calls the reading to the doctor, who is listening to the victim's heart through the stethoscope. The doctor says something to her and she leaves the room. A moment later she returns holding a tiny syringe and sticks it into the cannula in the victim's arm. The doctor places his stethoscope back to the victim's chest and nods. The victim seems to be breathing normally. He turns to leave.

"How is she?" Sherry asks as he passes by them.

"She had an anxiety attack, and I administered a mild sedative to calm her down. What happened in there?"

"I really don't know. One moment she was fine, talking to us, and the next she was sobbing, holding her chest and gasping for air."

"I guess that'll be the end of your interview today."

"Doc, I need her permission to revisit the crime scene."

"I don't know if she's in a position to give it. I've given her a sedative," the doctor says, "but you can try before the drug takes full effect."

They follow him back into the room. Era's eyes are closed and she is breathing normally.

"Miss Era, can I revisit your apartment to see if Forensics missed anything?"

Era cracks open her eyes momentarily and closes them again. Sherry turns to the doctor.

"That was one blink. And one blink always means 'yes,' right?"

The doctor smiles.

"Yes, one blink, and that was a yes," Deena concurs.

"Deena, can you get the apartment keys? We'll return them when we're done." Turning to the doctor, Sherry says, "Thank you."

5

THE PUTRA RIA CONDOMINIUM is a mid-range apartment complex with a swimming pool, tennis court, guardhouse, and covered parking lot. It was probably constructed a decade or more back when the area was being promoted as a new township in close proximity to the more well-known, overpriced Bangsar. The victim's apartment is on the ninth floor, a two-bedroom unit. The master bedroom is furnished, and the other room is used for storage. The living room has synthetic leather sofas, coffee tables, and a display cabinet with a flat-screen TV. What is conspicuously absent: family photos on the walls or on the display cabinet. A round dining table for four is set next to the wall partitioning the kitchen area. Dishes are neatly stacked in the dishrack on the kitchen counter. The kitchen is tidy, but Sherry doubts it's frequently used for cooking.

Inspector Sherry and Detective Deena are going through Era's bedroom when they hear the front door open. Hands on their weapons, they lean against the wall and watch the front door. Someone enters, closes the door, and heads for the bedroom. The person is about five feet two inches tall, with short hair and a stud in the left earlobe, dressed in a white short-sleeve shirt and dark pants. Waking past the dining table, the person calls out in a somewhat masculine voice, "Baby, are you home? Why haven't you answered my calls?"

The two officers step out from the bedroom. Surprised by the appearance of the two officers with guns by their sides, the person blurts out, "What the fuck?" and turns around to make a run to the front door.

"Stop," Deena calls.

"Fuck, who're you people? Where's Era?" the person asks, stopping midway to the front door.

"I'm Inspector Sherry, and this is Detective Deena. And who might you be?"

"Tim. What's happening here, and where's Era?" she asks, heading for the bedroom.

"She's not here," Deena answers, stopping her. "You're Fatimah, aren't you? I see you have keys to the apartment. Do you stay here with Era?"

"Call me Tim—*TIM*. On my days off, yes. Working days, I usually stay at my own place in Subang. Why d'you ask?"

"Who did you get the apartment keys from?"

"Era, of course."

Tim's answer confirms what the victim told them at the hospital.

"Have you ever given the apartment keys to anyone?" Sherry asks.

"No way, why would I do that?"

"I don't know, maybe to pick something up or to send something here."

"Never did that."

"If you only come on your days off, why was there a need for Era to give you the keys to her apartment?" Deena asks.

"My days off are her working days. Anyway, we're close friends, and sometimes she's out when I drop by."

"How close?"

"What's it to you?"

"How close?" Deena repeats, giving Tim a glare.

"Close," Tim replies, giving Deena a none-of-your-fucking business look. "You haven't answered my question. Where's Era?"

"As you're not family, I'm not authorized to tell you, but I can assure you she's fine. I'll need your particulars for records. Era will contact you when she wants to," Sherry replies.

Tim opens her mouth to say or refute something but doesn't. Instead, she hands the inspector her business card.

Sherry looks at the card. It lists Fatimah as Tim, Punk Bistro Manager, located in Section 17, Petaling Jaya.

"Where is she? Is she under arrest or has something happened to her?" Tim demands.

"No, she's not under arrest. That's all I can tell you. For now, I need you to leave and let us do our work."

"Typical police tactics," Tim says accusingly. "What's your name again?"

"Inspector Sherry from D11, KL police."

"You know we do have police officers as regulars at the bistro. Maybe I should just have a chat with them about your conduct," Tim says with a hint of intimidation.

"Maybe you should, and don't forget to offer them drinks on the house before you chat them up," Deena quips. "That'll surely buy you tons of free advice."

"And you are?" Tim asks, staring at Deena.

"The person that's going to kick your ass out if you don't leave quietly," she says with a swagger.

————

Deena follows the reluctant Tim to the front door. At the doorway, Tim spins around and then sidesteps the detective and shouts.

"I've every right to be here! This is my apartment, too."

"I'm sure you do, but not at this moment. Please follow Detective Deena out, and don't make me arrest you for interfering with a police investigation," Sherry replies.

"Investigation! What investigation?"

Deena tugs at Tim's arm, guiding her out of the door. She stands by the doorway, making sure Tim gets into the elevator and is gone before locking the door.

"Can you do that?" she asks, gesturing in the direction of the fuming Fatimah.

"What? Ask her to leave, or refuse to provide her with information about the victim?"

"Both."

"This is a crime scene. And as far as we're informed by the victim, Tim's not a tenant or housemate. I'm sure we're within our rights," Sherry replies, heading back to the bedroom.

"How about withholding information about the victim?"

"The victim explicitly expressed she doesn't want anyone to know. We have to respect her wishes. Anyway, Tim's not family. When Era's ready, I'm sure she'll tell her or anyone else she feels inclined to."

"Why do you think she doesn't want anyone to know? Victims usually want someone close to be informed and be with them, but Era doesn't. I think she has something to hide."

"What do you mean?"

Jerking her head toward the door, she says, "Like her. Did you notice her clothing, or hear her call out 'Baby' when she came in?"

Sherry glares at her detective. "She was probably in her working attire. I know a lot of pubs require their employees to wear white shirts and black pants. Anyway, they could simply be good friends. Many women call their close friends 'baby,' 'babe,' and so on. That doesn't necessarily imply what you're thinking."

"I know, I'm not judging her, but it just feels different coming from her. It's kind of lovey-dovey," Deena mocks with a wide silly grin.

"And you think Tim's the reason the victim doesn't want this known?"

"One of many."

"What are the others?"

"Like she said, the shame, the stigma, and could even be the fear."

"Fear of what?"

"Retaliation from the rapists. They took videos of the rape, and that tells me there'll be a comeback, a revisit. May not be an actual visit, maybe in some other ways."

"Blackmail?"

"That's one of them. She's a VP. I'm sure she's making good money." Sherry nods.

6

WHEN ERA OPENS HER eyes, her throat is dry and her mouth is sour. Sitting up and noticing a food tray on the edge of the bed, she reaches for a plastic cup of water and drains it in one gulp. *Is that lunch or dinner? What time is it?* She turns to check the wall clock: it's 2:20 p.m. *Is it Saturday or Sunday? Sunday, the party was Saturday evening, so today has to be Sunday.* Her throat is still dry, and she drinks from the bottle of mineral water bought by Detective Deena. She's still feeling dazed from the sedative. Closing her eyes, she tries to recall what's on her calendar for Monday and Tuesday. Her brain is fuzzy. She gives up trying, telling herself she isn't ready to go to the office and face her coworkers and bosses. Era decides to take a couple of days off. *I need to sort my nerves out. Need to come up with what to say if this thing comes out into the open. But what can I say?*

She gets off the bed and pulls the chair to the window. The noise of the city filters through the glass window, and she looks down to the street. At the steady flow of city dwellers in cars and on motorbikes going about enjoying a sunny Sunday, oblivious to her misfortune.

She calls her secretary, apologizes for calling her on her rest day, and informs her that she's down with flu and won't be coming into the office for two days. Then she summons the duty nurse.

"I'd like to be discharged."

"You're under Dr. Geetha's care; only she can discharge you. Let me check if she's on duty," the nurse replies.

When the nurse returns, she informs Era that Dr. Geetha is on the night shift and will only be in at eleven in the evening.

"Can't another doctor sign my discharge papers?" Era is getting agitated.

"I'm sorry, but your admission is part of a police investigation. I don't think a ward doctor can do that."

"Call the ward doctor and tell him I want to be discharged. If he's not willing to do it, I'll discharge myself. Give me whatever form you need me to sign, I'll sign it," she says firmly.

She gets off the chair, takes her overnight bag, and goes to the bathroom. The ward doctor enters the room, accompanied by the duty nurse, just as Era comes out of the bathroom, all dressed and ready to leave.

"Miss Era, I'm Dr. Lutfi. The nurse says you've requested a discharge. I strongly advise that you to wait for Dr. Geetha to examine you and let her decide."

"I appreciate your advice, but I'm fine now, and I want to go home. Don't worry, I'll sign the self-discharge form," she replies, continuing packing her belongings.

Familiar with obstinate patients, Dr. Lutfi nods at the duty nurse and they leave Era to her packing.

———

It is close to three in the afternoon when Sherry steps out of the shower and puts on a pair of loose satin shorts and an oversize Pink Floyd crewneck T-shirt. It had been a long and trying thirty hours, and she's looking forward to a nap. She makes herself a warm cup of jasmine tea, a drink that always calms her, picks a fashion magazine from the pile of unread magazines, and heads for the bedroom. Just as she lies in bed and starts flipping through the magazine, her cell phone rings. It's Dr. Geetha from Kuala Lumpur Hospital.

"Yes, Doc," Sherry answers, instinctively wary.

"I was just informed that your victim self-discharged," Dr. Geetha says, sounding concerned.

"When?"

"About fifteen minutes back."

"Did something happen?"

"The duty nurse says she called her and asked to be discharged. The ward doctor, Dr. Lutfi, was called. He advised her against it, but she insisted."

"I thought she was sedated."

"Yes, she was, but it was only a mild one to calm her down."

"Did someone visit her? Did she leave with anyone?"

"Not that the duty nurse is aware of."

"Did she say why?"

"She said she was feeling fine and wanted to go home."

"Couldn't the hospital stop her?"

"I'm afraid not. Since this is a police case, I was thinking the police could. Can you? I don't think she's in any condition to go home and be by herself. She could cause harm to herself. She needs professional help."

"I don't know if we have the authority. The court has, but that'll take some doing. And today is Sunday. Let me check with my boss and call you back."

"Sherry, the toxicology report just came in. There was no trace of semen. However, the lab did find traces of glycerine, propylene glycol—

"What are those?"

"Sexual lubricant, you know, like those pleasure-enhancing gels."

"Pleasure enhancing? Seriously . . . what pleasure?" Sherry sneers. "She was raped, what pleasure?"

"It's what the manufacturers claim on their product," Dr. Geetha replies defensively.

"I'm sorry, Doc, I didn't mean to take it out on you . . . just rattled by the victim leaving."

"No offense taken. I know you're concerned—so am I."

"Any chance the nurse knows if she got a phone call? Maybe overheard or saw her talking on the phone?"

"I can ask, but from where they're stationed I doubt if they can see or hear her on the phone."

"Thanks. Doc. Let me call my boss and see what we can do. I'll get back to you soon as I know. Thanks for letting me know, and again, sorry."

Sherry terminates the call with Dr. Geetha and dials Superintendent Lillian to update her and seek advice.

"Ma'am, sorry to call you on Sunday."

"No problem, what's up?"

"My victim just discharged herself from the hospital against the duty doctor's advice."

"When?"

"According to Dr. Geetha, about twenty minutes ago."

"Do they know why she discharged herself?"

"No. Ma'am, can we force her to return and remain in the hospital?"

"She's a victim. There's no provision in the law for us to do that. We can only send victims for medical examinations. Even then we need their consent for the examination and to take samples. Unless she's a threat to herself or others, which means she is mentally unsound, there's nothing we can do."

"I don't have any experience with such victims. Can she be deemed mentally unsound? I'm sure she's a threat to herself, if not to others, but that's only my gut feeling."

"Unfortunately, that'll not be enough for a court order. It has to be a medical diagnosis, I suppose by a psychiatrist."

"When I was interviewing her, she had an anxiety attack, and the doctor had to give her a sedative. I know she's emotionally unstable, and she's staying alone. I'm worried if she experiences another attack and nobody is around to help."

"I know, but she's of age, and she made the decision to discharge herself. There's nothing you can do, and there's no reason you should blame yourself should she get herself into a medical situation."

"Thanks, ma'am," Sherry says with a heavy sigh.

7

ERA AMILIA TAKES A cab to her apartment. She decides not to ask Tim or anyone to pick her up to avoid having to explain why she was hospitalized. She is in no condition, mentally or emotionally, to deal with probing questions and sympathetic gapes or pity-showering. She just needs to be by herself to work things out.

Stepping out of the elevator on the ninth floor, Era momentarily freezes at the lobby. Instinctively, she turns to look to her left and right, half-expecting someone to be lurking or waiting for her. Satisfied there is no one, she tentatively walks to her unit, the door keys ready in her hand. Standing in front of her door, she nervously turns to give the corridor another look before inserting the key. As she turns the lock, she remembers Sherry saying there were no signs of forced entry. A frightening thought crosses her mind: *The rapists probably have keys to my apartment, and they could be inside waiting for me to return.* Images of a knife-wielding man wearing pantyhose over his head and waiting for her in the bedroom flash through her mind. A cold shiver runs down her spine.

Steadying her trembling hand, she unlocks the door and quietly closes it, turning the dead bolt, pressing the doorknob button, and latching the night bolt. Once inside, she immediately steps into the kitchen, which is adjacent to the front door, drops her overnight bag, and grabs one of the knives from the knife holder. With her heart racing, Era presses her back against the wall, inching her way to the hall. Her eyes fixed on the open bedroom door, she watches for any sign of life, any movement of shadow while straining her ears for any sound. Seeing and hearing nothing, she carefully crosses the hall to the bedroom.

At the bedroom door, she hides behind the wall and peeks in. Her heart is throbbing so hard it feels like it's going to burst out of her chest. *It surely will if the pantyhose mask man is in there. What am I supposed to do, fight him with this?* She looks at the weapon in her hand. Era almost cries at the pathetic idea that she can take on the rapist with a kitchen knife.

Something inside her says, *It's better to fight and die than be subjected to the degrading act again.*

Era pulls herself together and scans her bedroom, looking for signs that the rapists are lying in wait. She sees nothing. She gets down on all fours and looks under the bed. Nothing. She lets out a sigh of relief.

While she's still on all fours, her cell phone gives out a series of knocking sounds, the notification of incoming WhatsApp messages. The noise makes her jump out of her skin. She scrambles to her feet, the knife gripped tightly, at the ready as she runs to the front door. Then she realizes what the sound was. With her heart still pounding like a jackhammer, she swears loudly. Fishing the cell phone from inside her pocket, she sees a string of WhatsApp texts from her secretary.

They read:

OMG boss.

Is it you?

Check out utube-era's salvation.

––––––––

Era rushes to her bedroom to get her laptop. Realizing she's still holding the knife, she throws it on to the bed. Grabbing her laptop from her work bag, she hurries out to the living room, sits on a sofa, and switches it on. She keys in www.utube.com on the search bar, her hands shaking. When the site appears, she searches *Era's Salvation*. A series of thumbnails of videos appear. One of them shows her tearful face.

She clicks on the video with a feeling of dread. Straightaway, she sees a pantyhose-masked man walking toward a sleeping figure on a bed. She cringes in horror as the voiceover says: *Freeing Era Amilia.*

"How did he know my name?" she whispers.

Her eyes widen, staring at the laptop unblinkingly.

The rapist covers her mouth with his hand, his face moving close to her ear. In his other hand a knife he held to her cheek. Her hand moves to her cheek. She felt the cold steel. She opens her eyes. The video zooms in on her terrified face, the blade pressed to her skin. The pantyhose man cuts her bra, and his latex-gloved hand fondles her breasts.

Era feels nauseated. The room begins to spin. *My secretary has seen this. That means the whole office must have seen it.*

The video is still playing. She can hear the pantyhose man's hoarse voice telling her she will be free. Era closes her eyes tightly, screams, "Shut up! Shut up! Shut up!" She clamps her ears with the palms of her hands, but she's still hearing him. Not from the laptop. The playback is in her head.

She springs to her feet, angrily swiping the laptop off the coffee table and sending it flying to the floor. Somehow, the crash causes the video to pause. The living room starts to spin slowly, then faster and faster. She feels like throwing up. Clutching her stomach, she dashes to the balcony for fresh air. Bending over the parapet, she tries to throw up— only water and tangy saliva come out. She bangs the railings repeatedly, sobbing and asking, *Why me?* Her mind races. *Who else has seen it? My boss, my clients, friends? Surely Tim. Oh my God, my parents, my sister, she's always on UTube. My life's ruined.*

The landscaping, the guardhouse, the swimming pool, the tennis court, the distant hill—they all are spinning. Era looks up to the blue sky, the puffy white clouds, and sees the smiling pantyhosed faces. Then she hears him asking, "Did you enjoy it?" and his laugh. The laughter grows louder and louder. Era turns away from the balcony, and she hears the apartment building's noises: children crying, the elevator bell dinging as it stops on the floor above, the thud of doors closing and the flushing of toilets in the building. All these welcome, familiar noises suddenly sound like they're mocking her, chanting, *"Era was raped . . . Era was raped."*

Era turns to face the balcony, gripping the concrete parapet tightly. The chanting in her head stops. Breathing heavily, she looks up to the sky. The clouds are coming together. It seems like they're coming closer. As they do, they change into the faces of her boss, coworkers, friends, even complete strangers. They are all grinning and sneering at her, chanting, *"Cleanse your body, cleanse your soul."*

"From what? I didn't do anything wrong," Era shouts to them and weeps.

"It doesn't matter. What matters is you were raped and you need to cleanse your soul."

"How?"

"Come with us, we'll help you, and you won't remember any of it."

Several white hands extend from the sky toward her.

"Trust us, this is the only way."

Era climbs onto the parapet, arms reaching for the white hands from the sky to freedom.

8

DETECTIVE DEENA IS AT the Putra Ria Condominium to look in on Era. Walking up to the apartment building from visitor parking, she notices a large crowd including two uniformed policemen at the upper-level open parking lot. She pushes through the crowd. A body dressed in jeans and a pink T-shirt is sprawled awkwardly on the tarmac in a pool of blood. The hands and legs are twisted, and bones can be seen protruding from them. It looks like the body fell from the building—probably a jumper. The jumper's face is facing the opposite direction—*If there is still a face*, Deena thinks, but from the body size and hair, she believes it is most likely a woman. Blood spatter can be seen as far as several feet around the body.

"What happened?" Deena asks the policemen.

"She fell from up there," one of the policemen says, pointing up toward the apartment building.

"Jumper?" she asks.

"Don't know."

"Who's she?"

The policemen shrug.

"What's the name of the deceased?"

Again the two policemen shrug.

"Didn't you ask around? What the hell are you here for?" Detective Deena snaps.

"We just got here," one answers.

"Era!" shouts a man in the crowd who was eavesdropping.

Deena turns to the man.

"Era Amilia, from the ninth floor?"

"Unit 9.01."

"Shit," she curses under her breath.

Deena steps away from the crowd and calls her boss. Sherry, who is driving out to meet friends for tea, calls one of them to apologize for not being able to make it. She makes a detour to Pantai Dalam. Deena is waiting for her at the visitor parking, and together they walk to the upper-level open parking.

The body is already covered with a plain light-colored blanket, probably given by one of the more sensitive residents. Deena introduces Sherry to the policeman on guard. They step up to the covered body. Deena lifts the blanket for her boss to take a peek. Sherry bends down, her lips moving as if saying something or offering a prayer. She inhales deeply, gestures to her detective to cover the deceased.

On the ninth floor, they find the assistant officer in charge of Pantai Police Station, Sergeant Major Rashid, and his team huddled in discussion in front of Era's unit. Approaching them, Sherry introduces herself.

"What's the situation?" she asks.

"The door is locked from the inside. I've called for a locksmith to pick it," Rashid says, pointing to a Chinese man sitting at the emergency staircase. "He managed to pick both the knob lock and the dead bolt, but we still can't open the door. The locksmith suspected it has a bolt, you know, the night latch."

"What's the plan?"

"We're waiting for the OCS's instructions." The OCS Rashid mentioned is his superior, the officer in charge of a police station.

"Have you called D10?"

Rashid nods. His cell phone rings, and he steps aside to answer it. Coming back, he displays a look of uncertainty. Sherry gives him a questioning gaze.

"OCS says to get one of the men to come in from the tenth floor through the balcony."

"That may not be a good idea," Sherry counters.

She asks for the OCS's contact number. Taking out her cell phone, she makes a call.

"Evening, sir, this is Inspector Sherry from D11. SM Rashid says you've given instruction for him to get a man onto the balcony from the higher floor."

"Hi Sherry, what's a Sexual & Child Abuse investigator doing at my suicide scene?"

"She's a victim in my case, or shall I say, was a victim in my case."

"Oh, I wasn't informed. SM Rashid says the door is bolted from the inside. Entering through the balcony seems the best option without breaking down the door."

"Sir, the balcony could be a critical site for recovering any evidence of struggle. Coming through it may destroy the integrity of any evidence there. Since the door is bolted from the inside, it's better to force it open, as I'm certain there would not be any tampering of evidence."

"You think it wasn't a suicide?"

"It probably was, unless there's another way out of the apartment. My victim was experiencing PTSD, and the doctor had admitted her for observation, but then she checked herself out. I just want to be sure that there was no foul play."

"PTSD? What's that?"

"Post-traumatic stress disorder."

"Wow. If you use big words like that, how can I say no?" the OCS jokes. "Go ahead. Do it your way."

"Thank you, sir," she says. Terminating the call, she says to SM Rashid, "We're going through the front. Where's the locksmith?"

A middle-aged Chinese man who was sitting quietly at the emergency staircase is pushed forward.

"Can you open the door by cutting around the night latch?" Sherry asks.

The locksmith knocks the door lightly with the handle of a screw-driver, listening to the sound.

"I have to cut a hole around here," he says, making a circle on the door with his finger. Then he flashes a youthful grin, saying, "I don't have my drill with me."

"Maybe the management office has a power drill?" Deena says. "I'll go ask."

"The management office is closed," one of the policemen informs.

"Can someone get the security to call the management staff in?" SM Rashid barks.

"Hang on," Sherry says. "SM, can you get me a carjack?"

Sergeant Major Rashid nods and instructs one of his men to get one from the patrol car. Turning back to Sherry he asks, "What do you want it for?"

"See those flip windows? We can go in through there. Use the jack to pry open the grille. That way, we won't damage the door, in case D10 needs to examine it."

"Good idea."

———

Using the carjack, they open a gap in the security grille of the kitchen window. The flap-window opening is small but large enough for a small person to squeeze in. Sherry looks around for someone small to climb through it, and her eyes stop at Detective Deena.

"Oh no," her detective says, backing away.

"You're the smallest."

"It's not ladylike," she protests. "And I don't want their grubby hands all over me," she says, indicating the policemen.

"Don't worry, we'll be gentle." one policeman says, and the rest laugh.

"Come on, Deena, show the men that we women are up to any challenge," Sherry coaxes her.

Deena grunts and relents. "Any one of you touches me in the wrong place and you'll be eating my shoes."

Two policemen lean against the wall and lock their hands together, creating a human ladder. Deena places her right foot on the hands of the policemen, holding on to their shoulders.

"Turn your faces away," she snarls at them.

She reaches up and grabs the lower frame of the window, and the policemen give her a lift.

"Stop, stop," she yelps. "I can't go in headfirst. I need to get my legs in before the rest of me."

She climbs back down. After a short banter with the policemen, she agrees to be hoisted up by two of them so she can push her legs through the window first.

"Careful that she doesn't cut herself on the broken grille," Sherry warns them.

Facing outward, Deena hangs on tightly to the window frame, feeling for a foothold on the kitchen cabinet, testing its strength. She spreads her other leg wide to distribute her weight on the cabinet top, before taking her grip off the window frame. One of her legs knocks over a cooking utensil, sending it tumbling to the floor with a racket.

"Oops!" she exclaims with a grin through the window.

"What was that, what did you knock?" Sherry asks.

"Frying pan. I'm in," she calls out, stating the obvious, drawing applause from the group outside.

"We can see that. Don't go breaking anything else," Sherry calls back. "Now, move along the wall and open the door. Be sure to put on your gloves."

"OK."

Sherry hears the sound of the night latch sliding. The door cracks open, and Deena's face beams at them.

"Yes, ma'am, may I assist you?" she jokes, role-playing a housemaid.

"Funny," Sherry says, glaring at her. Turning to the group, Sherry says, "SM, just the photographer in. The rest can wait outside."

In the living room, she spots the laptop on the floor and warns them, "Watch where you step."

They tread carefully through the living room to the balcony.

"Apart from the laptop, nothing else seems to be broken or out of place. No signs of struggle," Deena observes.

"What do you think happened here?" Sherry asks no one in particular. "Are you taking photos of all this?" she asks the photographer.

The photographer nods. Snapping on a pair of gloves, Sherry flips open the screen of the laptop and reads it. She makes a note and says to the photographer, "Can you bag the computer? I'll need Forensics to look at it later. Deena, can you look for her cell phone?"

Deena comes out of the bedroom with Era's cell phone and hands it to her.

"I think you should come and see the bedroom," she tells the inspector.

"Why, what's there?"

"There's a knife on the bed."

"Knife, you mean there's a sign of struggle in there?"

"Hard to say, the bed seemed to be the same as we left it last night. I mean bare after D10 took the bedsheet and blanket. But when we left there was no knife on the bed."

Sherry enters the bedroom, sees the knife on the bed. She examines the room for signs of commotion but does not see any.

"Why do you think the knife is here?" she asks her detective.

Deena shrugs.

"Deena, go check the kitchen and see if you find other knives. This looks like a kitchen knife."

Deena leaves the bedroom. Sherry tells the photographer to snap photos of the knife and bag it. Deena returns holding a similar knife but shorter than the one on the bed together with the overnight bag, showing them to Sherry.

"There's a knife missing from the holder," she says. "I believe it's that knife. It looks the same as this and others in the holder. Found her overnight bag on the floor."

Sherry tells the photographer to snap photos of the knives and holder. She checks the cell phone, and it is key-code locked.

"Here, bag this, too," she says, handing the cell phone to the photographer. "I'll need to ask our Forensic IT to unlock it." Turning to SM

Rashid, she says, "In the meantime, why don't you see if you can track down her parents to inform them of their daughter's demise?"

Sergeant Major Rashid nods.

"I noticed the address on her IC is that of a permanent address, not this unit. Chances are that's the parents' address."

Sherry hands over Era's purse containing the identity card to the sergeant major. "The IC is in there. There's nothing more for me to do here," she says and motions Deena to follow her.

"Why did you give the victim's personal belongings to the AOCS?" Deena asks. "Are we not handling the case?"

"What case?"

"This case."

"This is a suicide, since when do we do suicide?" Sherry asks, annoyed at her detective for not being able to distinguish the two cases.

"Yes, but she's our victim, our rape case," Deena presses on.

"So?"

"This should be our case."

Sherry lets out a tiny snort. "The rape case's still ours, but the suicide's the station's case. They may or may not be related, but they're different cases."

———

They take the elevator down and notice that the crowd has grown larger where the deceased lay. Sherry beckons the two policemen over and instructs them to disperse the crowd.

"This is not a freaking show," she admonishes them. "How would you like it if that's your sister or relative lying there?"

The policemen bow their heads.

"Now," she snaps.

"Yes, ma'am."

Walking to their cars, Deena says, "That was quick."

"What was quick?"

"Up there," she says, tilting her head to the apartment building.

"There was no sign of break-in, no sign of struggle, what's there to linger for?"

"Are you planning to go somewhere?" Deena asks.

"No, why do you ask?"

"You're all dressed up like you are."

"I was, but now I'm going to the office. There's something I need to check."

At the office, Sherry makes a call to Superintendent Lillian to update her on the suicide. Lillian hears the frustration and pain in her officer's voice. The hopelessness of not being able to stop an avoidable tragedy.

Lillian remembers how frustrated she herself was at not being able to act when the Australian police presented information and evidence on the infamous British pedophile Richard Huckle. Unlike in the United Kingdom, Malaysia's law required a complainant for a charge to be brought against him. Her team had to let the British police handle the case, although all the victims were Malaysians. That is the law: in offering protection, it blindsided the process.

"I'm sorry," Lillian offers. "I know you tried. Sherry, it's not your fault."

Sherry nods, although her boss cannot see her.

"The station's handling it?" Lillian continues.

"Yes, the AOCS was there."

"OK, get some rest, and we'll see how we'll go about the rape case."

"Night, ma'am."

"Night."

Sherry logs on to the Internet, goes to UTube, and searches for "Era's Salvation." With Deena standing behind her chair, she watches the horrific experience of the victim with disgust and understands why Era committed suicide.

"Deena, I want you to go to the condo management office and view all their CCTV recordings for yesterday and today. See if you spot anyone suspicious and check with the management if they're residents. If they are, find out their units. If they're outsiders, look at the security logs and take down their particulars. I'm going to stop by Forensics."

"Are you coming back here?"

"No, it's already late. I'll go home from there. See you tomorrow."

"Okay."

"Call me if you find anything interesting."

9

THE NEXT MORNING ON her way to the office, Sherry stops at a gas station to buy a newspaper. Sitting in the car, she reads the headline: Immediate Police Action Urged. The story that carried a photo of the victim says:

> *Era Amilia Zabidin, the vice president of marketing for Uptrend Advertising, was found dead at the foot of her apartment building last night. Police investigations allegedly found no evidence of foul play and classified the case as suicide. It was learned that she was allegedly raped in her apartment after returning from a party celebrating her promotion the night before. The alleged rapists recorded the entire episode and posted it on UTube. The video has since gone viral. The police confirmed a report was made, but have declined to comment further. A spokesman for the Malaysian Communication and Multimedia Commission (MCMC) said they were officially notified by the police to block the video and are looking into it. At press time, the video was still up with close to fifteen thousand hits. The victim's family said they had not been informed of the alleged rape. They want the culprits caught and charged for murdering their daughter.*

Sherry throws the newspaper onto the passenger seat and drives off.

Detective Deena is waiting for her in the lobby when she steps out of the elevator. "Ma'am wants you to go straight to OCCI's office. She's waiting for you there."

"Thanks. Can you take my bag to the office?"

Sherry turns and walks toward the emergency staircase to go up the two flights. Stepping into the OCCI office's waiting area, she is surprised to see it is full of reporters. She knows some of them, and she greets them with a smile. She glances at her watch. It is 8:10 a.m.

"Inspector Sherry, I was told you're the investigating officer in this rape-suicide case," one of the reporters says.

As she turns to the reporter, she is assaulted with a barrage of flashes from cameramen, blinding her temporarily.

"Yes," she answers, blinking repeatedly to regain her vision.

"Any comments?"

"You know I can't comment on an ongoing investigation. Hang around, maybe you'll get lucky." She motions to the office of the Officer in Charge of Criminal Investigation—aka the OCCI publicity junkie.

"You have any leads on who uploaded the video?"

"Sorry, I'm already late for a meeting. They're waiting for me," she says by way excusing herself and flashes a smile for the nonstop clicking cameras.

The OCCI's secretary greets her and points to a meeting room. "It'll be there."

Sherry returns her greetings with a smile and heads for the room.

———

Kevin Foo, head of Crime Forensics, D10, and Avtar Singh, the head of Legal and Prosecution, D5, are making small talk when Sherry enters. She greets the two officers, noting the absence of her boss and the OCCI.

"Sherry, you're the IO for the case," Avtar says rather than asks.

"Yes."

"The Chosen One," Kevin says with a chuckle.

Just then, the OCCI and head of D11 enter the room.

"Gentlemen, I suppose you know why you're here?" Senior Assistant Commissioner Burhanuddin Sidek says, somewhat exasperatedly.

Sherry tries to recall if she has ever seen the OCCI without that constipated look of his.

"Let's start with Sherry," he says.

Sherry looks at Superintendent Lillian, unsure where to begin. Seeing the look on her face, Burhanuddin snaps, "I've already been briefed on the case by your boss. Tell me what you've got on the rapists."

"So far, not much, except for the physical measurements of the rapist obtained from the video by Forensics."

"What good is that? After twenty-four hours, you're telling me you've no clue who they are?"

"The rapist didn't leave any forensic evidence on the victim or at the scene. Without that, we've nothing to go on."

Turning to Lillian, Burhanuddin asks, "That's it?"

Superintendent Lillian nods and opens her mouth to say something in defense of her officer, but before she can speak, the OCCI turns back to Sherry.

"What about witnesses? CCTV?"

"We viewed the CCTV recordings from the condominium but were unable to get anything from it. The condo only has two cameras, one at the guardhouse and the other in the main lobby. The guards on duty were unable to assist us in any manner."

"What do you expect from the security guards? How about our detectives? What's their excuse?"

"They've been asked to talk to the residents to see if any of them saw anything and to their informers—"

"Who are you kidding? What informers? You mean those bums hanging around roadside stalls full of gossip?"

Sherry winces and looks at her boss. She knows better than to explain the situation to a man who has no investigative experience and uses television crime series as his benchmark.

"I've revisited the crime scene—"

"What did you expect to find at the scene? Their photos? Better yet, their ICs?" Burhanuddin sneers at her.

That would be helpful, Sherry says to herself. To her relief, the OCCI turns his sights on Kevin Foo of D10.

"What about Forensics, what do you have?"

"From the video, it can be seen that the rapist had shaved his pubic hair. It could just be coincidental, or a precaution to ensure no pubic hair was left behind. As for bodily or oral fluid, the victim had already taken a shower when we arrived. That had washed away any evidence on her body. In the video, the rapist was seen sucking the victim's nipples, yet swabs taken by the doctor on her breasts and nipples yielded no trace of oral mucosa."

"With all the high-tech equipment available, you're telling me you have nothing. Do you, or your men, really know how to use the equipment?"

It is Kevin's turn to wince. He, too, knows it's useless to say anything.

"I have reporters outside waiting for my press release, and you people are telling me that you've got nothing. Do you know how stupid that makes me look?"

They all nod in unison, and Sherry cannot hold back a smile.

"You think that's funny?" he snaps at her.

She is about to answer when Lillian intercepts.

"We're forming a task force for this case. I'm putting in a request to Crime Forensics to assign one of their computer technicians to it."

"Good, good. I'll tell the press that. Now, we're getting somewhere. What else?"

"The task force will monitor any new posting. I don't know if it's possible, but if it is, I want them to monitor and also to analyze all social media comments on sites related to this video."

"I'm sure it can be done, I've seen it done on *NCIS*. That agent, McGee, and Abby, they can track anything on the net. With our technology, we can do anything they can. I like that. Go ahead and set up a task force immediately."

Sherry and Kevin exchange glances with each other.

The OCCI continues, "That's how seasoned officers think when confronted with situations like this. We don't sit around, make excuses, and wet our diapers." He looks at Avtar, the head of Legal and Prosecution (D5). "The parents are screaming murder. Can we charge the rapists for murder?"

"To charge the culprit under 3-0-2, we need to prove intent. I don't think we can. I suggest we go on 3-7-6, which carries a thirty-year prison term. We can also load the Communications and Multimedia offense on it."

"Go back and reread your law books. Find a way to charge them for murder," Burhanuddin retorts. "I'll tell the press our Legal and Prosecution is looking into the possibility. How does anyone expect me to serve the public when I'm surrounded by officers like you?"

The OCCI abruptly stands and leaves the room. The four officers look at each other, stifling smiles. When they are sure the publicity junkie is gone and out of hearing, Avtar breaks into a chuckle followed by the rest of them.

"Go reread your laws," Lillian mocks.

"I need to watch more *NCIS*," Kevin jests.

10

THE OCCI's WAITING ROOM is overflowing with noisy reporters and cameramen as well as NGO representatives. They've had a tip that the victim's delegation will be meeting with the OCCI. It wouldn't surprise anyone if the tip originated in the same office. Just as the tip said, Era's parents arrive accompanied by their state assemblyman, the Honorable Puah Chua Keng, his press secretary, David Lam, and a lawyer, Joganathan. The media leap into action, snapping photos and inundating them with questions.

"Mr. Zabidin, did the police say why you weren't informed of your daughter's rape?"

"That's one of the clarifications we'll be seeking," the Honorable Puah replies.

"Rumor has it that your daughter was schizophrenic and was on medication. Is that true?"

"Rubbish! Where did you hear that?" Puah lashes out at the reporter. "You should be more professional than to ask questions based on rumors, especially when the family has just experienced a tragic loss."

In the melee to interview the victim's parents, the reporters have surrounded them, pushing their chaperons aside. The assemblyman and his team claw their way back beside Era's parents, having no intention of being excluded from the photos, particularly now, with talk of the general elections on everyone's lips.

"Please, we're here to see Senior Assistant Commissioner Burhanuddin. We'll make a press statement after our meeting," Puah says.

"What're you demanding from the OCCI?"

"The family has no comments at this juncture," Joganathan says, making himself visible for the cameras. Grabbing the arm of a reporter making his way closer to Era's parents, he hisses, "Stop shoving."

"What're your comments on the UTube video?"

"It's an act of a mentally deranged person who should be charged with the murder of Mr. Zabidin's baby girl," Puah answers firmly. "And all those people viewing the video and cheering the rapists should be charged as accomplices. They're all equally guilty. The authorities should've acted immediately to take the video off the Internet."

"Are you planning on taking civil action against the MCMC for failure to block the video?"

"No comment," Joganathan barks, annoyed at losing his spot next to the parents in the scrum.

"Can you let Mr. Zabidin answer for himself? We want to hear what he has to say," one of the reporters shouts from the back of the crowd. The remark is met with loud approval from the other reporters.

"Please excuse us, we don't want to keep Mr. Burhanuddin waiting," Puah says, plainly annoyed by the call to shut up.

Concerned by the tense atmosphere, a uniformed policeman from the general office intervenes. He escorts the victim's parents and their political entourage through, telling the crowd to quiet down. The OCCI's secretary ushers them into the meeting room and informs them that SAC Burhanuddin will be with them shortly.

———

Senior Assistant Commissioner Burhanuddin is accompanied by the head of Legal and Prosecution when he enters the room, greets the entourage, and offers his condolences to the parents.

"What're you doing to bring the culprits to justice?" the Honorable Puah asks curtly, dispensing with pleasantries.

"I've issued instructions for a task force to be formed immediately, specifically for this case," the OCCI proudly declares. "I assure you that my officers, and our forensic experts, are looking at everything to identify the culprits."

"What about the video on UTube?" Puah asks.

"Again, I assure you there'll be no further postings. We're working closely with MCMC, that's the Malaysian Communications and Multimedia Commission, to block further postings on UTube."

"I know what MCMC stands for," Puah sneers. "They're not even able to block the existing video. What makes you so sure they'll be able to stop further postings?"

The OCCI leans toward his right and whispers to the head of Legal and Prosecution.

"Why the hell has the video not been blocked yet?" he demands.

"There's nothing we can do, it's not within our jurisdiction," Avtar whispers back.

"Are you planning to charge the culprits with murder?" Joganathan asks.

"My head of Legal and Prosecution is looking into that possibility, and I'm sure he'll come up with something."

Avtar glares at the OCCI, surprised by his silly answer.

"And what about those people who're cheering the rapists with their comments, are the police charging them, too? They're as guilty as the rapists," Puah butts in.

"We're just discussing it," Burhanuddin says, pulling another lie from his back pocket. "Again, D5 will be seriously looking into it."

"Mr. Burhanuddin, I don't think you understand what the family is going through," Puah stresses, clearly unhappy with the answers.

"Yes, I do, and I assure you that we're not insensitive to their loss and suffering. Mr. and Mrs. Zabidin, again, please accept my condolences." The OCCI stands, indicating the meeting is over, and heads out to an event he much preferred to be at—a press conference.

11

THE TASK FORCE COMPRISES Inspector Sherry, Detective Deena, and three additional detectives. Superintendent Lillian managed to rope in an IT technician, Saifuddin Rahim, from the Forensic IT section. She also allocated one of the smaller meeting rooms as the situation room.

Saifuddin has set up two desktop computers and a laptop in an arc at the end of the meeting table, with his chair in the middle. Four detectives sitting around the table watch with amusement as he checks the snaking cabling under the table and monitors. Now and then he nods to the monitors. It's like watching a man caring for his newborn triplets. A computer beeps, and he turns toward the monitor, punches some keys to silence it, and continues working.

"What's he doing?" one of the detectives asks.

"Playing games," one of them jokes.

"Checking his Facebook," says another.

The detectives laugh, and Saifuddin smiles. Inspector Sherry appears at the doorway, putting an end to their banter.

"Okay, let's set the ground rules," she says, taking a seat. "One, no one talks about the case to anybody, and I mean anybody, not even your spouse, imam, or priest. Two, you only go home when I tell you, and you come in when you're called. Three, you eat, drink, sleep, and breathe this case, and only this case. Anyone have any problem with the rules?"

"How about cases we're on now?" Detective Dorai asks.

"Refer to rule number 3. Anything else?"

The four detectives shake their heads.

"What about me?" Saifuddin asks from behind the monitors.

"The same applies to you. Deena, you partner with Dorai, and Mokthar with Yahaya. Deena and Dorai, go over the security videos again. We might have missed something. Visit the security guards again and jog their memories about people coming in and leaving that night. Then I want you to locate the victim's landlord, find out if he or she has a spare key to the unit. Mokthar and Yahaya, revisit the residents. There could be a few we missed. Shake all your informers and see if they heard anything. I also want to know if any convicted rapist has been released from prison recently and drifted into the city. Also, check with D7. Go around the cybercafes and do some digging."

Sherry waits for the four detectives to leave before questioning Saifuddin. "Did you make any headway?"

"The username used to upload the video is Emancipatist."

"Emancipatist? What does that mean?"

"I don't know, it's just a username. It doesn't have to mean anything. You can coin any name you like."

"Oh, OK."

"My honeypot's not picking up the username, and that could mean two things. One: the honeypot doesn't work, or two: whoever he or she is that's using the username hasn't logged on since the last time."

"I hope it's the latter. What's the progress on blocking access to the video?"

"No news yet from MCMC."

Sherry groans. "They need to do something quick. The media, the politicians, and NGOs are having a field day. The victim's parents came to see the OCCI with their state assemblyman and a lawyer. I'm sure he made a trainload of promises to keep them off his back."

"Is there anything politicians don't get involved in nowadays?" Saifuddin wonders with obvious scorn.

"Not now, OK, Sai?" she says. "Can you get into the victim's social media accounts? Check if she had Facebook, Instagram, Twitter. If she did, can you hack into her accounts?"

"I can go through her laptop logs and get her accounts, but isn't that illegal?"

"She's dead, OK? She isn't going to know."

Saifuddin gives her an I'm-not-sure look.

"Come on, Sai."

"You're kidding, right?"

"No. And, Sai, can you burn that video on a DVD for me?"

"Done." He flips through his DVD holder. "Here."

"Thanks."

———

Sherry locks herself in her office and watches the DVD. She freezes a frame with the rapist in it and scrutinizes it. *They can't be that good*, she tells herself. There must be something that gives them away. He is light-skinned, could be Chinese or Malay or Eurasian of average height and build. The head was covered with pantyhose. The hair looks dark but could be of any length. The pantyhose man stepped out of frame and the camera focused on the victim. When he comes back on, he is naked. The angle is from his back and side; there is no way to tell if he put on his condom or if his pubic hair is shaved. No distinctive mark on the body; no tattoo or birthmark, deformity or scar.

Sherry moves the video forward and searches for the frame that best captured the rapist's penis. She zooms in as much as she can without breaking the pixels. Staring at it, she believes the rapist's penis is circumcised. *What does it mean? That he's Malay, a Muslim? A lot of non-Malay and non-Muslim undergo circumcision for health and hygiene. Anyway, don't all erect penises appear circumcised? He spoke in a Malay-English mix, like most locals, with no particular accent.*

She replays the video, focusing on the body, its physical build. He doesn't appear muscular, like someone who worked out. But it does look like a workingman's body—not flabby. Her eyes strain from staring at the screen. "Damn it, give me something," she finally cries in despair, "something, anything."

Restarting the video, she turns up the volume, leans back in her chair, closes her eyes, and focuses on the dialogue. The rapist's low, hoarse, muffled voice sounded creepy, and it makes the hairs on the back of her neck bristle. Not once did the rapist raise his voice at Era.

She makes a call to Saifuddin. "Sai, can you enhance the vocals?"

"Yes."

"Can you make a copy of the video with enhanced audio?"

"Sure."

"When can I have it?"

"Give me until tomorrow. I need to do it at the lab."

"Okay, thanks."

12

It has been seven days since Era Amilia was raped. The case now has earned the moniker of *the UTube Rapist*. The first four days were hell for Sherry. The media had made a meal of it, covering the rape-suicide from every imaginable angle. Interviews with other rape victims were published or aired with graphic details, without regard to ongoing investigations or victims' feelings. One TV program went so far as to reenact the rape scene. Rape statistics for the last few years were repeatedly discussed at length by so-called "experts." Comments were sought from criminologists, psychologists, and NGOs. Politicians grabbed every opportunity they could for publicity. The police have been routinely condemned for incompetence and ineffectiveness. Social-media users have speculated on the what, why, and how. Conspiracy theories have alleged involvement of public figures, corporate bigwigs, and celebrities. The most common theory is that the rape was to stop the victim from revealing her affair with one such public figure or influential individual. NGOs have sent memoranda to the government demanding harsher punishments for crimes against women. Muslim groups blame alcohol and entertainment outlets for encouraging sexual freedom and moral degradation.

Although, after four days, the media have let up a little, Sherry still can't sleep at night. The rape scene keeps playing in her head when she closes her eyes. She hears the rapist's muffled scary voice asking the victim if she's enjoying it, if she came. She hears the victim's terrified pleading. She pictures the victim falling from the balcony, her sad pleading eyes staring at her.

Her cell phone rings.

"Yes, Deena," she answers, noting the time on the Astro decoder. It shows 3:10 in the morning.

"Ma'am, Wangsa Maju station just called, we have another case. They said D9 is already there."

"Special Investigations?"

"Yes, D9."

"Why's D9 responding to a rape case?"

"It was reported as murder, a 3-0-2, but then they learned that a housemate of the deceased had been raped. It's a bit sketchy. The station said something about a video. He's not sure if it was of the murder or the rape."

"What's the address? I'll meet the team there."

The crime scene is Unit 10-403 City Hall Public Housing in Setapak Jaya, a lower-cost walk-up apartment building. The cluster of blocks painted orange and yellow looks run-down and congested. Cars and motorbikes are randomly parked along the narrow streets. There is no guard post or any form of barrier limiting access to the area. Johan spots the blue-and-red light of an ambulance and drives toward it.

"It must be this block," he says as he parks next to the ambulance.

The D9 officers climb the stairs to level four. In front of unit 403 is a crowd of onlookers. Sleepy-eyed residents on the floor have started to emerge and gather on hearing the presence of the paramedics and policemen. Inspector Mislan Latif and Detective Sergeant Johan Kamarudin of Special Investigations find the patrolmen chatting with the paramedics. Mislan beckons a policeman over.

"Why are the paramedics here?"

"The initial call was for a medical emergency. By the time paramedics arrived, the victim was already dead, so they called us."

Mislan nods.

"Who's the IO?" Mislan asks, referring to the investigating officer.

"Inspector Low. He's inside with the victim."

"I thought you said the victim is dead."

"One of them."

"How many of them are there?"

"Two, one raped and one murdered. The station also called D11."

"Tell the medics to stand by. D11 may need them." Turning to enter the unit, he adds, "Don't let anyone in unless they're pertinent to the investigation."

From the doorway, he sees a body partially sprawled under the dining table, its head in a pool of blood. He observes blood spatters on the floor, the dining table, and the wall next to it. The blood on the wall formed a single jagged line from about five feet upward. He sees drops of blood on the floor, from the cadaver to the door. He beckons Johan over, pointing to the drops of blood

"Careful," he cautions his assistant.

From where he's standing, he notices that some blood drops have been smeared at the entrance and in the corridor.

"Shit," he cusses. "You," he barks at the policemen, "get all of these people out of here. Can't you see the blood on the floor?"

The crowd looks down.

"What're you waiting for?" he snaps. "And watch where you step." He waits for the crowd to leave before turning to his assistant. "Where the hell is D10?"

"On the way," one of the policemen answers.

"By the time they arrive, all the blood evidence will be destroyed," Mislan snarls. "Jo, get some glasses, cups, or plates from the kitchen and mark the blood drops so no one steps on them."

Johan and the two policemen mark the blood drops with whatever crockery they can get hold of from the kitchen. The corridor from the unit's front door leading to the staircase is littered with all forms and color of crockery.

"Great job," Mislan says.

"It reminds me of a domestic dispute call I responded to during my MPV days," Johan says.

"Not one of your own, I hope."

"I don't have that many dishes."

"Tell them," Mislan motions to the policemen, "no one takes pictures unless he wants to spend a day in the lockup."

Mislan reenters the apartment and takes another peek under the table. The deceased's head is lying in a pool of coagulated blood, her hair all matted and caked with dry blood, with wide-open eyes rolled back. The front of her black T-shirt is soaked in blood, and her right hand grips a chair leg that had fallen over. At a glance, the deceased appears to have two mouths—a clown-like mouth where dark red, thick blood leaked on the right side of her neck, and a wide gap where her real mouth is.

He lightly pats the victim's back pocket and pulls out a wallet. The identity card says the victim is Zaitun binti Zainal, age twenty-nine, listed home address in Taiping, Perak. The wallet also contains a driver's license with the same particulars, an ATM card, several commercial point-cards, and cash of thirty-six ringgit.

Johan enters the apartment. "Watch your step," Mislan warns him. "You know, it always amazes me how much blood a human body holds."

"It's a she!" Johan says, surprised.

"You were expecting?"

"Is that my rape victim?" Inspector Sherry asks, stepping into the unit unannounced, standing beside Johan.

Mislan turns to look at her.

"Sorry, Sherry from D11. You're Mislan D9 right? I've seen you around the office with Reeziana a few times."

Mislan nods,

"If she was, she's mine now," he says answering her earlier question.

"Where's mine then?"

Mislan motions to the bedroom. "In there with the IO."

"What happened out there?" Sherry asks. "There are cups, mugs, and plates scattered all along the corridor."

"Haven't you been told? Those are D9's new crime-scene exhibit markers. We don't want to create panic among the public by using the standard ones. So Forensics came up with this novel idea," Mislan says with a straight face.

"Seriously, what happened here?" Sherry asks, not amused.

"We just arrived. I haven't talked to your vic yet. Watch your step. Don't step on the blood spatters. Jo, where are the forensic guys?"

"On their way," Johan replies, heading to the kitchen.

"Sherry, I heard you've a task force working on the UTube rape. Did you bring them along?"

"Sure."

"Can I borrow your team to search the area for the murder weapon? Judging from the wound, it looks like it was a knife or some other sharp-bladed instrument. Jo, can you call for K9?"

"Dog unit?" Johan asks, uncertain of his boss's decision.

"Yes. Why?"

"The residents here are mainly Malay Muslim. I don't think they'd like having a dog running around."

"Just because they won't like it, we don't do our job?" Mislan questions sharply.

"You're the boss."

Sherry tells her three detectives to assist in the search for the murder weapon. She and Deena head for the bedroom.

Mislan calls out, "Sherry, please don't touch anything until the forensics team arrives."

———

Kevin Foo of Kuala Lumpur Contingent Headquarters Forensic (D10) and Chew Beng Song of the Crime Forensic Headquarters and his team arrive at the same time.

"Chew, why are you here?" Mislan asks.

"Superintendent Lillian asked my boss if we can assist, and here I am."

"Great. Kevin, why don't you go with Sherry? She's in there with the victim. Chew can do this with me."

"No problem."

"Good."

"My boss said it was a rape, so what's that body doing here?" Chew asks.

"I did ask her, but she's not telling," Mislan jokes.

"Oh I forgot, you can talk with the dead."

"Where did you hear that?"

"The DUKE murders, Detective Sergeant Johan told me you got closure by visiting the crime scene and speaking to the deceased," Chew replies and chuckles, joined by Johan.

"Let me have a peek at the rape case first so I can at least brief my boss when he asks," Chew says.

"Go ahead. Mine says she's not going anywhere."

"Who's the IO for the rape?"

"Sherry—she's in there. Chew, can you check my victim for her cell phone?"

"You haven't checked for it?"

"It's likely in her front pocket. Too much blood there. I'll let you have the honor of doing it."

"Thanks, that's thoughtful of you," Chew replies.

Mislan steps out of the unit and lights a cigarette. He walks to the staircase and inspects it closely. After several minutes, he summons the policemen.

"Were you the ones who responded to the call?"

"Yes."

"Who opened the door for you?"

"It was open when we got here. The paramedics were here first. I supposed the other victim opened it for them."

"Have you filed the report?"

"Not yet."

"OK, get those people off the floor and keep them off. File your report and send a copy to Detective Sergeant Johan."

———

The K9 Unit arrives and asks if there's anything belonging to the suspect that could be used as a scent for the dog. Johan replies in the negative.

"What do you want us to look for?"

"A knife or any sharp-bladed instrument covered with blood."

"I need something the dog can sniff to pick up the trail."

"How about the victim's blood?" Mislan suggests. "That should be all over the murder weapon."

"I'll give it a shot."

"Do the staircase first. See if the dog can spot traces of blood."

The dog handler nods.

"Cover a radius of about 250 yards. Start with the roadside drains and garbage bins."

"Yes, sir."

"Jo, let Chew know if K9 finds any trace of blood in the stairwell."

"Where're you going?"

"To walk about and check out the area. There's nothing here for me to do. I need to talk to Sherry's vic, but I can't do that until she has been processed." As Mislan walks to the staircase, he adds, "We're closer to HUKM than HKL, right?"

Johan shakes his head.

"Send the body to HUKM anyway."

"You want me to tell Inspector Sherry to send her vic there, too?"

"No, let her make her own decisions. See you back at the office."

13

ON HIS WAY BACK to the office, he stops by a roadside stall and buys breakfast for himself and his assistant. The Kuala Lumpur Police Contingent building is just beginning to come to life with officers, police personnel, and civilian staff coming in to work when he arrives. The greetings and hands rising in salute fill the lobby. *It must be bloody tiring for the policeman on duty in the lobby*, Mislan thinks. Even in the small and crowded space of the elevator lobby, there is so much ass-kissing and lobbying going on, so much office politics and gossip. When he steps out of the elevator, his cell phone rings. It's his assistant telling him the K9 didn't discover anything of interest.

"Jo, I got you breakfast."

"Thanks."

"Can you hang around until after the morning prayer?"

"Sure."

He makes a mug of black coffee and sits alone at the makeshift pantry to enjoy his favorite breakfast of nasi lemak with sambal sotong—squid cooked with chili paste—and fried egg.

Inspector Reeziana walks in looking as cheery as ever, drops her bag at her desk, and joins him.

"How was business?"

"Caught a late one this morning."

Reeziana raises her eyebrows.

"Rape and murder, Setapak Jaya."

"The vic was raped then murdered?"

"One was raped and another murdered."

"Same location?"

Mislan nods.

"Why wasn't the other one killed?"

"That's what I'm wondering."

Mislan lights a cigarette and passes the pack to Reeziana, who glances at her watch and declines, saying, "Morning prayer starting soon."

Inspector Tee walks in, drops his bag, and tells them the head of Special Investigations is already in the meeting room. Reeziana and Tee make their way to the meeting, leaving Mislan to finish his cigarette.

———

Superintendent Samsiah Hassan, the head of Special Investigations, is just about to start the meeting when Mislan enters. She acknowledges him with a remark: "Busy night."

"One of those days," Mislan replies, smiling.

Turning to the others, she asks, "Who has court today?"

Almost all the officers raise their hands.

"OK, let's start."

Mislan briefs the meeting on cases of interest reported within his twenty-four-hour shift. One armed robbery and one armed housebreaking, suspected to be by the same gang. One domestic violence, a housewife killed by her drug-addict husband, case handled by district. The last was a rape and murder in the same case.

"The vic, I mean the deceased, is Zaitun binti Zainal, twenty-nine, from Taiping."

"How's she connected to the rape vic?"

"Not established yet, most likely housemate. I've not been able to talk to the rape vic."

"OK, I want you to liaise with D11 before talking to their vic."

Mislan nods reluctantly.

"Ghani, what's the progress on the armed robbery and housebreaking cases?" Samsiah asks.

"So far, we've no solid lead on the gang," ASP Ghani Ishak, head of Special Projects, replies. "They seem to vanish after break-ins, and nothing taken has surfaced on the black market in the city."

"Widen your net. They may be from out of town. Check with other states and see if the loot surfaces in other areas. Let's wrap this up quickly." She turns to Mislan. "The rape and murder, I'm bringing in D11."

"Why?"

"Because we need them."

"But—" Mislan stops his objection, mouth agape, as the head of Special Investigations throws him a not-here-not-now glare.

She looks around the table. "Is there anything else?"

The officers shake their heads.

"For your information, our request for another investigator's vehicle was rejected. Off-duty investigations take second priority in the use of official vehicles. I'm still hearing complaints of vehicles being used by officers for catering services. I want this stopped immediately. Use your own vehicle to buy your meals, or get the detectives to buy your meals using their bikes. If you pay for their meal, I'm sure they'll be glad to do it for you," she says and smiles. "That's it, let's get some work done. Be safe."

Mislan follows his boss to her office.

"Ma'am, why're we bringing D11 into our case? Can't we keep it in-house?"

"You heard of the UTube rape case?"

"Yes."

"Lillian told me it's the same MO. The rape was recorded on video and she's expecting it to be posted on UTube."

"But we're investigating the murder. That takes precedence over rape."

"And you think I don't know that?" Samsiah snaps at him.

"I'm sorry. I didn't mean it that way."

"The problem with you is you only see the obvious. When are you going to learn? In the eyes of the law, murder is the ultimate crime, but in the eyes of the media, especially when a rape video goes viral on

UTube, that's prime-time news. With this second rape, the media will go wild with stories of a serial rapist on the loose. Now tell me, do you still feel your murder takes precedence?"

"But we still need one more rape to make it serial. It has to be three and more, right, for it to be classified as serial?"

"You think the media knows that? Even if they do, you think they care? Rape sells papers, and serial rape sells even more papers."

Mislan remains silent.

"You have a problem working with Inspector Sherry?"

"I don't know. I haven't worked with her before."

"Correction—you haven't worked with anyone before," she says.

"I work with Jo."

"He's your subordinate. Lan, I want you to stick around. Lillian and Sherry are coming over at ten."

———

Leaving his boss's office, Mislan heads straight to the emergency stair-case, his smoking area in a smoke-free building. Johan watches as his boss walks past without looking at him. Johan can see something is bothering him. He waits until Mislan disappears behind the emergency staircase door and gives him another minute to light up and take a few drags on his cigarette before getting up from his chair. While Johan is watching his boss, Inspector Reeziana is watching the detective ser-geant. She, too, has noticed something is brewing. As Johan walks to the emergency staircase, she follows.

Johan pushes lightly on the door and sees his boss leaning against the staircase handrail, smoking and staring down the stairwell. Mislan turns to stare at his assistant.

"What's up with you?" Johan asks.

Reeziana steps in from behind Johan, and they both look at her questioningly.

"You guys having a private party or something?" Reeziana asks, grinning.

Mislan flashes a tight smile.

"Can I have a ciggie?" she asks.

Mislan hands her the pack and lighter.

Lighting up, she hands them back and asks, "What's bothering you?"

"Nothing."

"It's the meeting with ma'am, right? What was it about?"

Mislan remains quiet.

"Her decision to being in D11, wasn't it? I saw your face when she said that just now."

"On what?" Johan asks.

"The rape and murder case," Reeziana answers.

"What's wrong with that?" Johan asks.

"You know your boss doesn't like sharing cases," she says.

"But the two cases are related," Johan replies. "It makes sense if we work them together."

"Tell that to your boss," Reeziana says, grinning.

Johan looks at Mislan.

"Your boss is afraid D11 will cramp his style," Reeziana says letting out a cheeky chuckle.

Mislan stares deadpan at her, and she laughs louder.

14

INSPECTOR SHERRY REACHES THE Kuala Lumpur Police Contingent headquarters at 8:15 in the morning and goes straight to her boss's office. Superintendent Lillian puts down her pen and invites her in. Sherry updates her on the latest case. The victim, although traumatized by the rape, was more devastated by the death of her housemate. The doctor had ordered her hospitalized for observation.

"The same MO," Lillian states rather than asks.

Sherry nods, taking out her notepad.

"The victim's name is Julie Maulana, thirty, born in Ipoh, Perak, works as a bank officer with CIMB. As in the first case, she woke up when she felt a hand over her mouth and found a man wearing a stocking over his head holding a knife to her cheek. He raped her while his accomplice videoed it. During the rape, he kept telling her he was freeing her, asking her if she was enjoying it and if she came."

Superintendent Lillian inhaled deeply, disgusted. "I'm guessing there was no trace of semen found."

"The GYN confirmed signs of vaginal trauma but didn't find any trace of semen. Swabs were taken for toxicology. I'm sure they'll find traces of the lubricant similar to that found on the first victim. Ma'am, I'd like to withhold that piece of evidence."

"From the press?"

Sherry nods. "Only on a need-to-know basis."

"OK, what about other bodily fluids?"

"None, although this time the victim didn't shower. The doctor examined her physically but couldn't find any trace. Forensics could not find anything, either."

"The murder victim?"

"Her housemate, Zaitun, was a waitress at the Beach Club. The rape victim said she heard a scream and peeked out from her bedroom and saw her housemate lying in a pool of blood under the table, groaning. She called 999, but by the time the paramedics arrived, she was dead."

"Who's the lead for the 3-0-2?"

"D9, Inspector Mislan."

"Hmmm," Lillian says. She had heard of the inspector's reputation. "Why?"

"Nothing. I'll arrange for a meeting with D9 at ten. Why don't you freshen up and get your notes in order?"

"Are they taking the lead?"

"I'm sure they'll want to. Let's see how the discussion goes."

———

Mislan makes a call to the Malaysia National University Hospital or HUKM (Hospital Universiti Kebangsaan Malaysia). He asks to be put through to the Forensics Pathology Department. Introducing himself, he mentions his victim's name and police report number and asks if the autopsy has been done. The woman on the line asks him to hold while she checks the schedule.

"It's scheduled for today, but it hasn't started yet."

"Who's on today?"

"Dr. Nursafia."

"Can you pass this call to her, please?"

"Hold the line."

A few moments pass, and a woman's voice answers, "Dr. Safia."

"Fie, it's me. You're working today?"

"Hi, how're you? Yes. Why?"

"Good, I got a case in your cold box: Zaitun. What time are you doing her?"

"Let me see. I've got three today. Ah, here, she'll be the last."

"What time will that be?"

"Around noon."

"Can you hold it until I arrive?"

"If you can be here by noon. What's special about this case?"

"Tell you when I see you. Give me a fifteen-minute window."

"OK, fifteen max."

"Thanks, see you."

————

He calls Crime Forensics and asks for Chew, who updates him on the preliminary findings.

"What about the murder weapon?" Chew asks.

"None found. The killer probably took it with him or ditched it out of the search area. Did you manage to lift prints from the stairwell?"

"No, too smeared to lift any."

"I didn't expect you to."

"Why is that?"

"If they're the same bastards from the first rape, they wore gloves. Any bloodstained shoe print we can use?"

"No. I didn't see any near the body, either. From the blood spatters on the table and the wall, I'm guessing it was a single strike, and the assailant didn't hang around to admire his handiwork."

"Ambushed?"

"Most likely. Normally, in such encounters the assailant would have blood spatters on him, too, but there won't be any footprints in the blood. By the way, the blood on the staircase is the same blood type as the victim's. I've sent the sample for DNA matching."

"I don't think the killing was premeditated. I think they were caught by surprise."

"Why is that?"

"The single strike and not hanging around to make sure the victim was dead before taking off."

"You've got a point."

"Chew, thank you. Keep me informed." He puts down the phone and says to Johan, "Jo, why don't you go home and get some rest? I've got a meeting with the boss and D11 at ten."

"You're sure?"

"Yes, I'll go home after the meeting and get some rest, too. The vic worked at Beach Club. Maybe we'll pay it a visit later tonight."

"What about the rape victim?"

"I'll ask Sherry if we can interview her and will let you know."

"Keep your cool," his assistant says as he packs up to leave.

Mislan gives his assistant a glazed look.

Detective Sergeant Johan smiles and leaves.

15

Superintendent Lillian and Inspector Sherry are already in the head of Special Investigations' office when Mislan enters. He acknowledges the head of Sexual & Child Abuse Investigations and her officer. The two D11 officers greet him with warm smiles, which makes Mislan uneasy. In his book, warm smiles always hide something unwarm behind them. Superintendent Samsiah addresses the two investigators.

"I know you're both tired, so let's make this quick. I'll skip the investigation's details for now and deal with it at the appropriate time." She pauses and gets a nod from each of them. "Has anything popped up on the net yet on this second rape?"

Sherry shakes her head. "My task force's monitoring it. So far, nothing."

"Maybe, with the murder, it might not be posted," Samsiah suggests.

"I'm sure it will be. It's a matter of when," Sherry counters.

"We'll deal with it when it happens." Samsiah addresses Lillian: "How do you propose we conduct this investigation?"

"We have a task force for the first case; Sherry's heading it. Mislan's the lead for the murder—perhaps he can be part of the task force," Superintendent Lillian proposes.

All eyes turn to Mislan.

"The task force is for rape, the focus may not be the same," he says, diplomatically.

"And how is it different?" Samsiah probes, inviting Mislan to argue himself into a hole.

"The forensics and leads," he gropes.

"Let me ask you this," Samsiah says. "Do you think the rapists and murderers are two separate sets of individuals?"

Mislan blinks, remaining silent.

"If the task force is going after the rapists, how does that interfere with you going after the murderers?" she presses on, knowing she has him cornered.

Mislan avoids her eyes.

Superintendent Samsiah's lips curve in a tiny smile. "I think it's an excellent suggestion, Lillian. Sherry will lead, and Mislan will play second. Who should the task force report to?"

"Since 3-0-2 takes precedence over 3-7-6, I think they should report to you," Lillian says.

Turning to Sherry, Samsiah asks, "Do you have a problem with that?"

Sherry casts a quick glance at her boss before answering, "No."

"Good, it's settled then, unless anyone has anything else to add." Samsiah pauses, half-expecting Mislan to make a last-minute pitch. When nothing happens, she continues, "There's one other thing. Whenever there's a need for Mislan to talk to the rape victim, I want Sherry to be present. I'm sure we'll be receiving more than the normal media coverage on these cases. We don't need them to start reporting about mishandling of the rape victims."

The D11 officers nod.

As they stand to leave, the head of Special Investigations says, "Sherry, the 'morning prayer,' sorry the morning briefing, is at 0830 hours daily."

Mislan remains seated as the D11 officers go out.

Superintendent Samsiah asks, "What's on your mind?"

"Ma'am, I don't know if letting Sherry lead is the right decision."

"And why is that?"

"She has no experience with murder and—"

"Look, Lan, she's not investigating your murder case. She'll be investigating her rape cases," Samsiah says, cutting him off. "And as I said earlier, and I'm sure you agree, the rapists and murderers are the same individuals."

Mislan looks at her, pleading.

"However, knowing you, I'm sure you'll bully your way into leading the investigation. Look, I need someone with you to make sure you don't create a media circus out of the investigation."

"But I've got you for that."

Superintendent Samsiah laughs. "Has that ever stopped you before? I can't watch over you 24/7, but Sherry can, because it's as much her case as it is yours. I'm hoping she's strong enough to stop you from making a fool of yourself with the media. Now, get out of here and get some rest."

16

Earlier that day, around 6:40 in the morning while he was at the rape-murder crime scene, the nanny had called to inform Mislan that Daniel was running a low-grade fever. He was coughing and had vomited all over his school uniform. Mislan told her to give him two children's aspirins and to let him sleep. He told her he would try to get home as soon as he could.

Arriving home, he goes straight to his son's room to find him curled up in bed watching TV: National Geographic *Monster Fish*. Somehow Daniel—or "kiddo" to him—has always been interested in watching monster fish instead of cartoons. Mislan has never taken his son fishing, and he himself was never interested in fishing. He finds it boring, as he has no control over the outcome, unlike with other sports. The channel is showing a guy that he always sees on the screen sitting in a sampan heading upriver somewhere in Vietnam.

"Hey, kiddo, how're you feeling?" Mislan sits next to his son, feeling his forehead.

"My throat hurts, Daddy. I vomited a lot," Daniel answers, his voice weak.

"I know. Sister told me. I'll shower and take you to the clinic, OK?" His son refers to the Indonesian maid as Sister.

"Daddy, you've got to tell my teacher. I didn't go to school."

"I'll do that, kiddo."

Glancing at the wall clock, he realizes he needs to get going to HUKM soon to catch the autopsy. After a quick shower, he drives Daniel to a nearby clinic. There are several patients ahead of them, and by the look of it he won't be able to make it to the autopsy. He makes a call to the hospital.

"Hi Fie, have you started?"

"About to. Where're you?"

"Sorry, I don't think I can make it. I'm at the clinic."

"What's wrong?"

"It's Daniel. He was vomiting this morning and says his throat hurts. Can we catch up later for dinner? We can update each other then."

"Does he have a fever? Have him checked for dengue. It's been on the rise in Selangor lately."

"I'll ask the doctor."

"Make sure you do that."

"Don't worry, he'll be fine. Got to go, the nurse just called his name. Call you later, OK?"

———

Reaching home, he gives Daniel his medicine and tells him not to drink anything cold until he recovers. He tells the maid to cook rice porridge and chicken soup for his son's lunch.

"Daddy, can I sleep in your room?"

"Sure, kiddo."

"Have you told my teacher yet, daddy?"

"Yes, I texted her. I also told her you'll be away for two days."

Daniel switches on the television and jumps on the bed. "Are you working today?"

"Later. Now I need to get some sleep."

"This Saturday, can we go to the driving range? I want to hit some balls."

"You want to restart your golf?"

"Yes, can I?"

"Sure, kiddo." He smiles. A couple of years back Daniel picked up the sport and was getting good at it. At his tender age of seven, he was able to drive the ball ninety yards. But for some reason, he lost interest, and now he wanted to restart.

He's delighted at his son's renewed interest in a sport he loves but doesn't have the time for. He turns on the air conditioner and climbs on the bed, and Daniel rests his head on his chest while he watches TV. He wakes up at a quarter to three in the afternoon, after only about two hours of sleep. Even after all these years of working twenty-four-hour shifts, he still can't get used to daytime sleep. Daniel is sound asleep, and the TV is tuned in to the golf channel. He touches Daniel's cheek to check his temperature; it feels normal. Climbing out of bed, he calls Sherry.

"Anything on UTube?"

"No."

"Maybe they're spooked, and there won't be any posting."

"Maybe, but I don't think they're going to let it pass."

"Why is that?"

"I've a feeling the rapes weren't the primary motive."

"I don't follow."

"Initially, my theories were trophy collection, power play they can revisit to jerk off. The possibility of extortion did cross my mind, too. But when they posted the video on UTube, my theories don't hold water anymore."

"OK, so what's your new theory?"

"The rapes are manifestations of their real motive. Something they did to prove a point, to demonstrate something."

"You lost me there."

"If it's rape for the pure purpose of rape, for sexual pleasure or a display of male dominance, why post it on the net? Perverts usually record it for their own viewing pleasure."

"Perhaps they're looking for fame or popularity."

"Maybe, except for one thing. If fame and popularity are what they're after, why haven't they posted something that'll make them iconic perverts in the cyber world?"

"Like what?"

"I don't really know how to explain it. Predators like to make some form of announcement or use macho-sounding names. You know what I mean?"

"Like Hannibal the Cannibal or the Green Man?"

"I've heard of Hannibal, but who's the Green Man?" she says, laughing.

"Go look it up. Anyway, the media have already dubbed the criminals the UTube Rapists."

"One more and the label will change to the UTube Serial Rapist."

"Hey, when can I speak to your victim?" Mislan asks, changing the subject.

"She's in no condition to be interviewed after the examination and has been taken home by her parents. They told me they'll bring her in tomorrow morning at ten. Why don't you sit in during the interview?"

"I thought she was hospitalized."

"She was, but the parents came down and that was that."

"Can't we do it tonight?"

"You've never handled rape before, have you?"

"No."

"Rape victims usually go through severe post-rape trauma. They need to be calmed down and be with people who love and support them. Interviewing them before they're ready will only add to the stress and increase the likelihood of them going into a state of depression and possibly blocking out the incident completely. I don't think we should risk that."

"But a delay might result in her forgetting vital details," he persists.

"Unlike in other crimes, rape victims don't forget what they've been through. They'll relive it over and over in their heads."

"I still say we should talk to her tonight."

"She's my case, I'm the lead, and I say we talk to her tomorrow," Sherry says firmly.

Sherry's words burned in his head. Terminating the call, Mislan angrily flings the cell phone onto the bed, annoyed at being reminded who the lead investigator is. His cell phone bounces off the mattress and hits Daniel on his back. The boy stirs in his sleep. Mislan pats him softly, saying, "Sorry, kiddo, go back to sleep."

Mislan meets up with Dr. Safia at the Lobster Curry Noodle Restaurant in Bandar Sri Permaisuri. Curry noodle is a Chinese dish that's also popular with other races; the river lobster makes it all the more tantalizing. Dr. Safia has been craving it since last week, when she heard of this place from a friend.

It's 6:30 in the evening, and the dinner crowd is building. They manage to get a table on the sidewalk and order their curry noodle with iced tea. The noodles come in a fair-sized red plastic bowl. The creamy curry is reddish-gold, accompanied by a couple of medium-sized lobsters. Mislan picks his lobsters up with the chopstick and puts them into Dr. Safia's bowl.

"Sorry, I forgot you're allergic," Dr. Safia says.

"Don't worry, it's not severe. I'm used to eating with those who aren't."

Dr. Safia takes a sip of the curry with a spoon. "Tasty."

Mislan tastes the curry and agrees. As they enjoy their noodles, he asks, "Anything interesting with the autopsy?"

"Nothing, straightforward, the COD is severe hemorrhaging. The left carotid was severed and part of the trachea, too. Judging from the wound, it's believed to have been caused with one upward slashing motion."

"Upward?"

"Yes," Dr. Safia says, putting down her chopsticks and running her finger on Mislan's neck. "From here upward to here."

"The victim's what, about five feet tall?"

"Exactly five feet one inch."

"Usually the strike is either a stabbing motion or downward strike, where it's easier to apply force. In this case it's upward, hmmm."

"The assailant could be shorter than the victim," Dr. Safia suggests.

"The victim is five one, how short could he be? Any shorter than that, he would be a midget."

Mislan closes his eyes, picturing the crime scene. When he opens his eyes, Dr. Safia is staring at him.

"What?" he asks.

"It scares me when you go into your shaman detective mode," Dr. Safia says with a sly smile.

"Sorry, I was trying to picture the crime scene."

Dr. Safia uses her hands to peel the lobster skin. Mislan watches as she savors it, thinking he has forgotten what it tastes like.

"Any defensive wound?"

"No."

Mislan nods slowly to himself. "I think she was caught by surprise. The assailant or assailants heard her opening the front door. They hid behind the partitioning wall at the dining table. When she walked past them to go to the bedroom they struck, catching her off guard."

"And how does that explain the upward strike?"

"They were most likely crouched behind the wall, shielded by the dining table. When the victim walked by, they sprang up and slashed her. Hence the upward motion. The blood spatters on the wall also ran upward, consistent with the slash motion."

"They were already inside the house waiting for her. Makes sense why there was no defensive wound on the victim."

After dinner, Mislan tells Dr. Safia he needs to go home. He had earlier promised his son that he could sleep with him tonight.

"How's Daniel?" Dr. Safia asks.

"The doctor says just a sore throat."

"Did the doctor do a blood test for dengue?"

"Yes, the result will be in tomorrow, but he doubted it's dengue."

"I'm glad."

Dropping her at her apartment, he wishes her good night. She kisses him on the cheek and says, "Night, and kiss Daniel good night for me."

17

THE NEXT MORNING AT 8:30, Inspector Sherry attends the morning prayer at Special Investigations Unit. She doesn't know what to expect. Entering the meeting room, she's greeted by the investigators who are already there. She knows Inspector Reeziana and Inspector Mislan but not Inspector Tee and ASP Ghani from Special Projects. Sherry introduces herself to them and takes a seat across from Inspector Mislan. Superintendent Samsiah joins them and starts by saying Sherry will be joining them until the rape-murder case is concluded.

"OK, let's start. Yana?"

Inspector Reeziana briefs the meeting on her twenty-four-hour shift: one shooting case in Brickfields, an attempted robbery of a goldsmith, but no one injured. The case is being investigated by the district, with D9 assisting. Three armed robberies, one using a knife and two with parang machetes. All were roadside robberies and are being investigated by the district.

The head of Special Investigations excuses those having to attend court cases, then turns to Sherry.

"Sherry, would you like to update us on your case?"

Inspector Sherry gives a summary of her case, including only what she feels should be public news and won't jeopardize her investigation.

"How was the deceased related to your victim?" Samsiah asks.

"My victim, Julie, says Zaitun, the deceased, was her housemate. They've been housemates for almost one and a half years. I've a feeling she wasn't telling the whole truth. I wanted to press her on it, but the doctor advised me not for the time being. It may aggravate her emotional condition."

"What made you think she was holding back?" Samsiah asks.

"The bedroom, when we searched it. We found personal belongings of the deceased: laptop, clothing, et cetera."

"So they're roommates rather than housemates."

"More likely."

"Intimate? A couple?" Mislan asks.

Samsiah, Sherry, and Reeziana look at him.

"Two women sharing a room doesn't automatically mean they're a couple," Sherry says, not liking Mislan's insinuation. "It could just be cost-saving, or they're close friends. Like men don't share rooms," she sneers.

"Why are you asking?" Samsiah asks.

"The vic was wearing sneakers, slacks, and a polo shirt. I thought women don't usually wear polo shirts. Jo also initially thought the vic was a male. I'm just asking if—"

"Your victim worked at Beach Club, what do you expect her to be dressed in—skirts, kebaya?" Sherry snaps back.

"You mean a *pengkid*," Reeziana interjects.

All eyes turn to Reeziana.

"The street slang for a girl that dresses and acts like a boy, who has girlfriends . . . beautiful girlfriends."

"Tomboy?" Samsiah asks.

"More than just tomboys. Tomboys are girls that like to do boys' activities. Pengkids are girls that want to be boys both in style and sexuality."

"OK, let's leave it at that," Samsiah suggests.

There is a knock on the meeting room door. Detective Sergeant Johan pokes his head in and informs Sherry that her IT technician has got something online. Sherry and Mislan look anxiously at the head of Special Investigations. Before she can nod her approval to excuse them, they're already out of their chairs dashing for the door.

"Let's take the stairs," Mislan calls, leading the way.

Saifuddin turns toward another beeping computer, saying, "I know, I know." He hits several commands and repeats the urgency for someone to call in Inspector Sherry.

"Done," Detective Deena replies.

Sherry, Mislan, and Johan barge into the room.

"What's happening?" Sherry asks.

"The Emancipatist is on the net," Sai says excitedly, his fingers rapidly working the keyboard. "He's logged on at Plaza Low Yat Starbucks' Wi-Fi."

Sherry instructs Deena and the team to scramble there.

"Spread out and observe. Do not make an arrest unless you're positive, a hundred percent positive, he's the Emancipatist. I don't want to show our hand."

She looks at Mislan and Johan questioningly.

"We're going," Mislan says. "Keep us updated."

Sherry nods. "Deena, go with Dorai." Once the team leave, she turns to the IT technician, "Sai, how can we identify him? Low Yat is a computer mall; I'm sure there're many people using the Wi-Fi there. We can't pick them all up. Can you identify him?"

"I can't. The thing is, he may not even be at Starbucks. He could be near Starbucks, within range of their Wi-Fi."

"And how far away would that be?"

"Depends on the signal strength, but I don't think more than twenty-five yards."

"That place has many fast-food outlets. There's no way Deena and the team can cover them all," Sherry agonizes. "And other outlets provide Wi-Fi, too. Why would he be somewhere else and use the Starbucks Wi-Fi? Wouldn't it be better for him to use the other outlets' Wi-Fi?"

"I'm saying he might not even be there, I could be wrong. However, if I were him, I wouldn't be sitting at Starbucks. That way, if my username was being monitored, the people monitoring would think I'm at Starbucks. If they hit Starbucks, I'll quietly turn off my computer and slip away."

"Arghh. It's always so simple on TV."

She calls Mislan to tell him what Saifuddin said.

"Start with Starbucks and spread out to the surrounding outlets."

"What do you want us to do? We don't even know what he looks like," Mislan says.

"Observe and try to remember as many faces as you can, look out for suspicious behavior or nervousness. You know the drill. Maybe next time, the face will ring a bell."

Parking is murderously difficult to find around the Low Yat Plaza. The narrow street between the buildings is constantly jam-packed. Mislan drops Johan in front of the plaza and drives on looking for parking. After double-parking, he walks over to the plaza and sees Johan standing by the entrance.

"Deena says he could be anywhere." Johan greets him. "Didn't the IT tech say he's logged on at Starbucks?"

"He could be anywhere within the signal range." He surveys the surroundings. "There're at least thirty people here with laptops or tablets. How the hell do we know which one is him? That's not counting smartphone users." He leans against the railing and lights a cigarette.

Detective Deena and Dorai appear from inside the mall. They stop to talk to Johan for a moment and walk away. Then Johan walks over to his boss.

"Deena says she tested the signal strength using her smartphone, and it doesn't reach inside the mall. It's only out here and over there," Johan says, indicating with a jerk of his head.

"Is he still logged on?"

Johan makes a call to Sherry, who says, "No, he just logged off."

"Don't you need to buy something before you can get the Wi-Fi password on the receipt?"

"I don't know, I don't drink expensive coffee," Mislan says.

"I forgot, you're cheap Charlie," Johan jests.

"What the hell do we do now?" Mislan is annoyed. "Let's get out of here, I'm double-parked. Jo, tell Deena to get the CCTV recording from Starbucks."

"What do you expect to find?"

"Nothing for now, but I'm hoping the next time the bastard logs on it'll be somewhere that has cameras."

"I see, you want to compare faces," Johan says.

"Make it fifteen minutes pre and post the login time."

"OK, I'll stick around with the team and catch you back at the office."

18

THE MEETING ROOM THAT has been turned into the task force center is silent except for the faint click-clack of the keyboard. Saifuddin is engrossed with his computers, with Sherry hovering behind him, feeling desperate and lost. She sees line after line of garbage scroll up the monitor screens, not understanding anything. Saifuddin keys in more commands, and more lines appear, some in white, some in blue, and mostly incomprehensible.

"What now?" she asks.

"I'm checking UTube for new uploads."

"Is it there?"

"Still searching."

"I don't see UTube site on the screen; where're you searching?"

"From the source."

"Why can't you go to the UTube site and search?"

"Too many uploads. UTube isn't only serving us here. It's all over the globe."

"Can't you just go to UTube and type 'Emancipatist' on the search?"

"Did that—nothing."

"Google it."

"Too soon for Google to pick it up."

"What about him, did we get anything on him?"

Turning to another computer, he says, "I'm trying to get into the Starbucks network."

"Can you?"

"It's an unsecured domain. How difficult can it be?" Saifuddin brags.

"If you say so, you're the expert. Why do you need to get into it?"

"To get his MAC and IP address and computer make and model."

"I know IP address stands for 'Internet protocol,' but what is MAC?"

"Machine Access Code."

"If you get them, what can we do with it?"

"It gives you the computer details. I can run a check on the manufacturer's distribution list."

"You can do it from here?"

"Yes, but only to the main or regional distributors. From there on, it has to be by personal inquiry."

"Meaning?"

"You have to go there, to the retailer and ask who bought the laptop." Then he says, "Shit."

"Why, what's wrong?" Sherry asks.

"I can't get into the Starbucks network."

"I thought you said it's easy, a public unsecured domain."

"Well, I thought wrong," Saifuddin admits sheepishly.

———

Mislan arrives at the Kuala Lumpur Police Contingent Headquarters and takes the elevator up to D11. He heads straight to the task force situation room. Sherry and Saifuddin can see how annoyed he is. They watch him without saying or asking anything, not wanting to aggravate him. Mislan walks to the window, unlocks its latch, and pushes it slightly open. He takes out his pack of cigarettes and lights up. Sherry glares at him and is about to say something when Mislan raises his hand to stop her.

Saifuddin stands and closes the door to the room, pressing the lock button.

"Good man," Mislan says, flashing him a smile.

The IT technician crosses the room, stands next to Mislan, takes out a pack of cigarettes, and flashes Sherry a schoolboy grin while lighting up.

"Great, just bloody great," Sherry remarks.

"Relax, will you? We just need some stimulant to work the brain," Mislan says. "What now? Where do we go from here?"

Sherry briefs him on what the IT technician was trying to do and how he failed to get into the Starbucks network.

"I worked with this geek before in one of my cases," Mislan offers. "What's his name . . . Hubble, yes Hubble, like the telescope. Anyway, he can get into anything and I mean anything."

"A hacker?" Sherry says.

Mislan shrugs.

"Has to be if he can get into anything," Saifuddin says.

"You want me to call him?" Mislan asks Sherry.

"Nooo. I'm not conducting this investigation your style. We'll do it by the book, every step of the investigation."

"What do you mean by 'my style'?" Mislan asks, staring at the D11 investigator.

Saifuddin watches in amusement as the two officers lock stares. Each not backing down or blinking. A knock on the door breaks the staring match. Mislan and Saifuddin flick their cigarettes out the window. Saifuddin waves his hands around to clear the smoke. Sherry goes to open the door, and Detective Sergeant Johan along with the rest of the team look at her inquiringly.

"What's going on?" Deena asks, seeing her boss's angry expression.

Johan looks toward his boss incredulously. Mislan gives his assistant a blank look. Saifuddin, on the other hand, is trying hard to stifle a smile. Johan knows his boss must have rubbed the D11 officer the wrong way.

"Got the video?" Mislan asks.

"Here," Deena answers, handing him the disc.

"Sai, can you hang on to it? We may need to review it if the bastard logs on again in another location with CCTV. Compare faces."

Saifuddin nods.

———

Sherry's cell phone rings. It's the front desk informing her that her victim, Julie, and her parents have arrived. She tells the front desk clerk to take them to the main meeting room and arrange for drinks if they want any. She makes a call to Superintendent Lillian to ask if she wishes to join in. Lillian declines, saying she has a meeting to attend, and tells her to go ahead and brief her later. She informs Mislan and signals for him to follow her. Stepping out of the situation room, Sherry tells him she'll lead the interview.

Julie Maulana sits sandwiched between her parents, staring at the wall in front of her. Her mother is whispering something in her ear when the two investigators enter. Sherry introduces herself and Mislan before taking a seat facing the victim. The victim's eyes are fixed on Mislan, and Sherry notices signs of uneasiness. Probably because Mislan is a male and she's not comfortable talking about her ordeal to a man.

"Julie, how are you feeling?" Sherry starts.

"OK," she answers almost in a whisper.

"I need to hear your version of the incident again to make sure it doesn't change from the first time it was told. If there're any disparities, we need to clarify it once and for all."

Julie nods, her eyes not leaving Mislan. Julie's mother puts her hand on her daughter's shoulder to calm her. Shifting her eyes to a spot a foot in front of her, Julie narrates her ordeal.

Sherry notes that Julie is able to speak with only slight hesitation, a sign the victim is slowly getting over her trauma. Going back with her parents must have helped her. There also seem to be no critical deviations from her earlier statement of the incident. When Julie is done, Sherry explains that Inspector Mislan is investigating the murder of her housemate. He needs to ask questions to assist in his investigation. Instantly, she notices the fear in Julie's eyes. She also sees pleading in them. She turns to Mislan, who eye-gestures that he notices them, too.

"Mr. and Mrs. Maulana," Mislan starts. "Is it possible for you to leave us while I interview Julie?"

"Why?" Mr. Maulana asks, his eyes narrowing at Mislan.

"In murder investigations, there'll be things that only the witness and killers know. These discoveries will be facts, evidence, or clues that can be used against the suspect when arrested. You know, like police stories on TV."

Mr. Maulana nods several times. "Like when the suspect said something and you'll ask him how did he know about it?" he offers.

"Yes, exactly," Mislan says, giving him a wink.

Mr. Maulana beckons his wife, and Sherry shows them to the waiting area at the front desk.

Julie looks at Mislan, puzzled.

"I need to ask you about your relationship with my victim, Zaitun. I know you don't want your parents to hear it."

Julie nods, mouthing "thank you." Sherry joins them and gives Mislan a smile.

"How long have you and Zaitun been . . . together?" Mislan asks, going straight to the point.

Julia nods her understanding and lets out a weary smile. "Almost two years."

"Before her?"

"No one steady, just . . ." Julie pauses, taking deep breaths. "I mean not staying together like with Zac."

"Zac?" Sherry asks.

"Zaitun, we all call her Zac."

"Was Zac with someone before she hooked up with you?" Mislan asks.

"I suppose so, but we made an agreement not to ask or talk about each other's past. No point revisiting it, for us it's just the present and future."

"Who do you think would do these things to you and Zac?"

Julie shrugs.

"Were you with any man before you, you . . ." Mislan searches for the right word.

"Discovered yourself," Sherry offers.

"No, I've always known what I am. As early as my school days."

"Do your friends know of your orientation?" Mislan asks.

"At the bank, I don't think so. People like me, we don't advertise ourselves. You know how it is here . . . how we're mistreated and persecuted by the religious maniacs." She pauses, taking deep breaths, realizing she's being emotional. "Sorry. At Zac's workplace, I guess they do."

Sherry flashes her a warm smile, telling her they understand.

"That night or morning, was Zac coming back from work?" Mislan continues.

"Yes, Zac normally comes home around 2:30 to 3:00 in the morning."

"Did you hear the door?"

"No."

"Were the rapists in the room when Zac came in?"

Julie closes her eyes, trying to remember, and slowly shakes her head.

"I can't say for certain, as my eyes were closed. I heard a groan, a chair fell, and then the slamming of the front door. I rushed out and saw Zac on the floor, her legs wiggling, and there was a lot of blood." Julie cups her face, sobbing and trembling.

Mislan waits for Julie to get hold of herself.

"I called 999, but by the time the ambulance arrived the man told me Zac was . . . ," Julia continues but is unable to say the word *dead*.

From Julie's statement, Mislan is quite certain the killing wasn't premeditated, and the killers reacted when caught by surprise. There is nothing much she can tell him that may lead to the killers. He decides to terminate the interview.

"Is there anything else you can tell us that may assist in the investigation?"

Julie shakes her head.

"If you do remember anything, give me a call," Sherry says.

———————

When the two investigators return to the situation room, Saifuddin informs them that he called the Starbucks main office and they're ready to assist.

"So you didn't manage to hack it," Mislan teases him.

"Nope," Saifuddin replies follows by a chuckle. "No need to."

Sherry decides Mislan and Saifuddin should follow her to the Starbucks office and for Johan to stay back to manage the team. Mislan offers to take his car. To Sherry's dismay, the instant they drive out of the contingent complex, Mislan lights up, followed by Saifuddin. She gives Mislan an admonishing glare. Mislan responds with a my-car-my-rules grin. Lucky for her, it's a short drive to Berjaya Times Square.

At the Starbucks office, Sherry introduces the team and is directed to the IT section, where Saifuddin takes over. The two geeks sit in front of a computer, talking and pointing to the screen. Saifuddin makes some notes and thanks the other geek. He gestures for the two officers to follow him out.

"Got it?" Mislan asks.

Saifuddin waves the piece of paper, indicating he got what they wanted.

"That was quick," Sherry says.

"When you know what you want and where to look, it's quick," he boasts.

"What did we get?" Mislan asks.

"The make and model of the laptop and the IP address."

"What can we do with it?"

"Go and check with MacStudio to find out who the Apple MacBook was sold to."

"That's at Plaza Low Yat, right?" Sherry says.

"Yup, in front of the mall."

Mislan's cell phone rings. It's his assistant calling.

"Yes, Jo."

"Where're you guys?"

"Going to Low Yat, why?"

"The computer is beeping like crazy. What do I do?" Johan sounds anxious.

"How the hell should I know?" Mislan answers.

"I know you know shit about computers—let me speak to Sai."

"Sorry," Mislan says, laughing, and hands the cell phone to Saifuddin.

"Yes?" Saifuddin asks.

"The computer is beeping like crazy. What do I do?"

"Which one?"

"The desktop on the left."

"Shit, that's the one monitoring UTube. OK, don't do anything, I'll come back now."

Handing back the cell phone, Saifuddin tells Mislan he needs to get back to the situation room.

"Shit," Sherry cusses.

"OK," says Mislan. "I'll send you back and then me, Jo, Sherry, and Deena can go to MacStudio."

19

COMING OUT OF BERJAYA Times Square, Mislan has to pass the Kuala Lumpur Police Contingent Headquarters and make a U-turn about a mile down the street. The other route, taking Jalan Pudu all the way into the heart of congestion back into Jalan Galloway, is longer. In the car, Sherry calls Deena and tells her to be downstairs with Johan. She tells Saifuddin to keep her constantly updated. When Mislan pulls up in front of the contingent building, Johan and Deena are already waiting.

"Get in," Sherry tells them as Saifuddin gets out.

"Where to?" Deena asks.

"Low Yat."

"Again?"

Mislan drives out onto Jalan Imbi and after Melia Hotel turns left onto Jalan Bulan 1. The street is narrow, sandwiched between aged shopping complexes. Finding parking is next to impossible, so he makes an illegal U-turn immediately after Plaza Low Yat to Sherry's disgust and double-parks in front of MacStudio. A car jockey, a street hustler who will park your car for a fee, approaches them, and Mislan waves him away, saying, "police."

He tells Johan and Deena to stay with the car. Turning to Sherry, who is still annoyed with him for making the illegal U-turn, he asks, "You coming?"

As soon as Sherry steps out of the car, her cell phone rings.

"The video is up," Saifuddin says.

She groans. "Sai, make me a copy and tell MCMC to get off their asses! They took four days to block the first one. Tell them that's not good enough. We're going to be lynched by the public if they don't block it immediately."

"Done. MCMC says they are acting on it. Again, don't hold your breath."

"Can you monitor it?"

"I am."

"Thanks."

Sherry calls the heads of Sexual & Child Abuse and Special Investigations to inform them about the video.

Stepping into MacStudio, Sherry introduces herself to a sales assistant and asks for the manager. The girl points toward a man attending to a Caucasian couple. She waits patiently at a distance as the man continues demonstrating the latest MacBook to his customers.

Mislan, not used to playing a secondary role, asks, "What're you waiting for?"

"For him to finish," she says.

"You're kidding, right? We're here on police business. We don't have time to wait for him to make a sale."

As he walks toward the manager, Sherry hisses, "Mislan, don't do something stupid."

Stepping up to the manager, he says, "Excuse me, I'm Inspector Mislan from Special Investigations. I'd like a word with you, please."

The Caucasian couple look at him, annoyed. He reciprocates with a what-the-hell-are-you-staring-at look. The manager apologizes to the customers and signals to one of his salespeople to take over.

"Is there a place where we can speak privately?" Mislan asks.

"Let's go into my office."

In the office Mislan makes a crack. "Space must be very expensive here."

"Yes, it is. How may I help you, Inspector . . . ahhh?"

"Mislan."

He holds out his hand at Sherry, asking for the piece of paper with the particulars of the laptop.

"I need to know who bought this laptop."

"May I know the purpose?"

"We're investigating a case."

"Don't you need a warrant or something?"

"I don't know, do we?" Mislan mocks him. "Look, are you going to peek into your system and give us the particulars, or do you want me to place two uniformed men here until we come back with a warrant?"

"OK, OK. I was just asking. I don't want anyone to sue the company."

The manager hits some keys on his computer, writes down the purchaser's name, and hands it to Mislan. As they step out of MacStudio, Sherry stops Mislan.

"Don't you ever do that again when I'm with you."

"Do what?"

"Be rude, sarcastic, and intimidating. I don't approve of it and will not tolerate such conduct as long as you're acting as my second."

"We got what we came for, didn't we?" he says, waving the Post-it with the buyer's particulars.

Sherry snatches the piece of paper from his hand and walks away, annoyed.

"You're just pissed off because I took the lead and got things done," he calls after her.

———

After what happened at MacStudio, they return to the office and Sherry decides to go in separate cars to the address provided by the manager, Johan riding with Mislan and Deena with Sherry. The address is one of several bungalows along Jalan Ara, Bangsar. Mislan decides to wait in the car and let Sherry deal with the inquiries and possible arrest.

"Why aren't we with them?" Johan asks.

"Because we're only playing second fiddle," he snorts.

"We're her team," Johan corrects him.

"I bet you the house owner is someone well-connected. Let her take the heat as the lead. Then, after this, she'll beg me to take over," he says, chuckling.

"What have you got against her leading?"

Mislan shrugs.

"Give her a chance. I hear she's OK," Johan says.

Mislan lights a cigarette and watches Sherry ring the gate bell. A woman approaches. He sees Sherry identifying herself and the woman opening the gate, letting her and Deena in. They disappear and a few minutes later, reappear walking toward them.

"She's at the college," Sherry informs Mislan.

"Which?"

"KLCAC."

"Kuala Lumpur Creative Arts College?" Mislan asks, wanting to be sure, as there are too many private universities and colleges in the city.

"Yes."

"Okay, let's pick her up."

"No. That's not the way we're doing it. The mother will bring her around to the office."

"Why did you allow that?" Mislan asks, annoyed.

"Because her father is Datuk Yunus, a senior immigration officer."

"So?"

"So he deserves some respect."

"That's not respect. That's jeopardizing our investigations, giving the suspect the opportunity to delete anything incriminating."

"Give me some credit, will you," Sherry snaps at him.

A car pulls out of the driveway and stops next to them. Detective Deena climbs in, and it drives off. As Sherry walks back to her car, Johan grins at his boss.

"Now, that makes you feel silly, doesn't it?"

———————

When they reach the office, the front desk clerk tells him that the head of Special Investigations wants him to stop by her office. Mislan tells his assistant to come along.

"How was your first day with the task force?" Superintendent Samsiah asks, as they sit.

"So-so."

"That doesn't sound good," she comments with a smile. "Any progress?"

"The IT tech managed to obtain the MAC address, and we obtained the buyer's details. She's at KLCAC, and the mother will be bringing her in."

"KLCAC?"

"Kuala Lumpur Creative Arts College. Deena has gone with the mother to take custody of the laptop," Johan says.

"Let me guess, she's the daughter of someone important."

"A Datuk, a senior immigration officer."

"It was Sherry's decision, but you disagreed with her."

Mislan wears a blank expression, but Johan nods.

"I sense things are not working out between the two of you."

Mislan responds with a sly grin.

"Is this going to affect the investigation?"

Johan shakes his head while Mislan shrugs.

"Now, I sense a difference in opinion between the two of *you*," she says, laughing. "Have you been told that the second video is up?"

The two officers nod.

"The OCCI, Lillian, and I were just summoned by Datuk CPO. The public's panicking and talking about a serial rapist on the loose." She sighs. "Datuk CPO has instructed the OCCI to head the investigation." CPO is short for Chief Police Office of the state.

"What!" Mislan exclaims, his jaw dropping in disbelief.

"He'll head, with Lillian and me assisting. Daily briefing at 0900, you and Sherry are to be present."

Mislan's cell phone rings. It is Sherry, telling him the Datuk's daughter has arrived.

"You go ahead," he says, switching off the cell phone.

"Who was that?" Samsiah asks.

"Sherry. The girl's at D11."

"And why are you still here?"

"She can handle it," Mislan answers, brushing it off. "Ma'am, you know what's going to happen if he—"

"Let's worry about that later. Go and conduct your interview."

Reluctantly, he stands to leave.

She gives him a smile, saying, "You do what you do best. Let me worry about the rest."

Mislan and Johan enter the task force room to find Saifuddin by himself. Mislan looks around at the whiteboard and the photos of the victims that have been posted, with details of the incidents written next to them. There are some flowcharts—with boxes containing data and arrows in red, black, and blue—neatly drawn up on another whiteboard. Saifuddin is perched in front of a computer screen.

"*Walau-eh*!" Johan exclaims. "Now, this is what an investigation is supposed to look like."

"In the movies, you mean. All we need to complete the setting are a few large touch-screen LCD monitors," Mislan says, mocking him.

"You did all these?" Johan asks, turning to look at the board.

"Me and the team," Saifuddin answers with pride.

"After he sends us on a wild-goose chase," Mislan sneers.

"It was not a wild-goose chase. He was there," Saifuddin says, taking offense.

Mislan waves away Saifuddin's response, "You techies can't take jokes, can you? You know what a joke is, don't you?" He laughs. "Can I have copies of the video?"

"Deleted," Saifuddin says.

"You didn't make a copy before it was taken off the site?" Mislan asks, ready to explode.

Saifuddin laughs. "It's a joke, OK. You crime-busters can't take a joke, can you?"

Johan laughs.

"Both?" Saifuddin asks.

Mislan nods, saying, "For a techie, you're OK."

Sherry pops her head around the door.

"The laptop owner Massayu's waiting in the meeting room."

Mislan ignores her and walks up to the flowchart.

"Can I see your investigation papers for the first case?"

"Remind me after the interview."

———

Massayu binti Datuk Yunus is a petite girl in her late teens, sweet-look-ing, with short hair and a fair complexion, dressed in an orange vintage, square-neck, button knitted top, jeans, and little makeup. The mother, on the other hand, is literally painted with cosmetics. The girl sits next to her mother engrossed with her cell phone, oblivious to what is going on around her. The presence of the two officers doesn't even distract her attention. Sherry introduces Mislan to them, which Massayu doesn't acknowledge.

A spoiled brat, Mislan thinks.

"You said you'd tell me what this is all about when we're at your office. We're here now, so what are we waiting for?" the mother demands.

"I'm sorry, Datin, I wasn't at liberty to tell you earlier, as you insisted on bringing your daughter here yourself. Massayu is registered as the owner of the Apple MacBook bought from the MacStudio in Low Yat in June of last year. We need to examine the laptop," Sherry says, unper-turbed by her demand. Datin is an honorary prefix for a wife of a person awarded the title Datuk.

"Why do you want to examine it?"

"We're investigating a case, and some information was uploaded using the laptop. Is that the computer?" Sherry asks, pointing to the one in the unzipped backpack on the table.

Massayu instantly grabs her backpack, saying scornfully, "No way."

Mislan makes a move to stand and Sherry kicks his leg.

"Massayu, we need to check the MAC address. If it tallies with the one our IT Forensics have identified, we may have to confiscate it for evidence. If that's the case, we'll make a copy of any private information or college material for you."

"No way! You're going to read all my personal things," she snarls, turning to her mother. "Mummy, call Daddy and tell him about these people."

Unable to control himself at her bratty behavior, Mislan leans forward and hisses.

"What's your father going to do, deport us? The laptop's evidence in a murder case. Hand it over, or we'll take it by force."

"Mummy!"

"What murder?" the mother asks, taken aback.

Her hand gropes the interior of her Louis Vuitton handbag. *Probably searching for her cell phone*, Mislan suspects.

"Everybody stay calm." Sherry butts in, taking control of the situation. "Massayu, we promise you, your personal information will not be revealed without your consent. Datin, there's no need to get Datuk involved. It may attract publicity that may not be pleasant."

"What murder is he talking about? You said the laptop was bought in June of last year?" the mother asks.

"Yes, June 14."

"That laptop was stolen. Daddy bought this notebook in August, after my notebook was stolen," Massayu asserts boldly.

"Was the incident reported?"

"Yes."

"Which police station did you go to, and do you remember the report number?"

"No, not to the police, to the college. They told me not to make a police report, and reimbursed me for the loss."

"Can you give me the name of the person who handled the report?"

"Mr. Lai, he's the Student Affairs manager . . . officer . . . whatever."

"Okay, but I still need to verify the MAC address of your computer. It can be done here in your presence."

Massayu places her backpack on the table and extracts the laptop.

———

After the mother and daughter leave, Mislan asks Sherry if the Datin looks a little too young to be Massayu's mother. Sherry is taken aback by his question and gives him a curious look.

"Why do you ask? What has it to do with the case?"

"Just asking."

"If you have money, cosmetic surgery can make a woman look forever young," Sherry says.

"No, I looked at her hands. They're the hands of a young woman. Massayu's what, nineteen, twenty? And the mum, she couldn't be more than forty."

"She probably married young, and Massayu did call her 'Mummy.' You heard her."

"That doesn't mean anything. The father might have insisted on it."

"Why are you so interested?" Sherry asks suspiciously.

"Not in the way you're thinking."

"Is there any other way?" she teases him.

20

DOCTOR SAFIA HAS HER mind set on chicken rice for dinner. Mislan suggests she takes the Light Rail Transit and meet him at Gloria Jean's in Sungei Wang Plaza. Johan declined his invitation to join them, saying he wants to visit the Beach Club to find out more about their victim. Mislan suggests, if he has the time, to pay a visit to Punk Bistro in Damansara Utama and speak to Fatimah a.k.a. Tim.

"Who's she?" Johan asks.

"The rape-suicide victim's housemate. Here, her particulars are in this file. She's the manager or assistant manager there."

"OK."

When Mislan arrives at Sungei Wang Plaza on Jalan Bukit Bintang, Dr. Safia is already at Gloria Jean's. Decades back, Sungei Wang Plaza was one of the hip malls. Now it is just another aged mall in a city flooded with malls, with the shinier Lot 10 and Pavilion just across the street. When the big-name retailers moved out of the newer malls, Middle Eastern and other Asian businesses filled the vacuum.

They walk across the street to BB Hailam Chicken Rice and pick a table along the sidewalk. Dr. Safia is casually dressed in jeans and crewneck T-shirt and open-toe sandals. Her thick black hair is tied in a ponytail. Mislan likes the way she's dressed—simple and practical.

"You been here before?" he asks, while waiting for a waiter to serve them.

"Yes, a few times."

Mislan orders chicken rice for two, one young mango salad, and two iced barley waters.

"Steamed or roasted?" the waiter asks.

"Roasted. Make the chicken in one plate."

The waiter nods and disappears.

"I like coming here. The chicken rice's good, and you get to watch all sorts of people. They used to be mostly whites, but now they're Arab, Vietnamese, or African. Look over there." He gestures with his head. "An entire row of Middle Eastern restaurants."

Dr. Safia turns to look. "You should visit Jalan Aman. The entire street is lined with Middle Eastern restaurants. It's a fad now. People like to hang out there, smoking shisha pipes and drinking their horrible spiced coffee." She laughs.

"Hookah or shisha, not pipe."

"Whatever. I thought it had been decreed haram, but I see them in almost all mamak restaurants!"

"Haram doesn't necessarily mean illegal. It's up to the people to smoke it, or not."

The food arrives, and the conversation stops as Dr. Safia attacks it with gusto. She cleans her plate in less time than it took the waiter to bring it. Mislan orders another round of iced barley and lights a cigarette.

"You must have been starving."

"Famished, I didn't have lunch. Finished the last case around two thirty and decided to skip lunch."

"Anything interesting about my cadaver?"

"As I told you, cause of death was a severed sternocleidomastoid, cutting through the digastric and mylohyoid—"

"Why do you always give me the medical mumbo jumbo whenever I ask you about the cause of death? Why can't you say it in plain English?"

"I was hoping some medical terms might rub off on you and boost your image as a homicide investigator," she says, grinning.

"I'm a real-life police officer, not a TV cop. I'm sure you know that by now," he says in good humor.

"Okay, in English, a main blood vessel had been cut, namely the common carotid artery behind the neck. In short, the victim died due to excessive bleeding and loss of blood to the brain. The cut was deep and clean. There was no bruising on her face or chest to indicate she was held from behind. No defensive wounds." Dr. Safia pauses and takes a drag on her cigarette. "I told you all this already. Why are you asking me again?"

"Desperate and hoping there's something new."

"Sorry, nothing new. Oh, I forgot, the victim's alcohol blood level was above the permitted level for driving."

"She worked at the Beach Club, which would explain the alcohol level. Jo is going there later this evening to make some inquiries."

"Now, this is not a scientific or medical observation . . ."

Mislan looks at her.

"This is from a woman's point of view," she says. "When I undressed the victim, I noticed that the bra was tight, much too tight. What was even more surprising were the pads. She had put hard padding into the cups to press down on her breasts."

"I don't understand."

"It's like she wanted to flatten her chest. You know, to look like she's flat-chested."

"The paddings, were there labels on them?"

"No, they looked self-made."

"You're a woman, you should know about these things."

"Thank you for noticing. No, it's not something I'm familiar with. Generally, women like to show off what they've got, not hide them," she replies.

"Maybe she was a different kind of woman. A *pengkid*."

"Ahhh, now that makes sense."

"You know what a *pengkid* is?" Mislan asks, surprised.

"Yes. Unlike you, I keep up with society and the world," she says, laughing.

Mislan gives her a disinterested stare. "Anyway, the rape victim admitted that they're a couple."

"So your deceased's the top."

"The what?"

"Top, meaning she's the dominant one in the relationship, the provider . . . giver."

"You mean the man in the relationship."

"In our world, you can say that, yes."

————

Driving Dr. Safia home, Mislan checks with Johan and is told the victim had worked as a waitress at the Beach Club for just over a year. The
staff knew the victim is a *pengkid* and called her Zac. Hard-working,
well-liked, and was earmarked to be promoted to supervisor. Before the
Beach Club, she'd worked at the Concorde Hotel as a room attendant.

"She was treated like the rest. I mean, like one of the boys."

"See if you can find out more about her relationship with the rape
vic."

"Will do."

"Jo, on your way home, stop by the Concorde and talk to the staff.
See what they say about her."

"OK. Are you coming back to the office?"

"No, let's call it a day. I'll see you tomorrow."

When they enter her apartment, Mislan goes to the kitchen and
makes himself a mug of coffee, while Dr. Safia goes into her bedroom.

"You want coffee?" he calls from the kitchen.

"Tea, please."

He carries the two mugs to the living room and slumps on the sofa.
Dr. Safia has changed into a black lace satin nightie. She joins him on
the sofa, leaning against the opposite armrest with her legs on his lap.

"This case, is there something bothering you about it?"

"What do you mean?"

"You seem detached. But I can see the usual MCCS."

"MCCS?"

"Mislan's compulsive closure symptoms," she says, giggling. "Want
to talk about it?"

He laughs. "You have a medical term for it? I mean the CCS part?"

She sits up and kisses him lightly on the cheek. "We have medical terms for everything."

They chat about everything but mostly nothing through the night until they decided to move to the bedroom.

Mislan wakes up to the ringing of his cell phone alarm. The faint odor of dried perspiration blends with her overnight Dolce & Gabbana perfume on the bedsheet. It reminds him of the intense and wondrous night they shared. Reluctantly, he disengages her arms from his chest, slides off the bed, and gets dressed in the dark. Kissing her lightly on the forehead, he leaves without waking her.

21

THE SPECIAL INVESTIGATIONS OFFICE is buzzing when Mislan walks in. He notices the detectives and clerical staff looking at him. Mislan gawks at them, thinking, *Shit, do they know I had a great time between the sheets last night and the religious police are waiting to arrest me?* He spots his assistant briskly approaching.

"The OCCI was here looking for you," Johan whispers anxiously. "When Reeziana told him you've not arrived he marched off to ma'am's office."

Mislan looks at the time on his cell phone.

"It's not even seven forty-five. What's he doing in the office so early?"

"Ass-hunting," Inspector Reeziana shouts from across the room. "To be specific, yours." The investigators and their assistants laugh with her. "What have you done to piss him off this time?"

"Now we'll all have to sit through his lion dance," Inspector Tee moans. "And Gong Si Fatt Choi was long over."

"He misses me," Mislan says with a swagger.

The front desk clerk pokes his head in and announces that morning prayer will start in five minutes.

"It's only eight, I haven't had my coffee. Shit, so now I've to sit through his blabbering on an empty stomach," Mislan grumbles.

"He must really miss you to get ma'am to start at eight," Johan teases him. "I hope you'll still be in the mood for breakfast after his lion dance, because I've got your favorite, nasi lemak with squid."

"Save it for me. I'll certainly need it to cheer me up later."

———

When the D9 officers file into the meeting room, they're surprised to see Superintendent Lillian and Inspector Sherry in there. The D9 officers greet them and take their seats. Lillian and Sherry return their greetings with tight smiles and baffled looks.

Senior Assistant Commissioner Burhanuddin barges into the meeting room like a raging bull. Everyone is silent. Sitting at the head of the table where Superintendent Samsiah usually sits, he immediately erupts into a stream of verbal diarrhea—accusing police officers of not having any respect for senior government servants, people who have dedicated their entire lives to serve the nation and the public, blah blah blah. When he finally realizes that most of those present are not paying attention and are either checking their watches or cell phones, his focus turns to Mislan.

"And you, Mislan," he roars, catching everyone by surprise, "who the hell do you think you are?"

All heads turn toward Mislan in unison.

"Going around arresting a girl at her school, embarrassing her in front of her school friends? Threatening her in front of her mother and slandering a Datuk, a senior immigration officer."

Mislan holds his tongue and gazes at the OCCI unblinkingly.

"What excuse do you have for such unprofessional conduct?" Burhanuddin barks. "He intends to sue the police for false arrest, intimidation, and slander, unless you apologize immediately to him and his family. And I've assured him that you will."

Mislan turns to his boss, his eyes pleading for permission to speak.

"May I know the actual allegations against Mislan?" Samsiah asks.

Burhanuddin turns to her, his face contorted with anger.

"False arrest, humiliating his daughter in front of her school friends, intimidation, and slander. If I have my way, I will add insubordination, too."

"Sir, the girl, Massayu, was not arrested. She was brought here by her mother, and Mislan was not even present. By the way, she's a college student. The interview was conducted by Inspector Sherry. Therefore, there is no basis for any of those allegations made against Mislan."

"I don't care who did the interview. He was there, and the allegations are against him," he growls. "I've promised Datuk that he will apologize, and he shall do so. You make sure of that."

Mislan opens his mouth to answer, but Samsiah beats him to it.

"I'm sorry sir, I don't think it's appropriate for my officers to apologize for wild and unfounded allegations. May I call Datuk to clear the air?"

"If you want to stick your neck out for him, it's up to you. However, if Datuk sues the police, I'll hold you responsible."

With that, the OCCI abruptly stands and leaves the meeting.

Superintendent Lillian, Inspector Sherry, and Mislan follow Superintendent Samsiah to her office. The D11 officers take the two guest chairs while Mislan stands leaning against the file cabinet.

"What a start to the day," Lillian says.

Samsiah smiles at her statement.

"Ma'am, what has he got against me?" Mislan asks.

"What makes you think he has something against you?" Samsiah answers with a question.

"If what just happened isn't sufficient proof of him gunning for me, then I don't know what is."

"Look, Lan, nobody is gunning for you. He's under tremendous pressure. Getting threatening calls from influential people can make even the toughest among us lose our cool. And you trying to stand your ground will only aggravate matters. Just let it slide and continue with your investigations. I'll handle Datuk."

"But why must we explain ourselves when we're only doing our jobs?" Sherry says in defense of Mislan.

"Because we're public servants, and the public has a right to know what we do and why we do it. Check out the concept of transparency and accountability. Once you understand that, you might even subscribe to it," Samsiah explains, all the while looking at her officer.

"I don't know how you swallow all this, ma'am," Mislan says, letting out a heavy sigh.

"What did we get from the daughter's laptop?" Samsiah asks, changing the subject.

"Her laptop was stolen, and the one she's using is new. Sai checked the MAC address and confirmed it," Sherry briefs.

"Have you checked out her story?"

"We're doing it today."

"Good. So we're back where we started."

"Looks like it," Lillian says.

"The new video, was it removed?"

"MCMC has been informed and they're working on taking it down. I'm hoping by today," Sherry answers.

"What've we found out about the deceased?"

"Johan did some inquiries at her workplace. It was confirmed that she was a *pengkid*. D11 victim confirmed it, too."

"What about the rape-suicide victim?"

"Johan is checking her background," Mislan answers. "He's also tracing her housemate—Fatimah, who goes by the name of Tim."

"Your angle?" Lillian asks.

"No angle, just trying to see if there's a link between the two vics," Mislan offers.

"Any theory?"

Mislan and Sherry shake their head.

"If there's no link between the two vics, then these are random acts and—" Mislan says.

"—it makes nailing down the perps more difficult," Samsiah finishes her officer's sentence.

The head of Special Investigations puts on her spectacles and opens a file, signaling the meeting is over. The D11 officers stand, thank her and leave, but Mislan hangs back.

"What?" Samsiah asks, staring at her officer.

"Maybe I shouldn't team up with them," he says, gesturing to the door with his head. "No point getting them into trouble on my account."

"I said you go and do your job and let me handle him," she says, tilting her head upward indicating the OCCI. "Now go serve the public and earn your salary." As he reaches the doorway, she calls, "Lan, watch what you say; it can get you in trouble."

22

JOHAN MAKES HIS BOSS a mug of coffee as Mislan unwraps his nasi lemak pack for his first meal of the day. With his mouth full of rice, chili paste, and squid, he asks, "What did you find out about our vic at the Concorde?"

"She worked there for about three years as a room attendant and was dismissed for sexual harassment."

"She was sexually harassed?"

"No, she harassed another room attendant, a recruit. The girl told her boyfriend, and he confronted the management."

"Is the girl still working there?"

"She left after the vic was dismissed."

"I need you to track her down and the boyfriend, too. Maybe there's more to the story. "

"Like what?"

"If I knew the answer to that, I wouldn't be asking you to locate them, would I?" Mislan says. "We've nothing to do anyway. Have you viewed the videos?"

"The whole thing is sickening."

"Spot anything that we can follow up on?"

"I really can't stomach it. Before I forget, Inspector Sherry called for the task force meeting at ten."

———

Mislan and Johan enter the Situation Room and find the four detectives chatting while Saifuddin sits alone behind his monitors and keyboards.

"Where is Sherry?" Mislan asks.

"With ma'am," Deena answers.

Mislan walks to the window, pushes it open, and lights a cigarette. His assistant and the four detectives look at him but say nothing. The IT technician stands, joins him by the window, and lights up, too.

"Don't you smoke when I'm not here?" Mislan asks him.

"Only if there's no one around."

"So I'm your ticket to smoke when the rest are here."

"Sort of," Saifuddin answers with a wide smile. "You're an officer. Who's going to tell you off?"

"Anything on the . . . what's-his-name?"

"Emancipatist. No, but I've programmed the MAC address and his username for monitoring. He hasn't logged on since the last posting."

"Maybe he knows we're monitoring him, so he only uses that computer for uploading the video and nothing else."

"In that case, he is no ordinary user. He could be a techie who knows about cyber monitoring and tagging."

Sherry appears in the doorway. Mislan drops his cigarette down the window, quickly followed by Saifuddin. She gives them the glare but says nothing. Mislan pulls the window shut as she takes a seat at the table.

"OK," Sherry says. "Yahaya, Mokthar, what've you got?"

"We talked to our snitches, but none of them heard anything on the rape," Yahaya, the spokesman for his partnership, says. "I mean they heard of the rape from the news and some even saw the video, but no one heard anything about who did them."

"Maybe they're not locals," Deena suggests.

"By local, you mean Malay?"

Deena nods.

"We talked to our Indon, Bangla, and Myanmar sources, but none of them heard anything, either."

"There's this one snitch, he said maybe the rapists are from out of town," Mokthar offers.

"That could be why our snitches didn't hear anything," Dorai theorizes.

"That could just be an excuse for you guys not shaking hard enough," Mislan sneers.

Detective Yahaya and Mokthar gaze at him, showing their displeasure at his remark. Mislan's reputation for being direct is well-known, and they say nothing.

"What about rapists recently released from prison?" Sherry asks, ignoring Mislan's remark.

"We've asked for a list from the prison authority. They're compiling it. Hopefully, we'll get it today. While waiting for the list, we've gone through old cases but failed to find any with similar MO," Yahaya answers.

"How far back?" Sherry asks.

"Five years."

"OK. Dorai?"

"I've gone through the CCTV for the first case. There're only two cameras, both at the guardhouse. A lot of vehicular traffic but no way of telling who is who or where the drivers were headed."

"What're the entry procedures?" Johan asks.

"The condo has an access card boom-gate. Tenants are provided with access cards so they just drive in. Visitors have to stop at the guardhouse and show their IC and are given a laminated visitor card to be displayed on their car's dashboard. The guard will lift the boom-gate for them."

"The ICs, are they recorded?" Sherry asks.

"Not all, you know *lah* guards."

"I don't think the perps would go through the procedures," Mislan says. "No way they'd want to be seen by the guards or run the risk of their particulars being recorded."

"What about motorbikes?" Johan asks.

"Outsiders' bikes park at an open space across from the guardhouse, and the riders walk in."

"No need to show their ICs?" Mislan asks.

"No, the open space is past the guardhouse. You park your bike and walk in."

"That's how they got in," Mislan emphasizes. "There're two of them, just one bike is needed. Nothing to bring attention to themselves."

"The second case?" Sherry asks.

"No CCTV, no guard," Dorai answers, shaking his head.

"Neighbors?"

"We interviewed most of them, but no one saw or heard anything that morning. In the second case, the next-door neighbor said she heard a scream but thought nothing of it. The units there are mostly rented by shift workers so you can hear all sort of noises at all hours," Deena reports.

"Shift workers, that means there're people going in and out of the apartment at all hours?" Mislan asks.

"Yes, we thought so, too, but then the incident happened around two to three in the morning, in between shifts going or returning," Deena says.

"Morning shift starts at seven or eight, and the graveyard shift workers will only reach home around eight or nine a.m.," Dorai explains.

"Interesting," Mislan says, tightening his lips.

"Jo, I understand you did a background on the murder victim and also the first rape victim's housemate," Sherry asks. "Like to share your findings?"

Johan briefs the meeting on what he found out about Zac and Tim, which was nothing much except they were *pengkid*.

"I also did a background on your victim, Julie," Johan says.

"Anything interesting there?" Sherry asks.

"One of the bank staff said she used to go out with one of her coworkers, a man, but they broke up after a few months."

"Was it amicable or nasty, the breakup?" Mislan asks.

"After the breakup, the victim asked for a transfer to her present branch."

"So it was nasty," Mislan says.

"Not necessarily, it could just be heartbreaking," Sherry counters. "Sai, anything on the social media angle?"

"Nothing of interest."

"And what's that supposed to mean?" Mislan asks.

"Nothing threatening or social-media stalking or personality-bashing."

"Looks like we've nothing to go on," Sherry admits with a sigh. "OK, keep at it and I'm sure something will come up."

———

Once they are in Sherry's office, Mislan closes the door behind him. She waits for him to take a seat before asking what he wants to discuss.

"Can I smoke?"

Sherry gives him a silent stare.

"I take that as a no," he says, grinning. "What do you people have against smoking? I'm sure you go out, right, restaurants, grills, and pubs? People there smoke."

"It's the regulation, I don't own this office, and neither is it a public place. What do you want to discuss in private?"

"The team's updates. In the first case, the perps know the entry procedures practiced by the condo guards. They also know there're no cameras except the two at the guardhouse."

"Meaning?"

"They know they can get in without showing their ICs at the guardhouse if they're on bike. They just need to park their bike at the allocated place and walk in. Two people on a bike attract less than two bikes coming in at the same time, or attract no attention at all."

"OK."

"The second case was during the in-between shift window. They know the apartment is mainly rented by shift workers. They also know the common shift hours. The incident was around two to three a.m. OK, the second shift starts at three p.m. and ends at eleven p.m. By the time they arrive home, it'll be around midnight or one a.m. The graveyard shift starts from eleven p.m., ending at seven a.m. Those going will leave around ten p.m. and those coming back will be there around eight or nine a.m. The widest nighttime window is between one to five a.m., just before those going for the morning shift leave their houses. The one to five a.m. window offers them the least chance of bumping into any of the tenants."

"Confusing," Sherry admits.

Mislan asks for a piece of blank paper and writes:

Morning shift – 0700 to 1500 (Leave 0600/Return 1600)
Second shift – 1500 to 2300 (Leave 1400/Return 0000)
Graveyard shift – 2300 to 0700 (Leave 2200/Return 0800)

"I'm giving a buffer of one hour for the travel to and from work. You can give two hours if you like," Mislan explains. "If you look at the timing, the widest nighttime window is between 0000, the time the second shift returns home, to 0600, the time the morning shift leaves for work."

"OK, got it. What's your theory?"

"Can I smoke?"

"Stop behaving like a child, will you?"

"No harm in trying. My theory is these are very organized perps. They observe and study their playground. They planned the entry, exit routes, and timing carefully. My theory is we're not dealing with brainless testosterone-driven creeps."

"And your suggestion?"

"At the moment, can't think of any."

"That's a lot of help."

Mislan smiles. "Once I have my nicotine fix, I may come up with something."

23

MISLAN GOES BACK TO the situation room, pulls up a chair, and sits facing the whiteboard. He lights a cigarette, and Saifuddin immediately locks the door and pushes open the window. Standing by the window, he capitalizes on the situation by lighting up while watching the inspector. Johan pulls up a chair and joins his boss. They both stare at the photographs of the victims and notes written beside them.

"What are you looking for?" Johan asks his boss.

"The link between the vics."

"One worked in a marketing agency and the other in a bank. There's nothing to indicate they knew each other or even crossed paths," Johan says.

"Yes, they did, without knowing it, they did cross paths."

"How so?"

"Their lifestyle."

"I don't get you."

"Their sexual orientation. Sai, you said you checked their social media accounts, right?"

"Yup," Saifuddin answers, stepping closer to them.

"OK, go into the first victim's social media accounts and read all her postings and comments. Search for Tim's accounts and do the same."

"What specifically are you looking for?" Saifuddin asks.

"Her relationship with Tim. I want to know for certain her sexual orientation. We know Tim is a *pengkid*, but I need to know the jumper was her partner."

"OK, on it."

The doorknob creaks, followed by angry-sounding knocks on the door.

"Open this damn door!" Sherry calls.

Mislan throws his cigarette butt out, pulls the window shut and opens the door.

"Sorry, I must have accidentally pressed the lock when I came in," he says.

"Yeah, right, like I was born yesterday." Sherry gives him and Saifuddin admonishing looks. "One of these days ma'am's going to walk in on both of you smoking and burn your asses."

Sherry walks in and takes a seat. Mislan sits next to her.

"Remember what you told me? About the rapes having hidden motives?"

Sherry nods.

"Well, as much as I hate to admit it, I have to agree with you. In your second case we know she's a lesbian, we can rule out jealous ex-boyfriends."

"Where did the jealous ex-boyfriend theory come from?"

"Experience," he chuckles.

Sherry laughs, "I hope it's not yours."

Mislan ignores her.

"The first vic, Era, was a marketing big shot. The second, Julie, works in a bank. Made the connection between the two?" she continues.

"Based on their backgrounds, nothing. They're not from the same school, neighborhood, or even state. They never worked in the same company. One lived in Pantai Dalam, and the other in Setapak Jaya, two different police districts. Roughly thirteen miles apart. They weren't in the same social circle," Mislan states.

"Random?" Sherry raises her eyebrows at him. She knows something is clicking in that brain of his, and she knows he is toying with her.

"Scary prospect isn't it, no pattern to map out, no specific target group to monitor. You won't be able to plan any preventive measures. Cases will mount, and you'll just be picking up the pieces as you go along. In the meantime, you'll be praying for Lady Luck to come to your rescue," he says, shaking his head.

"Me? It's we," Sherry reminds him.

"Me, I've only one case. The word 'serial' here is for the rapes, not the murder."

Sherry notices Johan and Saifuddin watching them, all ears. She beckons for Mislan to follow her back to her office. Once inside, she closes the door, walks to her chair, and stands next to it.

"Do you have a problem working with me?" she asks, looking intently at Mislan.

"I need a smoke, can I smoke here?"

"Damn you, Mislan, let's not make the situation worse," she snaps. "Do-you-have-a-problem-working-with-me?" she repeats. "You've been giving me the cold shoulder, second-guessing, and undermining me. I did not pick you to be my second, and I never looked at you as my second. If you want out, go talk to your boss."

Mislan purses his lips. "I like your spirit. Never knew you had that in you."

"What spirit? That's me, pissed off!" she explodes. "Look, I don't know what's bothering you about working with me, but if you're not going to give this one hundred percent, I suggest you talk to Superintendent Samsiah and get yourself off the case." She takes a long deep breath. "I've more than enough on my hands without having to deal with your attitude." She drops into her chair heavily. "Have you read the papers?"

"No. Why do you need to read them? You know firsthand what the case is about."

"They're talking about serial rapists on the loose in the city, that the police are clueless. The public is in a panic, and my boss's phone's ringing off the hook."

"That's why I don't read the papers. I don't know why you bother to. Look, Sherry, you know what you're doing and how the case is going. Just keep at it and let the papers publish whatever they want to sell papers."

"It's not that easy."

"It's that easy. Just ask yourself what you want. Play to the media or go for closure? In my case, I let the publicity junkie upstairs deal with the media."

"Let's get back to the primary issue. Are you with me or do you want out?"

"Let me be upfront, I'm with you, but there'll be times that I'll be against you. During those times, I'll do what I feel is the right thing to do. I suggest you do the same. How does that stand with you?"

She looks him in the eyes, "I'm fine with it, on condition that you must tell me when and why you're against me."

"Likewise. You want to seal it in blood?" he jokes.

"Yes, your blood."

"OK, let's go back to the situation room. At least there I can smoke."

———

They return to the situation room and find Johan standing next to Deena at the whiteboard as she writes more details about the second victim.

"Let's continue from where we left off," Sherry says, taking a seat.

"Where were we?" Mislan asks.

"Random. I know that screwed-up brain of yours is piecing together the jigsaw. Let's have it out in the open."

"Sai, anything?"

"Nothing concrete, but there were insinuations that they're a couple . . . Era and Tim."

"That's good enough for now. Keep working on it. We still need to be sure; otherwise my theory won't hold. Jo, I need you to confirm it. Talk to her and her friends."

Johan nods.

"We're talking about your first vic and Tim," Mislan explains to Sherry. "I've a strong feeling she's gay."

"Me too," Deena says. "The way she dressed and, when she dropped by the victim's unit, the way she called out to her. What was it, *Baby, where are you* or something like that."

"I believe the link between the two vics is their lifestyle."

"Meaning?" Sherry asks.

"There're gay, and that was where they crossed paths."

"You really have weird logic," Sherry says.

"I'll take that as a compliment." He smiles. "Sherry, why don't you and Deena talk to the first vic's coworkers, friends, and neighbors? Find out anything and everything you can about them, especially where they hang out."

"I thought you asked Jo to do that," Sherry says.

"Changed my mind. I'll go with Jo to KLCAC, check on the Datuk's daughter's claim of the stolen laptop."

"OK, but remember our deal," she wearily reminds him.

Walking out, Johan asks his boss what deal Sherry was talking about. Mislan smiles and shrugs.

"You took charge back there. What's the deal?"

"I don't know what she was talking about. She must have been mistaken. Maybe it was some deal she made with someone else. You know the pressure from these cases, not to mention the press and the public. It makes her a little mixed up."

"So now you're saying she's delusional."

"I did not say that. I simply said she must have me confused with someone else."

"So, who's the lead now, you or her?"

"Like ma'am said, she is."

Johan laughs. "You're just itching for trouble, aren't you?"

24

STEPPING OUT OF THE elevator at the ground floor, they bump into a large group of journalists and cameramen waiting for the elevator to go up. Mislan and Johan push their way through the impatient crowd that rushes in before they can get out and head for the parking lot. As they walk out of the lobby, Mislan hears his name being called. It's Rodziah, or Audi as she likes to be called. He quickens his steps toward his car. Audi calls out again running after them.

"Inspector, wait up, will you?"

Catching up, she greets Johan and says to Mislan, "Are you running away from me?"

"What gives you that impression?"

"Forget it," she replies, catching her breath. "You're the lead in the murder of the rape victim's housemate?"

"Shouldn't you be with them?" Mislan points to the crowd in the lobby.

"They're reporting history, I'm chasing stories," she crows. "Slow down, will you, my feet are hurting. So, are you the lead?"

"Inspector Sherry of D11 is the lead."

"Jo, is he telling me the truth?"

Johan nods.

"Why is Sexual & Child Abuse leading a Special Investigations case?"

"Don't ask me, I don't make the rules. I only follow them."

"Do I detect resentment?" she teases him. "Any lead so far on the murder and rapes?"

"I suggest you go to the press conference, or talk with Sherry."

They reach his car, and he unlocks and gets in.

"Can I come with you?"

"You don't even know where we're going," he says. "I'm sure you've heard how police officers like to malinger, you know, play truant at the taxpayers' expense? That's what we're doing. Go chase your story somewhere else."

Driving out of the contingent headquarters, he heads for Jalan Imbi and makes a right onto Jalan Sultan Ismail. Driving through Kampung Pandan, he hits Jalan Ampang and is caught in a traffic crawl.

"Where *are* we going?" Johan asks.

"Setapak Jaya."

"Why're you taking this street? You know this street is forever jammed."

Mislan grins.

His assistant is right. Jalan Ampang is the most congested artery and even boasts a title to be proud of—Ampang Jam. Inching along, they pass the Gleneagles Specialist Hospital where those with deep pockets go for treatment. Low-level public employees like him go to government clinics and wait for hours to receive treatment.

He makes a right after the Great Eastern Mall onto Jalan Jelatek and heads for the City Hall Public Housing in Setapak Jaya.

Turning to the apartment complex, he stops at an Indian Muslim or mamak restaurant across the street for a drink. Johan picks up a Malay daily lying on the table next to them. The headline reads, Rape Victim Housemate Brutally Murdered, with a photo of building 10-4-03 and a thumbnail of Zaitun.

"What does it say?"

"'The perpetrators of the UTube Serial Rapes are now involved in murder. The rapists call themselves the Emancipatist.' It mentions that the first rape victim committed suicide, etc. Oh, listen to this, 'The Kuala Lumpur Officer in Charge of Criminal Investigations, SAC Burhanuddin Sidek, says he's personally heading the task force and that they're looking into several promising leads. He's confident the police will have the rapists in custody soon,'" Johan says, laughing.

"It's easy to be optimistic when you don't know the first thing about what you're up against. Jo, look at the entrance. Cars, bikes, and pedestrians go in and out freely."

"That's common at most City Hall apartments: no budget for guards. They're for low-income people. I don't think there's a monthly maintenance fee charged."

"Jo, I thought I saw the management office in that block," Mislan says, pointing. "Why don't you talk to anyone there and see if they heard of any talk by the residents about the incident."

Johan approaches the office while Mislan walks to the crime scene block. He lights a cigarette and watches his assistant speaking to a couple of men. He notes that the block is old and under-maintained. Plastic bags litter the drives and drains. There is barely any landscaping, and whatever space there is is used for parking. The area next to the staircase is lined with parked motorbikes, an indication the apartments are mainly rented by the young working class. After a few minutes, Johan walks toward him.

"They heard a lot of gossip but nothing of any substance," Johan says.

"The killers would've parked their bike here," Mislan says, pointing to the motorbike parking area.

"They could park elsewhere, around the other end."

"Yes, they could, but I don't think they'd do that. Parking in non-designated areas may risk attracting attention of insomniac residents. And I'm sure they want to park where they can make a quick escape."

Mislan drops his cigarette in the drain.

"The staircase's over there, so parking here close to it makes the most sense. Eliminates the need to walk in an exposed area longer than needed. In the stairwell they're concealed from view."

Mislan walks to the stairwell and looks up. *Perfect for the killers' entry and exit route.*

"You know what I can't figure out about this case?" he asks.

"What?"

"How they gained entry into the vics' units. There was no sign of break-in. The first vic said she latched the door, and Sherry confirmed that."

"Yes, but it was a dead bolt that can be opened with a key from the outside, not the night latch," Johan says.

Mislan nods. "Still, the doorknob lock and dead bolt need two different keys. How do they know the second vic's boyfriend or partner's not home when they enter the unit?"

Mislan walks up the staircase, with Johan following close behind. He observes the missing light tubes in the stairwell.

"They probably observed the vic's unit," Johan offers.

"I'm positive they did, but with all their planning, our vic still caught them by surprise."

"And paid with her life."

"Jo, tonight, get the standby detective to talk to Zac's coworkers. Find out her work schedule and if she knocked off early that night."

"OK."

Mislan takes out his cell phone and calls Sherry.

"Yes."

"Sherry, can you send one of your team to the second crime scene?"

"What's there?"

"I need them to interview residents with bikes, see if they noticed any bike that's not usually parked here. If they hear of any biker complaining that his parking space was taken."

"Bike, how would they know? If it's a car I can understand."

"Before I could afford my old junk of a car, I rode a bike, OK. Like cars, we, too, have our regular spots. If someone parked his bike in our spot, we get upset and react."

"OK, how long do you want them there?"

"Until around midnight."

"That long?"

"You need to cover the office and shift workers that finish work at eleven p.m."

"I'll get Deena to organize it."

"Anything from your side?"

"Nothing so far. We just keep beating the bushes, eventually the snakes will come out," Sherry says.

Terminating the call, he turns to his assistant.

"Jo, those roadside stalls . . . they're open all night till morning, right? I'm sure if something happened around here, they'll know about it. Can you get the detective to talk to the operators and the owls and moths?"

25

From Setapak Jaya the two officers drive back to the city. At the junction of Jalan Tuanku Abdul Rahman and Sultan Ismail, they make a right onto Jalan Raja Laut and park on the street next to the building that houses the Kuala Lumpur Creative Arts College. Johan asks a group of students hanging about at the entrance for directions to the Student Affairs office. At the office, he introduces himself to a receptionist and asks for Mr. Lai.

"Mr. Lai's with the principal," the clerk says. "May I assist you?"

"Yes, a student by the name of Massayu Datuk Yunus reported her laptop stolen. May we see the report?"

"Give me a minute, I'll check with Mr. Sega, Mr. Lai's assistant."

The clerk disappears and returns with an Indian man.

"Sergeant . . . ?" the Indian man asks.

"Johan from Special Investigations, Kuala Lumpur, and this is Inspector Mislan. You are?"

"Gunasegaran, I'm the assistant manager of student affairs. Please come with me into my office. It's more private. Sorry, what's the student's name again?"

"Massayu Datuk Yunus. She reported her laptop stolen from the library bag depository pigeonhole."

"I remember that case was handled by Mr. Lai himself, with the chief of security."

"Can we view the inquiry file?"

"Let me check with his secretary." He makes a call and, replacing the phone, says, "She says there was no inquiry file opened."

Johan raises his eyebrows inquiringly. "Is there any reason why the case wasn't reported to the police?"

"I believe it was on the recommendation of the chief security officer, but I really don't know because I wasn't involved in it."

"Do you lose many laptops here?" Mislan asks.

"I think you'll have to ask Mr. Lai that."

"Are there cameras at the library?"

"Yes."

"At the pigeonholes?"

"Yes."

"Can we view them?"

"I'll have to check with the security chief."

"Can we meet this security chief?"

"Sure," Sega says, eager to be rid of the police officers. He phones someone, and tells them that the security chief is waiting in his office.

"I noticed a mamak restaurant next to the 7-E outside. Can you tell him to meet us there?" Mislan says.

———

The officers make their way back to the lobby and out the building. Walking to the restaurant, Johan asks, "Why the mamak?"

"I'm hungry and need to smoke," Mislan answers casually.

"What do you make of the lost laptop? You think they're covering up something?"

"I don't know. Ask the chief when you see him."

"You're going to have lunch?"

"Might as well."

He orders fried noodles with iced black coffee, while Johan walks to the mixed rice counter to check out the spread. He comes back with a plate of rice topped with chicken curry and vegetables. Just as Johan starts eating, a man approaches them.

"Are you Sergeant Johan?"

"Yes, and you must be the chief security officer."

"Yes," he says, extending his hand. "Najib."

"This is Inspector Mislan. Please sit."

They shake hands, and Najib slides into the seat next to Johan.

"I was told you're inquiring about Miss Massayu's lost laptop."

The waiter brings Mislan's fried noodles and asks Najib for his order, but he declines.

"Mr. Sega said you and Mr. Lai handled the case. Why was it not reported to the police?" Johan asks.

"Her father was insistent that the college reimburse his daughter in full for the loss. Since the college agreed to pay, I didn't see any reason to make a police report. We only make police reports to ward off liabilities or for insurance claims."

"Was there an official inquiry following the loss?"

"Yes, but we sort of stopped it when Miss Massayu was reimbursed."

"Was there a suspect?"

"No."

"Do you have CCTV cameras at the library?"

"Yes."

"Do you still have the recording?"

"We made a copy of the date of the incident. I think Mr. Lai has it."

"I'll need to view it. When can you give us a copy?" Mislan asks.

"I'll check with Mr. Lai."

"Do you lose many laptops?"

"A few, but since we increased security it has stopped. May I know the reason for the sudden interest in the case?"

"My boss was told about the loss by Datuk and we've been instructed to make some inquiries," Johan lies. "Can you confirm with Mr. Lai that he still has the recording? We'll wait here for you."

When Najib leaves, Johan looks at his boss.

"Something bothering you?"

"You're doing just fine," Mislan says with a sly grin.

———

Back to enjoying his fried noodles, his cell phone rings.

"Mislan."

"Mislan, Sherry, where're you?"

"KLCAC."

"What're you doing there? Please don't stir things up."

Ignoring her, he asks, "What's up?"

"We've uncovered something interesting about the first victim."

"Such as?"

"It's confirmed she had the same sexual orientation as the second victim."

"Gay?"

"Yes."

"That's interesting. Any other link between them?"

"That's the only commonality we have at this moment. Are you coming back to the office?"

"We're waiting for a CCTV recording. Let you know when we're back."

As Mislan terminates the call, Johan asks, "The first vic was gay? I thought 'gay' only applies to men."

Mislan laughs.

"'Gay' is often used to refer to homosexual men, but it can refer to both genders."

In a country where homosexuality is forbidden, there is a general lack of knowledge and understanding about it.

"I learned something today," Johan admits with a grin.

"Do you know that homosexuality also exists in the animal kingdom?"

"You're just making that up."

"I'm serious. . . . I did some research. The study was conducted in the early twentieth century but was suppressed by the Church authorities. It was argued that, if it was nature and not nurture because it existed in the animal kingdom, then it is God's will. That was why the study was suppressed."

Seeing Najib approaching, Johan warns Mislan with a tilt of his head. The security officer gives them a DVD and says he has to get back to the office.

"Thanks. I'll call you if there's anything else we need," Johan says.

26

SUPERINTENDENT SAMSIAH WAITS PATIENTLY as the operator transfers her call to the director general of immigration's personal assistant. When a woman at the other end answers, she introduces herself and asks to speak to Datuk Yunus Malik. After a few rings a man answers, "Yunus."

"Assalamualaikum, Datuk, I'm Superintendent Samsiah Hassan from Special Investigations, Kuala Lumpur."

"Waalaikumsalam. Yes, Superintendent, how may I assist you?"

"I was told by my OCCI, Senior Assistant Commissioner Burhanuddin, that you're disturbed about your daughter's interview by my unit. Let me assure you, Datuk . . ."

"Superintendent, I don't know what Burhanuddin told you, but I was only inquiring about the case and how my daughter is involved."

"Oh, I'm sorry Datuk. There seems to be some miscommunication. Since we're on the line, let me enlighten you. Your daughter Massayu is not a suspect, nor was she picked up by the police. I'm sure Datin has told you it was she who brought Massayu to the office. My officers needed to identify a laptop bought in June of last year, registered in her name, but it has been established that the laptop in question was stolen."

"Yes, and the college reimbursed her for the loss. I bought her a new one in August last year."

"Datuk, I'm sorry about the miscommunication with my OCCI, and I wish to inform you that Massayu is in no way involved with the case we are investigating. Thank you, Datuk."

Replacing the phone, she sighs and wonders how the OCCI could have misunderstood the Datuk's call. There was no reason for the director general to lie to her. What was the OCCI's motive for misrepresenting him? Apart from making an excuse to take Mislan off the case, she can't think of any. She brushes aside the thought, deciding to deal with it only if and when it arises.

———

Mislan and Johan enter the task force room, finding Sherry, Deena, and the techie Saifuddin huddled over a monitor.

"Come and read this," Sherry calls out to him.

"It'll be much easier if you print it," Mislan suggests.

Saifuddin sends the article to the printer, and Deena hands it to Mislan.

It's a story from *The Malaysian Insider* dated March 21, 2012, headlined BN Lawmaker Moots Gay Rehab Center. BN stands for Barisan Nasional, the ruling coalition party. It reads:

The government needs to create a "homosexual rehabilitation center" to combat the phenomenon in Malaysia, according to a Barisan Nasional MP who today claimed 30 percent of Malaysian men were gay. According to a Bernama Online report, Datuk Baharum Mohamad (BN Sekijang) said in Parliament today that this was to aid those with homosexual tendencies or engaged in same-sex relationships to stop such behavior.

Farther down, the article continues: "The lesbian, gay, bisexual, and transgender community is increasingly viewed as morally deviant and targeted for its nonheterosexual orientation."

"So?" Mislan asks.

"Read the last paragraph," Sherry says.

Mislan reads the last paragraph and says, "The Seksualiti Merdeka was last year."

Seksualiti Merdeka, or Sexuality Rights festival, is an annual event held in Kuala Lumpur featuring talks, forums, workshops, and art, theater and so on, organized by a coalition of Malaysian NGOs, artists, and individuals. It was first organized in 2008 and attracted nationwide protests from Malay/Muslim communities. In 2011, the police banned the event, and the High Court upheld the ban.

"I mean the part about a bureau chief at *Utusan Malaysia* attacking the Bar Council for its 'support' of homosexuality among Malaysians, calling it part of a 'deviant wave' fast gaining acceptance throughout the world."

"I've no idea what you're getting at," Mislan says.

"I'm saying it may be worth spending some time on that angle."

"You're the lead, whatever you say, ma'am," Mislan mocks.

Deena steps to the whiteboard and writes "Lesbian" below the photos of both the victims.

Johan tells her to change it to "gay" and gets a raised-eyebrow look from her.

"Johan isn't wrong," Sherry tells Deena, "but rub it off. I don't want that to be displayed up there."

———

Superintendent Samsiah and Superintendent Lillian appear in the doorway, catching them by surprise.

"Nice," Samsiah says. "I have always wanted my officers to be organized like this."

"Thank you." Sherry beams and introduces Saifuddin as the IT Forensic tech.

"Nice to meet you," Samsiah says, walking to the whiteboard.

"Have you found the connection between them?"

"Only that they're both lesbian."

"Hmmm. A coincidence?"

"Could be."

"Check out the gay clubs, find out if they frequented any or hung out together. If they did, that could be the lead you're looking for."

Mislan hands his boss the printout.

"What is it?"

"News article, Sai found it. Read it and tell us what you think?"

Samsiah reads it, and passes it to Lillian.

"I'd say, stupidity fueled by self-righteous ignorance."

"I second that," Lillian agrees.

27

MISLAN WATCHES THE VIDEOS of the two rapes for the third time. Like his assistant, he cannot stomach watching them. The fear on the victims' faces is like nothing he has seen before. What kind of a human does that to another? He lights a cigarette and stops the video. He also now understands why Sherry was very protective of her victims and respects her for it.

"You want to view the CCTV recording from the college?" Johan asks from his desk.

Mislan is deep in thought and doesn't respond.

"Boss, you OK?"

"Eh?"

"I asked if you'd like to view the CCTV recording from KLCAC."

"Sorry, I thought you were talking on the phone. Yes, bring it over."

"Why are you smoking in the office? Ma'am's still in here, you know."

"I am?" he says, looking at his hand holding the cigarette, as if he is not aware of his actions.

Mislan slots the DVD into his computer and runs it. A matrix of eight boxes appears, with footage of students walking across the screens.

"What the hell is this?" Mislan asks. "The matrix isn't labeled. How're we to know which locations the recordings are from?"

Johan bends closer to the monitor.

"Time and date are the same. The top boxes look like they're from corridors." He points to one box on the bottom row. "That's like the library entrance, and that's the lobby: See the top-right corner there? Looks like pigeonhole shelves."

They watch the stream of students moving about like ants in the eight boxes for about five minutes, then Mislan says, "This is not going to work." He presses the stop button and ejects the DVD. "Jo, take it to Sai and ask if he can separate each box."

"Can it be done?"

"He's the expert, he should know. Tell him to put it all on one disk."

He gives his assistant the DVD.

"Jo, check if Sherry has made arrangements for her detectives to go to the Setapak Apartments."

"Will do. I thought I'd spend some time at the roadside stalls across from the apartment, if we're not doing anything tonight."

"What time?"

"About seven, seven-thirty. We can have dinner there."

"I need to go home and check on Daniel. He wasn't feeling too good yesterday. I'll see you there after that."

———

On his way home, he calls the nanny to ask about Daniel's health and asks her to text the grocery list if she has one. The nanny informs him Daniel is still coughing a little and that he has taken his medication. Just as he gets to the supermarket, he receives the texted grocery list. He has no idea what some of the items are. He pushes the cart slowly along the aisles and scans the shelves. Too many items look unfamiliar. Giving up, he asks an employee stacking a shelf, wearing a "May I Help You?" T-shirt, where he can find baking chocolate. The obviously foreign worker looks at him blankly. He swears and moves on. He spots some baking flour on a shelf and pushes the cart toward it. He sees a woman, another shopper, approaching.

"Excuse me, please," he says. "What's baking chocolate?"

The woman smiles and leads him to the end of the aisle, "What brand?"

"Any brand will do, I suppose."

"What're you baking?"

Mislan laughs, "I don't even know how to cook, much less bake. My son's nanny asked for it, and I don't know what she wants it for," he says, showing the woman the text message.

"If she's baking a cake, then this is what she wants," the woman says, holding up a packet. "You should call her and ask."

"It has to be a chocolate cake, because Daniel loves it. Thank you."

"Maybe next time, your nanny should text your wife. I'm sure she'd know," the woman teases him.

"I'm sure she would, but I doubt if she'd get it for the nanny."

"Why's that?"

"She is staying in Johor," he says with a chuckle.

"Oh . . . single parent?"

"Yup."

"I'm Freda," she says, extending her hand.

"Mislan, pleased to meet you," he replies, shaking her hand.

"Call me the next time you need help when shopping for groceries. Here, take my number."

"Thank you, I may just take you up on it."

Freda walks away and, as she turns the corner, he notices her sneaking a peek at him. Smiling, Mislan now knows why many say supermarkets are good hunting grounds.

———

When he enters his apartment, he is greeted by Daniel saying, "Daddy, you need to buy me a recorder for my music class."

"Didn't Mummy buy you one some time ago?"

"That was when I was in kindergarten. I can't use that anymore as it only breaks into two. Teacher says I need one that can be broken into three."

"Where's the recorder? I can break it into three pieces, or more, if you want," he kids with his son.

"Dad-dy!"

"Sister says you're still coughing. Are you still drinking cold sodas?"

"A little."

"I told you not to."

"Sister gave me."

"He's the one insisting on it," the nanny shouts from the kitchen.

"Kiddo, please, no cold drinks until you're better."

"OK. When are you buying me the recorder?"

"This weekend. We can go shopping together."

28

MISLAN TAKES A QUICK shower and joins Daniel in his room. They watch his favorite documentary show *Monster Fish* together. When it is over, he tells Daniel that he has to go to work. Daniel looks at him disappointedly.

"Are you going to come home late?" His tiny voice catches in his throat.

"Most likely, kiddo. Don't stay up too late, and please take your medicine before you go to bed. Come here and give me a big hug. Love you, kiddo."

Before leaving, he reminds the nanny to give Daniel his medicine. Walking to his car, his cell phone rings.

"Yes, Sherry."

"Johan tells me you are meeting him at Setapak apartments. Can I come along?"

"Sure, but we're going to have dinner at a roadside stall. Are you OK with that?"

"What's that supposed to mean?"

"Word around the office is you've got class. Roadside-stall food may not suit you," he says.

"Has anyone told you that you're an asshole? Can I join you, or not!"

"Countless times," he says laughingly. "Dress casual."

———

He phones Johan to ask his whereabouts and is told he just arrived. He decides to take the DUKE expressway, driving past the site of one of his murder investigations that nearly cost him his job and prison time. It brings back memories. Exiting at Setiawangsa, he takes a left to Setapak Jaya. There are three roadside stalls, and they decide on the one in the middle. Mislan orders a bowl of oxtail soup, an onion omelet, and plain rice, while Johan decides to have Pattaya fried rice with mixed tomyam soup. Johan spots Sherry and Deena walking toward them.

"What're they doing here?"

"Joining us."

"You knew they were coming?"

"Only Sherry, not Deena."

"Is something happening?"

"Nope, we're just having dinner and snooping around."

"What're you guys having?" Sherry asks as they sit down.

"Rice," Johan answers, and signals to the stall operator.

Sherry and Deena order noodles and mineral water.

"Why are we focusing our investigation here?" Deena asks, sipping her drink.

They all look at Mislan.

"Are we?" he asks and smiles.

"We're all here, having dinner by the roadside. Why aren't we having dinner near the first crime scene?"

"Because it's too expensive in Bangsar," Mislan jokes.

"Seriously, sir, this is my first murder investigation, or sort of. I want to learn as much as I possibly can."

"Sorry. Well, it's not rocket science. For one thing, this is my crime scene." He glances at Sherry and waits for her disapproval. When nothing comes, he says, "It has been, what, nine days since the first vic was raped? By now, I'm sure you've interviewed most of the people you felt could help you and revisited every piece of information."

Deena nods.

"But you haven't come up with anything. Your second vic is alive, and the case is still fresh. Also, the rapists got into an unplanned situation and panicked. In the panic, they reacted rashly, which I believe was not in accordance with their playbook. But what's more important to me, I mean, to our investigation, is that panic often results in mistakes." He pauses and searches their faces. "That's why we're focusing our investigation here."

"Playbook . . . interesting," Sherry says.

Mislan smiles.

"May I know what was in their playbook?"

"I don't know, but certainly murder was not part of it."

"You come to that conclusion based on . . . ?"

"One, the perps only uploaded the rape but not the murder. That tells me killing is not what they were after. You thought earlier they're doing it for fame. Well, murder would certainly make them famous."

"You said one, what are the others?"

"I only have two," Mislan says, grinning. "Two, the manner in which the vic was killed . . . one strike, and they didn't stick around to make sure the vic was dead."

———

The dinner crowd starts building up, comprised mostly of young men in their early twenties coming down from block 10 and the surrounding buildings. Johan hops from table to table, introducing himself and chatting with the youngsters. When he returns, he says, "On the day of the incident at about three or four in the morning, a bike came out from the apartment compound at high speed and crashed into a parked car over there, making a turn. The biker and pillion rider picked themselves up and scooted off."

"The City Hall workers didn't say anything about the accident when I interviewed them," Deena growls.

"They probably didn't even know of the accident," Johan says.

"Whose car was it?" Sherry asks.

"They don't know, but they've seen it parked along the street before. A gray Kenari."

"Got the number?"

"All they remember was it had a Wilayah registration plate, and that the last two digits were 4-2."

"OK, let's finish eating and hit the ground and do some real police work," Mislan says. "Jo, you and Deena do the other stall. See if you can get any more info on the accident."

"Where'll you be?"

"Right here enjoying the company of Sherry, my coffee, and cigarettes."

Mislan's cell phone rings. It's Saifuddin.

"Inspector, I separated the CCTV recording Sergeant Johan gave me, and I think there's something here that you may want to look at."

"What is it?"

"The video might have captured the laptop thief. I suggest you view it and decide."

"OK, give me twenty minutes."

He informs Sherry of Saifuddin's discovery and tells Johan to go back to the office with Deena when he's done.

———

Saifuddin turns the large monitor toward them and runs the video on a split screen. Mislan and Sherry watch in silence as the three-minute video loops over and over.

"How do I pause it?" Mislan asks.

"Press this."

"Can I pause just one screen?"

"You press Alt and then 1 or 2 at the same time. Then this key."

"You do it. The first one . . . wait . . . now! Can you go back a little?"

Saifuddin punches another key

"Stop. Now, do the second box. OK, stop . . . The guy in the white-and-blue T-shirt with the baseball cap. He goes into the library without a backpack and comes out two minutes later with one."

"What's that dangling thingy? Sai, can you blow it up?" Sherry says.

Saifuddin punches several keys, and the image of a cute teddy bear on a keychain fills the monitor.

"Print the image of the backpack, with the brand and teddy bear. I'll confirm with Massayu if it's hers."

"What about the guy's face? Can you get a clear image of it?" Mislan asks.

"No, you can't, I've tried every angle. The baseball cap blocks his face. That was what attracted me to him in the first place."

"Let's view the video again. Try and track his movements, see if you can get a clear image of anyone he speaks to. They could ID him."

"I knew you'd ask for that." Saifuddin punches a few more keys, and a new video stream appears, with the baseball cap guy talking to a couple of other students while walking.

"This one has a clear shot of their faces."

"Great work, Sai. Print it out. Sherry, can you ask Masayu if she knows them?"

She looks at her watch. "It's late now, and we don't want another call from the Datuk to the OCCI, I'll do it tomorrow. Sai, can you print another set for the whiteboard?"

Mislan's cell phone rings, it is Johan telling him they've located the Kenari and its owner.

"Is the car damaged?"

"Yes, on the right bumper."

"Stay with the owner, I'll get Forensic over."

He calls Chew and asks if he can get his team over to the Setapak Jaya City Hall Public Housing.

"Yes, it's a car. I'll see you there."

29

JUST AS MISLAN TURNS right toward the flat, he swears, "What the fuck?" There is a massive jam from the turn-off right up to the roadside stalls. Parking the car on the street, he and Sherry decide to walk the two hundred yards to the front of the apartment.

"What's going on?" Sherry asks as they walk past cars lining the street.

Mislan shrugs. "Hopefully not another case."

Nearing the apartment building, they see a huge crowd on both sides of the narrow street. Yellow crime-scene tape stretches along the sidewalk, closing half of the narrow street and part of the entrance to the complex. Two mobile patrol cars, with their spiraling blue and red lights sweeping the night sky, attract onlookers.

"What the hell?" Mislan swears. "Switch off those damn lights," he barks at the patrolmen.

Johan hears his boss and waves him over.

"Jo, what's all this?"

"The owner of the Kenari, Miss Azura, says her car was parked here when someone crashed into it on the night of the killing. Deena and I checked the area, and we found some debris that could be from the bike. Then Deena spotted this," Johan says, pointing to a spot. "We think it's blood from the rider or the pillion."

"Good job, both of you. What's with the MPVs and those lights? They're going to attract the entire neighborhood, not to mention the press."

"We needed to contain the area."

"Tell the MPV to do traffic control and look out for the Forensic team."

———

As Mislan and Sherry walk away from Johan and Deena, he hears someone calling. "Inspector Sherry, is there another rape?"

He swings around to see a group of reporters and cameramen pushing against the crime-scene tape.

"Shit," he curses under his breath. "Sherry, you handle them, I'm going for a smoke." He briskly walks toward the flat.

Entering the compound, he hears a voice asking, "Leaving so soon?"

Turning around, he says, "Holy cow, you're like that crazy stalker-woman in *Fatal Attraction*."

"What woman?" Audi says.

"What're you doing here? The show is over there."

"Is that sooo . . . then why're you walking away?" she chuckles, walking by his side. "What's the story?"

"I don't know. I'm just going for a smoke. You can join me, or you can go back there and find out for yourself."

"I think I'll have a smoke with you, if you don't mind."

Sitting on one of the motorbikes, Mislan lights a cigarette and hands his pack to Audi. She lights one and says, "I heard the DG of Immigration's daughter was pulled up for questioning."

He ignores her.

"Why was she hauled up? Is she involved?"

He grins but doesn't answer.

"Oh, come on. I did some digging, too, you know. Let's trade."

Mislan squashes his cigarette. "You first."

"Trade, OK?" she stresses and waits for a response. "I know the two victims were lesbians. The murdered victim was a *pengkid* living with the second victim."

"Tell me something I don't know."

"How about this? The first victim's partner is on the organizing committee of Seksualiti Merdeka."

"That's not surprising. What has that got to do with the case?"

"I didn't say it had anything to do with the case, it's just something I found out. Now it's your turn, Trade, remember?"

"You know I can't tell you anything about an ongoing investigation. However, I can tell you the DGs daughter was not hauled up, she was brought in by her mother, and she has nothing to do with the case."

His cell phone rings. It's Johan informing him the Forensic team had arrived.

"Got to go and earn my keep," Mislan says. Walking away, he adds, "Keep the lesbian thing out. The families have already been through hell."

———

Mislan steps over the yellow tape as Sherry and Johan brief the Forensic team supervisor.

"Where is Chew?" he asks.

"He's at another scene and will come over if we're still not done here," the team supervisor says, signaling for his men to get moving.

Mislan and Sherry step back toward the yellow tape and watch the forensic technicians go about their work. Johan and Deena lead a couple of them to the Kenari parked about thirty yards away. Murmurs of excitement run through the crowd, as they're being treated to a real-life crime scene investigation. The media cameramen jostle with each other for a clear shot.

Two technicians systematically sweep the area with high-powered flashlights, marking every piece of debris that may be part of the killers' motorbike or the Kenari. They repeat the sweep to ensure they haven't missed anything. The team supervisor gives the nod, and the technicians turn on the floodlights. One of them is now armed with a state-of-the-art digital camera while the other holds a clipboard and evidence bag. They meticulously photograph, catalog, and bag everything they consider evidence. The team leader inspects their work and gives them more instructions. Two technicians disappear to their van and, after a while, return with orange goggles and flashlights. One of them has a large plastic container with a nozzle spray on his back. He distributes the goggles and flashlights among his other team members. They switch off the floodlights. The supervisor points to some areas and the technician with the plastic container pumps the handle and sprays a liquid into the spots, while other technicians examine the spots closely, take swabs, and test them with liquid from a small bottle, putting a few drops onto the cotton swabs. "We've got blood," one announces.

"Yes!" Sherry grins excitedly.

"OK, let's do the whole area," the supervisor says.

30

AT THE CONTINGENT HEADQUARTERS, Sherry walks into the Department of Special Investigations, where, by now, she's a familiar sight at the morning prayer.

"Heard you got a big break last night," Inspector Reeziana greets her.

"We got a break, but I don't know if it's big until Forensic comes back with the results. How's the coffee here?"

"As good as you can get anywhere. Here, have this, I just made it. I'll make another one for myself. You know, I always wanted to be in D11, but I don't think I could stomach it. How do you handle it? I mean the victims' trauma and suffering?"

Sherry smiles. "We all handle it differently. I suppose it's the same with you guys when you're dealing with the victims' families: all the questions, grief, despair, anger."

"Let's move on to something more cheerful. What're you doing tonight? I met this gorgeous guy at the courts yesterday. We talked and he invited me out. He told me to bring a friend if didn't feel comfortable going out with him alone on the first date. He said he'd bring his buddy. How about it?"

"A lawyer? Oh no, I don't date lawyers."

"Me neither. This guy is a musician."

"Musician . . . what the hell was he doing in court?"

"Arranging bail for a friend charged for using."

Sherry gives her a stare.

"He's not a user. . . . Well, that's what he told me. Anyway who cares? . . . He's cute," Reeziana says and laughs.

———

The front desk clerk announces the start of morning prayer in five minutes and adds, "Special appearance today by the OCCI."

The room moans.

The OCCI sits at the head of the table looking like he's about to explode, staring at the officers slowly filing into the room.

"How're we going to win the war on crime if we can't even start our meetings on time?" he barks.

Superintendent Samsiah, in a deliberate motion, turns around to look at the digital clock behind her. It's 8:27 in the morning.

"The meeting starts at 8:30."

SAC Burhanuddin follows her line of sight and declares, "This clock is slow; let's start."

The investigating officers give updates on cases of interest over the last twenty-four hours: two armed robberies, one kidnapping that turned out to be a case of a teenage girl going off with her boyfriend, and two sudden deaths.

"Ghani, what's the status on the VIP housebreaking and robbery gang?" Samsiah asks.

"It has sort of died off. We expanded our net, but there's still no report of the stolen goods surfacing anywhere."

"It could be shipped out to our neighbors, Thailand. I'll talk to Interpol and see if they can assist." She looks around the table. "Where's Mislan?"

The officers look at each other.

"Sherry, do you know where he is?"

Sherry shakes her head.

"Those with court cases, and on remand duty, can leave."

When the room settles down again, only Sherry and Ghani are left, much to the disappointment of the OCCI. He likes a bigger audience.

"Are you sure they all have court cases?" he asks Superintendent Samsiah.

She nods, knowing some of them do not but jumped at the opportunity offered. "Would you like to update us, Sherry?" Samsiah says.

"We managed to get a CCTV recording from KLCAC, and Saifuddin . . ." She stops when detective Deena appears at the doorway and stands to attention.

"Sorry, sir, may I speak to Inspector Sherry for a moment?" Deena stammers.

SAC Burhanuddin glares at her.

Samsiah nods, and Deena approaches her boss cautiously and whispers in her ear.

Sherry shuts her eyes and shivers.

"What is it, Sherry?"

"Saifuddin says another video has been uploaded."

The Officer in Charge of Criminal Investigations, the head of Special Investigations, the head of Sexual & Child Abuse Investigations, and Sherry stare in horror at the monitor, at the hissing rapist, the mouth behind the pantyhose, the gleaming steel knife pressed against the victim's cheek, the terror in her eyes, her desperate pleading, crying, and the final submission.

"Mute it, mute it," Samsiah barks at Saifuddin. "Have we received a report?"

"No," Lillian says.

"Where did it take place?" she asks Saifuddin.

"I don't know. There's no way to tell from the video."

"Check all the districts, find out where it happened."

Detective Deena enters the task force room and tells them none of the districts received a rape report.

"Could it be a hoax?" Lillian asks.

"If it is, they deserve an Oscar for their performance. Lillian, can you get on IPRS? It could be from another state. Who uploaded it?"

IPRS stands for Integrated Police Report System and enables tracking of police reports made within the country. Access is assigned to specific personnel based on need.

"Same username: Emancipatist," Saifuddin announces.

"Contact MCMC immediately," Samsiah instructs.

"Done."

"I promise you, heads are going to roll," SAC Burhanuddin growls. The officers stare at him.

Detective Deena comes back to inform them that the case was reported in Shah Alam, Selangor, at 3:40 in the morning. Selangor is the neighboring state to Wilayah Persekutan, where Kuala Lumpur is.

"Sherry, contact the IO and get more details on the case. Sir, can we get Selangor to work with us?"

"Why do you want that? We already have enough on our hands. Let them handle their own shit."

"There might be evidence there that may help us solve our cases," Samsiah says. "Lillian, can you call and ask them?"

The OCCI stands and walks to the door, "Update me at noon before my press conference this evening, and give me something worth telling the media."

"When was this video uploaded?" Samsiah asks.

"5:17 this morning."

"We've got one press day before it hits the nation. Let's make full use of it," Samsiah announces. She turns to Sherry. "Get Mislan and Johan in, now."

31

AT THE OFFICE, THE front desk clerk stops Mislan and points toward the office of Superintendent Samsiah.

"Where have you and Johan been?" Samsiah demands.

"Workshop. My car broke down, and Jo came to help me."

"And you couldn't inform the office?"

"I did. I WhatsApped you."

She snatches her cell phone to check and realizes her phone is on silent mode. The messages icon is blinking. She lets out a tiny laugh. "I'm sorry, with all these cases, and him appearing unannounced . . . I lost it for a moment. So how will you be getting around?"

"Jo borrowed a motorbike for me. Did something happen?"

"Another video has just popped up on UTube. This one was in Shah Alam."

"When?"

"Sai discovered it this morning, around 8:30 when he came to the office. The incident was reported around 3:40 and the video uploaded around 5."

Mislan arches his eyebrows. "Are we sure it's the same rapist?"

"Why?"

"The time between the rape and upload is very close, unlike in the first two cases."

"Maybe they're getting good, or more confident."

"Could be."

"Lan, I need you to focus on this case. Sherry tells me you guys may have the break you've been looking for. Run with it, and wrap this up before another wave of public panic."

"Can I take the lead?"

"No, Sherry remains the official lead, but from what I've been hearing, you've been running the show," she says, giving him the I-am-not happy-about-it stare.

"Where did you hear that?" Milan fakes innocence and stands to leave.

"I've ears and eyes everywhere, remember?" She waves him away. "Lan, don't aggravate the situation."

Sherry, Johan, and Deena are in the task force room when Mislan enters.

"Where have you been?"

"My car broke down. Ma'am says there's a new upload."

Saifuddin starts the video and moves aside to allow Mislan and Johan to slide closer to the monitor. The inspector takes out a packet of chewing gum, unwraps one, and offers the pack to the rest.

"What's with the chewing gum?" Saifuddin exclaims.

"I'm trying to cut down on cigarettes. It's burning a hole in my pocket."

"You should be more concerned about your health," Sherry says.

"What's the point of a long life if you run out of money?" he replies with a chuckle. He clicks "pause." "Sai, can you bring up the other videos on another monitor?"

Saifuddin wheels his chair closer and runs the first rape on the middle monitor and the second one on the laptop.

"What're you looking for?"

"Pause the video at the knife."

Sherry and Deena come up behind them.

"It looks like a different knife to me," Mislan says. "The knives in the first and second videos looked similar but not this one."

"Sai, zoom in on it," Sherry says. "Definitely different. They could've ditched the first knife after the murder and bought a new one."

"Maybe. Sai, can you get the best shot of the pantyhose guy, upright?"

"On all three?"

Mislan nods.

"I need to smoke," he gripes. "Can we open the windows and lock the door? Sai, when you're free, can you print a Do Not Disturb sign for the door?"

"Great idea, I'll do it immediately after this."

Sherry shakes her head at the two smokers.

"Deena, get the stand fan from the back room. The room is stuffy with cigarette smoke."

Deena grabs Johan by his arm and pulls him along with her, saying, "He's your boss." They return with a stand fan, plug it in, and open the windows. Sherry locks the door.

"Thanks," Mislan says, lighting a cigarette, with Saifuddin following suit. "Now, this feels like a real squad room, just the right ambiance for police work."

"This is the best footage I can get," Saifuddin declares.

"Tell me what you see?" Mislan asks the others, walking toward the open windows. The heat from outside hits him, and he decides to walk back to the middle of the room and stand under the air-conditioning vent.

"This rapist looks shorter and smaller than the guy in the first and second cases," Sherry says. "I don't think it's the same person. Look at his arm; he's darker-skinned, too. I think this is a copycat rape."

"Maybe it's due to the lighting and camera angle," Johan suggests.

"But the username is the same, Emancipatist," Saifuddin counters. "If it's a copycat rape, how did he upload it with the same username?"

"Same cameraman, different rapist," Johan offers an explanation. "Maybe they switched roles."

Mislan lights another cigarette and listens to the team. All of a sudden the room falls silent and all heads turn toward him.

"What?"

"I'm sure the nicotine has stimulated your brain sufficiently by now for you to pitch in," Sherry goads him.

"You don't need my input, you guys are doing fine," he says. "Let's leave this for a moment until we can get more on it. Sherry, why don't you meet Massayu and ask her about that backpack? Call me when you're done. We can meet to compare notes and plan our next move."

"Where'll you be?"

"Jo and I will pay the college another visit."

32

At the KLCAC Student Affairs office, Mislan and Johan introduce themselves and ask to see Mr. Lai, the manager. The clerk tells them, "He's in a meeting."

"Please tell him it's urgent that we speak to him," Mislan says politely.

The clerk hesitates. "Maybe Mr. Sega can assist you?"

"OK, we'll see Mr. Sega then," Johan answers, noticing that his boss is starting to get annoyed.

The clerk points them to a door and lets them pass through the counter barrier. Johan knocks, and Mislan enters without waiting to be invited. Gunasegaran is startled by their sudden entrance, frantically grappling with the mouse to minimize whatever he's watching on the computer monitor. A big mistake, as the audio of the video is still running. Mislan hears the soft moans of a woman coming from the computer.

"Want to share what you're watching?" Mislan says with a smile.

"No, I mean, yes . . . no . . . I was looking through some reports," Sega stutters, going red in the face. "Inspector, Sergeant, I didn't expect to see you again so soon. Please sit down. How may I assist you this time?"

His eyes flick from them to the monitor, and his hand gets busy with the mouse and the moaning stops.

Johan places the printout from the CCTV recording on the table. "Do you recognize these boys?"

Gunasegaran's shaky hand picks up the photo for a closer look. "No, I'm sorry."

"Is there any way to identify them? Your student records, perhaps."

"I don't think I can, not without the administrator's permission. I suggest you write officially with your request."

"Mr. Sega, all we need is the identities of the students. We'd like to talk to them. I'm sure you can assist us without making us go through the red tape." Johan says.

"I'm sorry, I can't help you, Sergeant. You have to—"

"I thought I heard a woman moaning when we entered," Mislan says to his assistant, cutting Gunasegaran off. Turning to the assistant manager, he says, "Were you watching porn on your computer?"

"I thought I heard it, too," Johan says.

"I bet our IT guy will be able to get into the history log and tell us just how many times he's been jerking off watching porn with the college's computer. Maybe he's also got some downloaded. Isn't that an offense under the Multimedia Act, Jo?"

Mislan sees Gunasegaran squirming.

"But we don't want to do that, do we Jo? We don't care what the Student Affairs assistant manager does in the privacy of his office, right Jo? We just want the particulars of the students in this photo."

Gunasegaran picks up the photo, saying, "Let me see what I can do," and leaves the office.

Mislan grins at Johan.

While they wait for him to return, the inspector's cell phone rings. "Mislan."

"Afternoon, Inspector. Chew, Forensic."

"Yo, Chew. I hope you have some good news for me."

"How about half-good?" he says jokingly.

"I'll settle for any percentage."

"The blood trace on the street at the Setapak Jaya flat is not of the same blood type as the murder victim. I sent it for DNA analysis and told them to rush it."

"That's something to look forward to."

"The debris was from a motorbike indicator light. We managed to piece it together and obtained a partial manufacturer's serial number. It's from Yamaha. That's all we can establish."

"That's not much to go on. When can we get the DNA results?"

"Tomorrow morning, earliest."

"Let me know when you get them, please."

"You'll be the first. Hey, Sai told me you have a third case. That makes it serial, doesn't it?"

"Legal definition, yes."

"Well, I'm sure you'll get them soon."

"I hope so."

Gunasegaran returns with two printouts and gives them to Mislan. Reviewing them, he asks, "Are they here in the college now?"

"Yes, but I'd like your cooperation and agreement not to pick them up here," he pleads. "Their lecture will be over in about thirty minutes. Perhaps you can detain them outside the college."

"Since you've been so cooperative, I think we can do that."

"Jo, why don't you wait outside the class and whisper to them to come for a drink with you." And to Gunasegaran, he says, "Thank you."

Gunasegaran scratches an imaginary itch on his head and mumbles, "About the moaning . . ."

"What moaning?" Mislan grins and turns to leave.

"Thank you, thank you," the assistant manager says.

―――――

Mislan heads for the mamak restaurant, orders an iced black coffee, lights a cigarette, and waits for his assistant to bring the students. His cell phone rings. It's Inspector Sherry.

"Yes, Sherry."

"Spoke to Massayu. She identified the backpack as hers but doesn't know who the boys are."

"Great. Ask her if she has a picture of her with the backpack showing the teddy bear. If she does, get one."

"OK. Where are you?"

"Having a smoke and drink outside KLCAC."

"You want me to come around?"

"I'll meet you in the office. Hey, have you contacted Selangor's D11?"

"Yes, they're sending a copy of their report over. ASP Luan is the IO. By the way, ma'am wants a sit-down at 2:30."

"Thanks for the heads up."

———

Mislan makes a call to his assistant and is told the class just ended. He watches as students pour out of the building, and some of them walk into the restaurant: teenagers and young adults, male and female in torn jeans, printed crewneck T-shirts, baseball caps worn backward, branded sneakers—kids from well-to-do families. Kids who couldn't get a place in public universities for whatever reason but with money are enjoying a Western university's lifestyle in a private college. None of the bullshit government-imposed activities and dress codes. He spots Johan with a young man walking toward the restaurant.

Johan tells the young man to take a seat and introduces him as Khairol.

"Where is the other one?" Mislan asks.

"He didn't show up today."

Mislan spreads the photos on the table. "Do you know who this is?" He taps the baseball-capped head in the picture.

Khairol picks up the photos for a closer look. "That's Wahab, a former student. Why?"

"Former? What was he doing walking with you in the college?"

"He said he was going to the bursary."

"Was he in your class?"

"Yes, in the first semester. Then he dropped out."

"Why did he leave the college?"

"I don't know."

"Was he expelled?"

"I don't know."

"What's his full name?"

"We only knew him as Wahab."

"Do you know where he's from, or where he lived?"

"No."

"Does he have a motorbike?"

"I don't know."

"Do you have his contact number?"

"No."

"What about this guy? Who is he?"

"Richard, he's from Sabah."

"Are you two close friends?"

"So-so."

"Was he close to Wahab?"

"I don't think so."

"OK, thanks, you've been very helpful." Mislan indicates the interview is over and signals the waiter for his bill. "Jo, get the particulars of this Wahab from the college. When you're done, come back to the office. Ma'am wants a meeting at 2:30."

33

THE HEAD OF SPECIAL Investigations and the head of Sexual & Child Abuse Investigations arrive together. Sherry greets them and starts her briefing immediately. With the help of the now almost fully covered whiteboard, she updates them on the discoveries at the Setapak Jaya City Hall Public Housing and the CCTV recordings from KLCAC.

"Anything from Forensic?"

"The blood from the street isn't that of the murder victim. DNA results will come in tomorrow morning. Forensic managed to put together the debris collected from the secondary scene and have obtained a partial manufacturer's serial number of the motorcycle indicator light cover, a Yamaha, but without a complete serial number, there's no way of identifying the model."

"What about the college? Any luck there?" Samsiah asks.

"Mislan and Johan spoke to one of the students, and he identified the baseball-capped guy as Abdul Wahab Majid, a former student who was booted out for failing to pay his second semester fees. His last known address is in Hulu Kelang, and the task force detectives are paying him a visit as we speak."

"Did the DG's daughter identify the backpack as the one she lost?"

"Yes, and the teddy-bear keychain as well."

"What about the third rape?" Lillian asks.

"The MO is similar. ASP Luan is the IO, and she'll keep us informed of any development."

"I heard you're thinking of a copycat rape. What is your theory based on?" Samsiah asks Sherry.

Just then, the door swings open, and the bulky figure of a fuming Senior Assistant Commissioner Burhanuddin Sidek fills the doorway, startling them all. "Why wasn't I informed of this meeting?" he roars.

"We're getting an update to brief you later," Samsiah answers for the rest. "But since you're here, do join us."

Sherry is asked to start again from the beginning. Mislan excuses himself for a call of nature, getting a suspicious glare from Samsiah and Sherry. He winks at Sherry, steps out of the task force room, heads for the emergency staircase, and lights a cigarette. He calls Johan, tells him to come into the task force room in five minutes and ask for permission to speak to him.

"Why?"

"I need to get out of there."

"Why can't you just tell ma'am?"

"Because the OCCI just came in."

"Oh, OK."

Mislan squashes his cigarette and goes back into the task force room, with Samsiah's eyes following him. After a few minutes, there is a light knock on the door and Johan appears with a serious expression.

"Sir, may I speak to Inspector Mislan?" he addresses the OCCI and, without waiting for an answer, walks toward Mislan and pretends to whisper in his ear. Mislan nods several times, and Johan makes a quick exit. Mislan leans toward his boss. "I need to organize a stakeout for Wahab, the former student."

"Can't Jo do it?"

"I don't want to chance it."

"Go, make the arrangement, and come back."

"I may be late."

"I want you back here. Go give your instructions to Jo, and come back here," she whispers firmly.

Mislan takes his leave, annoyed with his failed ploy to escape some verbal diarrhea. He goes to meet Johan, who is waiting for him outside. He shakes his head.

"Didn't work."

Johan laughs, "You've used that trick too often. What now?"

"She wants you to organize the stakeout for Wahab."

"Where did that come from?"

"I told her there was some problem and that I needed to organize a stakeout." Mislan chuckles. "Instead, she wants you to handle it."

Johan shakes his head.

"Anything from the detective?"

"They're still looking for him. He's not staying at the given address anymore. Syed says they've got a lead and are following up on it."

Mislan goes to the emergency staircase and lights a cigarette.

"I thought you're trying to cut down."

"Gave that up. Jo, I need you to do a background on the Shah Alam vic. Focus on her sexual orientation."

"You think she is, you know?"

"Two vics with the same sexual orientation may be a coincidence. Three . . . I'd say we're on to something."

"What about the stakeout?"

"What stakeout?"

Mislan's cell phone rings. It's Daniel, and he's excited. "Daddy, I got number one."

"Number one what, kiddo?"

"I topped my class. Teacher put the results up, and I'm the first in my class."

"Congratulations, kiddo, Daddy is proud of you. Have you told Mummy?"

"Why?"

"I'm sure she'd like to know, too."

"OK."

"Hey, I'm proud of you, my number one kiddo."

34

MISLAN REENTERS THE TASK force room just as Sherry is finishing her briefing. The room is silent as they wait for Burhanuddin's comments.

"This case is going to hit the news tonight and the press tomorrow. I still have nothing to give them. Do you know how bad that makes me look?"

"We do have a suspect." Samsiah says. "However, I do not recommend this information be revealed to the press just yet."

"When can you bring him into custody?"

"My men are tracking him down. Mislan has just arranged for a stakeout at his last known address," she replies.

Oh boy, Mislan says to himself.

"So you still have nothing."

"If you say so," Samsiah answers defiantly.

"What's that supposed to mean?" Burhanuddin snaps at her.

"We have a suspect. But if you feel that's nothing—"

"I know what it means. You don't have to be disrespectful. Lately, your attitude borders on insubordination. I told you to order him," he points to Mislan, "to apologize to Datuk Yunus. But, what did you do? You went behind my back and called Datuk."

Samsiah checks herself, not wanting to prolong the meeting.

"I want something that I can show the press. You've until tomorrow morning before I hand this case over to someone more competent." The OCCI issues the ultimatum and leaves the room.

As the door closes behind him, Samsiah says, "OK, let's get some work done. Sherry, you think the Shah Alam case is a copycat?"

"Yes, but Sai says the username of the person uploading the video is the same as in the previous cases."

"And that makes you think this is not a copycat?" Samsiah asks, turning to Saifuddin, who is still in a daze from watching the OCCI's performance.

"Ah? Sorry . . . yes. No two usernames can be the same on the same social network. The system will reject it and suggest additional numeric characters that could be added to differentiate it."

Samsiah nods. "Lan, you've been very quiet. What do you think?"

"I think both Sherry and Sai are right."

"I was afraid you might say that. So, you think there's more than one team?" Samsiah sighs.

Mislan nods. "That would be the most logical explanation."

"I don't follow you," Lillian says.

"If Sherry and Sai are both right, which they probably are, we are up against a gang that's going around raping women. So far, we can safely say there are two rapists, but God knows how many more there are in the gang," Mislan explains.

"Oh, my God," Lillian gasps.

"Several things are bugging me. One is the time lapse between cases. Seven days between the first and the second case, and between the second and the third case was three days."

"Explain," Samsiah says.

"I may be wrong, and we all should be praying that I am. Based on the short time lapse, I believe the rapes were planned and scheduled. What was left is for them to execute it in accordance to the schedule."

The room falls silent as they all realize the magnitude of Mislan's hypothesis. All eyes are glued on him.

"You said several, what are the others?" Sherry asks.

"In the first rape the perp was seen kissing or sucking on the vic's nipples. He was extremely lucky the vic showered and washed away the evidence before you arrived. In the second case, the perp didn't repeat the same mistake, and I bet you the same for the third case."

Sherry walks behind the IT tech and watches as he is already running the video while Mislan was explaining.

"Mislan's right," Sherry says, looking up from the monitors.

"Your point?" Samsiah asks.

"To me, it's like they or someone is reviewing the video and pointing out the perp's mistakes. Mistakes that could give them away through trace evidence."

"You mean to say they're trained, supervised, or coached?" Lillian utters.

"I'm not saying they were, but they've gotten better at what they do," Mislan answers. "Another thing is their script or dialogue. I've not listened to the third case, but the first two, the dialogue was almost the same. Like it was scripted and rehearsed."

"Sai, can you transcribe the dialogue?" Sherry asks.

"I don't want anything discussed here to leave this room." Samsiah says firmly. "If the press gets wind of this, there'll be nationwide panic."

Everyone solemnly nods.

"I'd say our best bet for closure is the video man . . . the Emancipatist," Mislan says. "He's the link to the three rapes."

"I agree with Mislan," Sherry says. "We get him, we get them all."

"Sai, can you monitor the username 24/7?" Samsiah says.

"Done. I've written a small program for the system to beep me when he's logged on. I can program it to notify any of you guys, too, if you wish."

Samsiah looks at the two investigators.

Both nod.

"What's the status on the former student?"

Mislan shakes his head.

"Put him on top of your list. Get him, and I'll let you smoke in your office for a week," Samsiah says.

"Just one week?" he teases her.

"Get him before midnight, and you get a month," Samsiah ups the bait and laughs. "And I'll throw in a packet of cigarettes as a bonus."

The meeting is adjourned, and, while walking out, Sherry asks him what his plans are.

"I'm going to get my one-month smoking privileges."

"I'll come with you."

"Don't you have anything else to do?"

"For now, only this case."

Mislan calls Detective Syed to ask for updates. Syed tells him they have information that Wahab works in a cybercafe called Hot Fingers in Bandar Baru Bangi. They are on the way there to check it out.

Mislan makes another call. "Hi, can you talk?"

"Yes, what's up?" Dr. Safia answers.

"Do you know cybercafes in the UKM area?"

"No, why?"

"You lived . . . I mean, your mom lived there, didn't she?"

"Yes, but my mom didn't go to cybercafes," Dr. Safia says with a chuckle. "You should ask students at the uni."

"Thank you, you've been a great help," he says sarcastically.

Dr. Safia laughs. "Want to meet later for dinner?"

"Love to, but can't decide now. Let you know later," he says and hangs up.

"Dr. Safia, the forensic pathologist?" Sherry asks.

Mislan nods.

"Heard you two are an item."

Mislan gives her his best none-of-your-business glare.

"Sai, can you google Hot Fingers cybercafe's location?" Mislan asks.

Saifuddin works his keyboard and reads out the address.

35

THEY TAKE THE NORTH-SOUTH Expressway and head for Bangi. Bandar Baru Bangi is a suburb bordering Selangor and Wilayah Persekutuan. The township was built around two public universities.

Detective Syed and Jeff are waiting for them as they pull up at the Hot Fingers cybercafe.

"Sir, ma'am," Syed greets them.

"Is he inside?" Sherry asks.

"I didn't get a good look. It's quite dark in there."

"Syed, cut off the back exit. Jeff, come with us and watch the front door," Mislan gives instructions. "Hold your positions for ten minutes after we take him out. Stop anyone making a run for the back exit. Any questions?"

The detectives shake their heads.

"Syed, you go in first."

Syed casually enters the café and walks to the rear as if he's going to the toilet. Mislan gives him thirty seconds before beckoning Sherry and Jeff to go in before him. Entering the dimly lit café, it takes a few seconds for their eyes to adjust to the low lighting. After Jeff sits at a computer nearest the front door, Mislan and Sherry walk toward the cashier. As they approach, Mislan notices the person behind the counter is a Chinese woman. He turns to Sherry.

"Why don't you ask her about Wahab? Tell her you're his sister or aunt."

"Aunt!" she hisses at him.

Mislan steps aside toward a computer and takes a seat as Sherry talks to the cashier. The front door opens. It's Wahab, carrying a packed meal. Jeff, who's next to the door, jumps out of his chair on reflex. Wahab, suspecting something amiss, throws his packed rice at Jeff, covering him with fish curry, rice, and vegetables and bolts out the door.

"Shit," Mislan swears, dashing to the door. "Stay here," he yells at Jeff as he flings the door open and gives chase, with Sherry close behind. He sees Wahab about fifteen yards ahead and shouts, *"Police! Stop!"*

The suspect looks back at him, quickening his pace.

"Damn you!" Mislan shouts, trying to catch up. *"Stop or I'll shoot!"*

Sherry runs past him. Mislan chides himself for being so out of shape and vows to stop smoking. Again. The suspect turns and makes a dash across the main street. An oncoming car grazes him, and he's thrown onto the curb. He falls on his back holding his leg, groaning in pain. Sherry expertly flips him onto his stomach and cuffs him just as Mislan reaches them, panting heavily, and kneels by the groaning suspect to catch his breath.

"My leg, I think it's broken," Wahab growls.

"Good. That's what happens when you run from the good guys," Mislan says, in between his panting.

Sherry examines the suspect's legs. "Try and move it."

When Syed and Jeff arrive, Mislan tells them to disperse the crowd. "Take down the particulars of the driver of the car for a statement later if required."

Wahab moves his leg and groans, "It hurts."

"You'll live." Mislan says. "Sherry, you want to bring the car around?"

"Shouldn't we call an ambulance?" she asks.

"No thanks, I'm fine. Just give me a minute," Mislan answers.

"For him, you fool," she says.

"What for? Wasting taxpayers' money on a piece of garbage? He'll live, it's only a bruise."

———

169

Mislan steps into his boss's office, beaming, "I'm collecting."

"You got him?" Samsiah asks.

"Room 1. By the way, I smoke Sampoerna Menthol, thank you."

"Good job. One month starts today. Let's see what he has to say."

Entering the interview room, Samsiah notices the bruise on the suspect's arm and his torn pants. She signals Mislan and Sherry to follow her out.

"What happened?" she asks, referring to the suspect.

"It's got nothing to do with me," Mislan instantly replies.

"He tried to escape and ran into a passing car," Sherry says.

"Why is he here and not at the hospital?"

Sherry looks at Mislan.

"It's superficial, nothing serious," he answers lamely.

"You want a police brutality case on your head as well? Send him to the hospital now!" Samsiah orders them. Turning away, she says, "Both of you, in my office in ten."

Sherry frowns at Mislan. "This is on you."

"Does that mean you're handing over the lead to me?" he kids.

"Arrrgh."

Mislan instructs Syed and Jeff to take the suspect to the hospital for treatment, and to bring him back immediately.

"Find a friendly doctor and whisper to him, 'no admission for observation.' Got it?"

The detectives nod.

Sherry shakes her head.

———

In the office, Samsiah makes herself a cup of tea, saying, "It's been a long day, so let's make this short." She walks back to her seat. "Lan, if the doctor so much as calls me, I promise you, I'll make you regret your actions today." She takes a deliberate sip, her eyes fixed on Mislan. Sherry shifts uneasily in her seat. Samsiah turns toward her slowly.

"Big mistake," Mislan whispers to Sherry.

"And you, Sherry, I expected better from you. There's a reason I assigned you as lead." She pauses, and takes another deliberate sip of tea.

It's the longest sip Sherry has ever witnessed. Mislan takes out a packet of cigarettes.

"What do you think you're doing?" Samsiah asks, with the teacup still at her lips.

"Cashing in on my reward," he answers, beaming.

"I said your office. This is my office," she snaps at him, startling Sherry.

Mislan grins sheepishly and puts the cigarettes back in his pocket.

Turning her attention back to Sherry, she says, "You let Mislan walk all over you. This case is going to be won or lost in the media. How do you think this will come out if the press gets wind of how the suspect was treated?"

Sherry starts to reply but stops when she feels a sharp kick on her shin.

Samsiah notices Sherry wince and thinks it's remorse in response to what she has said.

"Good, now you understand. For the victims' sake, I hope you take your role as lead more seriously and use extreme prudence."

Sherry nods.

"Lan, I expect you to lend her support and not make her fight you every step of the way."

Johan appears at the door, "Evening, ma'am. I need to speak to Inspector Mislan," he says excitedly.

Samsiah returns his greeting, "You looked like you're bursting to tell him something. Can we share the good news, too?"

"Inspector Mislan asked me to do some background checks on the Shah Alam victim. I talked to the neighbors, and they say she's one of them."

"Sexual orientation?" Samsiah says.

"Yes, that."

"By 'that,' you mean she's gay?"

The officers laugh at Johan's difficulty in saying it.

"Yes, the neighbors said she was discreet about her . . . you know . . . but they all knew."

"If she was discreet, how did the rapists know?" Sherry wonders aloud.

"You know how it is . . . Malay neighborhood . . . busybodies. Even at the mosque, the imam and the rest were talking about it. I stopped by her workplace at Subang Parade and talked to her coworkers. They confirmed it, too."

"This changes everything," Mislan says. "Three rape vics, all gay. That's too much of a coincidence."

"If Johan can find out about the victim's sexual orientation so easily, I'm sure the press will, too. If this comes out into the open, we'll lose any advantage we have," Samsiah muses.

"Can we get a gag order?" Sherry asks.

"We can, but the public has the right to know, especially the targeted group. If the information isn't made known and there's another incident, it'll be on our heads." She sips her tea. "I need to take this upstairs."

"The OCCI?" Mislan says derisively.

"Yes, that's if you don't mind," Samsiah replies sarcastically.

"I'm sorry, I didn't mean any disrespect, but consulting him is a sure way of making it public."

"Then we'll just have to solve these cases with that handicap, won't we?"

36

THE SUSPECT IS LED into the interview room by Syed and Jeff, bandaged and holding a plastic bag of medicine prescribed by the hospital. Syed gives him a glass of warm water and tells him to take his medication.

"It says here, 'after meal,'" Wahab says, holding up the medicine wrapper to Syed.

"So?"

"I've not eaten yet. I threw my lunch at him," Wahab says, indicating Detective Jeff and grinning.

"Funny. My new shirt's coming out of your next pay from the café," Jeff growls at him.

"Can I have something to eat? I'm starving."

"You got money?"

"In my wallet."

Syed looks in the suspect's wallet and finds a five-ringgit note.

"What do you want?"

"Rice, of course, with chicken, salted egg, and some vegetables."

"With five ringgit! Where do you think you are . . . Kedah?" Syed laughs.

"If you guys had done your job properly, that's what I'd be having for lunch," Wahab sneers at him. "Check his shirt if you don't believe me."

"You're a smartass, aren't you?" Jeff hisses, taking a step toward him.

Syed steps in between them, pulls out his wallet, and gives Jeff a ten-ringgit note. "Here, go get him his lunch."

Jeff snatches the money, glares at the suspect again, and heads for the door.

"Fried chicken. Drumstick please, and don't forget the salted egg," Wahab calls after him.

"Cut it out, and wipe that grin off your face," Syed snarls at him.

———

Mislan and Sherry enter the interview room just as the suspect is finishing his late lunch. Sherry takes the lead and reads the suspect his rights. Mislan switches on his digital recorder and places it on the table in front of the suspect, and waits patiently as Sherry goes through the formalities. He knows she's being extra cautious, doing everything by the book.

"Do you understand the caution I just read you?" she asks.

"Yes."

"Sign here and here," she says, pushing the caution form toward him.

"What am I being arrested for?" Wahab asks.

"For making me run," Mislan says. "Why did you run?"

"He startled me," the suspect replies, motioning at Jeff standing against the wall. "I thought the place was being robbed, so I took off."

Mislan and Syed laugh. Sherry cannot hold back a smile. Jeff fumes.

"You thought he was robbing the café? Does he look like a robber?" Sherry says, still smiling.

"Can't be too careful. You don't know how many times the café's been robbed. We're popular. I dunno what a robber looks like. These days, crooks wear ties and jackets, drive luxury cars, and sit in fancy offices. Who knows what they look like anymore?"

"Why didn't you stop when I shouted 'police'?"

"I look like a fool to you? Anybody can shout 'police.'"

Sherry gives Mislan a look that says "Let it go."

"Where's the Apple laptop you stole from KLCAC?"

"What laptop? I dunno what you're talking about."

Sherry shows him one of the photos from the college CCTV recordings. "Recognize these two guys with the person in the blue cap?"

Wahab shakes his head.

"Funny, because they remember the blue-capped guy."

"OK, it's me. So?"

She picks up the other two photographs and pushes them toward him.

"I'm sure you've played spot-the-difference before. Now, can you spot the difference in these two photos?"

Wahab takes a closer look at the photos, leans back, and grins, "There's a prize?"

Mislan sees a flicker of resignation in his eyes.

"Who are your partners?" he barks. "You cooperate and, maybe, we can convince the DPP to turn you into a prosecution witness."

"I dunno what you're talking about. What partners? What's DPP?"

"Deputy Public Prosecutor." Sherry answers. "Your partners in the rapes."

"Rape?!" he yelps, clearly taken aback. "Did the cashier put you up to this? There was no rape, it was consensual. Shit. Last night, before she knocked off from work, she got into the toilet while I was taking a leak and wanted it in there. If anyone has to make a report, it should be me for sexual harassment."

Seeing the two officers gawking, the suspect shuts up.

"We're not talking about you and the cashier," Mislan says angrily.

"We're talking about rapes that you posted on UTube," Sherry says.

"You're forgetting murder," Mislan adds.

"Rapes, murder! What you people talking about?" the suspect screams. "OK, I admit to stealing the laptop . . . In fact, I admit to stealing three laptops, but no way in hell I'm gonna admit to rape and murder."

Sherry and Mislan look at each other.

"Three laptops! Where're the laptops?"

"Sold. Why else would I steal them?"

"Who did you sell them to?"

"Anyone willing to buy!"

"The Apple laptop . . . who bought it?"

"Can't remember. It was months ago."

Mislan slaps the table hard. "Think hard or I'll hang the murder rap on your head."

Wahab looks terrified. "I dunno him. He paid me seven hundred for it. I don't ask for their names. It's not good for business."

"Where did you meet him?"

"Where we all usually hang out. I mean traders like me. The famous nasi lemak place at Sultan Sulaiman."

"You mean beside the sports club?" Mislan asks.

The suspect nods.

"What does he look like?" Sherry probes.

"Have you watched *Planet of the Apes*? He looks like the head ape-man, Thade."

"What do you mean?"

"You know, big boxer's nose, beady eyes," Wahab illustrates with his fingers, "stone-cold piercing stare, like he's looking for any reason to beat you up. I'm telling you, you can't make that shit up. . . . No way can you learn to look that mean. You gotta be born with it. He must have scared the shit out of the doctors and nurses in the delivery room," Wahab says laughing heartily at his joke. "Maybe even his mama."

Grinning, Mislan says, "So you can recognize him?"

"With a face like that, who wouldn't? I've seen him there several times, but in my business, I can't be too nosy. I'm telling you, he's not someone I'd wanna mess with. Ask too many questions, and I'll be lying in a drain with a knife in my back."

37

THE SPECIAL INVESTIGATIONS AND Sexual & Child Abuse Investigations team position themselves at the nasi lemak stall across the Dewan Sultan Sulaiman and at both ends of the street. Johan, Deena, and Wahab sit at one table, and Mislan and Sherry are a few tables away. The stall is crowded with long queues for the nasi lemak. It has been here since Mislan can remember. From humble wooded shed it has grown into a large concrete structure with a large open sitting space. To him, the nasi lemak or fragrant rice and the side dishes taste ordinary, but from word of mouth the place is packed with customers. Deena asks the others what they want to have and joins the queue.

"Anyone you recognize?" Johan asks.

Wahab scans the restaurant. "Some."

"Like to enlighten me what they do?"

Wahab chortles. "You guys think I'm dumb? I'm no snitch. So, what's this rape and murder about? What has the laptop got to do with them?"

"It's an ongoing investigation. I can't talk about it."

Deena comes back with a tray of banana leaf–wrapped nasi lemak and three glasses of iced coffee.

"These'd better be good, it's one sixty a packet," she groans.

"You see that guy in the black T-shirt joining the queue?" Wahab says.

Johan nods. "Is that him?"

"No, but he used to sit with the Ape-Man."

"Did he come in with anybody?" Johan asks.

"No, I saw him coming alone, probably to get takeout."

Johan makes a call to his boss to pass on the information. Mislan walks toward the queue pretending to examine the food, eyeballs the guy, and relays his description to his team. Returning to his table, Mislan instructs one member of the team to move to the front entrance.

"Do not apprehend. I want him followed. Get the address."

"Roger that."

Looking at the clock, Sherry asks what his plans are for Wahab.

"It's past ten. What're we going to do with him? We can't check him in now, seven hours after his arrest. His lawyer is going to scream."

"What're we charging him with?" Mislan inquires.

"Theft of laptops. He has admitted to three counts, but only from KLCAC. God knows how many more he has nicked from elsewhere."

"Where're the reports? The students didn't make police reports. We've nothing on him. On record, I've already released him, and he's just sticking around to assist us voluntarily as a concerned citizen."

"Does he know he's free to leave?"

"It must have slipped my mind to tell him," he says, grinning.

"You're going to get us into trouble again. Didn't you hear what ma'am said?"

"She says many things. It's impossible for an old man like me to remember everything." He tilts his head toward the man in the queue. "He's leaving."

Mislan walks to the entrance, lights a cigarette, and nods to his men. He watches as the man gets on his motorcycle and rides off, with two of his men on his tail.

————

At midnight, Mislan calls off the stakeout and drives back to the office, where he tells Johan to locate a sketch artist to do a composite drawing of the man Wahab dubbed Ape-Man.

"It's for our use only. Not for the public."

"What about him?" Johan asks, indicating Wahab.

"We can't assume his noninvolvement until we get Ape-Man into custody. Also, I don't want to attract attention to the case. Detain him for suspected housebreaking, and send him for remand."

"He seemed to be on the level, cooperative."

"They all do, Jo, until we get to the truth. Explain it to him. It's only a precaution we need to take."

Johan looks at Sherry, expecting an intervention.

"Mislan's right, we can't take the risk." she reluctantly concurs. "Take him out daily for a decent meal. The sooner we get Ape-Man, the earlier we can clear him."

Johan leaves to make the necessary arrangements.

"The detectives are still monitoring the house where the nasi lemak man is. What do you want them to do?" she asks.

"Anything interesting happening there?"

"Depends on what you mean by interesting. They noticed some young men coming and going."

"Gambling?"

"Could be."

"No women?"

"Just men."

"Hmmm."

When Johan returns to the office, Mislan tells him to check with Gaming, Secret Society, and Anti-Vice (D7) for any information about the apartment where the nasi lemak man is. Johan checks and tells him they have no information.

"Sherry, do your boys know who owns, or rents, that apartment?"

"They've asked around and have been told it's rented by college students. What're you thinking?"

"Tell your boys to find out the name of the student renting the apartment."

"Why?"

"A hunch, that's all."

Johan laughs. "Something's brewing," he says to Sherry.

Sherry calls her men while Mislan lights a cigarette, determined to fully enjoy his one-month privilege.

38

THEY REACH KAMPUNG BARU at 3:10 a.m. and park at the LRT station. Kampung Baru is a three-hundred-acre piece of prime land in the heart of the city. Designated by the government as Malay Reserve, the land there can only be owned by the Malays. It was an area where you went to delight in Malay architecture and heritage but not anymore. The area is dotted with new buildings and filled with Indonesian migrants selling their traditional food. Most of the houses are still wooden and clustered close together.

At Mislan's signal, Johan leads a team through the side and back lanes toward the target. Mislan and Sherry walk casually along Jalan Hassan Salleh toward the PKNS flats. When Johan reports that his team is in position, Sherry makes a call, and one of her detectives walks up the main street to meet them.

"Any developments?"

"The lights are on, but it's difficult to get close without being noticed."

"Is the nasi lemak man still inside?"

The detective nods. "Yahaya's watching the unit."

"Let's go," Mislan says.

On the ground floor of the block, Mislan heads for the elevator.

"It's out of order." Mokthar tells him.

"Shit. Which floor is it?"

"Second."

They go up the stairs to find detective Yahaya crouching on the second-floor landing, watching the unit.

Seeing the team arrive, he sighs in relief.

"So glad to see you guys. My back hurts from all that bending," he says.

"Let's move," Mislan says. "You two take this side of the door. Sherry and I will take the other."

As they walk past the unit, they hear conversation from inside. Once in position, Mislan nods to Sherry. She knocks on the door and announces, "Police, open the door."

The conversation stops, and they hear sounds of movement.

Sherry knocks harder and calls out more urgently, "*Police! Open the door!*"

Mislan puts his ear to the wooden door and hears murmuring. He tells Sherry to step aside and rams the door hard with his shoulder. The door rattles, but does not yield. Holding his sore shoulder, he barks at the two detectives to kick it down. They stand two feet away, ready to kick it down, when it swings open. The nasi lemak man stands in the doorway. Mislan pushes him into the house and steps in. He sees four other men on the sofa pretending to be watching TV. None of them look like Wahab's Ape-Man. Nasi lemak man begins to protest and demands the raiding party leave his apartment immediately.

"Shut up and sit down," Mislan snaps at him.

The nasi lemak man stands his ground and dares him, "If not, what?"

Mislan says to the two detectives, "Arrest him for obstruction."

When the two detectives approach, the nasi lemak man pushes them away, growling, "Obstructing what? You come into my house. I've the right to protect my property."

"Your rights ended when we introduced ourselves. Don't make it worse than it already is," Yahaya tells him.

The four men, who are pretending to watch TV, try to intervene, but Mislan holds his hand up and barks at the nasi lemak man, "Sit."

Sherry tells them they are from the Sexual & Child Abuse Investigations Division and asks who owns or is the main tenant of the unit.

The nasi lemak man says he is.

"This is a search warrant for the unit," Sherry says, handing him the warrant. "Can all of you produce your identity card, please?"

The four men on the sofa look at one another but do not move.

Yahaya steps toward them. "Are you deaf? Ma'am asked for your ICs."

When one of them stands to get his identity card, Sherry sees some documents on the sofa under him. She picks one up and studies it.

"What do we have here?" she says, handing it to Mislan.

He looks at it, and orders all of them to stand. Pulling the cushions off the sofa, he finds more fliers and booklets. He calls Johan, tells him to bring the cars around, and to come up to the flat.

"Sherry, search the apartment. I bet there's more."

"Do you think we should call in the SB?"

"Special Branch? Let the bosses handle that. I don't want them running away with our case."

———

When Johan arrives with his team, a crowd has already gathered on the ground floor and in the stairwell. As he's entering the building, he sees Audi, the investigative reporter, in the crowd. She waves to him.

"What's going on here?" she asks Johan, when he manages to push himself through the crowd.

"I don't know. Why don't you ask my boss? How did you know about this?" he inquires.

She laughs. "It's my job to know. Can you tell your boss I'm here?"

"Sure," he says.

Johan tells Mislan about meeting Audi outside when he finally gets to the unit.

"Jo, make sure the entire house is searched. I want to have a chat with Audi."

"Who's the lead for this?" Johan asks.

"Sherry."

———

Downstairs, Mislan beckons for Audi to follow him as he walks away from the crowd. He lights a cigarette and offers Audi one.

"What brings you here?"

"After your call, I did some digging and found an article about a gathering of NGOs and student bodies protesting against the 'alternative culture' at the UPM stadium recently. Then I got a tip about a raid on a student's apartment. I put two and two together, and here I am."

"You mean Universiti Putra Malaysia stadium?"

"Yes, it was held last week. They wanted to hold it at Dataran Merdeka, but their application was turned down by City Hall. They plan to hold a bigger one the next time."

"Can I see the article?"

"I knew you'd want to." She digs into her back pocket and hands him a paper clipping.

He reads it before putting it in his own pocket. "How big is this anti-LGBT movement?"

"I don't know. Remember the Seksualiti Merdeka event that was banned by the government? The most vocal protestors against sexuality rights were from Muslim NGOs and religious groups."

"You told me the first victim's partner is on the committee of Seksualiti Merdeka. How can I find out if the other victims are members of this Lesbian . . . Gay movement?"

"It's Lesbian, Gay, Bisexual, Transgender, and Queer, or LGBTQ. I guess you can call them and ask."

"Can you find out for me?"

"I can try. Wouldn't it be easier for you to check? You know, use your police powers," she says as a taunt.

"I don't want to stir things up. Not until I'm sure."

"Sure of what? What's your theory? Come on, Inspector, throw some crumbs my way."

"It's not like you to beg," he chortles. "Hey, thanks for this info, but I have to go. Got to clear this place up before it turns into a circus."

"Call me if something breaks."

39

IT IS 6:05 A.M. by the time the raiding party and their detainees reach the Kuala Lumpur Police Contingent Headquarters. Mislan suggests to Sherry that the five detainees be kept in separate rooms in the Special Investigations and Sexual & Child Abuse Investigations Departments.

"Keep them apart until we can establish what the hell we have."

"Are you going to update ma'am?"

"We both are, once we know what we've got." He looks at his watch. "It's almost six thirty; we start the interview at seven. Let's mess with their heads a little first. Tell the detectives to stand guard outside the room and not say a word, don't ask them anything or answer any questions."

Sherry smiles. "What's that supposed to do to them?"

"Under these circumstances, thirty minutes will seem like thirty hours to them. By the time we go into the room, they'll want to hug and kiss us," he says. "Tell the detectives to play with the lights as well. Switch it off for a minute now and then."

"You're a nutcase."

"Think about it, Sherry. Aren't they screwing with our minds, too, as they did with the victims'? I'm only playing their game and, hopefully, we'll come out on top."

———

Mislan and Sherry decide to interview the nasi lemak man themselves. The detective guarding the door hands over the nasi lemak man's identity card and tells them that the detainee has no criminal record. Entering the room, they are instantly bombarded with demands and threats. Mislan ignores him, takes a seat, and lights a cigarette. He reads the suspect's ID, then puts it on the table. The nasi lemak man keeps going on about his unlawful detention. Mislan gives him one of his oh-shut-up glares that stops him momentarily.

"Muhammad Jamali bin Muhammad Ali from Alor Setar, Kedah," Mislan reads out loud from the identity card. "Are you a radical?"

"I don't know what you mean by that," Jamali answers defiantly.

Sherry leans toward Mislan and whispers, "Don't you want to caution him first?"

Mislan signals Sherry to follow him out of the interview room. Closing the door, he says "We're not recording a statement from him. We'll leave that to SB. This is only an interview for information."

"What if he's connected to the case?"

"Then we're screwed," Mislan replies indifferently.

"I'm the lead, and I say we go by the book," Sherry says.

"What about the rest of them? Are you going to caution and interview all of them?"

"If that's what it takes to make the case, yes, I will. This is the only lead we have, and I'm not letting your street tactics blow it."

"Look, what do we know about the nasi lemak man?" Mislan says, softening his tone. "Wahab says he saw him with the Ape-Man. That's all. Ape-Man bought the laptop from Wahab . . . and he was alone. My theory is, our nasi lemak man knows who Ape-Man is, but my gut feeling is that he and the others aren't involved in the crimes. By now, news of the raid would have reached all other anti-LGBT groups, and we need to get Ape-Man's identity quickly before he hears about it and goes into hiding."

Sherry remains unconvinced and is adamant about going by the book. "I wish I were as sure as you are."

"Okay, let's do it this way, you go and make arrangements with SB for them to take over this case. In the meantime, I'll talk to the nasi lemak man. That way, we can still use the statement obtained by SB, which will be done by the book. And if ma'am questions you as to why the interview was done without the caution, you can play dumb and blame me."

"You have all the answers, don't you?"

"Not all, not yet."

When Mislan returns to the interview room alone, Muhammad Jamali starts his protests again.

"Shut up and listen," Mislan barks. "You've got a few minutes before the Special Branch officers come and take you away. Do you know what that means? You'll be locked up somewhere and forgotten." Mislan pauses, and watches the detainee's reaction.

"Why? I haven't done anything wrong," Jamali squeaks.

"Nothing wrong? What do you call these?" Mislan snaps at him, banging the leaflets on the table, making the detainee flinch. "Inciting violence against the LGBT . . . labeling them freaks, deviants, and polluters of society."

"Their lifestyle is against the teaching of Islam, and as a Muslim—"

"You're right. It's *their* lifestyle. Who appointed you the guardian of their lifestyle? They don't incite others to denounce yours," Mislan hisses.

Jamali starts to say something, and Mislan holds up his hand.

"I'm not here to debate with you, that's the work of the Special Branch." He digs into his back pocket and takes out a piece of paper and spreads it on the table. "Who is this?" he asks, staring unblinkingly at the nasi lemak man.

Jamali remains silent.

Mislan slaps the table again. "Who the fuck is this?"

"Radin. Radin Yasin," Jamali blurts out.

"How do you know him?"

"We met once at a gathering."

"How about at the Dewan Sultan Sulaiman nasi lemak stall?"

"I bumped into him there a few times, and we talked."

"Is he a member of your group?"

"No. He told me he runs his own group."

"Where can I find him?"

"I don't know. You can call him. His number is in my cell phone."

"Why didn't you tell me that earlier? Dickhead!"

Mislan goes out and asks the detective for Muhammad Jamali's cell phone. Back in the interview room, he has the suspect unlock the phone, then scrolls down the contact list for Radin's number, copies it, and deletes it from the phone's memory.

"What sort of group is he running?"

"Same as mine, I suppose."

"What did you talk to him about?"

"Stuff."

"What stuff?"

Jamali indicates the leaflets and booklets.

"And you think the LGBT people are sick? It's people like you who are sick," Mislan snarls at him and walks out.

40

THE HEADS OF SPECIAL Investigations and Sexual & Child Abuse Investigations sit quietly as the OCCI rants about the incompetence of their investigating officers.

"How many more rapes do we need before you break this case? Three, four, how many?" He grabs the newspaper lying on his table and slams it in front of them. "Have you read what they're saying about me?"

He grabs another newspaper and slams it on top of the first.

"Listen to this: *After the third case, the police still have no lead.* Do you know how that makes me look?"

Samsiah cracks a tiny smile.

"I want these cases solved immediately. I'm going to call for a PC and tell them the case will be solved in the next forty-eight hours."

"And if it's not?" Samsiah ventures.

"Heads will roll, and I'm sure you know whose."

"That's not important." Samsiah says calmly. "What's more important is how you will be perceived by the public, giving them an assurance that we've no certainty of delivering."

SAC Burhanuddin remains silent, and his face contorts with anger.

"May I suggest you proceed with your press conference?" Samsiah eases in slowly. "Tell them we're making progress, but we're unable to release specifics at the moment. We're also working closely with Selangor police, trying to establish the relationships between the cases." She notes a flicker of excitement in the publicity junkie's eyes. She throws in a sweetener. "Forensic managed to obtain blood samples from an accident scene that we believe are from the suspects. We're currently waiting for the DNA results."

"Samsiah's right. That'll satisfy the media," Lillian adds. "The task force is making progress."

The OCCI nods, and his expression softens.

"You can also tell them that you're bringing in investigators from Bukit Aman to join the task force," Samsiah suggests, pushing it.

"And let them take all the glory?" Burhanuddin sneers. "Get out of here and get me the culprits."

————

Sherry and Assistant Superintendent of Police Fakurrulah Mois from Special Branch are waiting for Superintendent Samsiah when she enters the task force room. Sherry introduces Fakurrulah and updates them.

"Where's Mislan?"

Sherry ignores Samsiah's question and hands her a leaflet and booklet. "These were recovered from the apartment."

Samsiah briefly reads the leaflet and booklet. Turning to the Special Branch officer, she asks, "Are you aware of this group?"

"Not specifically, but we're monitoring these anti-LGBT movements. They held a rally at UPM with student bodies and NGOs. They're planning to hold another one, on a bigger scale, soon."

"Are you aware of any violence by members of these movements?"

"That's hard to say. LGBTQ and anti-LGBTQ aren't registered bodies, so they don't have specific addresses or offices. Membership is loose, open. We know the main players, but there are hundreds of smaller groups. Even if a crime is committed against a person of such orientation, it doesn't mean it was instigated by the movement."

"Let us know if you discover anything that might assist with our cases."

Mislan, Johan, and Deena enter the task force room just as the Special Branch officer leaves. Mislan inquires, "SB?" tilting his head toward the man walking away.

Sherry nods.

"Sai, if I give you a cell phone number, will you be able to pinpoint its location?"

"You mean like on TV, no. But you can get the service provider to track it for you."

"They can?"

"Yes, if they want to."

"What do you mean?"

"Every few minutes, I don't know how many, your cell phone will check in with the nearest hub or transmitter. It's like a transponder in vessels and airplanes."

"Can you check with the service provider and locate it?"

"I'll try."

"Whose number?" Samsiah asks.

"Ape-Man."

"Who's the Ape-Man?"

"The person who bought the laptop from Wahab."

"How did you get it?"

"From a reliable source."

"Don't give me that. How did you get it?" Samsiah demands firmly.

"One of the detainees."

"You interrogated them?"

"No, we had a chat, he recognized Ape-Man from our sketch, and gave me his number. He was quite talkative and cooperative. He said he met Ape-Man at one of the rallies and bumped into him several times at the nasi lemak place."

Samsiah looks at him suspiciously. "I don't want to know any more details. Sai, can you get to the service provider and get the location?"

"It may take a while."

"I'm thinking of asking Wahab to call him and set up a meeting. Maybe offer to sell him another laptop," Mislan suggests.

"Does Wahab have his number? If he doesn't, Ape-Man may get suspicious, and you'll lose him. It's better for the guy who gave you the number to make the call."

"A bit difficult." Mislan hesitates.

"You just said he was talkative and cooperative."

"Maybe I exaggerated a little?" Mislan smiles.

"While Sai gets the service provider to locate him, the two of you get some rest and freshen up. You look like you've not slept in ages. I promise you, it's going to be a very long day."

———

When Mislan reaches home, he showers, slumps into bed, and tries to nap, but just as he's about to doze off, his cell phone rings.

"Inspector, Chew. Did I catch you at a bad time?"

"No. What's up?"

"The DNA results came in and the blood belongs to a female donor. No match on our database."

"Female?"

"Yes, but it could also be from another accident, unrelated to our case. The blood type is AB, which is not very common."

"Thanks."

"Inspector, the Chinese papers say the serial rapists are targeting lesbians. Is that true?"

"That's all newspaper talk . . . to sell more papers."

"How's the case going?"

"Tough."

"Wish I could do more to help."

"You already have, Chew."

Wide awake now, Mislan calls Dr. Safia.

"Hey Fie, busy?"

"Slow day, why?"

"Want to grab a bite? I've not had breakfast."

"Where are you?"

"Home. I can swing over to your place and grab a bite there."

"Why don't you stop by a McDonald's and get me a double fillet? We can eat here in my office."

"You want anything else? A sundae, or a pie?"

"Apple pie."
"OK, be there in thirty."

———

He arrives at Doctor Nursafia's office at HUKM with McDonald's take-out, and she clears the files from her desk to make room. Unfolding the wrapper of her double fillet, she asks, "What's on your mind?"

"Nothing. Just needed company, that's all."

"If it's company you want, there's Jo and others at your office. Tell me what's on your mind?"

He toys with his Quarter Pounder, then puts it down, picks up a french fry, and nibbles on it. Dr. Safia waits patiently, watching his face closely. She can see he's struggling with something. She bites into her fillet and puts it down, too.

"It's this case," he mumbles, picking up another french fry and dipping it in the chili sauce.

Dr. Safia waits for him to continue and, when he remains silent, she asks "What about this case?"

"The victimology."

"Wow, big word," she jokes. "What about it?"

Mislan smiles. "Learned it from watching *Criminal Minds*. All the victims are lesbians. That's the only connection between them."

"So, the rapists are targeting lesbians randomly."

"That's what it looks like. The question is, how did the rapists know the victims were lesbians? Is there a central source of information?"

"You mean, like a hangout, or a social gathering the victims went to?"

He nods. "We can't find any. The other puzzling thing is: how the hell did the rapists get into their houses? There're no signs of forced entry. All three victims were fast asleep and woke up to find the rapists standing over them. The first victim said she would put on the double locks whenever she was home, and that was confirmed by Sherry when she visited her. So, how the hell did they get inside the house?"

Dr. Safia takes another bite of her double fillet. "Maybe they were already inside when the victims came home. Hiding, until it was time."

"I thought of that. That would mean they had the keys to the houses. The next question is, how did they get them?"

"I can think of a few places. Car washes, service stations, jockey parking services . . . you know how we tend to leave our house keys in the car."

"Hmmm . . . and their windshield stickers would give away the location of their apartment. Car-jockey services, car washes, and service stations: that's a lot of places to cover."

"Lan, about this lesbian victimology, I read a story about it a few months ago. It said that such incidents have been reported in some countries. South Africa, Zimbabwe, even in Thailand. It's called 'corrective rape.' NGOs in those countries have so far been unsuccessful in pressuring the governments into classifying them as hate crimes."

"What do you mean by corrective rape?"

"Well, these men rape lesbians with the intention of turning them straight. You know, once they have had sex with a man, they're supposed to enjoy it and go straight."

"You violate a woman and expect her to love it or your kind? That's the dumbest thing I've ever heard."

"Well, men have been known to do dumber things," Dr. Safia laughs.

"But we're not living in some backward country."

"African, Malaysian, American, European . . . what does it matter? Men are men all over the world. They have two heads, and blood can only rush to one of them at any given time," she says, giggling.

"Funny," he says, and makes a face. "So you think these were corrective rapes?"

"I'm saying I read about it. The victimology seems to point in that direction. And the username 'Emancipatist' must come from the word *emancipate*."

"Like liberate. So they're 'liberators'?"

Dr. Safia nods. "Don't you think the username could imply corrective rape?"

"I totally missed that," he says. "I thought it was just a username they coined."

She sips her Coke.

"Sherry is a looker, isn't she?" she says, catching him off guard.

Mislan looks at her, bemused, and manages to say, "Do I sense jealousy?"

Dr. Safia blushes. "Jealous? Me? I was only making an observation."

"Yes, she is and, no, I'm not into her type."

His cell phone rings.

"Yes, Sherry," he answers. Catching a glimpse of Dr. Safia's expression, he smiles.

"Did I wake you?"

"No, I'm in Dr. Safia's office having brunch."

His answer brings a smile to Dr. Safia's face.

"Sai has managed to locate Ape-Man. I've already dispatched the team. You want to come?"

"You bet. WhatsApp me the location and I'll be there." He grabs his Quarter Pounder and Coke. "Got to run, they have a location on the Ape-Man. Call you later tonight."

"I like that . . . Sherry calls, and you jump," she kids with him.

"Yah, right," he laughs and dashes out.

———

He receives a WhatsApp message just as he turns on the ignition: *BSC. Meet u in front of Chilis.*

He calls back. "What's BSC?"

"Bangsar Shopping Center. You know where it is?" Sherry says.

"Bangsar."

"Yes, it's in Bangsar, but do you know where in Bangsar?"

"It's the shopping complex where that Chinese woman, what's her name, was abducted and then murdered and burned, right?"

"Yes, Canny Ong. I'll wait for you in front of Chili's. It's at the main entrance."

"OK, on my way."

On Jalan Loke Yew, he gets caught in a traffic jam. *Shit. Why is it that on TV the streets are always clear when the police dash to the crime scene?* He spots a patrol car in the right lane. Once level with it, he rolls down the window, introduces himself, and tells the driver to pull over to the side.

"I need to get to Bangsar in double-quick time. My team spotted a murder suspect there. Can you put on the siren and lead me?"

The obviously bored patrolmen jump at the opportunity for some excitement. The patrol car, with light bar on and siren screaming, guns down the emergency lane with Mislan tailgating, much to the annoyance of other drivers. Nearing the Jalan Maarof traffic lights, Mislan waves them off, not wanting the suspect to hear the siren. He turns right toward the Bangsar Shopping Center.

———

Walking up to the entrance of Bangsar Shopping Complex from across the road where he parked illegally, he spots an impatient Sherry by the florist next to Chili's Grill & Bar when he approaches.

"Where exactly is he?" he asks as she approaches him.

"Sai says he's here at BSC."

"Is there a car wash in the basement?"

"I don't know. Why?"

"Just a hunch. If there is, there's a good chance he's there. Let's go," Mislan says, entering the shopping complex looking for the staircase. "Get your men to cover all exits, especially the entrance and exit ramps."

Sherry gives orders over the walkie-talkie.

"You think he's going to make a run for it?" she asks him.

"I hope he won't, but I'm sure he will. Tell them to keep their eyes open. I want him taken down at all costs."

Sherry transmits more instructions over the walkie-talkie.

"And tell them not to move in until told."

They barge out of the emergency door and into the basement parking lot, with Sherry still issuing instructions.

"There," Mislan says, pointing to what looks like a car wash at the east end.

He quickens his pace, with Sherry scurrying close behind. The clacking of her heels on the concrete floor echoes through the half-empty lot, attracting attention. Mislan spots the Ape-Man, and for a moment their eyes lock. Ape-Man drops the sponge he's holding, and, crouching, he disappears behind a row of cars. Mislan dashes toward the car wash with his sidearm drawn and shouts, *Police! Stop!*

The word "police" instantly results in a group of foreign workers scampering in several directions. Some customers freeze motionless, gaping.

"Tell the men he's making a run for it!" he shouts to Sherry. "Shit," he curses.

———

He hears the roar of a motorcycle and stops in his tracks. He grabs the walkie-talkie from Sherry and yells into it.

"All exits watch out, he's on a bike. I repeat, he's on a bike."

Just as he finishes relaying the information, a motorbike roars out from behind the car wash and zooms toward the exit ramp. Mislan levels his Beretta at the speeding bike, and the gawking customers go hysterical, screaming and running for cover. Not having a clear line of fire, Mislan runs toward the exit ramp, shouting into the walkie-talkie.

"Ape-Man's on a bike, take him down, take him down!"

The motorbike disappears out of the parking lot. Mislan hears a loud crash, and he and Sherry run toward the sound to find Johan and Deena standing over the Ape-Man lying motionless on the street, with the motorbike wrapped around a lamppost, its engine still running.

"Is he dead?" Sherry asks anxiously.

"He's going to wish he is," Deena answers.

"What happened?"

"He slipped," Johan replies casually, bending down to cuff him. He picks Ape-Man up and pats him down for weapons and identification.

"He looks like an orangutan," Deena says.

A crowd gathers. Sherry tells her team to stand down.

"Jo, Deena, take him away before things get messy here. This place is crawling with human-rights activists and bleeding-heart liberals," she instructs them.

"His bike?" Deena asks.

"I'll call Bangsar police station and get them to send it to Forensic in Cheras," Mislan volunteers. "I'll tell Chew to expect it. I want him to examine the indicator lights, see if there's a match with the debris collected from the Setapak Jaya flats. Get one of the men to wait here, I don't want the bike going missing,"

"Also get Traffic to come in, just in case he decides to make a report against Jo and Deena," Sherry adds.

"For what? He slipped," Deena protests and then looks at Johan with a sly smile.

"Prudence," Sherry says.

41

THE OFFICE IS ABUZZ with news of an Ape-Man being captured. It is said that the Ape-Man, being six and a half feet tall and weighing almost three hundred pounds, was taken down by five detectives, two of whom suffered broken ribs. The elevator lobby is crowded with onlookers from other units. When Detective Sergeant Johan and Detective Deena emerge from the elevator escorting the suspect, the crowd lets out murmurs of disappointment.

"What was that about?" Johan asks Deena.

She shakes her head.

They take the Ape-Man to the interview room and wait for instructions.

Mislan gives Sherry the honor of informing the heads of Special Investigations and Sexual & Child Abuse Investigation of the arrest.

Superintendent Samsiah walks over to the general office and peeks into the interview room but quickly closes the door when Ape-Man turns to glare at her. Mislan steps up from behind, startling her.

"Ya Allah," she mutters. "Don't you ever creep up on me like that again."

"Nasty piece of work, hah?" he says with a chuckle. "Exactly as Wahab described him. Those eyes could scare even his mother."

"Why's he all bloody?" she asks, regaining her composure. "And don't tell me he ran into a car, and where's Sherry? "

"He fell. Jo says his bike skidded and he crashed at the exit ramp. Sherry's preparing her notes for the interview."

"Make sure Jo lodges a police report of the accident. Lan, work this one by the book. If he's somehow connected to the anti-LGBT movements, there will be thousands out there rooting for him and offering him free legal advice."

Mislan nods.

"I'd like to keep his arrest under wraps until we know what we're dealing with."

"Not even him?" Mislan jerks his head upward to indicate the OCCI.

"As long as I can."

"No disrespect, ma'am, but you may want to consider going above him on this one."

"That's disrespect in itself," she cautions him.

"If you say so. Ma'am, I want to search his place before word of his arrest gets around. Can you get me a search warrant?"

"I'll get Reeziana to apply for it. In the meantime, consider sending Jo and a team to monitor the house. Pick up anyone going in or out."

———

Sherry and Mislan enter the interview room, and Sherry releases Deena, to her dismay. While Johan leans against the wall near the door, Mislan and Sherry take a seat across the table from Ape-Man. Sherry recoils and looks away when Ape-Man glares at her. Mislan notices this and whispers to her.

"Don't do that again. Don't let him intimidate you."

He takes out the digital recorder and places it on the table between them, and reads aloud information from Ape-Man's identity card, "Radin Yasin bin Radin Alang, born July 25, 1986. Listed address, Kampung Pokok Sena, Sik, Kedah Darul Aman."

Ape-Man Radin glares at him, not answering.

"Radin, I'm going to caution you. Listen carefully to the caution," Sherry says.

Ape-Man Radin ignores her and continues staring at Mislan.

Sherry repeats her instructions, but Ape-Man keeps ignoring her. The room falls silent, and she can feel tension rising. She looks at Mislan, who appears calm, unperturbed by Ape-Man's glare. Mislan's hand slowly reaches out to his digital recorder. He switches it off. Then, like lightning, the hand slams down hard on the table and, in one movement, he is up on his feet and leaning across the table. He grabs the front of Ape-Man's shirt, pulling the detainee forward, their faces inches apart. When Sherry and Johan recover from their shock, they try to intervene.

Mislan snaps at them, "Stay out of this." The two officers stop and watch anxiously.

Yanking Ape-Man closer, Mislan hisses venomously, "Did you hear what Inspector Sherry said to you?"

Ape-Man blinks, and Mislan knows he has won.

"Is that a yes?"

"Yes," he snarls, grinding his teeth.

Mislan smiles, releases his grip on the detainee's shirt, and smooths the garment. "Now, that wasn't so hard. Let's try again." He nods to Sherry, "Go ahead."

Mislan switches on the digital recorder and leans back with a cigarette as Sherry administers the caution and goes through the formalities, with reluctant cooperation from Ape-Man.

"What's your current address?"

"The same as in my IC."

"That's your permanent address. I mean, where're you staying in KL?"

Mislan jots down the address and gives it to Johan, who immediately leaves the room and sends a text message to Inspector Reeziana, who is waiting at the courthouse to apply for the search warrant. Mislan leaves the interview room and comes back with a box of Kleenex, which he pushes toward Ape-Man, pointing to his bleeding elbow. Ape-Man pulls out a few tissues, dabs the blood, and looks around for a trash can. Mislan leaves the room again. A moment later he comes back with a wastepaper basket with a new plastic liner. Sherry glances at him, as if saying, *why the sudden compassion?* Mislan gives her a *what?* look. Sherry ignores him and continues with the interview.

"Between June and August, did you buy an Apple laptop from a man named Wahab?"

"I did, but I don't know his name. He said he needed cash and wanted to sell his laptop. There's no crime in that."

"For your information, disposing of and acquiring stolen property is a crime," Sherry says.

"I didn't know the laptop was stolen. He told me . . ." Ape-Man rambles.

"How much did you pay for the Apple laptop?" Sherry asks cutting him off.

"Seven hundred, I think."

"Where's the laptop now?"

"I sold it."

"To whom?"

"I don't know his name. I spread the word around that I had a MacBook for sale. One day, this guy showed up and I sold it to him for a thousand."

"When did this happen?"

"About a month ago."

"Where?"

"At the mamak stall behind BSC."

"Describe the man who bought the laptop from you."

Mislan listens patiently, studying Ape-Man's face as he answers Sherry's questions. On one occasion, he thinks he sees a glimmer of joy in the detainee's eyes. *What is he happy about?* Mislan wonders. He is bloodied, probably in pain, his motorbike is damaged, and he won't have an income for the next few days. He observes the calm confidence in the detainee's manner and voice. Mislan moves his chair to face the detainee, leans forward, and gazes into Ape-Man's eyes. *No, that's not joy, that's vanity. He is toying with Sherry, taking her for a ride and enjoying it.*

The interview room door bursts open, and the OCCI stands in the door. Sherry jumps to her feet. Mislan hears hurried footsteps and sees Superintendent Samsiah appear behind the massive figure of SAC Burhanuddin.

"So, this is the culprit?" Burhanuddin snarls, holding the door ajar. "What's your name," he barks at Ape-Man.

Ape-Man looks at him, his eyes narrowing like a diamond-head cobra ready to strike, but says nothing.

"I asked you your name!" Burhanuddin barks louder. "Do you know who I am?"

Ape-Man grins.

"Radin Yasin Radin Alang," Sherry answers.

Burhanuddin steps closer to Ape-Man. "Look at me when I'm talking to you, you piece of garbage," he snaps.

Ape-Man glares at him and smirks, "I know who you are. You're the Chief Garbage Collector."

Mislan hides a smile as Superintendent Samsiah steps in to intercede.

"Sir, the detainee is in a 113 interview. I suggest we let them complete it first."

Burhanuddin turns to her, his face red with anger at being mocked by a detainee and interrupted by a subordinate.

Before he can reproach her, Samsiah says, "Unless you want the cautioned statement to be thrown out in court. It's your call."

Burhanuddin storms out of the interview room fuming and shouts for her to follow him. He stops in the hall and confronts her.

"Don't ever tell me what to do in front of your officers."

"It's my duty to remind you of the consequence of interrupting a cautioned interview. This suspect is critical to our investigation. My officers and men have not slept for forty hours tracking him. I'm not about to let their efforts be wasted—"

"Watch it. You're talking to your superior."

"I'm fully aware of that, sir, and I'll do the same if it happens again." she answers firmly.

"I'll deal with you later. I want the suspect's details and a brief of his arrest on my table in half an hour." Turning to leave, he says, "If you know what's good for you, don't delay it."

"Sir, I have to caution you, if the suspect's details are released to the press, it will jeopardize our investigation."

Burhanuddin ignores her remarks and walks out.

42

THE TWO INVESTIGATING OFFICERS join Johan and Deena for lunch at a roadside stall close to Danau Rebung Apartments in Sungai Buloh, Selangor, a township about thirteen miles north of the city. Sherry decides to have lunch, too, while Mislan orders an iced black coffee.

"Who's watching the apartment?"

"Syed and Jeff on the outer, Dorai and Mokthar the inner perimeter. We'll take over from Dorai and Mokthar after we're done here, so they can have their lunch," Johan says.

"Any movement so far?" Sherry asks, returning to the table with a plate of vegetables and fish.

Johan's cell phone rings. "Yes . . . OK . . . Stand by." He ends the call and says to Mislan, "Dorai says a woman just came out of the apartment."

"Tell him and Mokthar to follow her, Syed and Jeff to take over the inner perimeter," Mislan instructs him. "Let's get moving."

Johan asks for the bill as Sherry and Deena hurriedly clear their plates.

"Who has the warrant?"

"Me," Deena says, patting her pocket.

"Deena, I want you to go to the apartment and ask for Radin. Pretend you're a relative from Kedah and ask to use the bathroom. I need to know how many people are in there," Sherry instructs her.

"What if there's no one?"

"Then it will be another long night for you guys," Mislan says.

"Another stakeout? At this rate, I'll be lucky if I'm married by for-ty-five," Deena groans.

"Can you speak the Kedah dialect?" Sherry asks.

"*Awat, Puan ingat cek tak tau ke?*" she answers, mimicking the northern Malay dialect. *Does ma'am think I cannot?*

"You sounded like a duck trying to mimic a chicken," Johan laughs.

At the apartment building, Johan follows Deena to the fourth floor and walks to the other end of the common corridor. Deena knocks on the Ape-Man's unit door and calls out, "Brother Radin." She waits and looks at Johan, who's pretending to check apartment numbers two units away against a piece of paper in his hand. Deena knocks at the door again, calling out the Ape-Man's name. The door cracks open, and a man peers through it and tells her that Radin isn't home.

"I called earlier and he told me he's home," Deena says, mimicking the northern Malay dialect.

"Wh . . . wh . . . who are you?" the man stutters.

"I'm his niece from Sik. Can I use the washroom? I can't hold it any longer."

The man hesitates, unsure of what to do. Deena wiggles her body, bringing her hands down to her front, and shuffling with her feet.

"Please, I really can't hold it any longer. It was very cold in the cab."

The man unlocks the door grille and lets her in. He pokes his head out and looks out into the common corridor in the direction of the stairwell while Deena goes to the bathroom. She locks the door behind her and waits for a while before flushing the toilet. She turns on the tap to wash her hands before coming out.

"Aaah, what a relief," she says, smiling. "Who're you?"

"Ka . . . Karim, Di . . . Di . . . Din's friend."

"Housemate?"

"No, I co . . . co . . . come here ss . . . sssometimes," he says, his stut-ter worsening. "Wh . . . when there is n . . . n . . . no class."

Deena moves toward the single sofa in the living room. "What're you studying?" she asks.

"I th . . .th . . . think you sh . . . sh . . . should leave. I'll tell Di . . .

Di . . . Din you ca . . . ca . . . came," he manages with difficulty, blinking his eyes rapidly.

"I'm looking for a place to rent, how much do you pay for this unit?"

"I . . . I . . . don't know, you should as . . . ask Din."

"How many of you stay here?"

He raises four fingers.

"Including you?"

"N . . . n . . . no. Ca . . . can you please leave?"

———

Deena briefs the team on her observations inside the apartment and her conversation with Karim.

"Notice any laptop?" Mislan asks.

"Not in the living room. The bedroom doors were closed."

"What do you think?" Sherry asks.

"We need some evidence on Ape-Man or he won't break. Notice how he was messing around with you during the interview?" Mislan asks.

Sherry nods.

"If we go in now and there's nothing there, we'll show our hand," she cautions.

The team is silent.

"What about the woman who left the apartment?"

"Sherry, call Dorai to find out what they have."

Sherry tells them to intercept the woman before she reaches her destination. "I want her and the car at the office. She may be helping them remove evidence."

"Deena said Karim was nervous, edgy. I think he must have heard about Ape-Man's arrest and is cleaning up for him," Johan says.

"Jo and Deena, come with us," Mislan jumps in. "Syed and Jeff, I want you guys to stay on the perimeter. Allow in anyone approaching the apartment, and only detain them if they try to walk or run away. OK, let's go in."

At the apartment, Sherry introduces herself to Karim and serves him with the search warrant. The team searches the two bedrooms for a laptop and a video camera but comes back empty-handed. Mislan tells them to go over the bedrooms, kitchen, and bathroom again. He pulls Karim into the living room.

"Who else lives here?"

"M . . . M . . . Man, R . . . R . . . Reza, and A . . . A . . . A . . . Ali."

Mislan draws his sidearm, and it shocks Karim into losing his stutter. "Where're they now?"

"Class, I think. I don't know."

"That's better," he says, holstering his sidearm. "Where's class?"

"Ma . . . Man and Reza go to K . . . KLCAC." Karim pauses, breathing in deeply. "Ali to INTI."

"I want you to call them back now."

Karim gawks at the inspector.

"Tell them the house has been broken into, and that they need to come home immediately."

Karim's eyes follow Mislan's hand pointing toward a cell phone on the coffee table.

"Do it now," Mislan snaps at him.

Sherry comes out, shaking her head. Mislan puts his finger to his lips, pointing at Karim on the cell phone. Sherry jerks her head in surprise.

"Calling his housemates to get them to come home," Mislan whispers. "Can you get D10 here?"

"Why?"

"I need them to bag Ape-Man's pants."

"Why?"

"The rapist didn't dispose of the condom at the vics' houses. Meaning he would have to zip up his fly with the condom still on his dick."

"So there could be vaginal fluid transferred to the pants," Sherry says. "That's a brilliant deduction, Inspector Mislan. I'm impressed."

"Thank you, Inspector Sherry."

"I also think we should get him a clean set of clothing. We don't want him going on remand wearing bloodied clothes and telling the magistrate he was tortured."

Mislan laughs. "You're getting good at this."

Johan comes out and whispers to Mislan that Dorai and Mokthar have lost their suspect. Mislan gestures to his assistant to follow him outside.

"How did that happen?"

"She took the expressway, and the boys couldn't keep up with her on their moped."

"I hope they got the car number."

"They did, and I told them to go to the JPJ office to obtain the owner's details. Do you want them to come back here or go back to the office?"

"We're about done here. Check with Sherry."

———

Sherry, Johan, and Deena are going through the rooms again just in case they missed something. Mislan stays outside looking at Karim. *He cannot be one of the perps. His stuttering is too obvious, and that could easily be a giveaway.*

The walkie-talkie crackles with Syed's voice warning them of two men approaching the unit. Mislan and Sherry take cover, one on each side of the door. Johan and Deena take Karim into one of the bedrooms.

Two men barge in calling for Karim. Mislan's frame fills the doorway behind them, blocking their exit. Sherry introduces herself and tells them to sit on the sofa. Johan and Deena bring Karim out and seat him at the dining table. The two men stare at Karim menacingly.

"There'll be another one coming," Mislan tells her.

43

THE CHIEF POLICE OFFICER's secretary nods at Superintendent Samsiah Hassan and tells her she can go in. She knocks lightly on the door, opens it, and stands to attention. "Good afternoon, Datuk."

"Samsiah, how have you been?" the Deputy Commissioner of Police, Datuk Zaid Zainal, greets her.

"As well as can be, under the circumstances," she replies, smiling.

"The UTube Serial Rapist cases swamping you?" He smiles back. "My secretary says it's urgent, so let's hear it."

She hands him the case brief and waits as he reads it. He lifts his head from the case brief and laughs. "Burhan?"

"How did you figure that?"

"It's not that difficult, Sam. No way would a publicity junkie like him let this one pass. He'll go into withdrawal for days," Zaid jests heartily. "Do you want me to stop it?"

"In my opinion, it's good to hold a press conference. The newspapers are talking about serial rapists on the loose. It's good to keep the public informed and contain the growing panic. However, I don't think we should reveal the identities of detainees or that they're members of anti-LGBT movements. That could spark a confrontation."

The Chief Police Officer nods in agreement.

"May I suggest that you conduct the PC?" she asks.

"When is it scheduled?"

"I was told that it's at four today."

Zaid calls his secretary. "What do I have today at four?"

"You're scheduled to officiate the closing of the refresher training for the general elections."

"Get my deputy to close it. Call Burhan's secretary. Move the scheduled four o'clock PC to the conference room. Tell her I'll be doing the PC. I want Burhan, Samsiah, and Lillian to be present." Then, turning to Samsiah, he says, "Give me what you want made public."

"Datuk, I'm sorry I have to come to you, but . . ."

"Don't be. I'd do the same in your position. Just be prepared for more heat from him," he warns with a chuckle.

"Always am, Datuk, thank you."

44

THE SPECIAL INVESTIGATIONS OFFICE becomes crowded with detectives and detainees as the four men are brought in. The escorting detectives ask the front desk clerk where they can hold the detainees. The clerk shrugs and tells them to check with Mislan. A detective disappears and, coming back, he signals for Karim to follow him and shouts to his colleagues to hold the rest in the detectives' room.

"Make sure they're kept apart, and no talking."

The detective escorts Karim to the investigators' general office.

"Jo, have we got the details of the car owner yet?" Mislan shouts from across the room.

"They're on the way back."

"Put Deena in charge of processing and remand. I want you to work on him," he motions to Karim. "Keep the rest in the detective room until we need them."

"Never had so many of them in the same time. This looks more like Ops Sapu," Johan says, referring to the periodic cleanup operation conducted on druggies or beggars and the homeless.

"I need to speak to ma'am to see if she can get Yana to assist us."

"I'll come with you," Sherry offers.

"Who's sending Ape-Man's pants to Cheras?" Johan asks.

"Check with Kevin, maybe he can send us one of his boys," Sherry suggests.

"I need to pass this on to Chew for DNA testing," Mislan says, taking an exhibit bag out of his drawer.

"What's that?" Sherry asks.

"Bloodied tissue from Ape-Man."

"So that's what the display of compassion was all about. And I thought you had gone soft," she laughs. "Didn't the high court throw out the DNA evidence in Anwar's case because it was obtained from a towel offered by the police?"

"Ape-Man disposed of the tissues on his own accord, so it's public property. Anyway, the DNA of the sample at the accident scene indicated a female."

"So why do you want his DNA?"

"For now, I don't know, but since the opportunity presented itself, why not? Let's hope Ape-Man's pants will yield traces of DNA of one of the vics. That may be our silver bullet. Tell me when the exhibits are delivered, I'll call Chew to rush it."

Superintendent Samsiah lifts her head from her laptop as the two investigators stand at her door. She beckons them in. "Good work by your team."

"Thanks, but it may be a little premature. We have many bodies but nothing to nail them with," Sherry answers.

"Good work, anyway."

"None of them are on our records. Sai has been through their laptops. Nothing," Sherry says, sounding tired and frustrated. "I was sure we were on the right track, but it looks like we were chasing the wrong lead."

"I'm not too sure about that," Samsiah says encouragingly. "Wahab led you to Ape-Man. That's solid evidence, and you can use Wahab's testimony to tie Ape-Man to the Apple laptop."

"Ape-Man says he sold the notebook to an unknown person," Sherry groans.

"That's crap," Mislan butts in. "He was toying with you because he knew we have nothing. He's not a trader."

"Based on what?"

"He works in a car wash, how much do you think he earns a day? Thirty . . . forty ringgit? Where would he get seven hundred ringgit for a laptop, taking into account the rental for his apartment—mind you he's the main tenant—the installment on his motorbike loan, and his daily expenses? He'd have barely enough to survive."

"So, what are you saying?"

"Someone is financing him. He's in this circle, the loop, so he was used to buy the laptop."

"Who's this mysterious financier?" Sherry asks.

"That's our jackpot." Mislan grins. "We're going for the jackpot. Ma'am, can we get additional support?"

"An additional man?"

"Officer."

"There're already two of you."

"Sherry and I need to work on the detainees, and I was hoping Reeziana can help us with some legwork. The men saw a woman leaving Ape-Man's apartment, but they lost her when she got on the expressway. They're on the way back with the particulars of the car's owner. I was hoping Reeziana might lead the men on this."

"You think the woman's involved?"

"We won't know until we get her in. Karim said she came over to collect some project assignments. He could be telling the truth, but the timing is suspicious, and I don't like coincidences."

"What you don't like doesn't fly by me."

"I knew you were going to say that," Mislan answers smilingly. "Chew tells me that the DNA sample we collected outside the Setapak Jaya flat was from a female."

Samsiah raises her eyebrows.

"Don't get excited, the samples collected could be from another accident. I asked the standby detective to make some inquiries to find out if there was another such event recently."

"What else are you withholding from Sherry?" Samsiah demands.

"I take offense at that, ma'am," Mislan replies, faking hurt. "I only just found out about the result and did mention it to her in passing."

"OK, I'm sorry. It was uncalled for," Samsiah apologizes with a smile.

"Apology accepted."

Sherry smiles in amusement. "You buy that, ma'am?"

"I'm giving him the benefit of the doubt. What else do you have?"

"This is just a hunch. I've been studying the crime scenes and their victimology."

"Victimology. Big word," Sherry kids.

"TV's a good teacher," he replies. "So what's the link between the vics? Two things, the crimes were committed in apartments, and the vics were lesbians."

The two women eye him, attentively.

"Ma'am, can I smoke? It's been a long day, and my brain doesn't work too well without nicotine," he asks sheepishly.

"Get the ashtray yourself. Lower shelf."

Sherry shakes her head in amazement at Mislan's audacity.

"Thanks." He opens the cabinet, takes out the ashtray, and, leaning against the cabinet, lights a cigarette. "The way I figure it, the selection of the crime scenes was not by choice but by convenience."

"You lost me there," Samsiah says.

"What do gated high-rise tenants have in common?"

"Car stickers," Sherry answers.

"Not all, many of them have done away with car stickers," Samsiah says by way of refuting his argument.

"But not all, and our two vics lived in high-rise apartments that still use windshield stickers. I bet the third vic's management does, too."

"But that still doesn't mean anything," Sherry says.

"It does if the car is sent for servicing or a wash or given to a car jockey. The culprit eyeballs the driver who has been marked as lesbian, notes the name of the apartment, and makes a duplicate of the apartment keys left in the car. They would have all the time in the world to look in the glove compartment for bills or documents for the unit number. Even if they don't find any, how difficult would it be to get that information once you know the apartment building?"

"Good theory, but too elaborate and painstaking," Sherry muses.

"I watched the videos five or six times, and the more I view them, the more convinced I am that the crimes were painstakingly planned and executed. There's nothing to indicate these were crimes of lust or opportunity. The vics were selected, possibly monitored for days, weeks, even months, before they were raped." He shakes his head. "These are definitely not two-men jobs. And I won't be surprised if they have a list of potential vics."

Sherry shivers. "That's frightening."

"You theorize that Ape-Man was financed. What do you mean by that?" Samsiah probes. "Are you saying there's an individual, or a group, behind him . . . a brain behind these rapes?"

"I don't think Ape-Man has the resources—or the brains. So far, we know of two laptops and, probably, two video cams. There could be more, and that takes financing. We also know there are, at least, two rape teams using the same MO. There could be more out there, waiting for a signal from their controllers like suicide-bomber squads waiting in their cells, brainwashed for the 'cause,' whatever that may be. These are simple-minded men and women who don't have the money to finance, or the capacity to plan, the crimes."

"That's one hell of a theory," Sherry says.

"You're saying Ape-Man and others like him are being manipulated or brainwashed into raping lesbians?" Samsiah prods him. "How did you come up with that?"

"I was prompted by Dr. Safia. She drew my attention to the user-name, Emancipatist, which should be 'Emancipator,' a person out to free others, a liberator. Initially, I took that as a creative username that they coined. But she told me about an article she read on rapes in South African, Zimbabwe, and Thailand. Put the username together with the anti-LGBT movement and the victimology, and it all adds up."

The two women stare at him.

"To be specific, corrective rape," he whispers, as if the term is taboo.

45

SHERRY'S CELL PHONE RINGS, and Saifuddin's excited shouts can be heard by others in the office without being placed on speaker.

"The Emancipatist's online again. He's now at Pelita restaurant Jalan Ampang . . . yes . . . a minute ago . . . no, not the same computer . . . the MAC address doesn't match," he says, answering a salvo of rapid questions from her.

"Pelita Jalan Ampang," she says to Mislan while still hanging on to the phone with Saifuddin.

Mislan is already on his cell phone to Johan, barking instructions for the task force team to get moving.

"Get the team to Pelita Jalan Ampang . . . Yes . . . close to KLCC."

"Give me more," Sherry asks.

"I'm trying to get more," Saifuddin replies agitatedly.

"OK, stay on him."

"Another posting?" Samsiah inquires.

"Is he posting a video?" Sherry asks.

"No . . . I mean, not yet."

"OK, we're on the move. Keep us updated," she says, terminating the call.

"Jo has mobilized the team," Mislan says.

"Let's go."

"Be careful," Samsiah calls after the two officers.

Outside the police headquarters, they hit the evening crawl. Mislan squeezes the car to the side, half-riding the curb, annoying other drivers, who honk, swear, and give him the finger. He almost rams into a motorbike.

"You're going to get somebody killed," Sherry scolds him.

"Where the hell is Jo when I need him?"

"What has Jo got to do with this?"

"He was once in the MPV squad and he does this better than . . . Fuck! . . . asshole."

"Watch out!" Sherry screams as a car cuts in front of them.

"Call Sai, and ask him if Emancipatist is still on the net."

Sherry puts the call through.

"Yes."

"What about the team, are they there yet?"

"They'll call in once they're there. Here, here . . . Cut through here and go onto Jalan Sultan Ismail, next to Sungei Wang Plaza. Then you take Jalan Perak and P. Ramlee. That's the shortest route."

Mislan swerves into a side lane, missing a hawker by inches. He is instantly rewarded with honking from vehicles behind and screams from pedestrians.

"That was close," he says in relief.

Sherry's cell phone rings. The task force is in position.

Sherry calls Saifuddin. "Is he still on?"

"Yes, and I've got its MAC address. It's a Samsung."

"Good job. Keep us informed." She calls the task force to tell them the Emancipatist is still online. "Spread around and monitor the situation. Identify Samsung users."

"Tell them to cover all exits but not to move in until we arrive," Mislan tells her.

Approaching the junction of Jalan Sultan Ismail and Jalan Raja Chulan, he hits the accelerator.

"Slow down, take a right at the traffic light, then keep left until Jalan Perak," Sherry says

"It's quicker this way. I'll cut into P. Ramlee at the next traffic light."

Passing the Petronas Twin Towers entrance, Mislan swears.

"Damn it, we're on the wrong side of the street. We'll have to go all the way to Ampang Park to make a U-turn."

"Park on this side of the street, and we'll walk across to Pelita," Sherry suggests.

He sees an opening on the street and pulls in recklessly, amid loud honking and screeching tires.

"Are you crazy?" Sherry screams.

He kills the engine and gets out of the car. "Nothing's happened, right?"

As they cross the street to Pelita, they see two task force members at the two gates and several more seated inside. Mislan counts nine customers with laptops, and about an equal number using tablets.

He turns to Sherry, bewildered. "How the hell do we know who he is?"

"Look for someone with a Samsung."

He walks into the restaurant as if looking for a table. Sherry notices him nodding to the task force members seated around the restaurant. Before she can say anything, Mislan walks to the center of the restaurant, his sidearm drawn and displayed high in the air.

He shouts, "Police . . . don't anyone move!"

The crowd falls silent, shocked by the sight of a man holding a gun. A heavily built customer sitting near Mislan panics and scampers out of his chair. His foot catches the leg of a table, sending him tumbling. The lightweight aluminum tables go crashing to the floor, and the occupants scuttle away as plates of curry, roti canai, and drink glasses fly through the air.

Sherry hurries to the front holding her authority card above her head, shouting.

"We're the police, please calm down, and be seated," she appeals, repeatedly.

She tells some customers to help the large man back to his feet, but they only stare at her blankly. Mislan steps in, barking more orders.

"This is a police raid. Please stay where you are. Anyone trying to leave will be arrested."

His tone, the handgun, and Sherry's authority card finally get the message across to the customers.

Coming close to Mislan, Sherry says, "What the hell were you thinking?"

"Trying to catch the Emancipatist, remember? The rapist, the killer," he hisses back.

Stepping away from her, Mislan announces.

"Listen up, please place your laptops, tablets, and cell phones on the table and remain seated."

He signals to the task force members to close in, telling them to detain anyone with a Samsung. He paces around, looking at the customers. Moving from table to table, he apologizes for the inconvenience, telling owners of equipment other than Samsung to keep it.

Sherry sees a laptop on an empty table. She walks to one corner and scans the growing crowd on the street. After a while, she's convinced the occupant and probable owner of the laptop on the empty table has disappeared. Most likely during the commotion when her crazy partner decided to play Dirty Harry. She signals him over and points to the laptop.

"It's a Samsung. Where's the owner?" Milan asks her.

"Gone."

He turns to the next table and asks the occupants if they'd noticed the person at the table with the laptop.

"A man was using the laptop," one of them says.

"Can you look around at the crowd, tell me if you see him," Mislan says.

The man looks around and shakes his head.

"Do you remember how he was dressed?"

"He was wearing a white T-shirt."

"Thank you. I need you to describe him to my men."

Mislan sees a closed-circuit camera on the wall and asks Sherry to check if the cameras are operational and if they can get a copy of the recording. He instructs Johan to get a full description of the missing man and bag the laptop.

"Jo, send it to D10 for prints before handing it to Sai."

46

SUPERINTENDENT SAMSIAH SITS QUIETLY as Burhanuddin rants on and on about the incident at Pelita restaurant, the calls he has been getting, and the promise of civil action against the department.

"Who the hell does he thinks he is? Threatening customers at gunpoint, causing panic at a tourist spot? The Pelita management has him on video and is threatening civil action against the police. I promise you, when this hits tonight's prime-time news, his ass is fried. You can expect yours to be, too." He pauses for breath. "I told you, he's trouble. Does he think he's above the law? But you choose to keep him and protect him. You disregarded my instructions to cut him loose, to transfer him to a desk job. What have you got to say for yourself now?"

Samsiah isn't in the mood for a confrontation and remains quiet.

"I've asked ISCD to deal with him. I've suggested he be immediately suspended from active duty. He's a bloody disgrace to the force."

ISCD refers to Integrity and Standard Compliance Department, previously known as Disciplinary Department, the equivalent of Internal Affairs.

———

Mislan and Sherry are waiting outside the office of Superintendent Samsiah when she returns. She signals them to follow her. Sitting down, she calmly says, "Explain to me what happened, and why."

Sherry glances at Mislan, as if saying "Let me explain." He nods and leans back. She starts from when Saifuddin told them that the Emancipatist was online and finishes with the abandoned laptop.

"Enlighten me. Why did you feel a need to display your handgun?"

"This may sound silly," Mislan says sheepishly. "At that moment, I felt it was the only way to get the customers' attention and ensure they follow my instructions."

"By intimidation and threat?" Samsiah mocks him.

"There was no intimidation nor was any threat made or intended. The handgun was not pointed at anyone. I wasn't even holding it in a shooting grip. I held it in a display grip, in my palm."

"Couldn't you have attracted their attention or gotten them to follow your instructions by displaying your authority card?"

"In my honest opinion, no. Not instantly, as they were engrossed with chatting and their food. I wanted to stop the culprit from deleting evidence from the laptop," he says in earnest. "Sherry held up her authority card. A lot of good that did."

Sherry tries not to roll her eyes.

"The thing is, ma'am, our authority cards look like company IDs," Mislan continues. "Unless one looks at it closely, no one knows what it is. It's not like TV cops that carry badges or shields. I didn't have the time to walk around the restaurant showing my authority card to every customer and to wait for them to read it before moving to the next. But a gun—well, everyone knows what that is."

"You have an answer for everything, don't you?"

"Certainly not *everything*, ma'am."

"Try and find an answer for this. The case has been referred to ISCD, and the OCCI is demanding that you be suspended from active duty immediately, pending inquiry into your conduct."

Somehow Mislan doesn't seem surprised. He shrugs and smiles.

"He can't do that," Sherry bursts out in defense of her partner. "We're so close to solving the cases."

"Go tell him that," Samsiah snaps at her.

The two officers are silenced.

"You said the restaurant has CCTV cameras. Have you got a copy of the recording?"

"Yes, it's with Sai."

"Did it also capture the gun-toting fool?"

"I'm not sure. I've not viewed it yet," Sherry says.

She calls Sai and, cupping the mouthpiece, tells them that there is footage of Mislan with his handgun.

"Wonderful, tell him to make a copy for me," Samsiah says, swiveling her chair toward the window. Without looking at them she continues, "Today's Friday, I'll try and delay ISCD. You'll have until Monday before they come after you. You've got the weekend: use the time to close the case."

"Thanks, ma'am," Mislan says.

"Don't thank me. I'm doing it for the victims and their families and because Sherry says you're close to solving the case. They've suffered enough, and taking you off the case will only prolong their suffering. This time, I'm throwing you to the dogs. Now, get out of here before I change my mind."

————

They stop by Forensic, and Kevin tells them his team managed to lift several fingerprints from the laptop. He has also taken swabs from the keypad and sent them for DNA analysis.

"Any match on the prints?"

"No, but I've asked my men to try the national registration data-bank. That'll take time."

"Thanks."

Johan and Deena are watching the video from Pelita when the two officers enter the task force room.

"Boss, you look good on camera." Johan jokes.

"Sai, have you made a copy for ma'am?" Sherry says, ignoring Johan.

"Done."

"Deena, can you send it to ma'am's office?" she tells her detective.

"Let's see who was at the table with the Samsung," Mislan says.

"The table is not covered by the cameras," Saifuddin says.

"Shit," Mislan swears. "What about the laptop, is it the one used to upload the video?"

"The MAC number matches, and I'm going through its activity log now."

"Is the video still on the laptop?" Sherry asks.

"It has been deleted, but I'm performing a diagnostic on the hard disk to see if it was once stored there."

"If it has been deleted, how can you find it?"

"When you delete something, it doesn't mean it's wiped out. It's still on the drive, and that's where geeks like me come in," Saifuddin says. "Deleted material is only wiped out or overwritten when all available storage space in the hard disk is used up."

"Are you able to check the Emancipatist's emails?"

"No. Having somebody's computer doesn't mean you have the password to the owner's email account."

The computer next to him beeps. Saifuddin turns to check the screen. "OK, the video was once stored in the hard disk. I can say with certainty that this was the laptop used to upload the rape video."

"Jo, find out where this Samsung was retailed and get the buyer's particulars," Mislan tells him. He then walks to the window, pushes it open, and lights a cigarette. "Chances are it was stolen, just like the Apple," he says as an afterthought. Leaning out the open window, he says to himself, "We've the Ape-Man, the nasi lemak man, a Samsung laptop, some fingerprints, and a DNA profile. Put them together, and we've nothing. We're running in circles: how the hell do we link them?"

The task force team watches him silently, hardly hearing what he's saying as his voice is drowned out by the noise of traffic from the open window. He turns abruptly and faces them.

"What about the woman?"

Johan pulls out his notepad, "The car's registered to Umi Kalsom Ali, a single mother living at 24, Medan Athinahapan 2, TTDI. She says her son Hisham uses the car. Syed and Jeff have gone to his workplace to pick him up. They should be back soon."

"You think the woman is part of this?" Sherry asks.

"I don't know what to think anymore," he says with a sigh. "I feel like we're chasing soap bubbles. Every time we get close to a bubble, it bursts." He turns toward the window and flicks his cigarette out. "Sherry, can you get the case files? We need to go over them to see where we are and what we need to do. In the meantime, I need the task force to go through the daily routines and movements of the three vics."

"Any specific areas?"

"Anything to do with their cars. I want to know where they're repaired, serviced, washed, and parked. And who used them apart from the vics."

"OK."

"And no one goes off for the next forty-eight hours." He lights another cigarette, "Jo, have you eaten?"

Johan shakes his head.

"Can you pick something up? I'm hungry." He gives Johan fifty ringgit. "Get me spicy mee goreng with a fried egg on top, iced black coffee, and a packet of cigarettes. Ask the others what they want."

Johan's cell phone rings. He answers it and tells Mislan that Syed and Jeff are back with Hisham, the car owner's son.

"They can get the food then. You and Deena interview Hisham."

———

Mislan and Sherry are going through the investigation papers when Superintendent Samsiah comes into the task force room, followed by Johan and Deena.

"What a mess," Samsiah says. "Is this how you guys work? Can you clear away all the empty Styrofoam packets and plastic bags? And get a proper ashtray, if you want to smoke."

Sherry and Deena clear the table.

"We missed our lunch," Mislan answers lamely. To Johan, he says, "What did you get from Hisham?"

"His girlfriend borrowed his car, and he's asking her to come down to the station to talk to us. Jeff and Syed are with him. They'll call me when she comes."

"Where's the car?"

"Downstairs. We inspected it. Nothing."

"Did he say why his girlfriend borrowed the car?"

"She needed to pick up some college assignments from her study group."

"That's what Stutterer said."

"His name is Karim," Sherry reminds him. "We're going through the statements and evidence to see if we can link what we have. Ma'am, would you like to sit in?"

"Yes, but first, Jo, can you get a fan in here and open a few more windows. This place stinks like a cheap bar."

Johan and Saifuddin disappear and come back with a stand fan and an ashtray.

"Let's start with the first case," Mislan suggests. "Sherry, you want to take us through that?"

Sherry stands beside the case's whiteboard display, and goes through the evidence, then moves on to the second case. When she finishes, Mislan suggests that she leave aside the third case for later.

"Why aren't you considering the third case?" Samsiah asks.

"We only have the case brief at the moment, and it could mislead us. We need to sight the IP. For our investigations, I'd like to treat that case separately."

"And?"

"From the video recordings, we can establish that the rapist in the Shah Alam case wasn't the same person as in the first two cases. However, my gut says they're linked."

"OK, let's see what the first two cases have in common," Samsiah agrees.

"The MO. Both victims claimed the rapists woke them from their sleep," Sherry points out. "Both crimes occurred in high-rise apartments, and there're no signs of forced entry. And, as Mislan has pointed out, both victims were gay."

"Don't forget, the knife used was also identical," Saifuddin butts in. "Both videos were uploaded by a person with the username Emancipatist, using the same Apple laptop."

"Wahab, a petty thief, steals a laptop and sells it to Ape-Man, who claims to have then sold it to an unknown person. Nasi lemak man, who heads an anti-LGBT group, knows Ape-Man through their activities, but is not associated with him," Sherry continues.

"You now have the Samsung laptop, which was used to upload the third rape video," Samsiah states. "Have you checked who the owner is?"

"It was bought by a company, ACE Constructions in Sungai Buloh, and issued to their project manager. His car was broken into at Damansara Uptown about seven months ago, and the computer was reported stolen," Johan answers.

"Was Wahab questioned about it?"

"Yes, he denies having anything to do with it. It's not his style, he says. He prefers easier targets, like spoiled rich college kids. Less chance of it being reported to the police."

"Smart man," Mislan says, running his fingers through his hair. "So, what are we missing?"

"The Apple laptop," Deena says.

"And how's that going to link Ape-Man to the rape and murder?" Mislan asks.

The team looks at one another for answers.

"One, it's going to link the person in possession of it to the murder-rape. Ape-Man may not be the rapist, but it will definitely link him to the crime," Sherry says.

"What if the Apple laptop had already been disposed of? And the Samsung's what they use now?"

The team looks at Mislan.

"Do you think they'd do that?" Johan asks.

"I would, if I found out the police have IDed my laptop."

"How would they know that?"

"Criminal intuition, paranoia, I don't know. I'm only asking what if."

"Sai, you've been quiet. This is your area of expertise, what do you think?" Samsiah asks, catching Saifuddin off guard.

"Eh, sorry."

"From the IT point of view, is there any way you can tell who used the computer and get a lead on them?"

"There's no way I can tell that until he goes online and I catch him red-handed. However, evidence-wise, I can. Like this Samsung computer, the log shows that it was used to upload a video."

"Hmmm. So we still need a suspect to crack the case." She turns to Mislan and Sherry, "How sure are you that Ape-Man is the rapist?"

Mislan shrugs.

"Can I suggest something?" Saifuddin says meekly.

All eyes turn toward him.

"It can't be used in court, but it may give you some indication if Ape-Man was the rapist. I downloaded a voice comparison software and have been toying with it for a while. The spectrographic analysis of my voice was amazingly accurate and—"

"Skip the technicalities and get to the point," Mislan cuts him off.

"Why don't we get Ape-Man to record the exact words in the video? I'll run it through the software and see how they match. You can take it from there."

"Good suggestion," Samsiah compliments him. "I want it done on video, so we can read his face as well. Sherry, I want you to do it. Perhaps a woman will bring out the real him."

"Ma'am, anything from SB?" Sherry asks.

"I don't know. They've not come back. I'll call them later."

"I'd like to work on the suspects we gave them," Mislan says. "The SB interviews won't focus on our cases, and I'm sure those guys know, or at least heard, of the events. I mean, the vics were their targets."

"I'll speak to SB and see if they're done with them. Lan, there's another thing about the victimology. They're all Muslim women."

"I thought of that, too, but I've been trying to avoid stepping on a religious minefield," Mislan admits, smiling.

"This is a murder and rape investigation; race and religious sensitivities have no place in it." Samsiah says. "So, what are your thoughts about that?"

"LGBT people have been labeled as deviants who are threatening the faith and are polluters of society. They're condemned on a daily basis in the media." He lights a cigarette. "So I wouldn't be surprised if an extremist group has decided on its own remedy."

"So you think the rapes are the result of strong anti-LGBT sentiment running through a particular group?"

Mislan nods.

"OK, I'll talk to SB about that, too, to see if they can give us any inside info on these groups." Samsiah stands to leave. "At least one thing's on our side."

"That is?"

She points to the Samsung, "They know we're on to them. Let's hope that stops the rapes."

"Until they feel it's safe to continue," Mislan broods.

"Get cracking. The clock's ticking."

47

MISLAN GLANCES AT HIS cell phone screen. It is 4:10 p.m. He tells Sherry he wants to revisit Ape-Man's apartment.

"Why?"

"I can't just sit around, I need to do something. In the meantime, can you go over Ape-Man's cell phone and identify as many of his contacts as you can? For that, you may want to ask his housemates."

"Anything else?"

Mislan shakes his head.

"Can we meet back here at eight? We'll go through what we have."

"Sure thing."

———

Leaving the contingent headquarters, they drive to Danau Rebung Apartment in Sungai Buloh in silence. Johan takes the North-South Expressway and exits at Sungai Buloh toll. Traffic is building up as office workers leave for the day. Mislan's cell phone rings.

"Mislan."

"Hey, what're you doing tonight?" It's Dr. Safia.

"Working."

"I thought it's your day off." She sounds disappointed.

"It was, but something came up. What's up?"

"Some friends asked me to join them for some music and drinks, thought you might want to come. Take your mind off the case for a bit," she tempts him.

"I'd love to, but I don't know what time I'll be free."

"It's OK. Call me when you're free, and, if we're still there, you can come join us. Hey, take it easy."

Johan glances at his boss.

"Why don't you go join her after this? Music, drinks, and good company will do you good. Clear your head a little and maybe find a way to work around this disciplinary thing."

Mislan is silent.

"That thing you said about extremist religious groups, you know you can get into trouble for that," Johan cautions his boss.

Mislan looks at his detective sergeant but doesn't respond. He doesn't want a debate or argument. He knows there's little point in getting worked up about things he can't change. Johan drives into the compound of the apartment block and finds a parking spot.

"You've got the keys?" Mislan asks.

Johan nods. "I brought a search list, just in case. Don't you think it'd be better if we had brought him along?"

"We'll look around first. If we find something, then we'll do the search again with Ape-Man present."

"You're the boss."

As they step out of the elevator on the Ape-Man's floor, Mislan notices a pair of male shoes in front of the unit. He signals to Johan to stop and points to them. It's common practice for shoes to be taken off before entering a house, especially a Malay house.

"Someone's home."

He motions to Johan to take one side of the door and takes up his own position on the other. Drawing his sidearm, Johan bangs on the door and shouts, *"Police! Open the door!"*

They hear something crash inside the apartment. Mislan gestures to Johan. The detective sergeant slots in the key and cracks the door open. A man appears from the kitchen, holding a knife threateningly.

Mislan points his gun to the man's head.

"Police. Drop the knife and get down on your knees."

The man continues to glare at them, twirling the knife menacingly.

Mislan smiles. "You want to take the chance and see if you're quicker than a nine-millimeter bullet?"

The man smirks and drops the knife.

"Get down on your knees and put your hands behind your head."

The man growls and takes his time to get down on his knees.

"That's my boy, kneel to Mr. Beretta."

He signals to Johan, who leaps forward, kicks the knife away, and cuffs the man. Johan pulls out the man's wallet and reads his name from his identity card. "Azuandin Hamzah." Johan grabs him by the collar, jerks him to his feet, and pushes him onto the sofa.

"Mr. Azuandin, let's introduce ourselves. I'm Inspector Mislan, and this is Detective Sergeant Johan. Now, it's your turn to tell us who you are and what you're doing here."

Azuandin stares at him unblinkingly, biting his lower lip.

"I know you don't live here, or do you?"

Mislan walks toward the kitchen and notices a table and a fallen chair in the bathroom.

"What do we have here?"

Stepping into the bathroom, he sees a half-opened ceiling board.

"Ah-hah, were you keeping something or looking for something?"

Johan grabs the detainee by the shirt, dragging him to the bathroom. "What were you looking for?"

The detainee wriggles away from his grip, swearing under his breath.

Johan grabs the detainee's hair with one hand and, with his other hand, holds his chin in a viselike grip.

"What were you looking for up there?" he says into the detainee's ear.

The detainee twists his head, glares at Johan, and hisses. "Your sister."

In one motion, Johan's hand goes from Azuandin's chin to his testicles. "What were you looking for?" he asks again, coolly.

The detainee squirms. "Your . . . arrrgh," he screams in agony as Johan squeezes his balls.

"I didn't hear you, what did you say?"

The detainee drops to his knees and Johan does likewise, maintaining his grip.

"Again, what were you looking for up there?" he asks calmly.

The detainee falls backward, freeing his testicles from Johan's grip, and rolls on the floor yelping.

Mislan signals to Johan with his eyes, giving a slight shake of his head to tell his assistant that's enough.

Johan stands, staring down at the detainee. "Don't you ever bring my family into this, you piece of dung."

To divert his detective sergeant's anger, Mislan says, "Jo, call D10 and ask them to send a team here. Get Syed and Jeff to bring Stutterer here, too."

"Karim?"

Mislan nods and makes a call to Sherry.

48

WHILE WAITING FOR FORENSIC and the detectives to bring Karim, Mislan steps out to the corridor for a breath of fresh air. *This has to be it. This has to be the break we need.* He has forty-eight hours to get closure before he is pulled off the case and placed under suspension.

Come Monday morning, the Integrity, Standard Compliance Department will serve you your suspension letter. Well, you deserve it for being such an idiot. This time, even ma'am can't help you. You'll be lucky if you don't take her down with you or, for that matter, Sherry.

He takes a long deep breath, filling his chest.

"If they want my job, they can have it," he says aloud, letting out his frustration.

He sees the Forensic vehicle pulling into the compound, followed by Sherry's car. He watches as Sherry and Deena lead Karim to the staircase. He glances at the time on his cell phone screen and sighs, acutely conscious of the passing minutes. The D11 officers appear with Karim from the elevator, followed by the Forensic team. He tells Sherry and the Forensic supervisor to check the bathroom ceiling.

Pulling Karim aside, he points to Azuandin sitting in the living room.

"Who is that?"

"Az . . . Az—

"I know his name's Azuandin," Mislan retorts. "Is he one of your housemates?"

"N . . . n . . ." Karim shakes his head. "He's Ra . . . Ra . . . Radin's friend. I, I, I don't know him. He al . . . al . . . always goes out w . . . w . . . with Ra . . . Ra . . . Radin only."

"Is he a member of the same anti-LGBT group as Radin?"

"I . . . I . . . I only hear them ta . . . talk about it. Ra . . . Ra . . . Radin never t . . . ta . . . talks about it to me."

"What did you hear them talk about?"

"Me . . . me . . . meeting."

"What meeting, where?"

"In P . . . P . . . PJ."

"Where in PJ?"

"I . . . I . . . don't know."

"Who else from this house goes to the meeting?"

"I . . . I don't know."

Johan alerts Mislan that Forensics found something hidden in the ceiling near the water tank. Mislan tells Deena to watch Karim and goes into the bathroom, where a Forensics team member is standing on a chair placed on a table, his head and shoulders above the ceiling.

"What is it?" Mislan asks.

"Looks like a backpack wrapped in a garbage bag," the technician says.

"Snap some photos of it first," the supervisor instructs him.

"OK, hand me a camera," he says to the team's photographer.

"It's on auto; just click the shutter. Take a few shots to be sure."

The technician returns the camera when he's done.

"Now, take out the bag and hold it at the opening in the ceiling. I need pictures of you doing that," the photographer says.

Sherry, who has already snapped on her latex gloves, grabs the backpack as it is lowered, unzips it impatiently, and exclaims: "It's a laptop."

The cameraman takes a few more pictures of the backpack with the laptop inside.

"Please let it be an Apple," Sherry says softly, as she pulls out the computer. She sees the Apple logo and cries out excitedly.

"We've got it."

Deena comes running to the bathroom, dragging Karim by his shirt. "Let me see it, let me see it."

Mislan and Johan laugh at the sight of her dragging the terrified Karim. Just then, Johan realizes no one is guarding Azuandin in the living room. He dashes out just in time to see the detainee's leg disappearing out the door.

Johan shouts, "He's getting away!" and runs after him.

Mislan and Sherry rush to the living room. They hear a heavy thud followed by a scream as Johan's flying rugby tackle brings down the escaping Azuandin in the corridor.

Mislan catches up with them and yanks the detainee up by his hair. His clenched fist is ready to deliver a blow, when Sherry catches hold of his hand.

"No Mislan, you don't want to do that," she says calmly.

"Like hell I don't."

Johan gets up and pulls the detainee away from his boss. Even so, Mislan manages to deliver a kick to the detainee's buttock. Then he leans against the railing and lights a cigarette. Sherry joins him and asks for one.

After several quiet puffs she asks, "You OK?"

"Why shouldn't I be? We've got the evidence to link Ape-Man and that asshole to the case."

"Yes, we do, and all due to your instincts and perseverance. Look, Mislan, I'm not going to bullshit you. It's not easy working with you, and your methods are beyond anything I've experienced. But I can see you always devote yourself to the case, and you're hell-bent on getting closure. Those are qualities I don't really possess or have observed in others I've worked with." She takes a light puff on the cigarette. "If you need me to testify on your behalf at the disciplinary hearing, I'm all yours."

He glances at her.

"I mean it. Just say the word."

"Thanks, but I don't need you to lie for me. I did what I thought was best. I don't regret it. I only hope I don't take ma'am or you down with me."

"In these investigations we're partners, remember that."

She crushes her cigarette and walks back into the apartment.

Mislan's cell phone rings.

"Yes, ma'am."

"I heard the news, well done. Are you still there?" Samsiah asks.

"Yes, Sherry is tidying up."

"Is she still holding a team debriefing at eight?"

"Yes," he says, looking at his cell phone screen, "but I guess it'll be slightly delayed. We have to clean up here first."

"Let me know when you arrive. I'd like to sit in."

"You're still at the office?"

"Yes. Lan, tell the team 'well done.'"

49

Superintendent Samsiah and Assistant Superintendent of Police Amir Muhammad from the ISCD watch the video obtained from the Pelita restaurant. The footage started with the customers suddenly looking up from their food at something that caught their attention. Some customers were seen hastily backing away. Inspector Sherry appeared with a hand raised over her head, holding her authority card. She appeared to be saying something. Moments later, Inspector Mislan stepped in front of her with both hands raised to the ceiling. In his right hand his service Beretta and his left palm opened facing outward. He, too, seemed to be addressing the customers. The two officers exchanged words, and Inspector Sherry disappeared from camera range. After a few seconds, Inspector Mislan also disappeared from the frame.

"What do you think of it?" Samsiah asks.

"Looks harmless enough, but drawing his sidearm in a situation like that is going to be hard to justify," Amir says.

"I'd love to know what he was saying," she says. "On second thought, it'd be better if we don't."

"What was his justification?"

"That the public doesn't recognize police authority cards and that he needed the customers to stop whatever they were doing instantly."

Amir looks at her quizzically.

"They're looking for someone who was online at the restaurant at that moment. He was afraid the suspect would delete evidence from the laptop. In his skewed mind, the public recognizes handguns and will respond to a demand by a man with a gun. In some ways, he's right. Look at Sherry holding up her authority card. No one seems to give a damn."

"He may be right, but the rule for drawing a sidearm is clear: only when the officer's life, or that of others, is in danger, and I don't see any of that," Amir says. "He was using his sidearm as an authority card to attract attention and to get the public to comply. That's a no-no," Amir summarizes.

Samsiah agrees with him. "Do what you need to. Hopefully, it'll knock some sense into his thick skull."

"But there is something else, right?" Amir says, noting the look on Samsiah's face.

Samsiah nods. "I need you to slow-paddle this one, maybe to Tuesday. He's making headway into the cases and taking him out now will delay it. . . . I don't know how long. It could even turn the cases cold."

"The UTube Serial Rapes?"

Samsiah nods.

"No promises, ma'am. I'll see what I can do."

———

The task force members wait anxiously. Saifuddin has announced the raiding team is on the way back. The atmosphere is one of jubilation and celebration. Someone suggests food and drinks for the raiding party, who would surely not have had dinner. Detective Dorai volunteers to procure some karipap and packed nasi lemak. Detectives Mokthar and Yahaya wash the mugs and make fresh pots of coffee and tea. Saifuddin, who is cleaning the ashtray, suggests they bring back the stand fan.

"Knowing your Inspector Mislan, I expect a long night."

The raiding team comes into the task force room in high spirits and to a rousing welcome. Sherry instructs Deena to put Azuandin in the interview room and send Karim back to the lockup. She informs Superintendent Samsiah that debriefing will start in fifteen minutes.

"What's this?" Sherry asks. "I've never had such a reception from you guys before."

"We thought you'd be hungry," Dorai says. "We all chipped in and got karipap and nasi lemak."

"Thank you. That was really thoughtful of you guys."

Mislan goes for the coffee and lights a cigarette. He looks at the clock and asks Sherry if there's a TV set in the office.

"There's one in the detectives' room. Why?"

"To see if we made the news," he says and heads for the door.

Superintendent Samsiah appears at the door just as Mislan is about to leave. "Where are you going?"

"To the gents," he lies.

"To catch the news on TV, to see if he's made prime time," Sherry snitches, chuckling.

Mislan gives her a dirty look.

"Since when have you been interested in making the news?" Samsiah says, and points him to a chair. "What are you guys celebrating? Has the detainee admitted to the rapes?"

Some shake their heads, and Dorai explains it's in anticipation of a long night.

"Let's start then. Who's chairing?"

"Sherry's the lead, therefore she chairs," Mislan answers, still annoyed with her.

The team is updated on the latest raid and evidence uncovered. Sherry pauses and turns to Mislan with a do-you-want-to-take-over-from-here look. Mislan, who seems to be disengaged from what's going on, misses her offer. Samsiah, noticing the exchange, senses something amiss.

"Lan, what's bothering you?" she asks.

Mislan lifts his head. "Eh?"

"You seem disinterested. Like . . . perhaps we're wasting your time."

"No, no. I'm sorry if I gave you that impression. I was only going through all we have in my head. How do we connect the evidence to our suspects?"

"Would you like to share your thoughts?"

"I think we should let Sherry finish the briefing and instructions so we can let the men off to do what needs to be done."

Samsiah nods to Sherry to go ahead. She concludes her briefing, assigns tasks, and dismisses her team. As the men file out, she asks Johan and Deena to remain. When they've left, she asks, "Sai, what's the result of the voice-match you did on Ape-Man?"

"Inconclusive. Some similarities but not sufficient for a positive match."

"It's Forensic's way of saying they got nothing," Mislan mocks him.

"Not exactly, but close," Saifuddin says, defensively. "You have to understand, voice analysis isn't as simple as fingerprint matching. Pitch and tone vary with situations and moods," he explains. "Even the recording medium—"

"OK, OK, I got it. I'm sorry," Mislan apologizes. "Can you do one on Azuandin?"

"If we can get him to talk," Johan says.

"Make him talk. Get a court order for him to talk, if that's what it takes."

"Can we do that?" Deena asks.

"You can get a court order for anything," Johan jokes.

"Use your charm. We're not going to use the evidence in court," Samsiah says. Addressing Mislan, she says, "Let's hear your thoughts, before we all die from your secondhand smoke."

"Can I make a quick call first?" he asks, pulling out his cell phone.

He walks out of the room and calls home.

"Hey, kiddo. Had your dinner yet?"

"Yes, where're you? Aren't you coming home early today?" Daniel asks.

"Daddy's still at the office. You sleep with Sister tonight, OK."

"OK."

"Kiddo," he takes a deep breath. "About going to the driving range tomorrow, Daddy doesn't think we can. Daddy's got this—"

"It's OK, I want to go play football with Nasir. Can I, Daddy?"

"Sure, kiddo," he says, relieved. "Take some pocket money for drinks and have fun."

"OK, Daddy."

"Daddy's got to go. Love you, kiddo."

"Love you, too."

50

MISLAN GOES OVER THE evidence and facts presented by Sherry. He looks at Sherry, Johan, Deena, and Saifuddin and sees their initial exhilaration being burst. When he finishes, he takes a deep breath.

"I'm not trying to throw a wet blanket over all your achievements. You all did a great job. However, all that we've got till now is circumstantial—incriminating but still circumstantial."

Superintendent Samsiah nods in agreement.

"Where are the direct links between the murder and rapes to the suspects? We can't put any of them at the scene of the crimes, not even in the video." He pauses and takes another deep breath. "No murder weapon, no DNA, no semen-stained clothing, no eyewitness. Hell, we don't even have a solid motive." He sighs. "If we take the case to him now," he says, jerking his head upward, "he'll persuade our ambitious DPP to charge the suspects just so he can look good. The case will get thrown out, and the two will walk."

Samsiah sees the frustration in her investigator's eyes and hears it in his voice. He is a reckless nonconformist and high-handed sometimes. But she has never doubted his dedication.

"Do you have a suggestion?" she asks.

He simply looks at her, defeated.

"We work on the suspects," Sherry says. "We work them until either they break or we do."

"Sai, what else can you give us from the two laptops?" Samsiah asks.

Saifuddin hesitates. "I'm not sure where we stand on this legally."

"What do you mean?"

"I can, if you want me to, break into their emails, but I'm not sure if that'll be breaking any law. It'll be like hacking."

"Do it. We'll think about technicalities later," Samsiah says firmly, taking charge. "Lan and Sherry, organize interview teams for the two suspects. I'll get SB to lend a hand."

The room goes quiet as Samsiah pauses to collect her thoughts.

"What scares me most is the interval between the second and third cases. Only three days."

"They're getting bolder," Sherry says.

"Or they got the go signal," Mislan counters.

"What do you mean?"

"At the risk of sounding like a broken record, I'll say it again. These rapes aren't acts of opportunity or lust. The way I see it, there are several teams out there, waiting and ready to go. Targets have been selected and monitored, preparations have been made, and they're only waiting for the go-go-go order."

"So, who's making the call?"

"I don't know, but if we nail him, the rapes will stop."

"We could work on the ones we have to try and ID him," Sherry says.

"Jo, you and Deena go through all their phones. Look for common contact numbers. Find out whose numbers they are, and get a list of calls made over the last three months."

"Wow, that's going to take ages," Deena says.

"Get the service providers to do the cross-checking; they have the software. It'll only take minutes if you provide them the numbers," Saifuddin interjects. "If they're not willing, I can write a short program for it."

"Good. Let's see if Mislan's right," says Samsiah, ending the briefing.

———

Samsiah signals for Mislan to follow her as she leaves. Sherry stands to follow, too, but Samsiah holds up her hand to stop her. As they walk to the elevator, she asks, "How are you holding up?"

Mislan smiles. "I'm not even thinking about it."

"Is there anything I can do for you?"

"No, ma'am, thanks," he says. "I suppose it's long overdue, and I'm kind of glad it's finally happening. Will be a good experience to see what it's going to do to me. I'm only sorry if my conduct has gotten you or Sherry into a situation."

"You're one weird man. Any other officer would be devastated, but you want to see what it feels like. I should send your DNA for analysis and see if you're human," she jokes. The elevator door opens. Stepping in, she says, "Let me know if you change your mind."

"There's one thing you can do for me."

Holding the elevator door open, she asks, "Name it."

"Can you pressure Fakurrulah? I'm sure the SB has something on these guys. Maybe some low-grade intel about LGBT persecution. That information might give us the lead we need."

"I will," she says, disappointed, having expected something else, something personal.

51

IN THE INTERVIEW ROOM, Mislan is having a staring match with Azuandin, who hasn't said a word since being brought in two hours back. The suspect totally ignores his questions but stares at him expressionlessly. Mislan has no success in breaking him with talk of prison terms. His attempts to provoke him into a debate on LGBT lifestyles ended with similar results. Mislan looks at his cell phone screen for the time. He calls the standby detective to guard the suspect and leaves the room.

His legs wobble. He's mentally and physically exhausted. He tries to remember when he last slept. By reflex, his hand reaches for his pack of cigarettes. "Shit, the last stick." He lights it, crushes the box, and throws it away. He pokes his head through the door of the second interview room, where Sherry is interviewing the Ape-Man, and beckons to her.

"Any progress?"

She shakes her head.

"Still giving me the same story. Yours?"

"Not a word. Can you believe it, two hours and not a damn word," he swears, crushing his cigarette. "Hey, can you get one of the detectives to buy me a pack of cigarettes? I'm all out."

Sherry calls one of the detectives.

"You should slow down a little. Those things are going to kill you."

Mislan ignores her. "How are Jo and Deena doing?"

"I don't know, let's go ask."

———

Stepping into the task force room, he asks no one in particular, "How's it going?"

They look up from their work, and Saifuddin says, "I've gone through the laptops, there're email logs of the original owners but nothing from our suspects."

"How do you know it's the owners?"

"Usernames. One is a company account, and the other is Massayu's. There're no other usernames in the logs. It looks like the laptops were never used for communication."

"It was used only to upload the videos?"

"That's what the logs show."

"I hope you two have better luck," Sherry says to Johan and Deena.

"Records called, said one of the fingerprints lifted from the Apple laptop matched Azuandin but not the Ape-Man. Two more sets are unknown."

"Sherry, can you get Massayu's prints for matching so we can identify the two unknown prints? Ask her if anyone else used her computer and get their prints, too. I don't like loose ends. What about the contact numbers?"

"We've almost finished capturing them," Deena says. "I should have listened to my mother and taken up typing, it's definitely a required skill for a police officer," she quips.

Mislan pulls Sherry aside.

"We need to try some other way to make them talk."

Sherry looks at him suspiciously.

"No, I don't mean beating the shit out of them. That would be very un-police like," he says.

"Then what?"

Detective Dorai enters the room beaming and hands Mislan a small black plastic bag. Mislan peeks at the contents and smiles.

"You can have them after I'm done with it."

"No, thank you. Not my cup of tea," Dorai says.

"Can you organize a computer?"

"On it."

"Let me know when you're done," Mislan tells the detective.

―――――

Sitting next to Sherry, Mislan explains to her what he has in mind. Sherry gazes at him skeptically.

"You think it'll work?"

"I don't know. Worth a try to see the reaction."

"You're desperate, aren't you?"

Mislan nods.

"I don't know if I can pull it," she admits.

"Do the best you can. Work it out with Deena."

"OK, let me discuss it with her."

Sherry gestures to Deena to follow her to her office. Johan looks at her, then his boss questioningly. When Sherry and Deena leave, Mislan explains to Johan what he has in mind.

"Jo, I'm willing to try anything to break these bastards," Mislan admits.

"And if it doesn't work?"

"We'll think of something else."

"Ma'am knows about this?"

"Does she need to?"

"I don't know, does she?"

Mislan shrugs.

"You're already in deep shit with ISCD. Won't this makes it worse if they knew about it?"

"One additional charge won't make any difference to the outcome, would it?"

"If you say so."

―――――

He walks to Sherry's office to find her with Deena intensely discussing their roles.

"You follow my lead." Sherry says, "and don't you go overboard."

"But if I'm to be your bitch, I'll have to be lovey-dovey don't I?" Deena insists playfully. "Otherwise, he'll see we're faking it."

"It's nice to see you both getting into your roles. Make it casual, a slight touch of the hands, a TLC glance, a whisper, a light brush of the lips on the ear," Mislan suggests. "Don't come on too strong. You girls are conducting an interview. It has to look real."

"Wow, never would've thought you'd know so much about it," Sherry mocks him.

Mislan smiles. "I'm good to go. Can you girls finish your rehearsals soon? I want to do it simultaneously."

"Give us five," Sherry says.

———

Mislan sits facing Azuandin, while Johan takes the DVD out of a small black plastic bag and slots it into the computer drive. He clicks play and lowers the volume. The suspect watches with unblinking eyes.

"I brought you a treat," Mislan says.

The image of a woman touching herself appears on the monitor. After a few minutes, another woman appears and they start caressing and kissing.

Mislan notes the suspect looks uneasy, his breathing labored, face contorting, and eyes narrowing. Mislan sees rage, burning rage. The suspect turns his head away from the monitor and screams, "Shut the bloody thing off, you disgusting bastards."

Mislan laughs. He's got the suspect's attention. Johan stands behind the suspect, holding his head firmly, and turns it to face the monitor.

"What's the matter, you don't like seeing sexy naked women?" he asks.

"Go to hell," the suspect curses, shutting his eyes tight.

Mislan increases the volume, and the room is filled with the moaning of pleasure from the two women in the video.

The suspect shakes his head wildly and screams. "Go to hell, traitor of your race and religion, you shall burn in hell. You and the rest of them."

"Not before you," Johan mocks him.

"*Them*, who are *them*?" Mislan asks. "The women you raped?"

The suspect continues to swear at them, screaming for the video to be turned off, accusing them of being heathens and committing mortal sin by enjoying deviant sex.

"How dare you call yourselves Muslim? It's people like you, and those deviants, who defile our religion. Infidel . . . *infidel*. Lesbian lovers . . . infidels!" he sneers.

Mislan and his assistant watch in disbelief as the suspect yanks at the handcuffs, trying to break loose, wailing and cursing. *Shit, this guy is a lunatic. He's willing to break his damned hand to get at the computer.* He signals Johan to turn off the computer. Instantly, the suspect stops yanking at the cuffs and stops swearing, opening his eyes.

Mislan motions to the suspect's bruised hand.

Johan shrugs. "He did it to himself."

Mislan's cell phone rings.

"Mislan."

"Inspector Mislan, Fakurrulah here. Are you still at the office?"

"Yes, sir."

"There's something that might interest you. I'll be there in twenty."

"Sir, we're at D11."

"OK."

———

He tells Johan to organize for a standby detective to guard the suspect. They walk to Interview Room 2, and Mislan signals to Sherry and Deena to step out.

"How?"

"Not biting."

Johan laughs. "Maybe you're not convincing enough."

"How to be convincing? I touch her a little, and she pulls away," Deena complains. "How about yours?"

"Went berserk the minute Jo played the video. He condemned the two of us to an eternity in hell," Mislan says, shaking his head. "It was unbelievable."

"So why are we out here?" Sherry asks.

"Giving him a break, before we screw up his head again," Mislan teases her. "ASP Fakurrulah is on the way here. He says he might have something that could help us."

"I need some coffee. Is there still some?" Sherry says.

"I told Dorai to make a fresh pot."

52

Assistant Superintendent of Police Fakurrulah sips the coffee and frowns. "What's this?" he says, holding up the mug.

"PM," Deena laughs. "Police meth. It's totally legit, designed to keep you awake and hyper all night."

"I thought coffee this bad only existed on TV," Fakurrulah jokes.

He puts the mug on the table and pushes it away.

"OK, going through our files, I noticed this. I thought it might be useful to you."

He pulls out a file from his briefcase and slides it across the table to Mislan.

Sherry leans closer to Mislan, and reads it with him. Her eyes widen.

"How credible is this intel?" she asks.

"Low. It's something we heard on the streets, but we've not assigned resources to it. You know how it is. We get information by the truckload every day. We don't have the resources to follow up on everything we hear out there. If there's no threat against national security, it gets filed away, unless something else comes up."

"You're saying that anti-LGBT movements are not considered a threat to national security?" Mislan asks.

"Not as it stands."

"What about this?"

"As I said, it's something we picked up on the streets. No one gave it a second thought, and that was that."

"What about those guys we picked up, you heard anything about them?"

"Rumors, street gossip, coffee-shop talk." Fakurrulah takes another sip of the coffee and grimaces. "I'll never get used to this. Who drinks this?"

All heads turn to Mislan.

"I guessed as much. You must have the taste buds of a crocodile."

"I thought crocodiles didn't have taste buds," Sherry remarks.

Fakurrulah nods, grinning, and stands.

"You might want to get your men to dig a little deeper, see what comes up."

Mislan closes the file and returns it to him.

"Keep it. That copy is for you. Good luck, and thanks for the coffee, or whatever it was."

The room is silent after Fakurrulah leaves, as if no one wants to be the first to talk. Finally, Saifuddin breaks the silence.

"What's in the file?"

Johan is unsure if Saifuddin, a civilian, is allowed to read a Special Branch file. He looks toward Mislan. Mislan nods, and Johan gives the file to Saifuddin.

"Wow," he exclaims. "Is this for real?"

"I need to talk to ma'am," Mislan declares.

"At this hour? Can't we wait until tomorrow morning?" Sherry asks.

"I need eyes on him. Immediately," Mislan says.

"You really think he's involved?"

"I don't know, but I'm not taking any chances. You're the lead: what's your decision?"

Sherry stares at him awkwardly. "What would you do?"

"Go with it, but then I've got nothing to lose."

The room falls silent again.

"I'm with Inspector Mislan. I say we go for it," Johan says.

"OK, we put eyes on him tonight." Looking at the clock, she corrects herself: "This morning. I'll brief ma'am, first thing when she comes in. In the meantime, let's use this info on our suspects to see their reaction."

"Sai, I want you to search the net for everything you can get on him," Mislan instructs.

"Like what?" Saifuddin asks.

"What don't you understand about the word *everything*?" he barks. "The rest of you, this is on a need-to-know basis."

Deena leans closer to Johan and whispers, "What about the team?"

"In order to be safe, not even them, unless you're sure they're in the loop," Johan whispers back to her.

"Sai, what's the outcome on cross-matching the phone numbers?"

"There're twenty-two common numbers on the three phone lists."

"That's too many. Take out numbers belonging to women. How many would you have left?"

"Let's see . . . nineteen."

"Still too many. OK, get me the numbers calls were made to between midnight and morning, say around seven."

"Why seven?" Sherry asks.

"That's roughly after morning prayers. I figured, if they reported their deeds to anyone, that would be the time, just before or just after the morning prayer."

"Hmmm."

"Two numbers."

"Sherry, can you get one of your men to get the details of the owners from the telco first thing tomorrow morning?"

"I'll get Mokthar to do it."

"You want to continue with Ape-Man?"

Sherry shakes her head. "I'd like to join you with yours."

"Best if you keep at yours with the new info, see if he talks."

53

MISLAN REENTERS THE INTERVIEW room and notes the time on the wall clock. It's just after 3:30 a.m. He sits facing the suspect and nods to Johan, who in turn nods at the detective to leave the room. The suspect glares at them with bleary eyes, his fury still evident. He hisses at them and goes back to his original position, head resting on his folded free arm at the table. Mislan looks at Johan and gestures with his head toward the suspect. Johan takes a step forward and slams hard on the table with both palms. The impact makes the suspect jump off his chair, dragging the table with him with his hand still cuffed to it.

"Fuck you!" the suspect screams at Johan, who steps back smiling and leans against the wall.

"No, thank you," Johan says with a grin.

"Sit down," Mislan says firmly.

The suspect keeps staring at Johan menacingly, ignoring Mislan's instruction.

"Sit down," Mislan snaps.

Azuandin turns his attention to him, staring like a cornered tiger standing his ground.

Mislan smiles at him, making him furious. "*Sit down.*"

The suspect remains standing, glaring at him.

"Suit yourself," Mislan says and tells Johan to remove the chair.

Johan does as instructed and yanks the table back to its original position, tugging the suspect's cuffed hand with it.

Azuandin growls at him.

"Who's Pak Non?" Mislan asks.

"Your bastard father," Azuandin sneers.

Mislan calmly lights a cigarette and takes a drag.

"Who's Pak Non?" he repeats, unruffled.

"Your—"

"Don't," Johan cuts in before the suspect can finish answering. Stepping closer to the suspect, he says, "You don't want to try me."

The suspect makes a mocking face at him. With lightning speed, Johan's hand digs into the suspect's stomach, holding the flesh with his thumb and index finger. The suspect tries to pull away and Johan locks him in an embrace and twists the stomach flesh. The suspect screams. He turns his head around and tries to bite Johan's arm. The detective sergeant twists the flesh harder, and the suspect finally gives in. His face turns red, then white.

"Don't be disrespectful. Don't ever bring family into this. Do you understand?" Johan whispers in his ears.

The suspect yelps, "OK, OK." Saliva drools from his mouth.

"Good."

Johan releases his grip and slowly moves back to his position against the wall without taking his eyes off the suspect. Mislan gives the suspect a few seconds to catch his breath and lick his wounds, before asking him again.

"Who's Pak Non?"

"My uncle."

"What's his full name?"

"Zainon."

"Zainon what?"

"I don't know, just know him as Pak Non."

"Where does he live?"

"PJ."

"Where in Petaling Jaya?"

"I don't know."

"How did Ape-Man, I mean Radin, get to know him?"

Azuandin's eyes widen.

"How does Radin know him?" Mislan repeats.

The suspect remains quiet.

"I'll ask you again, who is Pak Non?" Mislan says, leaning across the table toward the suspect.

Johan straightens, cracking his knuckles.

Sherry pokes her head into the room. "Radin broke. He's given Pak Non away."

The suspect hangs on every word Sherry says. His head bows, and he stares at the floor.

"Great. Offer him a deal. We don't need this fool," Mislan says. "We'll pin the murder on him and make sure the DPP asks for the death penalty."

The suspect lifts his head.

"I didn't murder anyone. You can't frame me for that!" he yells. "I'll talk, if you make me a deal."

Mislan turns to Sherry and winks. She gives him the tiniest of grins and disappears. He places his digital recorder on the table, and Azuandin starts spilling, and by the time he finishes, it is 5:55 in the morning. Mislan instructs Johan to arrange for the suspect to be remanded into custody.

"Get some rest. Tell the team we'll meet at eight. I'll call ma'am to see if she wants to join us."

He goes to Sherry's office and finds her napping.

She sits up with bleary eyes when she hears the door. "So, how did it go?"

Mislan slumps heavily into a chair. "Before I forget, that was a good bluff. Scared him shitless."

"You said it yourself: TV is a good teacher," she says with a laugh. "Did he admit to the rapes?"

"No, but he gave us many leads."

"You mean more work," she says and sighs. "And we don't have much time left."

"You mean, *I* don't have much time left," he corrects her. "Whatever happens, the case is in good hands. How did it go with Ape-Man?"

"Stuck to his earlier story like superglue."

"Doesn't matter, we'll break him later. He's just one of the procurement agents and a target spotter."

"What do you mean by one of? How many of them are out there?"

"Azuandin doesn't know. He doesn't know the others. He only deals with Ape-Man and Pak Non."

"What was his role?"

"It's a damn labyrinth."

54

THE SMELL OF FORTY-HOUR unwashed bodies, soiled clothes, cigarette smoke, stale coffee, and overnight nasi lemak is overpowering. Samsiah gags on entering the task force room. Saifuddin sleepily turns his head from the monitors, flashing her a smile. "Morning, ma'am."

"Morning Sai. It smells like fish-manure in here," Samsiah says. "I know you guys are exhausted, but you don't have to look like bums."

The bleary-eyed officers and detectives straighten up.

"Now that's better," she comments with a warm smile. "Take five minutes and go freshen up. Sherry, get some cleaners in here to clear the mess. I'll stay and make sure they don't get nosy."

The officers and detectives file out, leaving Saifuddin alone with Superintendent Samsiah.

"Why're you still here?"

The Forensic IT technician gawks at her.

"You're part of the team, aren't you?"

Saifuddin nods.

"So?"

Saifuddin jumps off his chair and heads for the door, beaming.

She calls a standby detective and asks him to buy two cans of air freshener. The team filters in looking fresher but smelling the same.

"Now you guys look exhausted but not beaten. Who's chairing?"

All eyes turn on Sherry.

———

Sherry updates her but deliberately leaves out the late-night visit by ASP Fakurrulah from Special Branch and the interview with Azuandin.

"So we still have nothing?" Samsiah sighs.

Mislan asks if Sherry could dismiss the detectives except for Johan and Deena. She agrees and tells them to get some rest in the detectives' room and await further instructions. When all of them leave, she hands the floor to Mislan.

"ASP Fakurrulah came in and gave us this file," Mislan says.

Handing Samsiah the file, he watches her face closely as she reads.

"Interesting. What's the classification on this?" she asks, closing it.

"Low," Sherry answers. "Mostly street talks and gossip. That's the reason they've not allocated too many man-hours to it."

"Who else knows about this?"

"Here, only us. At SB, I don't know, probably many."

"OK, let's keep it small."

"I need eyes on him, but if we're going to keep it small in here, we'll need SB's assistance," Mislan suggests.

"I'll talk to Fakurrulah."

"Sai, can you brief us on what you found out about him on the net?" Sherry asks.

"Not much on him, but I found several blogs with anti-LGBT content. There's this one in particular, AmanatIslam.blogspot.com. Most anti-LGBT stories reiterate the teachings of Islam, nothing radical or inciting. However, some of the comments by followers are pretty provocative and inflammatory."

"Like what?"

"There's this one by SatuUmmah: '*The LGBT movement and proponents of their immoral lifestyle are destroying the nation's image and our religious values . . . We must put a stop to them by whatever means.*' Then there's this other by MelayuJati; '*These practitioners of unnatural sex must be condemned and severely punished according to Islamic laws. They're a serious threat to our race. . . . Either they repent and seek help to revert to the path of God, or face the consequences of their choice.*'"

"Hmmm, can you identify the blogger and the two followers?" Mislan asks.

"It's not easy, but I can try," Saifuddin says. "That's provided you don't ask me how I do it."

"OK, do it. And we don't want to know," Samsiah confirms.

"Be sure you don't get caught," Sherry cautions him.

"How about the suspects? By the way, sorry to disappoint you: you did not make prime-time news," Samsiah says, clearly happy about it. "Maybe there's still hope for you yet."

"Azuandin broke and spilled."

Mislan briefs them on what the suspect has admitted to. When he finishes, he asks Deena if she can make coffee.

"So, Ape-Man is the procurer and spotter, Azuandin is the IT man, and they don't know the identity of the rapists on the videos. And this Zainon, alias Pak Non, is the go-between?"

"Looks like it. According to Azuandin, he gets the CDs from Pak Non, full name Mohd Zainon Mohd Hadi, and uploads them. The username and password come with the CD. That's why it's the same username for all three uploads."

"This means the rapists are still out there," Samsiah emphasizes, her voice filled with concern.

Mislan nods.

"Pick up this Pak Non," she orders them. "Let's see where he leads us."

One of the computers beeps repeatedly and Saifuddin jumps into action.

The IT technician punches a few keys and calls out, "We've got another video."

Everyone around the table scrambles off their chairs as screams of a terrified woman comes over the speakers.

"How could it be? We have their IT man in custody!" Sherry says.

"He's just one of them. Mislan's theory is proving to be right. There could be many more out there." Samsiah steps back from the monitor. "Find out where it happened." When she sees no one making a move, she snaps, "Now!"

Sherry pokes her head out the door and yells for the standby detective. It's Saturday, and only her task force members are in the detectives' room. Her voice echoes eerily through the empty main office. She yells louder, and Mokthar comes running.

"There's been another rape. Find out where it happened. Call the CCC and MCC."

"Freeze it," Mislan says to Saifuddin. "Back a bit. Can you zoom in on the knife?"

Saifuddin crops the knife and brings it up.

"Can you run the third rape video and do the same on the knife?"

Saifuddin turns to the next computer and repeats the process, and brings up the image of the knife into focus.

"It looks the same."

"That doesn't mean anything," Sherry says. "It's not a custom-made knife."

"Look at how he held it. How the thumb's pointed forward along the grip. It's the same person. I bet you this case is in Selangor."

"Good eyes," Samsiah praises him.

Mokthar pops in just then and tells them the case was reported in Kajang, Selangor. Sherry calls the Kajang police and speaks to the investigating officer. Terminating the call, she says, "Same MO. The victim was awoken by the rapists around three in the morning. No sign of break-in, pantyhose over the head, and the condom."

"I'm guessing the crime scene is an apartment, and the vic is a Muslim woman with gay orientation." Mislan says it more as a statement than a question.

Sherry nods.

"Expect more, unless we get the brain, the controller," he says.

"This is getting out of control. We're going to be crucified by the public and the press," Samsiah says, walking back to her chair.

Mislan lights a cigarette and turns to Deena. "Where's the coffee?"

"Sorry, sorry." she says, and rushes out of the room.

"Who's picking up Pak Non?"

"Syed, Jeff, and Dorai."

"Find out what their status is," Samsiah instructs Johan.

55

MISLAN PACES THE TASK force room, chain-smoking. The others watch him silently, fearing the worst. Saifuddin pretends to focus on the monitors, and tries to make himself invisible. Deena comes in with a fresh pot of coffee. Mislan stops pacing to pour himself a mug and notices all the weary eyes on him.

"What?"

They look at one another, and laugh.

Johan tells them that Syed and gang are on the way back with Pak Non. "Where do you want him? Here or in our office?"

"Take him to our office," Samsiah replies.

"Syed says he has a lawyer with him."

"There you go, a sure sign of guilt," Mislan says.

"Sai, where are you with identifying the bloggers and the two followers?"

"Still working on it."

"Work faster," Samsiah says, standing to leave. "Let me know when Pak Non is in. I want to sit in during the interview. Lan, you and Sherry handle it." Walking to the door, she says, "Sai, try to get their identities before the interview is over. If he's the blogger, or one of the followers, we can use that to squeeze him."

————

Superintendent Samsiah's cell phone rings. "Samsiah . . . Yes, Datuk . . . At the office . . . Was just viewing it . . . Yes, Datuk . . . Yes, Datuk."

Switching off the cell phone, she lets out a long sigh.

"What's wrong?" Mislan asks.

"Datuk KP is calling for a meeting at ten." KP stands for Ketua Polis and means chief of police.

Mislan looks at the clock. "About?"

"This case, and D11 Bukit Aman is attending."

"They're taking over?" Sherry asks, clearly sounding unhappy.

"I don't know. Probably. In the meantime, the cases are still ours. Go talk to this Pak Non and see where he leads us."

―――――

Kuala Lumpur's chief police officer, Deputy Commissioner of Police Datuk Zaid Zainal, is in his office, dressed casually. Senior Assistant Commissioner of Police Faridah Manap of the Sexual & Child Abuse Investigations, Federal Headquarters in Bukit Aman, and two other women, also casually dressed, are making small talk when Samsiah enters. She stands to attention in the doorway, and Zaid invites her to join them.

"You know Faridah," Zaid says, "and this is . . . Sorry, I didn't get your name."

"Dr. Suthisa Ritchu, rape behavioral profiler from the Royal Thai Forensic Academy," Faridah introduces her. "And you know DSP Chandramala. Dr. Suthisa is here on the SEA Enforcement Exchange Program."

"Pleased to meet you," Samsiah says, shaking Dr. Suthisa's hand and smiling at Chandramala.

"Where the hell is Burhanuddin?" Zaid looks at his watch. "Let's give him a few more minutes before we start. In the meantime, can I offer you ladies a drink?" He calls his helper, and asks for coffee and tea. "Dr. Suti . . ."

"I know it's not a common name here, but call me Sophia," Dr. Suthisa says.

"Dr. Sophia, how long have you been on the program here?"

"On and off for about four months. I was told of the UTube Serial Rapist by Faridah and asked if I could be part of the team," she says, in a Thai-American accent that makes her sound exotic.

"You specialize in rape behavioral profiling? How's that different from normal criminal profiling?" Zaid asks.

"The fundamentals are the same. The difference, if any, is the forensic community's idiosyncrasy of separating one from the other. Scientific territorialism," Dr. Suthisa jokes. "I see that you've just been out in the field. Golfing?"

"How did you know? I was on the fourth tee when the Director of CID called and told me about this meeting."

"I see pieces of fresh grass and topsoil on your pants."

"Good observation," Zaid compliments her. "Let's not wait for Burhan any longer. The UTube Serial Rapist is whipping the public into a frenzy. Women, especially single women, are afraid of staying alone in their homes. The director is being bombarded with calls, and he wants this case wrapped up before the public starts taking matters into their own hands. Faridah, what do you think?"

"The Director of CID wants us to take over the investigations, but in my opinion that'll set everything back by at least a week. The new team will need time to familiarize themselves with the cases and the evidence gathered so far. Time is what we don't have. But, at the same time, I don't wish to defy the director's order."

Zaid nods. Addressing Samsiah, he asks, "Any suggestions?"

"Before we decide, may I update you on the progress the task force has made in the last twenty-four hours?"

"Excellent," Dr. Suthisa agrees.

Samsiah gives them a quick rundown of the arrests, the seized anti-LGBT booklets, the recovery of the laptops and information obtained from the suspects and the Internet. She leaves out the Special Branch file and Mislan's gun-toting episode at Pelita restaurant.

"Your team has been busy," Faridah compliments her.

"Good work," Zaid says. "So, Faridah, what do you think?"

She leans in for a quick consultation with Deputy Superintendent Chandramala.

"I have to abide by the director's instructions, so we'll be taking over the investigation," Faridah says.

The disappointment on Samsiah's face is obvious.

"However, Samsiah's task force has done a wonderful job in getting to where we are, and we've no intention of taking that away from them. Datuk, may I suggest that, on record, we take over and lead in the investigations. Meaning all formal reports and press releases will come from Bukit Aman. The actual investigation, however, will be done by Samsiah's present task force, with Mala as lead, reporting to Samsiah as her immediate supervisor," she says, referring to DSP Chandramala.

Zaid turns to Samsiah, "How does that sound to you?"

"Thank you, ma'am," Samsiah says, beaming.

"What about Dr. Sophia?" Zaid asks.

"If Samsiah has no objection, I'd like for her to be in the task force," Faridah requests.

"We need all the help we can get," Samsiah says. "At present, we have two officers, Inspector Sherry from D11 and Inspector Mislan from my department, with six detectives. Would it be possible for ma'am to assist us with more detectives?"

"Mala?"

"I can mobilize my team. They're on slack time after that last case in Johor," answers DSP Chandramala.

"Good, that's settled then," Zaid says.

The Officer in Charge of Criminal Investigations appears at the door, panting and sweating profusely.

"Datuk," he manages between huffs and standing at attention. "Sorry for the delay. I was trapped in the elevator for almost an hour," he exaggerates.

"Burhan, you know Faridah, and this is Dr. Sophia and DSP Chandramala."

He nods half-heartedly, preferring to devote his attention to the Chief Police Officer, the only person who matters to him in the room. "I'm really sorry, Datuk. The admin officer should be hauled up—"

"This is not the time or place. There are six elevators, and trust you to take the one that breaks down," Zaid jokes. "Anyway, we're all done here. Faridah is officially taking over the case. All communication with the public and media shall from this moment go through her."

Burhanuddin glares at Faridah. "But—"

"That's final. You have many other cases you can give PCs on. I remind you again, this case is off-limits."

Zaid stands, offers his hand around, thanks everyone, and wishes them luck.

56

DR. SUTHISA AND DSP Chandramala follow Samsiah down to the Sexual
& Child Abuse Investigations office, where they are introduced to Inspector Mislan and Inspector Sherry. Samsiah tells Sherry to take them through
the case to bring them up to speed. When she finishes, she informs her
guests that Sherry and Mislan are about to interview Zainon, a.k.a. Pak
Non. Dr. Suthisa asks if she can witness the interview.

"Yes, you're most welcome, but we don't have a one-way mirrored
observation room, like on TV," Samsiah explains. "You'll have to sit in
with them."

Mislan turns to his boss and raises his eyebrows.

Samsiah ignores him.

"Can I make a video of the interview for review at a later time?"

"I don't see why not."

Mislan objects to his boss, speaking to her in Malay. To his embar-
rassment, Dr. Suthisa assures him in fluent Malay, "Don't worry,
Inspector, I won't interfere with your interview. "

Samsiah, Chandramala, and Sherry smile at the look on Mislan's
face.

Pak Non and Khairul Annuar, his lawyer, stop whispering when the
interviewing team, four women and a man, enters the room. Mislan
tells detective Syed to bring in more chairs. At which point Khairul
jumps into action.

"Why has my client been arrested?"

"Abetting if not involvement in criminal activities: rape and murder to start with," Samsiah answers.

"That's preposterous. My client's a respectable government official, a senior assistant director at the Ministry of Higher Education. The Ministry'll hear of this and—"

"We're aware who he is. The Ministry will be duly informed of his arrest," Chandramala says, cutting him short.

Sherry opens the interview room door and holds it.

"Now, if you'll please allow us to do our work. You can see your client once the interview is over," Samsiah says.

Khairul demands he be allowed to sit in during the interview, citing precedence where politicians have been allowed to be accompanied by counsel during police interviews.

"In those cases, they came in voluntarily to assist police investigations, and I shall not comment on them. Mr. Zainon has been arrested for suspected involvement in criminal activity. Are you a trial lawyer?"

Khairul nods with pride.

"Then you should know the difference."

"I want copies of the statement made by my client," he demands, knowing that, as Zainon's counsel, he's entitled to it.

"Please put in a formal request," Chandramala replies, ushering him through the door.

Syed comes back with several chairs but can't get them all into the cramped interview room.

Mislan says to his boss, "It's obvious we can't fit everyone in here."

"Let's step outside for a moment," she says. Once outside, Samsiah says, "Mislan's right."

The others agree.

"Can we view the interview from a remote location?" Dr. Suthisa suggests.

They all look at her, unsure what she means.

"I mean, through a video stream. Do you have a remote camera that can be linked to a computer?"

"I'm sure that can be arranged." Samsiah says. "Sherry, get Sai to set it up. We can watch the interview from the task force room."

"I'll get Technical Aid to assist with the equipment," Sherry suggests.

———

Saifuddin turns the monitor toward the women and explains the controls. "Press this to zoom in and out, and this one for volume control."

"Is it being recorded at the same time?" Dr. Suthisa asks.

"Yes. I'll burn a copy for you later."

"Thank you."

Samsiah sends a WhatsApp message to Mislan, informing him they're all set up and he can start. Mislan nods to Sherry, switches on his digital recorder, and places it on the table. Sherry introduces herself and Mislan, then she explains to the suspect what is going to happen and administers the caution.

"Do you understand the caution I've just given you?" she asks.

Pak Non nods.

"Is that a yes?"

"Yes."

Pushing the cautioned statement form toward the suspect, she says, "Please sign here to acknowledge that you understood the caution." After he signs, she pushes the document aside and starts, "Would you like to say anything or answer our questions regarding the posting of several rape videos on UTube?"

"What rape?"

"I take that as a yes."

She nods to Mislan. He boots up the laptop, and turns the screen toward the suspect.

A still image of a man wearing pantyhose over his head, holding a knife, and standing over a terrified woman, appears on the monitor. The suspect strains his eyes at the monitor. Mislan watches him closely, but doesn't see any sign of recognition on his face.

"This and several others," Sherry says, pushing the laptop closer to the suspect.

"I don't know anything about it."

"What if I tell you we have a written statement from a man who claims you gave him the videos for upload?"

"You're lying."

"Do you know this man?" Sherry shows him a photo.

Pak Non winces slightly and his eyes narrow, but he replies, "No."

"He claims to be your nephew, Azuandin Hamzah. Don't you know your own nephew?"

"He's lying. I don't know who he is."

"How about this man?" Sherry pushes Ape-Man's photo toward him. "He, too, has given us a written statement saying he knows you."

Pak Non winces again before saying, "I don't know him, either. They're both lying."

"We're lying, they're lying, everybody's lying except you," Mislan sneers. The suspect leans back in his chair, clearly intimidated by him. "And what's the reason for us, and them, to lie?"

The suspect blinks rapidly but doesn't answer the question. Sherry allows a few moments to pass before continuing.

"Do you think we'd arrest a senior government officer without being sure of the evidence we have?"

"Don't take us for fools," Mislan says, leaning back in his chair.

"You come clean with us, and we'll report to our bosses that you're cooperative, and you may still have a job after all this is over. This is your last chance. Once we walk out that door, the offer walks out with us. The next thing you know, you'll be standing in the dock, facing charges for multiple rapes and a murder," Sherry adds.

"You may win the case with your high-priced lawyer. It really doesn't matter, because the media will turn up in droves at your trial. They may even want to talk to your family for stories. What do you think?" Mislan says, toying with him.

From the task force room, Dr. Suthisa watches the suspect's face, body language, and speech patterns, making notes on her tablet.

"Is there a way to communicate with your officers?" she asks.

"I can call them," Samsiah replies.

"Tell them to freeze the video on the victim's face. I'd like to study the suspect's reaction."

"They only have one laptop with them: it'll take time to go through all the four videos of the rapes. Can they do it with still photos?" Samsiah suggests.

"Yes."

"Sai, print out the victims' faces, including the murder victim."

"Clean or gory?"

"The goriest you've got," Dr. Suthisa says.

"Ask the woman officer to show it to him, and do it slowly, one at a time. Give him time to react. Before that, ask him if he has daughters. If he does, suggest to him that one of them could've been his daughter."

Saifuddin hands Dr. Suthisa the photos.

"Here, let me pass these on to Sherry," Chandramala says. "I'll brief her on what to do."

As she leaves, Dr. Suthisa asks if she can smoke.

"Yes, you may," Saifuddin says, jumping off his chair to grab an ashtray from the top of the cabinet. Samsiah smiles at Saifuddin while politely declining Dr. Suthisa's offer of a cigarette. As soon as she lights up, Saifuddin takes out his own pack and lights one himself.

Sherry's voice comes over the speakers. She's asking the suspect about his family. The suspect says he has three children, one boy and two girls. The older girl is fourteen. Dr. Suthisa zooms in to the suspect's face, watching it closely. The suspect flinches slightly when Sherry shows him a photo of the first victim. Dr. Suthisa zooms in on his eyes, and then zooms out to capture his whole body. When Sherry pushes the second victim's photo toward him, he recoils visibly. When Sherry shows him the picture of the murder victim, the suspect turns pale, looks away, and pleads.

"Stop it. Stop it."

"Did it cross your mind that these are somebody's daughters?" Sherry presses. "What if this was to happen to one of your daughters?"

"How dare you?" the suspect says, glaring at her. "My daughters are not lesbians."

"How did you know these women were lesbians?" Mislan pounces. "How the hell did you know that?"

"Yes, how did you know?" Sherry inquires.

The suspect is clearly shaken by his revelation. "It's in the papers."

"No, that has never been reported. How did you know they're lesbians?" Mislan bellows at the suspect. "The only way you could've known is if you're the rapist or the murderer."

"No, no, I didn't rape or murder anyone."

"I don't give a damn if you did or didn't. I've two witnesses linking you to the UTube rape videos, and you've just made a statement that reveals intimate undisclosed knowledge of the crime . . . facts that only the police and the perpetrators knew." Mislan laughs. "That's good enough for me. I'm going to charge you for the four rapes and a murder. I get to close my case, and it's up to you to prove in court that you're innocent."

"You can't do that. I didn't rape or murder them."

"You think the media is going to give a shit?" Mislan hisses, standing to leave. Addressing Sherry, he tells her, "Lock him up and charge him on Monday."

———

After Mislan leaves the interview room, Sherry says, "Well, Pak Non, you heard my boss."

"I swear, I didn't rape or kill anyone. You've got to believe me," the suspect pleads with her.

"If you want me to help you, you'll have to talk to me. Tell me where you got the videos, and how you know Azuandin and Radin."

The suspect lowers his head and stares at the floor in silence. Sherry waits a moment before moving toward him, pretending to unlock his handcuff.

"That's it, then. You can forget about seeing your family as a free man ever again. Rape and murder are not bailable offenses. Come, let's go."

"No, no. I'll talk. Promise me, I'll not be charged."

"No promises. It would depend on what you tell me. I'll take it to my boss."

"Call him back, your boss," Pak Non pleads.

Stepping out of the interview room, she finds Mislan leaning against the wall outside. She smiles at him. "Great move."

"He crack?"

"Like groundnut, and he wants you back."

57

SUPERINTENDENT SAMSIAH, DEPUTY SUPERINTENDENT Chandramala, Inspector Mislan, and Inspector Sherry listen to Dr. Suthisa Ritchu explaining her observations. Freezing an image from the Pak Non interview, she points out, "Here, you see him flinch when he sees the first victim's photo. It becomes more obvious with the second one." She runs the video and pauses it. "This is when he sees the picture of the murder victim. He turns away in horror. That's not the behavior of a psychopath. Psychopaths show no remorse. They're devoid of such emotions, and they usually take pride in their criminal work."

"So, do you think he was a participant in the act?" Samsiah asks.

"His hatred for gays is obvious. Here." She stops the video at another point. "Here you see how he backs away, trying to distance himself from any discussion concerning LGBTs. In his mind, it's taboo and un-Islamic even to discuss it."

"Could his hatred have driven him to commit the crimes?" Chandramala asks.

"Involvement, that's for certain, but as I said, directly participating in the act . . . I doubt it. However, due to his hatred toward LGBTs, he's a choice recruit for a psychopath, easily manipulated and dominated. Most people tend to underestimate psychopaths, thinking they're merely stupid or crazy. On the contrary, psychopaths are highly intelligent individuals."

"So, we're looking for an intelligent man who hates gays. How difficult can that be?" Mislan says. "There are only about a few million of them."

"It's not a lost cause," Dr. Suthisa says, smiling reassuringly. "The suspect that you're looking for is a man or a woman of influence, could even be a man or woman of power. He or she is patient and extremely devoted to his or her faith and cause." She pauses to light a cigarette. "This idea of emancipating nonconformists is common in Christianity, Islam, and Judaism but less so in polytheist religions, though it's not unknown. Since your victims are all Muslim women, I'd say the person you're looking for is also a Muslim."

"You said we're looking for a man or woman," Samsiah says. "I've heard of women assisting rape, but would a woman get someone else to go around raping other women?"

"I believe we're all in agreement that these rapes were not committed out of sexual drive or male dominance. In other words, they were committed not with the common motives of most rape cases."

The officers nod.

"These rapes were motivated by a specific cause, thus the username Emancipatist, which should be actually be Emancipator. Now this is just my theory, and I may well be wrong."

"We're open to any theory," Samsiah says.

"The username 'Emancipatist' may not be a spelling mistake or from lack of English as we thought. And I don't think it's that the username 'Emancipator' was taken, as Sai explained, with the need to come up with a different one. I think 'Emancipatist' was deliberate and intentional."

Dr. Suthisa notices the confused look on the officers' faces and smiles.

"This individual we're dealing with sees him- or herself as a specialist. Not just an emancipator or liberator but an *emancipatist*. Let me try to explain. A doctor is general, but a cardiologist is a specialist. A preacher is general, but an evangelist is a specialist. Do you see the difference?"

"Like a grave robber is general, and an archaeologist is a specialist," Mislan says.

Dr. Suthisa laughs. "Something like that. My feeling is that 'emancipatist' was specifically coined by them to suggest that they're specialist doing god's work. That's the objective, or so the offenders intended. He, or she, feels the act of rape will liberate the victims from their wayward behavior and allow them to revert to the ways of their faith. So yes, it can be a male or female behind it. The reason I profiled him, or her, as Muslim is because there would be no reason for a non-Muslim to liberate a Muslim."

"But the act of rape and murder is evil and un-Islamic," Samsiah points out.

"Again, you have to understand, this is not a matter of being evil or un-Islamic. In the psychopath's mind, there's no conflict in being evil to fight evil, to fight a war or self-destruct as a suicide bomber for the glory of your faith. . . . Doing the Lord's work, as they said in Christianity. Here, observe the suspect's expressions and body language when the subject is raised. Note the horror but also the absence of sympathy."

"And you're saying this unknown brilliant psychopath is the rapist and murderer," Chandramala interjects.

"In this case, I don't believe that to be so. In most cases, psychopaths commit crimes because of their big egos and pride. They'd want the crime committed exactly the way they'd planned and pictured it. However, there've been numerous cases where psychopaths employ others to do their dirty work. Detailed and very specific instructions will be issued as to how to commit the criminal act."

"That's why the same MO was used," Sherry says. "And as Mislan pointed out, they corrected their mistakes, and the dialogue was all scripted and rehearsed."

"And the same username," Saifuddin butts in from behind his monitors.

Dr. Suthisa nods.

"If that's the case, only the rapists would know the psychopath's identity," Mislan theorizes.

"Yes and no," Dr. Suthisa says. "The instructions could be given through phone calls, emails, letters, or go-betweens, in which case there's no face-to-face contact between them."

The room is silent.

"In my view, your best chance of identifying this suspect is to go back to the anti-LGBT movements. Your suspects claim to have met one another at these gatherings. When recruiting individuals, a psychopath needs to be sure they share the same sentiment and subscribe to the same ideology or cause. Secondly, the psychopath needs to ensure that he or she won't be exposed or snitched on should the venture fail."

"That makes sense," Chandramala agrees.

Sherry steps across to her whiteboard and starts pinning up the mug shots of the suspects, linking them in an organizational chart. She puts a question mark above the image of Pak Non.

"I don't think Pak Non has a direct link to the mastermind," Mislan says. "He has admitted to passing on envelopes that he believes contained money to Azuandin, twice. This is corroborated by Azuandin's admission that he got the money to buy the laptops from Pak Non, which he then gave to Ape-Man. Pak Non further claims that the videos were dropped into his letterbox by an unknown person. He then got a call from a man who identified himself as the Dispatcher and instructed him to call Azuandin and hand the videos over to him. He says the arrangements were made by a man known to him as Halil. They had met once at an anti-LGBT gathering and a few more times casually after that. Halil had then recruited Pak Non to be the mailman for the cause. I suspect there may be more layers between this Halil and the mastermind."

"Are we checking on this Halil?" Samsiah asks.

"Deena and Dorai are on it," Sherry says.

"The way I see it, this Halil could be the head of only one cell, or he could be controlling multiple cells. Pak Non admitted to handing over three videos to Azuandin, and the fourth rape was uploaded while Azuandin and Ape-Man were in our custody. Either Halil is controlling two cells, or there's another Halil out there controlling more cells," Mislan theorizes.

"Inspector Mislan may be right," Dr. Suthisa agrees.

"The third and fourth cases were in Selangor. That's another reason why I believe there may be other cells. Probably one or several cells in each state."

"Scary," Sherry remarks.

"Whatever it is, let's find out who this Halil is," Chandramala says, "And bring him in for questioning."

58

Senior Assistant Commissioner Faridah Manap and the head of Public Affairs welcome the media and thank them for making time to be present. She apologizes for the short notice given.

"I called you here in the hope that you will, as usual, give us your fullest cooperation. As you're all aware, there was another rape video posted on UTube this morning by the Emancipatist." She pauses to evaluate the reaction and doesn't like what she sees. A few reporters are already eagerly raising their hands to ask questions. She hears a voice call out, "You mean the UTube Serial Rapist?" The room erupts with questions shouted by the rest of them.

Faridah holds up her hands, and after several more shouted questions the ruckus subsides sufficiently for her to be heard.

"Let me finish before I take questions," she says, flashing a bright smile.

It takes another minute for the crowd to quieten down.

"The cases have attracted much media attention and, unfortunately, appear to have caused undue panic in the community. Please don't take this the wrong way: the police aren't blaming the press for doing your job. We're appealing to the media for a temporary moratorium on all news pertaining to these cases. We don't want mass panic or to cause people to take matters into their own hands. Innocent people could get hurt, and things could get out of control. We fully appreciate that the public has a right to know and to be warned of any danger. However, we must bear in mind the consequences of a nationwide panic. So, on

behalf of the police force, we ask for your understanding and cooperation to temporarily suspend all stories about these serial rapes."

She takes a deep breath and turns to look at the head of Public Affairs,
who smiles and shakes his head, indicating he has nothing to add.

"Now, I'll take questions."

"Ma'am, have the police made any progress in the case?" someone
shouts from the back row.

Holding up her hands again, she says calmly, "I'll answer questions
on the condition it will not be reported. For the moment, it will be
for your ears only, to erase any doubts that you may have. Are we in
agreement?"

She hears a resounding, "Yes!" from the crowd, which comes a little
too quickly for her liking.

"OK, please raise your hands, and I'll invite you to speak. Do introduce yourself before asking your question."

Hands shoot up, instantly.

"Yes, you sir, in the third row with the blue shirt."

"Ma'am, I'm Harun from *Metro*. Is Bukit Aman taking over the
investigation?"

"As of today, we'll be leading the investigation. You, ma'am, in the
back row in the yellow baju kurung."

"Assalamu'alaikum, I'm Zahara from *KOSMO*. Have the police
arrested any suspects yet?"

"Waalaikumsalam. Yes, we are interviewing several individuals to
assist us in the investigations."

She scans the room, "You, ma'am, here in the front row, yes you."

"I'm Audi from Astro Awani. I have information that the task force
has conducted several raids and arrested a number of people who are
believed to be members of anti-LGBT movements. Is that true?"

"As I said earlier, we're interviewing several individuals who are
assisting us with our investigations."

"Are the individuals members of anti-LGBT movements?"

"My understanding is that LGBT and anti-LGBT are not registered
bodies. Therefore, legally, they have no members. Next, you, ma'am, in
the second row?"

"Legally or illegally, they do exist," Audi persists, unhappy with the answer.

Faridah ignores her. "Yes, what's your question?"

"I'm Cindy from the NST. The rapes seem to be happening two to three days apart. Are they all committed by the same individuals?"

"We're still investigating that, and we hope to announce our findings soon. OK, one last question."

The announcement draws disgruntled murmurs from the crowd, and hands start waving wildly to attract her attention.

"You sir, in the front row."

"I'm Liew from *Sin Chew Daily*. Why was SAC Burhanuddin the OCCI taken off the case?"

"SAC Burhanuddin has not been taken off the case. The Director of CID is of the opinion that this case should be handled by Bukit Aman." Faridah picks up her notes and says, "Thank you very much for your time, and I would like to remind you that no information discussed today will be printed or broadcast. Again, on behalf of the police force, I thank you for your understanding and cooperation. Have a good weekend."

As they leave the meeting room, the head of Public Affairs asks, "You think they'll hold the story?"

Faridah gives him an "are-you-naïve" look.

"So what was that all about?" he asks, jerking his head back toward the meeting room.

"Buying time."

Faridah walks into her office and makes a call.

"Where are we with the gag order?"

"All signed and ready. The men are hand-delivering copies to all print and electronic media."

"Good, well done."

59

IT IS 3:20 P.M., and the hunters are nowhere near their quarry. Halil, the man Pak Non claims to be his controller, hasn't been found. The cell phone number Pak Non provided turns out to be a phantom prepaid line. A check with the telco reveals the number was last used four weeks ago. No one from the mamak stalls and restaurants where Pak Non claims to have met Halil for teh tarik remembers them.

"Who the hell is this guy?" Mislan says to no one in particular.

"I can't understand how a person like Pak Non can take instructions from this Halil person without even knowing who he is! He's not an uneducated man. He also holds a good position in the government," Johan wonders aloud.

"Being educated doesn't mean you can't be fooled or just be stupid," Dr. Suthisa comments. "People like Halil can easily spot weakness in their prey."

"Jo, bring Pak Non into the interview room. Let's have another crack at his memory on this Halil," Mislan instructs. "Sherry, in the meanwhile, tell the team to keep at it until we can get something." He takes a deep breath. "We've got about forty-one hours left to get closure."

Dr. Suthisa and DSP Chandaramala look at one another, and then at Sherry.

"He's got forty-one hours left before he's taken off the case," Sherry explains.

"Why's that?" asks Chandramala.

"It's a long story. The OCCI wants him suspended for the raid at Pelita."

"I wasn't told about this."

———

Mohamad Zainon a.k.a. Pak Non slumps glumly on the hard steel chair, his eyes on the floor as Mislan tells him that Halil doesn't exist.

"Who else knows this Halil?"

"The people at the rally, I saw him talking to them."

"What're their names?"

"I don't know."

"How did you know about the rally?"

"I heard about it from some students."

"What students?"

"I'm in charge of Student Affairs for Higher Education. Sometimes, we'd hear of their activities and we'd do some inquiries. I heard that some students were going to hold a rally to protest against Seksualiti Merdeka. I went to the rally to gather information, and that's where I met Halil. We spoke and exchanged telephone numbers."

"Was he alone or with a group?"

"I don't know. I only spoke to him."

"When you met for teh tarik, was there anyone else with him?"

"No, he always came alone."

"How about his car, do you remember what car he drives?"

"Harrier, black, I don't know the plate number. All I can remember is that it's the new model."

"When was the last time you met him?"

"Ten, maybe twelve days ago."

"Where?"

"Bangi Kopitiam at Bandar Baru Bangi, Section 9. He said he was around the area and asked if we could go for a drink."

"Did he drop names?"

"I don't understand."

"Did he ever mention names of prominent individuals or politicians and claim to be close to them? Individuals who are supporting the movement or are backing and protecting him?"

Pak Non's forehead wrinkles as he searches his brain. "He did mention YB this, YB that, but never mentioned names."

"YB meaning a state assemblyman or member of parliament? What did he say about this YB?"

"He sort of insinuated that the YB is backing the movement. But he didn't say how."

"You said you met him at the Sexuality Rights protest rally."

"Yes."

"I want you to try and remember: who else that you know saw you there or spoke to this Halil?"

Mislan leaves the interview room and calls his boss. "Sorry to disturb you, ma'am. I need a favor."

"You're still at the office?" She sounds concerned.

"Yes. Ma'am, can you ask ASP Fakurrulah if the SB took videos or photographs at the anti–Seksualiti Merdeka protest?"

"Why?"

"Halil, the man Pak Non claims to be his handler, is like a ghost. Pak Non says they met at the protest rally. If the SB has videos or photos, there's a chance this ghost would be on them. If Pak Non can pick him out, at least we'll have a face to work with."

"Let me call Fakurrulah and find out. Hey, Lan, in the meantime, why don't you and Sherry get some rest?"

"I'll tell Sherry. As for me, I can sleep all I want come Monday," he says, chuckling. "Thanks, ma'am."

———

Mislan walks to the task force room, and Saifuddin tells him he managed to obtain the particulars of the blogger and two followers.

"How accurate is the information?"

"There's no way of knowing until you visit the address. Many give false details when registering on social networks. There's no way for the networks to verify the information."

"Jo, send a detective to check them out."

"And if it's them?"

"Persuade them to come in for a chat."

Sherry and Johan laugh.

"Where are DSP Mala and Dr. Sophia?"

"They've gone back to freshen up. They'll come in around seven. Why?"

"Just asking. Why don't you go home, too, and get some sleep? Freshen up and put on some fresh clothes. You look like—"

"An old hag," Sherry finishes his sentence for him.

"I was about to say, like you need sleep, but old hag sounds better," he kids her.

"Like you don't need some sleep."

"I've got a change of clothes in my car. I'll freshen up in the toilet and change into a clean shirt. I'll hold the fort. You take off and come back around seven. I'll call you if something comes up."

"Promise?"

Mislan laughs. "Yes, Inspector Sherry, I promise. Now, get out of here."

"What about me?" Saifuddin asks.

"If the toilet is good enough for Jo and me, it is good enough for you."

His cell phone rings.

"Yes, ma'am."

"Fakurrulah says they have many videos of the protest. Can you send someone to pick them up from his men?"

"Sure, who do we ask for?"

"Sergeant Jhoti."

"Thanks, ma'am."

"What was that?" Sherry asks.

"I've asked ma'am to get some videos from SB on the anti–Seksualiti Merdeka protest. Hopefully, Pak Non will be able to identify this Halil."

"You want me to stick around and help you view them?"

"No, you go home and get some rest. We may need your fresh eyes later."

"OK, see you at seven."

60

SAIFUDDIN SETS UP THE biggest monitor he has and runs the video. Deena is tasked to sit with Pak Non.

"Pause it when he recognizes the ghost," Saifuddin says. "I'll crop it out."

"Once we identify him, do we still view all the other videos?" Deena asks.

"You have to check that with your boss."

"There are what, five DVDs? It's going to take all night."

"Can't help you there," Saifuddin says, leaving the interview room.

Turning to Pak Non, she asks, "You ready?"

The suspect nods.

Images of young men holding placards and banners and shouting slogans pop up.

"Do you want the audio?" Deena asks.

Pak Non shakes his head, and she mutes the audio.

"Let me know when you see him," she says, already losing interest in the images of shouting, jeering, and booing hooligan-like students.

Pak Non notices her disinterest. "You one of them?"

"One of who?"

"Them . . . you know."

"What gives you the idea?"

"Your uncovered hairstyle, the way you dress and talk. You act like you're one of the men."

"You're extremely judgmental, aren't you? Typical. Just because I dress or act differently, and not the way you and people like you want me to?" Deena rebukes him. "Anyway, so what if I am? What's it to you?" Pak Non opens his mouth to answer, but Deena snaps at him, "Take care of your grave, and I'll take care of mine. Now shut up and watch the video." She abruptly stands and drags her chair away from the suspect. "People like you make me wish I were a lesbian so that I could give you all bloody heart attacks," she scorns.

———

Mislan is taking a catnap in the task force room when his cell phone rings.

"Hi," he answers sleepily.

"Hi, where are you? Why so quiet?" Dr. Safia asks.

"In the office."

"You're working today?"

"No, but we're working on the cases, you know."

"Just heard there was another one this morning. There's talk going around at the hospital that night-shift nurses aren't coming to work for fear of being attacked."

"It's that bad, ah?"

"Any progress so far?"

"Some, but could do with more. Fie, tell the nurses there's nothing for them to fear, OK?"

"You know something?"

"Yes, but I can't reveal it. Just tell them there's nothing to fear, and don't spread panic among the staff. That'll only play right into his hands."

"I can try, but I don't think it'll do any good. It's the only thing they talk about. Anyway, you take care, OK?"

"Always. Catch you after all this is over."

"Miss you."

Hanging up, he says, "Sai, you want to take a shower?"

"With you? No thanks," Saifuddin sniggers.

"Why? Afraid you can't fight the temptation of my gorgeous bod?"

"I'm straight, OK?" he says.

Mislan laughs and goes to the washroom.

———

Johan is waiting for him when he returns. He tells Mislan that the detectives came back empty-handed. None of the addresses exist.

"I wasn't hopeful. Sai, what about the IP addresses? Or better still, work your magic and get the MAC number."

"Got the IP addresses but still working on the MAC number."

"Let me know when you get them. How are Deena and Pak Non doing?"

"They finished the first video and are just starting on the second. Did you know there are five videos altogether? It'll take a while."

"Jo, why don't you go and freshen up before the women come back? You, too, Sai. You two are beginning to smell."

Just then, Deena bursts excitedly into the room, and announces that Pak Non has identified the ghost. Saifuddin kicks back his chair and literally runs after her, followed by the two Special Investigations officers.

———

The three bend over the monitor.

Saifuddin inquires, "Which one?"

"The one in the white shirt," Deena points out.

"This person?" Saifuddin hovers the cursor over the figure of a man.

"No, the other one . . . yes, him."

Saifuddin notes down the time and stops the video. "I need to run it on my laptop. The software is on it." He reaches out to eject the DVD.

"Sai, why don't you bring your laptop here? Let him positively identify the ghost first," Mislan suggests, jerking his head toward the suspect.

"OK, hang on." Saifuddin heads for the door.

"Are you positive that's Halil?" Mislan asks the suspect.

"Yes, I was standing alone when he came toward me. Back the video up a bit."

Mislan drags the timer back, slowly.

"That's me, and there, you can see him approaching me. . . . There . . . there," the suspect gets excited.

"Good, let's see if Sai can enlarge his face. What's taking him so long?" Mislan growls impatiently.

Saifuddin comes back with Dr. Suthisa and DSP Chandramala.

"Saifuddin says the suspect has identified his handler," Chandramala says, as they enter.

"It's too small to see clearly, Sai's going to run it on his laptop," Deena answers.

"Where's Inspector Sherry?" DSP Chandramala asks.

"I told her to take a break and freshen up. Deena, why don't you call her? I'm sure she'll want to be around."

Saifuddin announces he's ready to run the video on his laptop. He stops at the frame where the "ghost" appears. He crops the ghost's face and zooms in so it fills the entire monitor.

"It's him," Pak Non exclaims.

"Sai, can you rewind the video a little? See if you can get a better image of him," Mislan says.

Saifuddin drags the timer back a little.

"Pause . . . pause," Mislan says. "Back a little. That's a clearer image. Can you pull that up?"

Saifuddin repeats the cropping, and the image of the "ghost" once again fills the monitor.

"Anyone know who he is?" Chandramala asks.

"He looks familiar, but I just can't place him," Johan agonizes.

"Relate or associate him to a profession," Dr. Suthisa suggests. "Police, customs, politician, it might be easier for you to recall who he is that way."

Johan mumbles to himself, "Where, where? Arrrgh . . . I've seen him before, but can't figure out where."

"Relax. The more you torture your mind, the farther you're going to push it away. Position his image in your mind and step outside, away from the distractions here," Dr. Suthisa advises him.

All eyes follow Johan as he leaves the room.

"How about the rest of you, any idea who this ghost is?" Mislan asks. They shake their heads.

"Sai, email the photo to me and print out some copies."

———

Mislan calls the head of Special Investigations to update her.

"You have a face but no idea who he is?" Samsiah asks.

"That pretty much sums it up. Do you want to have a look at him?"

"Why not? Mail the image to me."

"OK. Will do it now."

"You may want to put out a bulletin to see if anyone can identify him. Do it internally. I'll talk to SAC Faridah to see if she wants to make it public."

"OK."

"Tell the team they did a good job."

"Thanks, ma'am. I will let them know."

———

Johan comes barging into the room, excitedly announcing, "I know where I've seen that face before."

Everyone stops talking.

"Where?" Mislan barks at him when Johan hesitates.

"Oh, I thought I interrupted something, and you guys were annoyed with me," he says, grinning. "Remember the murder case some time ago, where a *pengkid* killed her partner in the car?"

"Vaguely. It was in Kedah, wasn't it?"

"Yes. I read the story in *KOSMO*, and I remember there was a side article about the decaying morals of our youth—by him. His picture was with the article."

"You're sure about this?"

"Yes, because I discussed the article with my, you know, and she was really pissed off with some of the comments he made."

"Call *KOSMO*. Find out who wrote that article," Mala instructs.

287

"I found it on the net," Saifuddin calls out. "It was last year. I have the article with his photo."

They crowd behind him and peer at his laptop.

"Sai, print out that story and surf the net for any more information on him," Mislan says.

Saifuddin does it immediately, and Mislan reads aloud, "Dr. Haliman Illyas. He holds a doctorate in social science."

"He's well-documented on Google," Saifuddin announces with a whistle.

"Print out anything you can get on him."

"On it."

"Inspector, can I get a translated version of the stories?" Dr. Suthisa inquires. "I speak Malay, but I read better in English."

Mislan turns to Chandramala just as Sherry appears at the door. They both look at her.

"What?"

"How's your Malay?"

"Scored Al," she declares proudly.

"English?" Mislan asks.

"What's this all about?"

"Dr. Sophia needs a translation of this," Mislan says, handing her the article. "I suppose you're the most qualified candidate for it."

"Why not you?"

"I don't have the patience. Besides, I got a C in Malay," he says.

Sherry looks at the article and says, "I'll give it a shot. Can someone update me on what I missed?"

While DSP Chandramala briefs her, Mislan and Dr. Suthisa review some of the articles written in English. Haliman a.k.a. Halil has a doctorate in Social Science from the University of Wales and was attached to the Institute of Strategic and International Studies in Kuala Lumpur before he moved on to lecture at a private university. He is also the author of several articles on the influences of Western lifestyles on Eastern culture.

"Listen to this." Mislan says.

"*The acceptance of same-sex marriages by some Western countries has given hope to the local LGBT movement. Seksualiti Merdeka was mooted to test public acceptance.*"

"I don't see anything in his articles that could be deemed provocative," Dr. Suthisa says.

"An intellectual reading another intellectual's paper will deem it so, but a nonintellectual, like me, will interpret it differently," Mislan rebuts.

"Point taken."

61

IT IS AFTER MIDNIGHT when Mislan and Johan walk into the *KOSMO* office in Jalan Chan Sow Lin. They introduce themselves to the security and ask to see the person in charge. The security guard tells them the office is closed and suggests they come back on Monday.

"Is there anyone working in there now?"

The guard nods.

"Who's in charge?"

The security guard telephones someone.

"The editor, Mr. Aziz, is still in the office, but he's leaving soon."

"Tell him we need to see him urgently."

The guard telephones again, then tells the police officers he's coming down. Mislan lights a cigarette, walks back to the car, and leans against it. Johan watches his boss and knows he must be exhausted, mentally and physically. He also knows that stepping away to be alone is his boss's way of controlling his temper. But Johan knows that, most of all, Mislan is worried he won't be able to get closure before he's suspended on Monday.

A man comes out of the main building, walking toward them. Johan calls his boss, and jerks his head at the approaching man.

"Mr. Aziz, good morning, thank you for coming to meet us. I'm Detective Sergeant Johan from Special Investigations, Kuala Lumpur."

"Yes, Detective Sergeant, how may I help you?"

Mislan approaches them, and Johan makes the introductions.

"Mr. Aziz, we need particulars about one of your contributors, a Dr. Haliman Ilyas," Mislan says.

"I'm not sure if I can do that without a court order."

"Mr. Aziz, I don't think you want us to do that," Mislan says.

The editor stares at him challengingly, and Johan steps in.

"Mr. Aziz, we're investigating a murder and series of rapes. We believe Dr. Haliman can assist us in our investigation. Delaying our opportunity to talk to him may result in another woman being raped. I'm sure you don't want that on your conscience."

"Don't pull the conscience bullshit on me. We only report the news, we don't make it," Aziz reproves.

"How would it look if word was to leak out that your paper refused to give vital information to the police that could have prevented another rape?" Mislan asks.

"Are you threatening me?"

"Threatening? No. We're officers of the law. Threatening the press is unconstitutional and a serious offense," Johan says. "We're just seeking your cooperation."

The editor is silent and looks around as if to ensure that no one is listening. "I suppose it's OK. He's not listed as a confidential source. Let's go up to my office."

As they walk out of the building with the particulars, Mislan calls Sherry and gives her the address.

"Can you lead the pickup of the suspect?"

"Are you not coming?"

"No, I'll wait at the office."

"Mislan, are you OK?"

"Never felt better."

"Seriously, are you OK?"

"Yes, just a little beat. I'll wait for you at the office. Hey, don't start getting yourself into the news: that's my job," he kids.

———

After Mislan's phone call, Johan asks him, "Why don't you want to go pick him up?"

"I don't want to start something I can't finish."

"Meaning?"

"It's already Sunday, and by the time we get anywhere with him, I'll be on my way home for a long rest."

Johan looks at his boss, not knowing what to say. Having worked together for more than five years, he knows what closure means to Mislan. They drive back to the office in silence.

In the task force room, he finds Dr. Suthisa still reading the articles on or by Dr. Haliman. Saifuddin and Deena are napping at the table. Saifuddin opens his eyes when Mislan enters and smiles apologetically.

Mislan winks at him and says, "It's all right, you need it."

Saifuddin returns to his original position, resting his head on his folded arms, eyes closed.

"How's the reading, Doc?"

"Fascinating."

"In what way?"

"His arguments are interesting, yet he isn't supporting them with any data. He has formatted the articles to resemble scholarly papers, and they could even deceive some academics. I think he published them on the net because they fall short of the strict requirements of academic journals."

"I'm sure he chooses his media carefully."

"By that, you mean?"

"How many readers would he get if his works were accepted and published in academic journals, a handful of intellectuals? Then he'd have to deal with rebuttals and dissenting opinions." Mislan lights a cigarette and offers one to her, which she declines. "However, if these are presented in the public media, they'll be read by the uninformed members of the public who'll more than likely take them as true."

"True."

"His target's the layperson, people who are easily incited and manipulated."

62

DSP CHANDRAMALA AND INSPECTOR Sherry escort the suspect, Dr. Haliman, into the interview room equipped with the remote camera. Their image on the monitor attracts Mislan's attention, and he looks closer. He shakes Saifuddin gently and points to the monitor.

"Is this being recorded?"

"No," Saifuddin answers, rubbing his eyes. "You want to record it?"

"Yes."

Saifuddin hits some keys. "OK, now it is."

Dr. Suthisa puts down her reading material and stands behind them. "Can you zoom in on his face?"

Saifuddin punches a few more keys. Dr. Haliman Illyas's face fills the screen.

"Tell me, Inspector, what do you see?"

"It's what I don't see that worries me," Mislan says, staring at the monitor.

Dr. Suthisa nods.

"Most people read the obvious. Interestingly, you read what's missing from the face."

They see DSP Chandramala leave and, moments later, appear at the task force room door.

"That's one confident man," Chandramala says. "When we introduced ourselves at his house, he invited us in politely and even offered us drinks. Imagine the police knocking at your door at two in the morning and you invite them in for drinks?"

Dr. Suthisa asks, "How did he react when you told him he was under arrest?"

"When Sherry told him, he was calm, he made no threats, dropped no names . . . nothing. He only asked if he could change into something more appropriate."

"I'm not surprised. He was probably expecting us and was prepared," Mislan says.

"In other words, you're telling us to expect a tough nut."

"If we can crack him at all."

"You and Sherry will be doing the first round. I'll take over with Dr. Sophia next."

"With due respect, ma'am, I don't think Dr. Sophia should be involved in the interviews. She has no legal standing here."

"I agree with Inspector Mislan," Dr. Suthisa says.

"May I suggest ma'am and Sherry conduct the interview? I'd like to sit this one out."

"Any reason?"

"Just tired."

They look at him suspiciously but let it pass.

"Can I have Sherry in here first?" Dr. Suthisa asks. "I'd like her to wear an earpiece so I can prompt her."

"Certainly. Mislan, can you get D6 to fit her with one?" Chandramala asks. D6 is the Technical Aid Department.

Sherry takes the suspect through the formalities. The suspect acknowledges he understands the caution and signs the caution form. His manner is polite and cooperative.

"Do you wish to be addressed as Dr. Haliman, or can I drop the title?" Sherry asks.

"Just Halim, please. Thank you."

Sherry asks if he wishes to make a statement or answer questions regarding a murder and four rape cases they are investigating.

"I'm sorry, I don't have any statement to make as I don't know anything about the cases, except for what I read in the papers. However, I'll cooperate fully and answer any questions to the best of my ability and knowledge."

"Thank you, we'd appreciate that," Chandramala says, mocking his politeness.

"Can you tell us your relationship with Mohammad Zainon Mohammad Hadi?"

"You mean Pak Non? Well, there's no 'relationship,'" he says, holding up his hands and making quote marks in the air. "I knew him casually when I was lecturing. I believe he's with the Higher Education Ministry."

"Smooth," Mislan says, listening in from the task force room. "Come on, Sherry, throw him a curveball. Catch him off guard," he says, into her earpiece.

He notes Sherry imperceptibly glance at the camera before asking, "And, what did Pak Non regard you as?"

"You know, I really don't know," he answers with a fake laugh. "But if I were to guess, it would be as a doctor. That's what nonteaching academics holding a PhD are called."

"Really?" Chandramala interjects.

"I'm sorry," he says, sounding surprised. "Did he claim it to be something else? Is he here, too?"

"How do you know we have him in custody?" Sherry asks.

"Oh, Sherry, you jumped the gun," Mislan groans into the microphone. "You're giving away information."

"I don't. I'm merely guessing that you do, based on your questions," the suspect replies smugly.

"It's OK, we play it straight. Admit to it and throw him the sucker punch," Mislan whispers into the microphone.

"Yes, we do have him in custody. And he claims to have a relationship with you . . . a special relationship. He even called you by your nickname, Halil," Sherry smiles at him sweetly.

Dr. Haliman seems taken aback by Sherry's comment.

"Got you," Dr. Suthisa says. "Nice work, Sherry."

Mislan, Saifuddin, and Dr. Suthisa are so engrossed in monitoring the interview that they don't notice Superintendent Samsiah arrive.

"How's progress?" she says, standing behind them.

Startled, Saifuddin almost jumps out of the chair, exclaiming, "Ya Allah."

"Sorry, didn't mean to startle you," Samsiah smiles. "Doctor," she acknowledges Dr. Suthisa.

"What brings you here at this hour?" Mislan asks, his eyes glued to the monitor.

"Sherry told me you guys had the 'ghost' in custody. I just had to come and see him for myself. So, how're they doing so far?"

"Slowly, but surely," Dr. Suthisa answers. "We caught him reacting at the mention of his alias."

"Why're you not in there with Sherry?" she asks Mislan.

"I prefer to sit this one out and learn a thing of two from Dr. Sophia on behavioral profiling. It's not every day I get a chance to learn like this."

Samsiah eyes her officer doubtfully but refrains from probing further.

"There's that eye twitch," Dr. Suthisa announces. "See how he avoids eye contact when answering. He's lying or hiding something."

"Sherry, probe him on the photographs from the anti-LGBT rally and mention the teh tarik sessions with Pak Non. Doc says he's hiding something," Mislan says into the microphone.

They watch as Sherry continues to push the suspect.

"Ma'am, can we get a search warrant for his house and his office and vehicles?" Mislan inquires.

"At this hour on Sunday, you'd have to have a really good reason."

"This guy's not going to sing unless we link him directly to the cases. The only way to do that is to present him with something solid, something he cannot talk his way out of."

"Can we get his wife's cooperation to grant us permission to search his house and vehicles? We can do the office on Monday if need be," Samsiah suggests.

"He lives alone, a divorcee."

"Hmmm, let me check with Legal and see what they can cook up. What, specifically are you looking for?"

"This guy's an intellectual, an academic. What's the one thing all intellectuals and academics have in common?"

Dr. Suthisa and Samsiah look at him askance.

"I'm interested to know the answer to that, Inspector. What's the thing intellectuals have in common?" Dr. Suthisa asks, amused.

"Taking and making notes, documenting. He may be brainy, but I don't think he's street smart. I bet if we search his house, vehicles, and office, we will find some incriminating records or notes."

"Inspector, I'm amazed at your, shall I say, shrewd observations."

"OK, let me wake up the head of D5 and see if he can work out something," Samsiah says, leaving the room.

63

It is 8:30 a.m., and the task force room table is stacked with packets of nasi lemak, fried noodles, roti canai, tea, and coffee. Detective Dorai and Deena are busy arranging them when SAC Faridah arrives with Superintendent Samsiah.

"What's this, a welcoming spread? I should visit you more often," Faridah quips.

Detectives Dorai and Deena look embarrassed.

"Where're the rest?" Samsiah asks.

"Freshening up. They should be coming back soon," Deena answers.

The team members start arriving, looking like zombies after not having slept for more than forty hours. Samsiah tries to energize them with warm and cheerful greetings.

"As we enjoy breakfast, generously sponsored by DSP Chandramala, let me introduce our guest," Samsiah says. "Senior Assistant Commissioner Faridah Manap is the head of the Sexual & Child Abuse Investigations Division in Bukit Aman. She's currently in charge of this investigation, having taken over from the OCCI. Ma'am, would you like to say something?"

"Thank you, Samsiah. Let me first congratulate you on your great police work. I can see you're all exhausted. From what I've been told by Samsiah and Mala, I'm confident the cases will be solved soon." She pauses. "And Mala, thank you for this breakfast."

———

After breakfast, Samsiah requests that the officers Johan and Deena remain and the rest wait in the detectives' room. Sherry, as the lead investigator, brings Faridah and Samsiah up to speed. She finishes with, "We still do not have anything concrete to link him to the other suspects."

"How about his phone record, the contacts?" Faridah asks.

"The one he has with him shows no match. I believe he uses another cell phone to communicate with them. The number given by Pak Non was of a prepaid number with false registration."

"Mislan has asked me to try obtaining a search warrant for his house, vehicles, and office," Samsiah interjects. "I've spoken to D5, and they're working on it."

"That could yield something," Chandramala says. "I agree with Mislan: the only way we can break this man is with direct evidence."

Samsiah's cell phone rings.

"Good morning, sir."

"I was told you have Dr. Haliman in custody," SAC Burhanuddin says.

"Yes, we do."

"Do you know who he is?"

"In relation to the cases we're investigating, yes."

"Not that," he snarls. "He was a director at the Institute of Strategic and International Studies. He has access to some ministers. Why was I not told before your team made the arrest?"

"The arrest was made this morning based on information the team obtained from one of the suspects."

"My question was, why was I not told?" he retorts.

Samsiah sighs. "SAC Faridah was informed of the arrest, and she's here next to me. Would you like to speak to her?"

The line goes dead, but as she's about to pocket the cell phone, it rings, and all eyes are on her again.

"Samsiah."

"Samsiah, I'm Datuk Abu Sahid. Burhanuddin gave me your number."

"Good morning, Datuk. How may I assist you?"

"I was informed that your team arrested Dr. Haliman this morning. May I ask on what charge?"

"I'm sorry, Datuk, but I'm not at liberty to divulge information regarding an ongoing investigation. Datuk, may I ask the reason for your interest?"

"He's a close friend of mine and many others like me."

"Sorry, but I don't understand what you mean by that."

"You'll find out soon enough."

Again, the line goes dead.

"The pressure's mounting, and that can only mean one thing," Mislan says.

"That we're on the right track," Sherry says.

Samsiah turns off her cell phone. "It's Sunday . . . too many distractions."

"Now that the pressure is on, what's our next course of action?" Faridah asks.

"Ma'am, if you can handle the inquiries and the politics, we'll push on," Chandramala suggests. "And work on the search."

Faridah turns to Samsiah. "What's the status on the warrant?"

When Samsiah switches on her cell phone, she hears the "missed-call" tone. She ignores it and phones Legal. Then she says to her team, "They're waiting for the magistrate to finish his round of golf before they can get him to sign the warrants."

"Tell them to get a buggy, go to whichever hole he's at, and get it signed," Faridah orders. "Tell them it's urgent."

Detective Syed knocks on the door to tell them there are two men claiming to be from the Ministry of Higher Education waiting to see Inspector Sherry. "They want to speak to Pak Non."

"Tell them that today is not a working day and to come back tomorrow," Faridah dismisses Syed. "Mala, organize the search team. I want the suspect to be present during the search. Get D6 to be part of the team."

"Ma'am, may I suggest we get Forensic involved as well? Dust for prints at all locations to match those of the suspects or future suspects. Any match can be used against him," Mislan says.

"Good suggestion. In the meantime, show his photograph to all the suspects. See if any of the others know him. Samsiah, direct all inquiries to my office. I'll stall them as long as I can."

64

THE TASK FORCE LED by DSP Chandramala, accompanied by personnel from Technical Aid and Forensic, ask Dr. Haliman to lead them to his study, if he has one. The suspect leads them to his bedroom, and Chandramala tells the suspect to sit on his bed and signals to the team to start. Mislan leans against the door, studying the suspect. Technical Aid personnel photograph the entire room while the Forensic team dusts doorknobs, the desktop, and every other item for fingerprints. The suspect appears unconcerned with the search. The only time he turns to look at them is when he's attracted by the sound of something falling. After a few minutes, the suspect says, "I'm tired and sleepy. Is it all right if I lie down?"

"Suit yourself," Chandramala says bluntly.

The suspect lies down, closes his eyes, and crosses his arms over his face. Mislan watches him, wondering if his supercool demeanor is an act or if he really has nothing to be afraid of. The suspect opens his eyes and asks if he can switch on the air conditioner.

"Don't get too comfortable. After we're done here, we'll want you to come with us to search the rest of the house," Mala says.

"I know you want me to be present during the search, but I'm waiving my rights to be present. I trust the integrity of the police. Wake me up when you're finished," he says smugly.

Mislan signals Sherry over, and they step out of the room.

"We're wasting our time here," he says.

"Why?"

"Can't you see how confident he is?"

"But you're the one who said he's the type who'd document his activities," Sherry reminds him. "He could be trying to fool us."

"I still believe he documented the events, but I doubt the evidence is here."

"I'll talk to DSP Chandramala, but since we're here, we might as well carry on."

"OK, I'll hang out in the living room and have a smoke. Make sure there's someone with him at all times."

Mislan steps out to the living room, lights a cigarette, and walks to the front door. When he opens it, the bright late-morning sun hits his face. His body feels sticky and his face oily. The heat dissuades him from going outside to smoke. He flicks his cigarette out, closes the door and walks back into the living room; switching on the ceiling fan, he slumps heavily onto one of the sofas. Its soft comfort, the dimness of the room, and the silence soothe his exhausted body.

Mislan sees himself walking into the ego-chamber. The OCCI is standing in the middle, waving a piece of paper and laughing like a villain in a low-budget movie. He frantically waves and calls to the Mislan he sees, urging him to get out of there. The Mislan smiles at him and calmly continues into the ego-chamber, stopping face-to-face with the OCCI. Burhanuddin leers, his eyes lighting up with triumph as he bellows: *I got you, you are hereby suspended.* Out of nowhere, two bulky policemen appear, grabbing him by his arms. Mislan sniggers at the OCCI as he's escorted out. In the general office, a group of officers are gathered, among them Superintendent Samsiah, Inspector Sherry, Detective Sergeant Johan, and the entire task force. Even Dr. Safia is present. They jeer and shout angrily, *You let us down, you're a disgrace to the team.* The elevator door opens, and he is shoved in. The elevator cab is pitch-black, and as he falls, he realizes it's bottomless. He screams in horror.

"Sir, sir, are you all right?"

Mislan twists on the cushion, mumbling, "I'm sorry, I'm sorry." He turns, kicks, and struggles upright on the sofa. He takes deep breaths to calm himself, trying to recollect where he is.

"Are you all right?" Johan asks.

"Yes, yes. Why, what happened?"

He notices the entire team and the suspect standing in a semicircle at the foot of the stairs, staring at him,

"You were rambling and screaming."

He takes a few more deep breaths, shuts his eyes, and rubs his face. "A bad dream, just a bad dream," he says. Looking at the gawking gallery, he asks, "Are we done here?"

"Yes."

"Found anything?"

Johan shakes his head.

Mislan looks at the time on his cell phone. It's almost noon.

———

The team makes their way to Dr. Haliman's office in Shah Alam. The search there takes almost two and a half hours. As it's late, DSP Chandramala decides to search the vehicles at the police headquarters. When they return to the task force room, the team hands over the laptop, the compact discs, and thumb drives they confiscated to Saifuddin.

"What am I looking for?" Saifuddin asks.

"I don't know, anything incriminating."

"Like?"

"Like a picture of him raping the victims," Mislan snaps at him angrily. The rest stop whatever they are doing and stare at him.

Chandramala beckons Saifuddin and tells him to examine documents in the laptop and external storage drive with Dr. Suthisa. Stepping out of the room, she signals Mislan to follow her to Sherry's office.

"You want to explain what happened just now?"

"Sorry, I've no excuse for it."

"I know you're under pressure," she says. "I know about your impending suspension." She glances at her watch, "You still have about fourteen hours to work the case. Losing your temper will only eat into those hours."

Mislan nods.

"What happened at the suspect's house?"

Mislan looks at her. "A bad dream."

"When was the last time you slept?"

Mislan smiles.

"Why don't you get some sleep while we go through the items? I'll send someone for you if we find anything interesting." She stands, "Use this room, I'll let Sherry know."

65

Mislan lights a cigarette and stretches out on the chair in Sherry's office, unable to nap. He looks at the time. *It won't be long now. Can't expect a miracle.* He calls home.

"Hi, kiddo."

"Daddy, where're you?"

"At the office. Had your dinner yet, kiddo?"

"Not yet, we're waiting for Sister to cook."

"Are your friends there with you?" he asks, hearing kids' voices.

"Yes, Nakip and Omar."

"Tomorrow's a school day. Don't stay up too late, OK?"

"Daddy, what time are you coming home?"

"Late, kiddo. Make sure you prepare your books for school tomorrow before you sleep."

"Hmmm hmmm."

"Are you still coughing?"

"No more."

"Good. Love you, kiddo."

"Love you, too."

He then calls Johan over.

"Jo, at Dr. Haliman's house and the office, did you notice any letters or bills?"

"I don't understand."

"I mean, personal letters or utility bills, like for cable, water, electricity . . . especially at the house."

"I didn't, maybe the others did."

"Can you check with them?"

"Why's it important?"

"It may not be, just curious."

———

Johan comes back shaking his head.

"Deena did the general search. She didn't notice any in the house."

"Don't you find that odd?"

"You mean the bills?"

"We've done hundreds of house searches, right? There're always bills. But in this case, nothing, not in the house or the office."

"So you're saying somebody is paying his bills?"

"Even if someone's paying his bills, he'll still keep them for records or reference."

Mislan makes a call.

"Hi, can we speak?"

"Yes, what's up?" Audi says. "Hey, there are whispers going around that you've got a big fish. Is that true?"

"Don't know what you're talking about."

"Yeah right. So what's up?"

"I need to use your resources, your informants."

"What's in it for me?"

"Public appreciation," he says. "Can't you, for once, help others for the sake of helping?"

"I've finished my quota for this year. What info are you looking for?"

"I need you to find out all you can about Dr. Haliman Ilyas, an ex-ISIS guy."

"ISIS!"

"Not that ISIS, the International Strategic whatever."

"Oh, OK, the big fish they were talking about?"

"I don't know. Can you do some digging?"

"And look for what?"

"Everything, personal, politics, marriage, children, property . . . everything."

"Whoa, Inspector, do you know what day this is? *Sunday*."

"That's why I called you. I know you have information archives . . . property archives. Otherwise, I could get my men to work the government agencies. OK, forget the marriage and children. I'll get my men to handle that."

"It'll take a while. Get back to you by tomorrow evening, earliest."

"Not good enough. Need the information by today, midnight latest."

"What's brewing? Something big, right?"

"Nothing's brewing. I'm considering going on a long vacation starting tomorrow. Can you get them for me?"

"I'll see what I can do."

––––––––

Terminating the call, he strolls over to the task force room. DSP Chandramala, Dr. Suthisa, Sherry, and Saifuddin are hunched over the documents recovered from the suspect's house and office. Sherry is doing her best at translation from Malay to English for Dr. Suthisa. Saifuddin is probably enjoying himself being closely surrounded by three women and just sits there.

Mislan beckons his assistant to the window.

"Jo, get Syed and Jeff to track down the suspect's ex-wife. Talk to her and find out anything they can about their marriage, divorce, and children, if any."

"What're you on to?"

"The suspect was very confident when we searched his house, office, and vehicle. No objections, no signs of fear. I said earlier that he's not street smart, but what I failed to realize is that he's book smart."

"He holds a doctorate. He has to be book smart."

"That's it. People like him read lots of books. But where're the books? They weren't in the house. In novels, perverts and predators often operate from safe houses, dens, or lairs."

"That's why he was so confident we won't find anything. But why his ex?"

"Perhaps she can give us an insight into him. Anyway, we have to cover all bases."

"OK, I'll get Syed, Jeff, and Deena on it. Perhaps with a woman present she'll open up."

"Good. Any luck on the prints lifted from the house and office?"

"Nope. No match to any of the suspects."

"I didn't expect any. This guy is too careful to make silly mistakes like that."

Johan stops at the door, turns around, and asks, "Are you all right now?"

Mislan grins at him.

———

Mislan stands behind Dr. Suthisa and DSP Chandramala, peering over their shoulders.

"Anything useful?"

"This man is really into LGBT bashing. He has many articles on the decaying morals of modern societies, especially in the Western world, and attributes most of it to the acceptance of LGBT people. As I said earlier, his articles appear to be scholarly, but they're not."

"So, there's nothing we can use to pin him to the cases?"

Dr. Suthisa shakes her head. "Not even incitement. However, there's one article where he does blame the government for not taking firm action against the growing LGBT community. He claims that studies suggest that being gay isn't genetic but a mental state and that it's reversible."

"Is he right?" Chandramala asks.

"I've heard and read this argument before. Never any mention of success, just a lot of assurances and promises with no supporting data."

"What's your profile on this guy, Doc?" Mislan asks.

"He certainly has the intelligence to come up with the plan . . ."

"But?"

"What compels him? What's his motive?"

"Perhaps he's not the one sitting at the helm. Maybe there's someone else pulling the strings."

"Could be."

"Keep at it, Doc. I don't think we can hold him much longer. Come Monday . . ."

"I'll do the best I can."

———

Dr. Safia pulls up alongside the guardhouse and slips over to the passenger seat as Mislan takes the wheel. He drives to Jalan Sultan Ismail and turns right just after Parkroyal Hotel.

"Thanks for coming."

"Are you sure you can take the time off?"

Mislan nods. "There's something I need to tell you, but it can wait until after dinner."

"Sure," she says, knowing not to push. "Where are we going?"

"There's a Chinese stall around here. I think you'll like the chili crab."

"I've heard of it, but I don't know where, exactly."

He maneuvers the car along the narrow dimly lit street with cars parked on both sides. She spots a space, and he squeezes her compact into it. They walk to the stall and choose a table. He orders chili crab, fried water spinach with shrimp paste, fried rice, and two sugarcane drinks. Waiting for their orders, he lights a cigarette for her and another for himself.

"You look dejected. Are you all right?" she asks.

"Superb."

She reaches over the table and squeezes his hand. "That means you're not."

He grins, saying nothing, and looks at the time on his cell phone.

"Are you expecting something or someone?"

He shakes his head.

"You keep looking at your phone. What's wrong?"

Their orders arrive, and Dr. Safia digs in. He knows she loves sea-food, especially crab and prawn. He watches her nibbling on the fried spinach.

"How's the case coming along?"

"Not too good. Have you heard of Dr. Haliman Illyas? A former ISIS guy."

"No, why? Is he involved?"

"Not sure."

"You're not sure, or you don't have any proof yet?" she inquires, as she cracks a crab claw open to get to the meat. "This crab's really good. Why haven't you brought me here before?" she teases him.

"Too expensive on a policeman salary," he jests.

"This former ISIS guy, Dr. Haliman, is he in custody?"

Mislan nods.

"How's he involved?"

"The hierarchy leads to him."

Licking the chili gravy off her fingers, she says, "So, he's the master-mind, or, in your jargon, the handler or controller. What's his motive?"

He shrugs.

"Not being able to figure out the motive is not what's really bother-ing you, is it? There's something else you're not telling me."

His cell phone rings.

"Yes."

"Got what you asked for, but I have to tell you that this is from our property archives. It could be outdated, or there could be more if you check the public records," Audi says.

"I'll take anything for now. Shoot."

After terminating the call, he makes a call to his assistant.

"Jo, I want you to get a team out to apartment 6-1 at the Tropika Paradise Condominium, Jalan USJ 17/8, Subang Jaya. I want them to sit on the unit and stop anyone going in or coming out. . . . Yes, now."

He then calls DSP Chandramala, asking if she can get a fresh search warrant for the new address.

"Why? Who's staying there?"

"I don't know, but it's registered under the suspect's name."

"How did you get this information?"

"From a reliable source, but I can't reveal it. Can you get a warrant?"

"At this hour? I'm not sure."

"How about using the existing warrant? It does say house and/or houses belonging to the suspect, right?"

"Let me check. . . . Yes."

"Then the warrant is valid. I've told Johan to get a team to sit on the unit. Can we get the suspect out and search that unit?"

"I'll get Sherry to organize it. Where're you?"

"Having dinner. I'll be there in thirty."

———

Dr. Safia cuts her savoring of the chili crab short. Mislan protests and says that they should finish dinner, apologizing profusely. She signals to the stall operator to pack the dishes.

"I'm sorry."

"Hey, it's OK. Thanks for bringing me here, and we can do it again."

Mislan sighs.

"Look, there's this TV program on in about thirty minutes I've been meaning to watch. Thanks to whoever called, now I can sit in front of the TV, watch it, and enjoy the crabs," she says, flashing him a sweet smile.

Mislan replies with a tight smile and pays the bill.

"I'll drive you back to the office, no need to get a cab, you go do what needs to be done and stop brooding. It's really OK."

"I'm really sorry. I promise we'll come again."

She smiles and pats his hand, "Go, get your closure."

66

IT IS CLOSE TO 11 p.m. by the time the team drives out to the Tropika Paradise Condominium. Mislan sits at the back, next to the suspect, with Johan at the wheel and Sherry in the front passenger seat. The suspect continues to wear his smug and confident expression.

"I see you've decided to take me on another outing. That's nice. It was starting to get a little stuffy in the cell," Dr. Haliman taunts his escorts. "So, where're we going this time?"

Mislan says nothing.

"You know what goes well with a night out, apart from the fresh air? Good company," the suspect says with a chuckle.

Johan steps on the accelerator, heading toward the North Klang Valley Expressway. Mislan lights a cigarette. Sherry asks for one, too. He gives her his, and lights another for himself. He rolls down the window and the whoosh of wind from the open window is a welcome sound to the three officers. As Johan cuts into Subang Jaya, Mislan catches the suspect looking out the window.

"Where are you taking me?" he asks again.

Mislan notes a slight anxiety in his tone. He allows himself the tiniest bit of pleasure at the suspect's apprehension, but remains silent. Realizing that Mislan isn't about to enlighten him, the suspect bends forward to ask Sherry.

"May I inquire as to where you're taking me?"

"For an outing, for some fresh night air," she answers.

The suspect leans back, knowing he's being mocked, and continues to look out the window. When they stop at a traffic light, Johan points for Sherry.

"That's the condo."

The suspect instinctively looks out the front windshield. Mislan smiles. The suspect turns toward him.

"Who lives there?" Dr. Haliman asks, trying hard to maintain his composure.

"I don't know, you tell me," Mislan says.

"Then why're we going there?"

"Jo, why're we going there?" Mislan asks his assistant, toying with the suspect.

"I don't know. Ma'am, why're we going there?" Johan asks Sherry.

The suspect realizes the officers are toying with him and leans back, his jaws clenched tight.

Johan pulls up to the guardhouse, and Mislan notices the suspect turning his face away from the window, pretending to look for something on the seat. Johan flashes his authority card and states their destination to the security guard. After recording the car's registration, the guard directs them to the visitor parking bays. Mislan sees closed-circuit TV cameras at the entrance and tells Johan to get the complex manager's contact details from the guard. The team takes the elevator to level 6 to find two detectives in front of unit 6-1.

"Anyone inside?" Sherry asks.

The detectives shake their heads.

Johan gives Mislan the complex manager's telephone number. He puts the call through, introduces himself, and requests that the manager make his way to Unit 6-1 with a record of owners and tenants. Neighbors start coming out to investigate the noise and presence of a large group of people. Sherry approaches them, introduces herself, and asks if they know who the occupant of Unit 6-1 is. They tell her it's empty most of the time, and that sometimes they see a middle-aged Malay man come and go. When she asks if they see that man in her group, they shake their heads and quickly disappear into their apartments.

"I'm going to ask you a question, and I want you to think carefully before answering," Mislan says to the suspect. "Who owns this unit?"

The suspect stares at him, biting his lower lip. Mislan waits patiently. His eyes are cold and emotionless.

"You know the answer to your question," the suspect finally snarls.

"Yes, I do, but I want to hear it from you."

"You want the satisfaction to hear me admit defeat," Dr. Haliman says. "I'll grant you that. It's mine, but I don't live here. It was rented out and now it's empty. Satisfied?"

"Totally. Please open the door for us to do a search."

"I don't have the keys with me. It's with my realty agent, who manages the apartment."

"Who's the agent? Here's your phone. Please call him or her and tell him or her to come here now."

"At this hour? I don't think he'll come. Anyway, don't you need a warrant to search the apartment?" Dr. Haliman asks defiantly.

Mislan pulls out the warrant and holds it inches from his face.

"That warrant has already been executed, you cannot use it again," he says smiling.

"It says here house and/or houses," Mislan says, pointing to the words. "Now, open the door or we break it down, your choice."

"If you so much as touch the door, I will sue you for all you're worth," Dr. Haliman hisses at him.

"Well, I'm sorry, but you won't get much by suing me," Mislan chuckles, and nods to his men to open the door.

———

A detective steps forward and unzips his tool bag. Kneeling, he starts picking the lock. Mislan steps away, lights a cigarette, and watches the suspect. He knows they're standing at the threshold of closure, yet the suspect's air of confidence unsettles him. The only hint of anxiety he witnessed was when he produced the search warrant. What does the suspect know that he does not? Maybe he knows they'll come out empty-handed again, that the apartment had been cleared of all incriminating evidence when his people were arrested.

Mislan starts toward the door and stops. *You are letting him get to you. Follow your investigative instincts. They've served you well before. Stop over-analyzing the situation.*

He squashes the cigarette and walks to the detectives crouching by the door.

"Do you really know how to do it?" he asks impatiently.

The detective nods. "I'm trying to find the second lever."

Mislan steps back and lights another cigarette. A man appears with a security guard, coming out of the elevator. He asks for Inspector Mislan.

"That's me. Mr. Tan?" Mislan asks.

"Yes. You said you wanted to look at the record of owners and tenants," Tan says, handing over some papers.

Mislan riffles through the listing and smiles.

"Thank you. I noticed you have CCTV installed. How many days' record do you keep?"

"Fourteen."

"I'll need a copy of all the recordings up till today."

"Anything else?"

"That's all for now. Thanks for your cooperation."

As the manager walks away, Mislan calls after him, "Tan, do you have a locksmith on standby?"

"Yes."

"Can you call him? It's urgent."

Tan looks at his watch. "Who does he charge the service to?"

"The Royal Malaysia Police," Mislan replies.

"OK, got it!" the detective announces just then. He turns his metal clip slowly in the lock, there's a click, and the door opens.

Mislan's cell phone rings.

"Mislan."

"Mislan, Chandramala. Where're you?"

"Just about to enter the apartment."

"Stop, don't go in."

Holding the mouthpiece, he tells Sherry to hold the team until he gives the go-ahead. He steps away from them, and as he turns he thinks he sees the suspect sigh in relief.

"Sorry, ma'am. Why?"

"I just got a call from SAC Faridah to stand down until further instructions."

"I don't understand. Why does she want us to stand down? We have him cold. The warrant is valid, and we're standing at the threshold of closure. Soon we'll have enough evidence to fry this guy and his band of rapists," he pleads.

"She has called for an eight o'clock meeting tomorrow morning. She'll explain then. For now, her instruction is for all activities to be put on hold."

"But I'm gone tomorrow. I need to do it now, tonight."

"Mislan, I understand what you're going through and how you feel, but orders are orders. Please don't make things worse for yourself."

"Can't you just tell SAC Faridah you couldn't reach me?"

"You know I can't do that."

"You can't or you won't?"

"Stop it. Let me speak to Sherry."

Mislan passes the cell phone over to Sherry. He walks toward the elevator. Losing control, he kicks the trash can in the lobby, sending it flying against the elevator door, creating a din. Some startled members of the team draw their weapons. Neighborhood lights come on and heads peer through curtains. Johan runs toward his boss to calm him, and Sherry tells the team to holster their weapons. The dented trash can is quickly retrieved and placed in its original position. Mislan looks at the suspect, who is grinning. He moves toward the suspect, but Johan grabs him firmly. "He's not worth it," he whispers.

Sherry walks toward him briskly, holds his arm, and drags him to the end of the corridor.

"What the hell do you think you're doing? You want us all to get into trouble?" she snaps at him. She tells Johan, "Jo, arrange for the suspect to be sent back to the lockup." She waits until the suspect is in the elevator, then says, "Ma'am wants me to escort you back personally, so please don't make a scene."

Mislan glares at her, his eyes red and teary. With shaking hands, he lights another cigarette and turns away from Sherry to stare at the sky.

"Look, Mislan, I don't like it, either, but it's an order."

She whispers to Johan to stay close to his boss. "Give him a few minutes to calm down and then bring him to the car."

Johan nods. He stands next to his boss, not saying anything, but making sure Mislan knows he's there.

————

After Sherry leaves, Mislan looks at his assistant. Johan can see the pain, anger, and frustration in his boss's face.

"Jo, I want you to be in charge. Arrest anyone going into the unit and confiscate whatever they have on them," Mislan finally says.

"Sure, I'll take care of it."

Mislan looks at the elevator, then at Unit 6-1. In the commotion, the team forgot to close the apartment door. Johan sees the sly smile on his boss.

"What are you thinking?" Johan is suspicious.

"Watch the elevator and signal me if it comes up. Give me two minutes."

"You're going to jeopardize the investigation and get us into shit."

"The case's already down the toilet," Mislan says. "I just need to know." Snapping on a latex glove, he disappears into Unit 6-1.

67

At the police headquarters, Mislan excuses himself, saying he's tired and wants to go home to rest. Sherry looks at him but doesn't object. Not to arouse any suspicion, Johan follows the team up to the office. Sherry orders the team to stand down and report back by eight in the morning for a briefing by SAC Faridah. Sherry beckons Johan to follow her to her office.

"How is he?" she asks.

"OK, I guess."

"Did he say anything?"

"No, just kept smoking."

"What took you guys so long to come down?"

"Did we? I waited for him to decide to move, didn't want to rush him," Johan says, shrugging.

Sherry looks hard at him. "Was that it?"

"Unless you know something else," Johan says with a straight face.

"I know you're loyal to him, but don't let him take you down with him."

Johan smiles. "You don't know him as well as I do. He'll never take anyone down with him."

Sherry nods.

Leaving Sherry's office, Johan heads for the staircase and calls his boss.

"Where're you?"

"Like I said, I'm going home. Why?"

"There was something in the suspect's apartment, wasn't there?"

"What makes you think that? I'm tired, the case is dead, and I'm going home."

"Whatever you're planning, you know you can count on me."

Silence.

"I'll wait for you at the LRT station. Jo, come alone."

The line goes dead.

———

Mislan drives past the old National Palace, then to Jalan Bangsar. As they pass the National Museum, Johan asks, "You want to tell me where we're going?"

Mislan gropes under his seat and pulls out a thin paper file labeled in bold, Subject No. 3, and hands it to him.

"What's this?" Johan asks, switching on the cabin light.

"Read it."

Johan reads and exclaims.

"The third rape, it's all here." Closing the file he asks, "What're you going to do with this? We can't use it as evidence; it was obtained illegally."

"Don't you think I know that?" Mislan snaps. He lights another cigarette. "Is there a twenty-four-hour shop somewhere here with a photocopy machine?"

"Look for a KK Store."

"I know there's one in Bangsar Baru," Mislan says, turning the car into Jalan Maarof.

"What're you planning?"

"We can't give the original away because that will lead the trail back to us. We need to make a copy and send it anonymously to ASP Luan. She's the IO on the third rape case."

"And what if she's asked where she got the information from?"

"She'll tell the truth. It was sent to her anonymously." Mislan grins. "Possibly by someone who suddenly developed a conscience."

Johan laughs.

"What're you going to do with the original?" Johan asks.

"Return it to where I found it."

68

IT IS ALMOST THREE in the morning when they get back to the city. Mislan drops Johan outside the contingent headquarters and tells him to walk to the office.

"If anyone asks, say you went out for a drink and met an old friend."

Mislan gives his detective sergeant a twenty-minute lead before driving into the parking lot. Walking into his office, he throws his backpack on the desk and drops heavily into his chair. The duty investigator, Inspector Reeziana, raises her eyebrows at Johan, and he shakes his head. He sits at his desk and watches as his boss squirms and twitches in his chair. In a few hours it will be daylight, and his boss will be suspended from active duty, ending his hope of getting closure. They were so close to nailing the suspect.

It is 3:15 in the morning, the sun is still sleeping but the streets of the city are waking up, traffic noises filter through the building walls. Reeziana and Johan are just about to take their catnaps, when suddenly Mislan sits up, drawing his sidearm. Reeziana and Johan's hands instinctively drop to their own sidearm, eyes watching the inspector unblinkingly. Mislan raises his Beretta, unclips the magazine, and clears the chamber. The sound of metal rubbing against metal is loud and eerie in the early dawn. The two officers sigh as Mislan lays the Beretta on the desk, next to the magazine.

"Jo, can you call the armorer and surrender these? I don't want them with me when they serve me the letter, I might just lose it and use them," he jokes.

The two laugh, a tense laugh. Johan calls the armorer and, replacing the phone, he says awkwardly, "It's all going to be all right."

"Thanks, Jo. I marvel at your naivety and your faith in the system."

———

The armorer arrives, and Johan hands over the Beretta and magazine to him. The armorer asks why Mislan is surrendering his service weapon, and Johan tells him his boss is going on a long-overdue vacation abroad. However, he knows all sorts of speculations and rumors about his boss will be flying around soon. As the armorer leaves, Superintendent Samsiah walks in, surprising them. She beckons for Mislan and Johan to follow her.

A tired-looking SAC Faridah, DSP Chandramala, Inspector Sherry, and Detective Deena are all seated in the task force room when they enter. Faridah greets them.

"Samsiah said you're here. I know I said I'll call for a meeting at eight, but since you're all here, let's do it now. Mala can use the eight o'clock meeting to brief the task force team. Before I start, please help yourselves to the terrible coffee Deena made," she jokes to lighten the mood. "Mislan, I understand you survive on nicotine, so feel free to pollute the room and share some of your secondhand smoke with us."

The others smile.

"The director and I have just come out of a meeting with the AG and several others." She pauses, scanning the surprised faces of the officers. Six pairs of tired eyes instantly widen. "Yes, at this hour, and I'm sure you can guess the subject of the meeting."

Mislan lights a cigarette. Sherry reaches out for it and he lights another for himself.

"The long and short of it is that Dr. Haliman will be released unconditionally by nine and there will be no further investigations carried out on him."

Mislan chokes on his cigarette smoke and coughs. It feels like ten minutes before Faridah continues.

"That is, until we have solid concrete evidence against him." She sips her coffee. "At which point, the AG will review the evidence and, if found to be sufficient, will arrange for him to surrender. That is the extent I'm authorized to brief you. Mala, please stand down and disband the task force. I thank you for your dedication, especially Mislan, Sherry, Johan, and Deena. I'll make sure your exemplary performances will be documented in your personnel records."

"That's it?" Mislan hisses, unable to control his anger any longer.

"Yes, Inspector Mislan," Faridah answers.

Mislan jumps to his feet, "I—"

Samsiah immediately snaps at him, "Sit down and behave yourself."

Sherry tugs at his hand, pleading with her eyes for him to calm down.

He slowly sits down, murmuring, "I'm sorry."

"No need to be sorry, I would have reacted the same way in your position."

————

Johan catches up with his boss and offers to drive him home. Mislan declines, saying he's all right and wishes to be alone.

"You sure?"

"Yes, thanks. Why don't you go home and get some rest? I'll see you later."

"Call me if you need company."

Sherry and Deena catch up with them at the elevator.

"Where're the bosses?" Johan asks.

"Still in there."

"You OK?" Sherry inquires.

Mislan nods.

"Mislan, for what it's worth, I enjoyed working with you. I don't agree with many of your methods, but we all have our ways," she says and smiles.

"Likewise." Mislan smiles back.

Downstairs in the lobby, he bumps into detective Syed and Jeff coming back from their assignment.

"We're told to stand down. What happened?" Syed asks him.

"Briefing at eight. By the way, what have you guys found?"

Syed tells him they managed to locate the suspect's ex-wife and had a pleasant chat with her. She was hospitable and cooperative.

"Lovely woman, charming, and not to mention beautiful," Jeff adds.

"How long were they married?"

"About seven years."

"Children?"

The detectives shake their head.

"Did she tell you why they divorced?"

"Not in so many words."

"What do you mean?"

"She now lives with her partner . . . a woman."

"Oh. Did she say when they were divorced?"

"Two years ago in August."

69

IT IS CLOSE TO five in the morning as Mislan enters his house and heads for Daniel's room. He carefully opens the door, kneels, and kisses him lightly on the head. Daniel's fever has subsided. In his own room, he dumps his backpack on the bed, and he automatically reaches for his gun. A fleeting moment of panic hits him when he doesn't feel his sidearm. He sighs with relief when he remembers. He drops on the bed and, within minutes, is lost to the world.

He is jolted awake by a loud crash and reflectively reaches for the bedside table drawer. Stopping in mid-motion, he swears. *Shit, Lan, you don't have your sidearm anymore.* The sunlight from a split in the window curtain hits him directly in the face. He wonders what time it is. Bleary-eyed, he strains to look at the cell phone. "Oh hell, twelve ten," he murmurs and checks his cell phone. Fifteen missed calls and six messages. He jumps off the bed to check out the sound. The maid tells him the wall mirror in her room fell for no apparent reason.

"Well, that sums it all up. A broken mirror and seven years bad luck," he says, and looks at his cell phone again. The missed calls were from the office, Sherry and Johan. The text messages were also from them asking for his whereabouts, except one from Audi and one from Dr. Safia. He calls Johan, telling him he will be in about 1 p.m., and replies to Dr. Safia's messages.

On the way to his office, he calls Audi.

"Where have you been?" she asks angrily.

"Asleep. Why?"

"I heard from my source, Selangor police made several arrests in relation to the UTube Serial Rapes."

"They did? Great."

"You don't sound surprised. Why are you not angry that they beat you to it?" Audi probes.

"What difference does it make? We're all on the same side."

Audi laughs. "Excuse me, am I speaking to the Inspector Mislan Latif from Special Investigations?" she mocks.

"Funny."

"I heard rumors about your big fish."

"What sort of rumors?"

"That he was cherry-picked for some secret work. His lecturing was only a front. Is this true?"

"And what else are you hearing?"

"Depends on where and whom you ask. Coffee-shop talk is always about a Jewish conspiracy, at kopitiams they're pointing fingers at political figures, at Starbucks Muslim extremists. And in pubs, they're too drunk to care." Audi laughs. "So, is any of it true?"

"The truth is whatever you want to believe."

Mislan leaves his car on the street and walks toward the guardhouse. As he approaches the gate, his pace slows; he's half-expecting to be stopped by the guard. The fact that he was not at the office at eight has automatically made him AWOL. The guard greets him as he walks by cautiously. *Phew. They probably haven't received the order yet.* In the lobby, it feels like all eyes are on him and every whispered conversation is about him.

In the elevator, he moves to the rear of the cab to escape imaginary prying eyes. As soon as the elevator stops on his floor, he rushes out and walks briskly to his office.

"Where've you been?" Johan asks.

"Overslept. Why, what happened?"

"Everyone has been asking for you. They thought you might have gone after you-know-who."

"Not a bad idea," he kids. "Is ma'am in?"

"I think she is."

"Might as well get it over with," he says, walking to his boss's office.

"Hey, let's go for a drink after you're done with ma'am," Johan calls after him.

———

Superintendent Samsiah is having her tea and reading the newspaper. Putting it down, she invites him in.

"Close the door, please. So, where've you been all morning?"

"Sleeping. Did I miss anything?"

"Only the disappointed looks on the faces of the task force members. Did you hear that Selangor made progress on their case?" Samsiah says, watching her officer closely.

Mislan shakes his head.

"I spoke to ASP Luan. She told me she received some very accurate anonymous tips . . . very accurate."

"Good for her. We never seem to get that lucky."

"A piece of documentation with a list of names of the people involved," Samsiah says slowly, gazing at him.

"Are you suggesting I had something to do with it?" Mislan asks, poker-faced.

"Did you? Sherry says you were alone on the sixth floor with Johan. It was a while before the two of you came down to the car."

"I'm hurt you could think we did something illegal."

"Since you brought it up, did you do something stupid while the two of you were up there?"

"No. What did Johan say?"

"I've not asked him, yet. I thought it would be better to ask you first, knowing how Johan will lie to his mother for you." She sips her tea. "I suppose now Selangor can wrap things up, including our cases."

"What about him?"

"Dr. Haliman?"

Mislan nods.

"It all depends on the song the suspects detained in Selangor sing."

Mislan nods and says, "Let's get it over with."

"Get what over with?"

"You know."

"Oh, you mean the suspension. I totally forgot about that. SAC Faridah says the matter has been resolved, and no action will be taken against you."

"Was that part of the deal?"

"No, it was not. She raised it with Datuk CPO, and it was his decision."

"Can I?" he asks, holding his packet of cigarettes.

"You know where the ashtray is."

Mislan walks over to the cabinet and takes out the ashtray. Placing it on the top of the cabinet, he lights his cigarette.

"Syed and Jeff tracked down his ex-wife," Mislan says.

"Sherry told me."

"She told you the ex is, you know, and she left him to be what she is, the real her."

"Yes, and I don't think it's for us to judge her."

"No, I'm not."

"Then why're you raising it?"

"Did it occur to you that his actions may have nothing to do with his religious beliefs or defending Islam? He's a scholar, and he used his knowledge to hide his true cause, which in my opinion is his vendetta against his wife leaving him to be her true self, but made it look like a religious crusade."

Superintendent Samsiah thinks about what her officer said.

"You know there're thousands if not millions of suckers out there easily and eagerly drawn in when it comes to religion. I'm not saying it doesn't happen with Christians, Jews, Hindus, Buddhists, and others, too, but this is especially true for us here . . . the Malay Muslims."

"You may be right," she says, "but there's no way for us to know now."

"What was the meeting with the AG about?"

"About nothing that concerns you."

"Four women were raped, one murdered, and one killed herself. Zaitun, remember them?" he says.

"What about them? Don't you accuse me of selling out the victims," she snaps, glaring at him.

"I'm sorry. I didn't mean it that way." He leans against the cabinet and sighs. "Don't you think, at least, Sherry and I deserve an explanation?"

"I don't have an explanation to give."

70

LEAVING THE HEAD OF Special Investigations' office, Mislan walks to the elevator. He is in no mood to hang around the office, even if his suspension order has been revoked. Down at the lobby, he walks briskly to his car and makes a call.

"Hey, I haven't had lunch, you want to meet up?"

"Sure, if you're buying. Where?"

"Meet you at the nasi padang place in Kampung Pandan. Remember, where we met the first time?"

"Yes."

"OK, see you there in thirty."

At the restaurant, Audi is already waiting for him at the entrance.

"You look depressed . . . no, defeated," she remarks.

"Thanks," he says, walking into the restaurant and picking a table farthest from the entrance.

"So, why're you buying me lunch?"

"Can't I do something for you without a reason?"

"You can, but you don't," she says, giggling. "So come on, spill it, so I'll know whether I should eat lots or just watch you eat."

"My ex-wife likes coming here, she loves the dishes, especially the grilled fish," Mislan says, reminiscing.

Audi listens without saying anything.

"You want a story?" Mislan suddenly asks, snapping out of his memories.

"That's a dumb question. Of course I want a story."

"Dig deep into the UTube Serial Rape case. I heard Selangor police has got an anonymous document listing in detail the who's who."

"You're kidding."

Mislan looks up her and smiles.

"You're not kidding," she says, gawking at him.

Mislan shrugs.

"Why can't you give me the information?"

"Because I only heard of it, and I don't want to mislead you."

"So you're saying the rumors about the former ISIS guy are true?" Audi asks excitedly.

"Let's enjoy our lunch," Mislan says.